KU-571-415

THE FLAW IN HIS RED-HOT REVENGE

ABBY GREEN

THE ITALIAN'S DOORSTEP SURPRISE

JENNIE LUCAS

MILLS & BOON

First Published in Great Britain 2021
by Mills & Boon, an imprint of HarperCollins*Publishers* Ltd,
1 London Bridge Street, London, SE1 9GF

www.harpercollins.co.uk

HarperCollins*Publishers*
1st Floor, Watermarque Building,
Ringsend Road, Dublin 4, Ireland

The Flaw in His Red-Hot Revenge © 2021 Abby Green

The Italian's Doorstep Surprise © 2021 Jennie Lucas

ISBN: 978-0-263-28256-6

07/21

MIX
Paper from
responsible sources
FSC™ C007454

Printed and bound in Spain
by CPI, Barcelona

THE FLAW IN HIS RED-HOT REVENGE

ABBY GREEN

MILLS & BOON

This is especially for Anne McAllister.
I told you I'd get 'Eamon' into a book one of these days.
Now all you have to do is find him! xx

PROLOGUE

ASHLING DOYLE WAS so nervous that she was taking short panting breaths and it was making her light-headed. She had to force herself to take deeper breaths. She just hadn't expected this place to be so…intimidating.

She was tucked behind a large plant, hidden from view, in one of London's most iconic and historic hotels, which was hosting one of the city's most exclusive events in its annual social calendar.

Even the air smelled expensive. She'd only realised a short while before that it was scented, which added to the very rarefied atmosphere and the gobsmacking luxury of the place.

She touched her hair again nervously, even though the wig felt secure. She wasn't used to long hair tumbling over her shoulders in sleek waves. Or the vibrant red colour that gave her a jolt of shock whenever she caught a glimpse of her reflection.

She shivered slightly when someone opened a door nearby and the frigid winter air touched her exposed skin. Of which there was a lot. She looked down at the tight black strapless dress and tried to tug it ineffectually higher over her breasts. It sat an uncomfortable few inches above her knees and it sparkled when she moved, from the crystal embellishment in the material. Discreet, it was not.

She spoke to the man in the suit beside her, Carter. She'd only met him this evening and he had given the spec for the job. He would supervise her. 'Every other woman is wearing a long evening dress…won't I stick out?'

Carter flicked her a glance. 'It's perfect. Remember you're playing a part. You're not a guest here.'

As if she needed reminding that she didn't belong in a

place like this, and would never, in normal circumstances, be mixing with this rarefied crowd. But then, this was not a normal circumstance. She was only here as a massive favour for a friend from her amateur dramatics group, who couldn't make it.

She looked back out to the crowd through a gap in the foliage. 'That's him? The man in the middle? With the dark brown hair?'

In a classic black tuxedo, he shouldn't be standing out from hundreds of other men similarly dressed but he did. And not just because he was taller and broader than everyone else. It was something the eye couldn't see, but which Ashling could sense even from this distance. Power. Charisma. Sexual magnetism.

'Yes, that's him. He's talking to a blonde woman.'

A prickle of foreboding went up Ashling's spine. There had been no mention of a woman.

Carter took her arm and thrust her out from behind the plant and towards the crowd. 'This is the moment. Do it now.'

Ashling hesitated.

He spoke from behind her. 'If you don't go now the moment will be gone and you won't get paid.'

Ashling's belly lurched. She needed the money to finish her yoga teacher training course or she'd never establish herself. She took a deep breath to quell her nerves and threaded her way through the crowd until she was right behind the man.

He seemed even taller up close, almost a foot over her very average five foot five. And she was wearing heels. His back looked impossibly broad and imposing. His suit was lovingly moulded to his powerful body as only a bespoke suit could be.

Ashling had no idea who this man was—only that he was the one she had to target with the script she'd been given. An elaborate practical joke, she'd been told. She'd put it down to the crazy whims of rich people, who did strange things because they could…because they were bored.

She wasn't going to get anywhere looking at his back, so she stepped around him and stood right in front of him.

And promptly lost the ability to breathe and form a coherent thought.

He was…breathtakingly gorgeous. Short dark hair, dark eyes, and an unashamedly masculine bone structure. Hard jaw and high cheekbones softened only by a surprisingly sensual mouth, a lush lower lip.

He'd been smiling at the tall blonde woman by his side, but now the smile faded as he looked at Ashling. His eyes dropped, taking in the dress which Ashling realised had been picked for exactly *this* effect.

Even though it had a designer label, she stuck out like a tacky bauble amongst clear bright gems. The woman beside him was wearing a white dress, cut with the kind of elegance that could only be manufactured by hand in an atelier in Paris. Ashling registered all this without even looking at the woman.

'Just stick to the script and then leave.'

The words of instruction came back to her. She came out of her trance and nerves started to bubble upwards.

Emptying her mind of everything but the role she was playing, Ashling launched herself at the man, wrapping her arms around his neck. *'There* you are, darling, I've been looking everywhere for you.'

She pressed a kiss to his jaw—the only part of his face she could reach. Her lips came into contact with granite-hard bone and stubble. Her body was pressed against a wall of steel and flesh. His scent filled her nostrils—deep and woodsy, with a hint of something more exotic, causing a quiver of sensation in her belly. More than a quiver.

A wave. It was such a shock to find herself reacting with this much intensity that she froze.

The man put his hands on her arms and pulled them down, unpeeling her from his body, pushing her back but not letting her go. His face was thunderous. 'Who the hell are you? I've never seen you before in my life.'

Ashling didn't have to call on any acting skills to portray her dismay. His touch wasn't harsh, but his expression and tone were horrified. She'd known to expect exactly this re-action—after all she *was* a complete stranger to him—but she hadn't counted on his response affecting her so viscer-ally. It made no sense.

She blinked and felt moisture gather under her lashes. His gaze narrowed. She said, in a tremulous voice that she didn't really have to manufacture, 'But, darling, last night was the most amazing night of my life. You told me I was special. How can you say you don't know me?'

For a split second Ashling wondered what it would be like to have a man like this tell her that she was special. Then she lambasted herself, disgusted at getting caught up in dangerous fantasy even for a moment. This kind of man, this kind of place, was not her world and she never wanted it to be. It had rejected her a long time ago.

Out of the corner of her eye Ashling could see the woman in white go rigid. Dimly she wondered about their relationship, but she'd gone too far now.

'What the hell...?' he said now, sounding genuinely mys-tified. 'You are a complete stranger to me.' He looked her up and down again, cold disdain etched all over his face. 'I would never touch a woman like you.'

Ashling went cold all over. Suddenly she forgot why she was there. All she knew was that she was standing in front of a man who fascinated her and who had a powerful effect on her. And who was rejecting her.

Echoes of another, too similar situation came back to

haunt her… Approaching a man in the crowd. Tapping him on the shoulder. Him turning around. Him not recognising her. She'd had to tell her own father that it was *her*—his firstborn daughter. His illegitimate daughter.

At first there had been no recognition and then, slowly, comprehension had dawned. And with it not surprised delight, as Ashling had hoped, but horror. He'd grabbed her arm, pulling her away. Aside. Out of sight…

Ashling pushed the memory down where it belonged, hating it that this situation was precipitating its resurgence. But the tendrils lingered, and irrational hurt at this stranger's response made her pull free of his hold. She could never have suspected that this incident would be a trigger for her. But she was triggered. And caught between two worlds.

She tried desperately to focus on the job at hand, but the recent past and present were meshing painfully as she said, 'So now, here with your friends, I'm not worthy of you?'

His lip curled. 'You're talking nonsense—you don't belong here.'

The inexplicable hurt inside Ashling solidified, making her want to protect herself. Words that she wasn't even aware of formulating fell from her mouth. 'From what I recall, there wasn't much talking last night. How many times did we *not talk*? Two? Three? You told me I was the best you'd ever had.'

There was an audible intake of breath from someone. The blonde woman? Ashling couldn't break free of that dark gaze. A breeze skated over her exposed skin, making her shiver. Sanity trickled back slowly.

She realised that she'd gone way beyond the original spec and that she had about a second before the man reacted and her very flimsy disguise was exposed for the sham it was.

She lifted her chin. 'I know when I'm not welcome. I'm good enough to take to bed, but not to stand by your side in your world.' Tears gathered, because she felt that sentiment down to her very bones. She wasn't acting any more. Her vision turned blurry. 'You just used me because you were bored, or jaded, or…something. Well, I'm worth more than that.'

She turned and pushed her way through the silent crowd, trembling with the overload of adrenalin and emotion. Emotion that had no place here.

She went straight up to the suite where she'd changed beforehand. Carter was waiting. She ripped the small microphone from under the bodice of the dress and handed it back to him. She felt nauseous as the full impact of what she'd just done sank in.

Carter was grinning. 'You did a great job—the ad-libbing was a brilliant touch. We have a Murder Mystery Weekend coming up in a castle in Scotland…you'd be perfect for it.'

Ashling recoiled at the thought. 'I only did this because Sarah wasn't feeling well. It's not really my scene.' In fact, she wasn't sure she'd want to keep up the amateur dramatics after this.

The man looked her up and down, and Ashling didn't like the assessing gleam in his gaze.

'Shame, you're a natural.'

He handed her an envelope full of cash. 'This might help change your mind.'

Ashling looked at the envelope, suddenly reluctant to take it. It felt tainted. Dirty. She said, 'This was meant to be a practical joke…it didn't feel like a joke.'

Carter's eyes narrowed. 'You're the one who turned it into something else. You only had two lines to deliver and then you were meant to get out of there.'

Shame rose up. He was right. She'd overreacted and over-acted because she hadn't expected the man to affect her like that. She hadn't expected his rejection to feel so personal.

She asked, 'Who is he anyway?'

Carter shrugged, bored. 'Just some billionaire. Believe me, he'll have already forgotten about you.'

That stung more than she liked to admit. 'Then why hire someone like me in the first place?'

Carter's expression hardened. 'I don't ask questions when someone wants to hire one of my actors for a private event, once I know there's no funny stuff involved. This was one of the easiest jobs. Who knows why people do the things they do?' He thrust the envelope at her again. 'It's money for old rope—now, take it and go. If you want more gigs like this, you know where I am.'

Ashling took the envelope, but when she was walking away from the hotel a short while later, minus the wig and dress, back in her own clothes again, she felt sick. She was passing a homeless shelter, and on an impulse she couldn't ignore she went in and handed the money over to the manager.

He looked at it and her with shock. 'Thank you, miss, are you sure?'

She nodded and fled, putting the whole evening down to an unsavoury experience not to be repeated. She thanked her lucky stars that she would never meet that man again.

CHAPTER ONE

Four years later...

IT WAS A warm late summer's evening and Ashling Doyle was half walking, half running down a Mayfair street, white stucco houses towering over her on each side. She imagined all the windows were like eyes, judging her for sullying this exclusive part of London with her bedraggled, sweaty self.

She felt a bubble of hysteria rise up from her chest, but she pushed it back down. It was only masking the severe anxiety that had been gnawing at her insides since her best friend Cassie had asked her to do her a favour. A very doable, innocuous favour.

All she had to do was pick up and deliver a tuxedo to Cassie's boss for a function that evening. She couldn't have refused. Not when she knew her friend's PA was out sick and Cassie was under pressure—she'd left London earlier that day to go to the United States for a two-week work trip.

Ashling also couldn't have refused because Cassie would have wondered why on earth she couldn't do this really minor little thing.

But Cassie had no idea why this was not a minor little thing. It was huge. And it was the reason why, ever since Cassie had started working for her boss, and had then worked her way up the ranks to become an executive assistant, Ashling had always found an excuse not to come to Cassie's workplace or attend any social work events.

Cassie had put it down to Ashling's distaste for all things corporate and regimented.

But that wasn't the reason why Ashling had to avoid Cassie's boss. Zachary Temple. A man who had single-handedly become one of the most powerful financiers in the City of London. Temple Corp dwarfed every other financial institution with its innovative ways and ruthless ambition.

Zachary Temple was the man the government called on for help. He was the man who, with a click of his fingers, could make economies falter. And what he could do for the companies he invested in didn't bear thinking about unless he thought they were worth it.

He was also, far more importantly, the man who Ashling had hoped never, ever to meet again. The man she had confronted at an event four years ago, when she'd been just twenty years old and dabbling in amateur dramatics.

She'd only realised who he was when Cassie had pointed out a picture of him in a newspaper, saying, 'That's him! That's my new boss.'

Ashling had told her friend about that night after it had happened, but of course she hadn't had a name for the man then. Now she did. A feeling of sick dread had sunk into her belly. Guilt. She hadn't had the guts or the heart to tell Cassie that *he* was the man she'd publicly shamed for no good reason.

Her guilt and shame had only grown over the years, as Cassie had spoken of Temple in hushed, reverential tones. She'd never been able to understand Ashling's antipathy or studied lack of interest in the man. 'Wow, he really gets up your nose, doesn't he, Ash?' her friend would say. 'You've never even met the man!'

But it didn't stop Cassie blithely tell Ashling about his legendary attention to detail, which extended beyond the office to his personal life, and to the women he carefully chose to take as his lovers—none of whom seemed to last long.

Ashling could recall only too well the woman at his side that evening, and she'd barely glanced at her. Tall, Hitchcockian blonde. Refined. Sophisticated. Everything Ashling hadn't been that night. And still wasn't.

She slowed to a walk. Temple's house was in front of her now. It stood on its own among other houses. A detached townhouse in the middle of London would be worth more money than she could earn in about ten lifetimes. Not to mention, according to Cassie, Temple's palatial country home outside London, his penthouse apartment in Manhattan and his pied-à-terre in Paris.

Ashling doubted she'd amass enough money in this lifetime even to buy a modest studio flat. Oh, she earned enough money to support herself, and she was proud of her independence. But her payment came in in fits and starts, due to the nature of her myriad revenue streams.

Trepidation pooled in her belly at the thought of seeing the man face to face again. At the thought that he might somehow recognise her, even though she looked nothing like she had that night four years ago.

She had blonde bobbed hair, currently pulled back into a messy ponytail. No make-up. Athleisure wear instead of a black minidress. She still cringed when she thought of all the other women that night, in their long evening gowns.

She forced herself to walk up the steps. As it was, she was late with the tuxedo, and she did not need to add fuel to her reputation for scattiness, which Ashling always thought it was a bit unfair—until Cassie invariably pointed out the numerous occasions when Ashling's attention to detail had been somewhat lacking. Like the time she'd left Cassie sitting in a restaurant for an hour because she'd been so engrossed in a book at the library. Or when she'd forgotten to stock up on milk. Or missed her bus stop because she'd been too busy daydreaming.

She shoved aside the reminder that she was behaving true to form and regarded the massive matt black front door in front of her. It was flanked on either side by small potted trees. She instinctively reached out and touched a leaf, to see if they were real, and at the same moment the door opened—which was just as well, because Ashling hadn't seen any sign of a bell or knocker.

She blinked at the uniformed butler. He looked exactly the way she would have imagined a stern, silver-haired butler to look.

'Good afternoon—' She winced inwardly. 'I mean, *evening*. I'm Ashling Doyle—Cassie…er… Cassandra James's friend—Mr Temple's executive assistant? She asked me to bring a suit for him, for an event.'

Ashling lifted her arm to indicate the suit draped over it in its protective black zip-up bag.

She could have sworn she saw the butler wince as he reached for it, saying, 'Mr Temple is most anxious for this as he's already late—'

'Peters, was that the door? Is that the damn girl with my tuxedo?'

Ashling's insides dropped at the censorious tone. She'd hoped that she would be able to get away without seeing him.

At that moment Zachary Temple appeared behind the butler, towering over the older man, who was saying, 'Yes, sir, it's your suit. I'll deliver it to your suite right away. The car will be in front in fifteen minutes.'

Ashling was left standing in the doorway, looking up into the forbidding features of Zachary Temple, who was as darkly gorgeous as she remembered. She felt as if she was trapped in the blinding beam of powerful headlights. Unable to move. His dark eyes were totally unreadable, just as they'd been that night four years ago.

She didn't see a spark of recognition, and wasn't sure if she was relieved or disappointed—ridiculously. *Not disappointed*, she assured herself. She definitely did not want this man to recognise her.

He seemed taller than she remembered. Broader. The muscles of his biceps bulged from beneath his black polo shirt sleeves and the open buttons drew her eye to the bronzed column of his throat. His chest was wide, and the shirt did little to disguise taut musculature underneath.

The thick dark hair was still kept almost militarily short but even with that she could see that it had a tendency to curl. And for some reason that detail made her pulse trip even faster. His jaw was as hard as granite, and at that moment she recalled how his stubble had felt against her lips when she'd pressed her mouth there.

But then he spoke. 'You'd better come in—you look hot.'

Ashling blinked, as if coming out of a trance, and became all too conscious of her 'hot' state. She'd all but run here from the local tube station. She must be a sight in her three-quarter-length joggers, sneakers, and a bra top under a loose singlet. It was, after all, still close to thirty degrees on a hot London summer evening.

No wonder he didn't recognise her...

But she couldn't risk it by hanging around. She backed away. 'It's fine. Cassie just wanted me to deliver the suit and I have—'

'About an hour late.' Zachary Temple looked pointedly at the watch on his wrist.

A shiver skated over her skin as she recalled how he'd looked at her before and said, *'I would never touch a woman like you.'*

Ashling stopped in her tracks. She bit her lip. A nervous habit. 'I'm sorry... I was on my way to the dry cleaners straight after my class, but one of my students—'

Temple frowned. 'Students?'

'I teach yoga.'

He said nothing to that, so Ashling did what she did best whenever an awkward silence grew. She filled it.

'Like I said, I was leaving to go straight to the cleaners,

but one of my students started having a panic attack, and I had to wait with her and help her breathe through it, and then I stayed with her until her boyfriend came to collect her... I couldn't leave her on her own in that state.'

Temple arched an unamused brow. 'Isn't yoga meant to have the opposite effect on people?'

'Actually, a practice or class can bring up a lot of emotions for people.'

He looked at her as if she'd just spoken in an incomprehensible dialect. But then he stood back from the door. 'You should have some water—you look like you need it.'

Contrary to what her head was telling her to do—which was politely decline and leave, and hopefully not lay eyes on this man again for at least a decade—Ashling found her feet moving forward and into the hushed and blessedly cool entrance hall of Zachary Temple's home.

It was a huge space, with a black and white chequered marble floor leading up to a central staircase. The sunlight caught the crystals of a massive chandelier overhead and sent out shafts of iridescent light just before Temple shut the door behind him, effectively muting the sounds of the city.

He must have telepathically communicated to a member of staff, because at that moment a maid in a black short-sleeved shirt and trousers appeared and handed Ashling a glass of water with ice and lemon.

'Thank you...' She took it from the young woman, who then vanished back down a corridor—presumably to wherever the kitchen was. She took a gulp to try and cool down.

Ashling wasn't used to being around someone as coolly impassive as Temple. She was an animated person and generally used to putting others at ease—the benefits of a peripatetic upbringing with a single mother who'd had a tendency to befriend total strangers.

She risked a look at him, to find him staring at her as if she was some kind of alien object. No wonder... He was used to mingling among people who looked a lot more put-together. She couldn't imagine Cassie, for instance, appearing before Temple in anything less than her sleek, elegant, business-suited perfection.

'You live with Cassie…you're her childhood friend.'

He stated this and Ashling nodded, mentally cursing her friend for asking her to do this favour. 'Yes, we've been friends since we were eight. My mother worked for her father as his housekeeper for about five years, so we lived together.'

Ashling blushed when she thought of how that sounded. 'Well, obviously not "together" like equals, because Mum and I lived in a flat in the basement beside the kitchen, but Cassie never made me feel *less than*—even though she went to the fancy day school and I went to a different one…' She trailed off. She was gabbling again.

'I really should let you get on with your evening, Mr Temple. I've delayed you enough. Sorry about that again.'

Ashling drained the icy glass of water in one go, which gave her brain-freeze for a few seconds. As she looked around helplessly for somewhere to deposit the glass Temple said, 'Here, I'll take it.'

She handed it to him and their fingers brushed against each other. The fleeting physical contact made Ashling jerk her hand back so fast that the glass almost slipped between their hands to the marble floor, but Temple caught it.

Before she could react to that, he said, 'The delayed tuxedo isn't my only problem.'

Ashling looked at him. 'What do you mean?'

He looked even more unamused now. 'Cassie's PA—Gwen—was meant to come with me to the function this evening, to take notes. Obviously she can't as she's unwell.'

'Oh, of course…' That was why Ashling had been drafted in to pick up the tuxedo at short notice.

Abruptly Temple asked, 'Can *you* take notes?'

Ashling had not been not expecting that. Almost automatically she responded, 'I've worked as a temp and a secretarial assistant—of course I can take notes.'

'Then you'll come with me this evening.'

It took a few seconds for what Temple had just said—announced, actually—to sink in.

'You want me to come with you?' Ashling's voice was a squeak. She balked at the thought of such a preposterous suggestion. At the thought of going anywhere with this man who she should be avoiding at all costs. Any more time spent in his company risked him recognising her.

'You did Cassie a favour by bringing the tuxedo…late, I might add…but without Cassie or her PA I'm still down a member of staff for the evening.'

At that succinct summary, Ashling couldn't think of anything to say. She had no plans for the evening other than to sip a cold glass of rosé while reading a good book on the terrace of the flat she shared with Cassie, but that looked elusive now, when she thought of Cassie, blissfully unaware of the fact that her boss was not happy.

Also, Ashling didn't really relish the prospect of Cassie getting to say *I told you so* when she found out about the delayed tuxedo. If she did this then surely the delayed tuxedo would be forgotten and all would be well again?

'I… Okay, I guess… If you really need someone.' She couldn't have sounded more reluctant.

Temple's dark, unreadable gaze looked her up and down. 'Do you have anything to wear? It's black-tie.'

Ashling went cold all over as she was reminded of that sparkly black dress. Too short and too tight. But, as it happened, she did have some clothes with her.

Cassie was due to attend a fancy wedding in San Francisco on her arrival in the States, and as her self-appointed stylist—because she knew more about fashion—Ashling had found her some options of outfits to choose from. She still had the rejected dresses in her bag as she'd been planning on returning them to the vintage shop, and luckily they had the same size feet.

And, as much as Ashling was tempted right now to say, *no*, she didn't have anything to wear, in a bid to get out of accompanying Temple, her innate honesty, coupled with her desire to prove—even just to herself—that she could be counted on, made her say, 'I do, actually. But it's a cocktail dress. Would that be suitable?'

'That'll be fine.' Temple headed towards the marble staircase. 'Follow me. I'll show you to a guest suite where you can get ready.'

She followed him up the stairs, her eyes on the broad back narrowing down to slim hips. The material of his black trousers hugged his buttocks as if tailored just to fit his muscular contours.

She almost ran into those muscular contours when he stopped suddenly at a door. She hadn't even realised they were in a long corridor, plushly carpeted in slate-grey, with doors leading off either side.

He opened the door and stood back. 'You can use this suite.'

She walked in, taking in the opulent luxury of the room.

He said from behind her, 'Have we met before? Perhaps with Cassie?'

Ashling was glad she was facing away from him, so she could school her features before she turned around. 'No,' she said, while mentally crossing her fingers, 'I've never met you with Cassie.' Which, technically, was not a lie. She *hadn't* met him with her friend.

He looked at her for a long moment, as if not entirely convinced. Then he glanced at his watch again. 'You have fifteen minutes. Come down when you're ready.'

The door closed and Ashling sagged. He hadn't recog-

nised her. Now all she had to do was get through this evening and hope that nothing sparked his memory.

He'd recognised her as soon as he'd laid eyes on her.

Zachary Temple paced back and forth in the reception
hall a short time later. Anger bubbled in his blood. Anger
and something a lot more disconcerting.

Awareness.

The moment he'd seen her standing in the doorway,
in spite of the fact that her hair patently *wasn't* long and
flowing and red, the sense of déjà-vu had almost knocked
him over.

He'd sworn he'd never forget that oh-so-innocent face
and those huge blue eyes…that lush mouth that had stayed
emblazoned in his mind for days afterwards.

And he hadn't.

He wasn't sure how he'd managed to contain his rage
just now, but it had taken levels of control he hadn't had to
call on since he was a teenager, being goaded by the school
bullies because he'd been an outlier in their midst.

Ashling Doyle was *her.* The mystery woman who had
appeared and disappeared like a faery sprite four years ago,
teaching him an important lesson in never being compla-
cent and always watching his back.

That night four years ago Zach had been publicly humiliated. Exposed. His years of working so hard to prove
himself had almost come to nothing. His success had still
been a fragile thing, easy to dismantle. He'd had to work
twice as hard to build his reputation back up again. Restore
people's confidence in him.

He never would have known that the friend Cassie spoke
of so fondly as she described her various scatty escapades
was the same woman who had left such a trail of destruction in her wake.

The two women had known each other since they were

children. What did that say about Cassie? He trusted her implicitly, but if this woman was her friend… He went cold inside at the thought that she might know.

He suddenly regretted his impetuous decision to take Ashling Doyle with him. To toy with her. He didn't have time for this. He should have confronted her straight—

But then he heard a sound from behind him. He turned around slowly, the back of his neck prickling with some kind of strange foreboding.

There was a woman standing at the top of the stairs in a black silk dress, and for a second Zachary wondered who the hell this stranger in his house was—before he realised it was her.

She was coming down the stairs slowly, because of her vertiginous black heels. His eyes travelled up from her feet, taking in slim calves and a toned thigh, peeking out from the slit in the dress. Gone were the hot pink Lycra leggings and the yellow singlet worn over an even more lurid purple sports bra.

She was transformed.

Cinched in at her waist, black silk clung to her breasts and then went over one shoulder, leaving the other bare. A vivid pink flower was pinned to the dress at the waist on one side. Her skin was lightly golden. Her hair was pulled back into a rough chignon, showing off the delicate bone structure of her jaw and face. Subtle make-up made her eyes huge, her lashes long and dramatic.

But it was her mouth that Zach couldn't take his eyes off. The mouth that he remembered so well.

It took a second before he realised the sound of roaring in his head was his blood.

He told himself it was anger. Not desire.

But he shouldn't be surprised. After all, he'd seen her transformed before.

He looked at the flower. It should look gaudy, but somehow…it worked.

She looked nervous—which was patently an act.

She gestured towards the flower. 'The dress just felt a bit…too black. I can take it off.'

That caused a vivid image of this woman stepping out of the dress, standing there naked, to enter Zach's mind. He cursed it and said frigidly, 'It's fine.'

She said, 'I've left my things upstairs… I'm not sure what to do with them.'

Suspicion coursed through Zach's veins. She was already sizing up the opportunity this turn of events had afforded her. He was doing the right thing. He wanted to see just how long she would keep up this charade.

'Leave them there. You can pick them up later or we can arrange to have them delivered back to you.'

'I don't want to cause more hassle…'

He curbed an urge to laugh at her theatrics. She really was very plausible. But then she'd had four years to hone her skills.

Zach put out a hand to indicate that they should leave. 'My driver is waiting.'

As she walked out ahead of him he noticed a sparkling diamanté clip holding her hair up at the back. A light but evocative scent of roses and something a little spicier caught his nostrils. It hinted at the sensuality she was hiding under her *Who me?* surface.

It wasn't usual for Zach to be taken by surprise by anyone or anything. It had happened once and never again. Even though it had only been a couple of minutes in time, four years ago, he'd never forgotten her—not her face, or how she'd felt pressed against him. Her soft mouth on his jaw… Her scent clean and fresh…

So different from the women he'd found himself surrounded by as his success had grown. As he'd become a man who was desired and sought after. As he'd become a target.

Ashling Doyle had reminded him that night that he was always going to be a target. She clearly had no idea of the damage her actions had done.

But she would.

CHAPTER TWO

ASHLING'S HEART WAS still pounding after the effort it had taken not to tumble down those marble stairs in the high heels and land in a heap at Zachary Temple's feet, and more so from the dark, brooding appraisal he'd subjected her to.

At every step down the stairs she'd imagined that he would be remembering who she was, and her skin had prickled all over with little needles of heat that she'd put down to self-consciousness, not awareness.

But he hadn't said anything. And, actually, when she thought about it now she realised it was really delusional of her to fear that he would remember her. Why would he, when it had been so long ago and he was habitually surrounded by the most beautiful women in the world?

How on earth would Ashling have made any kind of impression, except perhaps as an annoying fly that had had to be swatted aside?

Ashling was not his type. He'd looked at the flower she'd pinned to the dress as if it was a live thing. She'd seen his type. Tall, sleek, soignée… Cold. Oozing class and sophistication. They wouldn't be pinning flowers to their dresses to liven them up a bit.

The women a man like Temple pursued would have the right breeding and the intellect to match. Like him, they would have been born into this world—a world that didn't accept people from the margins. She should know.

His type of woman would have had a privileged and conventional path to success. Her CV wouldn't have an education littered with gaps and holes. Not to mention a list of myriad jobs such as Ashling had had over the years, none of which could be considered conventional.

But then, Ashling had never been destined to be conventional. Her single mother had loved Ashling fiercely and had taught her how to be independent and believe in herself. She'd believed in the school of life ethos—and Ashling had certainly seen a lot of life, going from living in a palatial house in Belgravia to living on a commune in the west of Ireland.

But convention and things like a solid base had not been her mother's priorities. Angela Doyle was a dreamy romantic who had taken a long time to get over the hurt and pain of rejection by Ashling's father.

But right now, sitting in a car next to one of London's giants of industry, was not the time for Ashling to be dwelling on her lack of credentials or thinking of painful memories. She just had to get through this evening and not cause a national incident. Or make him remember her and that night.

She sneaked a look at Temple, sitting on the other side of the car. She'd seen him in a tuxedo before, but the impact this time was not diminished. If anything, four years seemed to have enhanced his physicality. Her gut tightened at the sheer raw masculinity of the man. There was nothing soft about him. Not his expression, his bone structure, or his body. Just that intriguing tendency of his hair to curl.

No wonder she'd had to cling to the banister the whole way down those stairs. The man needed to come with a health warning. *Proceed with caution. May cause severe dizziness!*

He looked at her then, as if aware of her regard, and Ashling could feel the heat climb up her chest. In a bid to try and deflect his attention from her helpless reaction, she asked, 'What is the event this evening?'

'It's an awards ceremony for young entrepreneurs.'

'Oh, cool.'

He arched a brow. *'Cool?'*

As if Ashling needed reminding that she was so not his type. And glad of it.

Liar.

'I mean,' she said, aiming to sound knowledgeable, 'that should be interesting…seeing the next generation of talent…or competition?'

A ghost of a smile flickered at Temple's mouth so briefly that Ashling knew she must have imagined it.

He said, 'Competition for me? I don't think so.'

She might have thought he was joking if he hadn't sounded so utterly matter-of-fact. It went beyond arrogance to total certainty. And she knew he didn't joke. He didn't have time. Cassie had told her about his work ethic. This was a man who had his whole life mapped out.

Normally that kind of rigidity would disgust her, but she found she was more intrigued than anything.

'What exactly do you want me to do?' she asked.

He glanced at her. 'Listen…observe. Take notes.' Then he asked, 'You said you're a yoga instructor?'

She nodded.

'*Just* a yoga instructor?' he commented idly, qualifying it with, 'I can't imagine teaching yoga alone is enough to keep the wolf from the door.'

Ashling shivered slightly, but put it down to the air-conditioning in the car and not the sudden image she had of a slightly more wolfish Zachary Temple appearing at her door. Her imagination was far too vivid for its own good.

Conscious of her colourful CV, Ashling felt slightly defensive as she answered. 'No, it's not my only job, although I do consider it my main one. But, I also waitress in a local café. And I do some styling work for different clients.' They were friends, but Cassie had told her that referring to them as clients made it sound more important. She went on, 'I also care for an old lady who lives in our building for a few hours a week—do her shopping…things like that.'

'Anything else?'

Ashling looked at Temple. She sensed she was amusing

him. It made her prickly. 'Yes, as it happens. I did a course in cordon bleu cookery along the way, but I'm sure the minutiae of my CV really isn't that interesting.'

Something stretched between them—a tension that made Ashling nervous, because it felt charged with something she couldn't understand. And then it was broken when Temple looked over her shoulder.

'We're here.'

Ashling turned her head to see that the car was pulling up outside one of London's most iconic museums. Paparazzi lined a red carpet and A-list stars mingled with politicians and household names from the business world. One she recognised was from a well-known TV show, in which budding entrepreneurs were pitted against each other.

Well, this was one experience she'd never had...

She tried to quell her nerves as the driver came around to open her door. Temple was already waiting for her. He put out a hand to help her and she looked up at him for a moment. She was suddenly very reluctant to touch him, afraid of her reaction, but she couldn't ignore him.

She was right to be afraid. As soon as her hand touched his, electricity scorched up her arm. The palm of his hand was rough, not smooth. Not the soft hand of a man who sat at a desk all day. But then, she already knew there was nothing soft about him.

For a moment he just looked at her, almost as if he hadn't seen her before, but then he let her hand drop. He said, 'Stay close to me.'

Ashling had no intention of letting him out of her sight. As the reality of the situation sank in, she grew more terrified. The paparazzi were screaming out for people to turn and smile for them. She heard Temple's name being called but he ignored them, cutting a swathe through the crowd of preening people as if they were minions and not some of the biggest names in the country.

They had almost run the gauntlet of the red carpet when someone jostled Ashling from behind and she pitched forward. Even though Temple was ahead of her, he turned at that second and caught her as she collided with his body.

It was like running into a steel wall. The shock of contact drove the breath from her lungs.

He held her arms, looking down at her. 'Okay?'

She managed to nod, even as a wave of unbridled heat coursed up from her core and out to every erogenous zone. Exactly the way it had felt four years ago. An immediate rush of sensation, hot and overwhelming. No man had ever had the same effect on her—not before or since. In fact, she'd believed in the intervening years that she'd imagined it.

But it hadn't been imagination.

It had been very real. Powerful.

Her hands were splayed across Temple's chest, under his jacket. She wanted to press herself closer, but she exerted enough pressure to straighten herself, feeling hot and flustered. She felt a tugging neediness between her legs... an ache. Her breasts were bare under the silk of the dress because she hadn't had a suitable bra, and they felt tight, her nipples pricking into hard points against the sensuous material.

She took her hands down, avoided his eyes. 'Sorry about that. I... I lost my balance.'

For a moment Temple didn't move, and the air hung suspended between them as people passed by. She felt an icy finger touch her back. *Did he recognise her?*

But then he moved, manoeuvring her so she was in front of him.

Ashling told herself she was being ridiculous.

He put a hand lightly to her back, propelling her forward and into the lavishly decorated venue, where hundreds of people were already chatting, networking and sipping sparkling vintage champagne.

Ashling sucked in a shaky breath.

She was playing with him.

Zach felt a mixture of anger, consternation and very unwelcome arousal as he kept a hand lightly on Ashling's back as they walked into the function room.

That little stunt just now had been designed to let him know how her lithe curves felt pressed against him. Exactly the way she'd momentarily robbed him of his logical faculties for a dangerous moment four years ago. Giving her the chance to do her damage and get away.

The fact that she still had an effect on him was galling in the extreme. So was the fact that he could be caught by someone so full of guile.

As for the myriad occupations that she'd listed earlier... No doubt they'd been plucked out of thin air to disguise the fact that she only really had one job: con woman.

But he knew who she was now, and he wasn't going to be caught again. She wouldn't slip through his fingers this time.

Ashling sat down with a sigh of relief after what had felt like hours of trailing in the wake of Temple and his Midas Touch. He'd met with hundreds of sycophants, all vying for his attention.

The novelty of being on the other side of the red rope, so to speak, had worn off fast. The man's energy levels were indefatigable, and it had taken all her wits just to keep up and try to take notes on her phone.

There'd also been a steady stream of stunning women. All tall, statuesque, and exuding a sexual confidence that Ashling found both intimidating and fascinating. None of them had even spared her a glance. That was how little of a threat she was.

Ashling slid off her shoes under the table now and stretched her feet out. She stifled a yawn. Her busy day was catching up with her. She'd been up since five that morning and had packed in more than was usual, even for her. And that had been before the trauma of seeing Temple again and worrying that he'd recognise her...

'Are we boring you?'

Ashling looked to her right, where Temple was taking up far too much space. She smiled sheepishly. 'Sorry, it's been a long day.'

His dark gaze moved to her mouth and for a moment she couldn't breathe, remembering pressing her mouth to that hard jaw. The scent of him. Earthy and spicy all at once.

She blinked and Temple looked away, his jaw clenching. Ashling cursed herself again for being so weak. *Ugh.* What was wrong with her? She was disgusted with herself for finding him so mesmerisingly attractive when he inhabited a world she had no desire to explore.

Her father had been a successful financier—albeit nowhere near the league of someone like Temple. He had rejected Ashling and her mother because they hadn't fitted into his corporate world. They'd cluttered it up. Made it untidy. And so he'd jettisoned them in favour of a far more acceptable wife and family.

What Ashling had learned about Temple from Cassie had only reinforced the impression she'd got of him that night four years ago. That he had nothing but disdain for anything or anyone who put a wrinkle in the perfect surface of his life. The way he'd looked at her that night—with such horror. She'd never forget it.

It still hurt.

She shoved that memory down, rejecting the fact that it still had the power to affect her.

'Mr Temple? We need you backstage now, on stand-by to present the first award.'

A woman in a suit had appeared, breaking Ashling's circling thoughts.

Temple got up, buttoning up his jacket. He slanted a look to Ashling. 'Don't go anywhere now, will you?'

There was a distinct edge to his tone that made her nervous, but when she looked at him his expression was bland. She was imagining things. She shook her head and watched as he walked away with such innately athletic grace that every head and set of eyes was pulled in his direction.

Temple was up on the dais now, and people were clapping. At that moment Ashling had the fleeting thought of doing exactly what he'd just asked her not to. Get up and leave. Escape. Consign him to history, where he'd safely been until this evening.

But at that moment, as if hearing her thoughts, Temple's gaze stopped on Ashling. His focus was so intense that she saw people turning to look at her, wondering who he was staring at.

The whole way through his speech Temple barely took his eyes off her. There was absolutely no chance of her going anywhere. He'd as good as branded her.

'Really, you can just drop me at a tube station. I can come by tomorrow to pick up my things.' Ashling was still jittery after Temple's intense focus during his speech. She wanted to get out of his disturbing orbit.

'It's after midnight. You're not taking the tube alone at this hour.'

Ashling refrained from telling Temple that she'd been taking late-night tubes on her own for some time now. She was street-smart. His tone brooked no argument and they were already back in the leafy exclusive streets of Mayfair.

He'd undone his bow-tie and the top button of his shirt

and it was hard for Ashling not to look at him and notice how the stubble along his jaw and the loose bow-tie gave him a decadently sexy air. It added to the brooding energy that was almost palpable.

The car pulled to a smooth stop outside the house, and before Ashling could step out Temple was at her door, opening it and holding out his hand. She steeled herself, but it was no good. As soon as they touched, skin on skin, electricity pulsed up her arm and into her blood. She took her hand away as soon as she was standing.

He led her into the house, where all was dimly lit and hushed. Ashling suddenly felt self-conscious. Very aware of how he made her feel and the fact that he must be dying for her to go. As much as she was dying to leave! she assured herself.

'I'll just run up and change and get my things.'

Temple was pulling off his tie completely now, and undoing another button with long fingers. 'Take your time. The car will be waiting to take you home when you're ready.'

Ashling slipped off her shoes and hurried up the stairs, the marble cool under her bare feet. When she got to the luxurious suite she looked in dismay at the minor explosion she'd created when getting ready earlier.

She wasn't the tidiest person on the planet. And she wasn't used to wearing much make-up. So she gave in to an impulse to clean her face in the sumptuous bathroom. And then she saw the massive shower…and remembered that the shower in the flat she shared with Cassie was currently on the blink. A plumber was due to come tomorrow.

The lure of this massive state-of-the-art shower and the chance to wash off the grime and humidity of the day was too tempting. Assuring herself it would only take five minutes, Ashling stripped off and groaned softly as she stepped under a gloriously hot, powerful cascade of water.

* * *

Where the hell was she?

Zach put down his empty tumbler and looked at his watch. She'd been upstairs for thirty minutes now. It hadn't taken her that long to get changed earlier.

Frustration rising at himself for playing this game, letting her feign innocence and a lack of recognition, rose like fire inside him. She was probably upstairs laughing at him.

The thought of that propelled him out of the room, up the stairs and to the door of the guest suite to seek her out and—

Zach stopped on the threshold of the room.

Ashling was emerging from the en suite bathroom in a wave of steam. She wore nothing but a short towelling robe. The hem rested high on her thighs, showing off more of her slim shapely legs than he'd seen earlier. It was belted around her slim waist and the front gaped open slightly, giving a glimpse of the curve of a breast. Pale and plump.

Immediately Zach had an image in his head of her naked body in the shower, water sluicing over slender limbs, curves and pert breasts. Firm buttocks.

Desire was swift and hot, eclipsing the anger that had propelled him up here. He was rendered momentarily insensible. He couldn't remember the last time a woman had precipitated such intense need.

She hadn't seen him yet. She was rubbing at her damp hair with a smaller towel.

In that moment Zach clawed back control with an effort and fresh anger rose as he interpreted the scene.

Ashling only sensed she wasn't alone after she'd stepped into the bedroom and a crackling tension in the air skated over her skin. Her hands went still and she looked up to see Temple standing in the doorway, without his jacket, waistcoat and tie, the top buttons of his shirt open. But even the shock of seeing him standing there couldn't diminish her first helpless reaction—pulsing awareness and a flash of fire in her belly.

'I was wondering what was taking you so long,' he said, with no discernible tone to his voice.

Except Ashling fancied she could hear a steel undertone.

The full impact of having been found like this hit her, and an awfully familiar wave of guilt and shame overwhelmed her. She was trespassing. She didn't belong here. She saw the chaotic detritus from her bag strewn all over the pristine suite. Shoes on the floor near Temple's feet.

She took down the towel from her head and said, 'I'm so sorry. I saw the shower and I couldn't help myself. The shower in our flat is broken and it's been a long day and—'

'You don't need to explain. After all you did me a favour this evening, joining me at short notice.'

Ashling's mouth shut. Temple had stepped into the room. The door was still open behind him. Her skin prickled with heat as his dark gaze rested on her. The air suddenly felt thick with a kind of tension Ashling had never experienced before. It coiled tight in her gut. Down low.

She was very aware of her naked body under the robe.

She opened her mouth again, tried to form something that sounded coherent. 'I… It was the least I could do…for Cassie. I'm sorry I was late.'

Temple took another step into the room. He shrugged. 'We got there in time. It was really no big deal.'

Gone was the stern Zachary Temple, and in his place right now was someone Ashling found far more disturbing. His gaze dropped momentarily. Ashling realised the robe was gaping open.

Embarrassment warmed her face as she pulled it together. 'I should really get going. I've imposed enough.'

'There's no rush…is there?'

Ashling looked at Temple, wondering if she'd misheard

him. Why did she feel as if every limb was weighted down and she couldn't move? Didn't want to…

All she could see was him. Those impossibly broad shoulders. His hard jaw, dark with stubble, like it had been four years ago. The sensation of how it had felt under her lips was still vivid.

Oh, God. Now was not the time for memories. Not when past and present were colliding in a way that was seriously disorientating.

Then he said, 'You felt it between us, didn't you? From the moment we met?'

Ashling's mouth went dry. She'd been that obvious? 'I… um…what do you mean?' But her heart betrayed her, beating fast.

Temple's mouth quirked into a little smile. 'Do you really want me to spell it out?'

When had he moved so close that she could almost touch him? So close that she could smell his scent? Deep, and dark, and musky. Infinitely masculine.

And then mortification coursed through her when she realised that he hadn't moved another inch towards her. She'd moved towards him without even realising. As if pulled by some invisible force.

Temple's gaze dropped to her mouth and then down, before coming back up. 'You're a beautiful woman.'

Her eyes widened. She struggled to find her voice. 'I'm nothing special.'

'I disagree.'

This from the man who had once looked at her and said, *'I would never touch a woman like you.'* That memory still scored away at her insides, even though she'd told herself that she was over it.

Temple repeated his words. 'You feel it too, don't you? This heat between us.'

Ashling was fast losing any sense of reality or desire

to think coherently. Was Temple really saying he fancied her? Asking her to admit she fancied him too when it had to be laughably obvious?

Before she could articulate a word, he reached out and touched his fingers to her jaw. A touch so light she could barely feel it, and yet it burned like a brand. He traced the line of her jaw, his fingers under her chin, his thumb exploring her lower lip.

Ashling's breath was coming fast. She was drowning in a sea of melting sensations, desperate for Temple to bring her closer. Her eyes were fixated on his mouth, wondering what it would feel like on hers... She didn't recognise herself right now. She'd believed that she didn't have much of a sex-drive.

But at that moment Temple took his hand away and stepped back, his face shuttering. A small sound of pleading came out of Ashling's mouth. She barely noticed.

He said, 'I'm sorry. I misread the signals. I thought you were attracted to me too.'

It was such a reversal to hear this man say he found her attractive that it took her a second to realise that he thought she didn't fancy him. Ashling blurted out, 'No—*wait*. I mean... I am attracted to you too...'

Temple stopped. 'Are you sure?'

Ashling nodded and took a step closer, a boldness she'd never felt before giving her confidence. Confidence born out of this man admitting he wanted her.

She said, 'Please... I don't know...'

I don't know what to do.

She couldn't admit that she didn't know what to do. How did one behave with a man like Temple? He was so tall. Broad. Intimidating. He must be used to worldly lovers, taking the lead, showing him exactly what they wanted.

'Do you want me to kiss you?'

Relief mixed with excitement flooded Ashling's body,

making her tremble. She nodded. Temple stepped closer. He lifted a hand and cupped Ashling's jaw again, his fingers caressing the back of her neck under her damp hair.

Gently, he tugged her closer, until their bodies were almost touching. He looked down at her. Tipped her chin up. Lowered his head. Ashling's eyes fluttered closed as Temple's mouth hovered for an infinitesimal moment before closing over hers.

Nothing she'd imagined or held in her memory since that night four years ago could have prepared her for this… this immediate rush of sensations. Melting heat at her core, blood rushing to her head, and an urgency to get even closer, have him kiss her harder.

She didn't even realise her hands had tangled in his shirt, pulling him even closer. Her mouth moved under his, restless, seeking a deeper intimacy. And he obliged, coaxing her lips apart so that he could explore and deepen the kiss until Ashling was no longer conscious of anything but this exquisite moment in time.

With one hand at the back of her head, holding her so he could plunder her mouth, Temple drifted his other hand down along the front of the robe Ashling wore, his fingers teasing along the edge, close to her bare skin. Ashling's breath quickened under his mouth, where he held her captive to his masterful onslaught.

He pushed the robe aside. Ashling could feel cool air skate over the bare skin of her breast. She pulled back from the kiss reluctantly, opening her eyes. Temple was out of focus. She was breathing heavily. He was cupping her breast now, his eyes on her there. A thumb stroked her nipple. She could feel it tighten into a hard bud of need. She almost whimpered.

He looked at her as he teased her flesh. 'What is it? What do you want?'

Ashling bit her lip. Then she blurted out, 'I want you to touch me…'

Put your mouth on me.

She didn't have the nerve to say that. She was reeling from the fact that apparently she *did* like being made love to. That her previous experiences hadn't defined her.

Temple's fingers trapped her nipple. 'Here? This is where you want me to touch you?'

She nodded.

He smiled and it was wicked. 'You really want this?'

Ashling nodded. Almost feverish with lust. Begging silently.

Then he said lazily, 'I wondered how far you'd go…'

He was bending his head, his breath feathering close to her exposed skin, his mouth coming ever closer to her straining nipple… But something cut through the heat haze in Ashling's brain. Words that she hadn't really understood. A tone that made her uneasy.

She tensed. Pulled back.

Temple straightened up, his hands dislodged.

Instinctively she pulled the robe over her exposed breast. 'What do you mean by that?'

CHAPTER THREE

TEMPLE FOLDED HIS arms across his chest. She noticed then that he barely had a hair out of place, when she felt hot and dishevelled.

He said, 'You really don't have to put on this act, Ashling. The game is up. I know exactly who you are. I recognised you as soon as I saw you—and for what it's worth, the red wig was not a good look.'

Ice landed in Ashling's gut, dousing the feverish lust. *He'd known all evening.* She'd suspected, but she'd convinced herself that he couldn't possibly…

As if she had to hear him confirm it, she said faintly, 'You knew?'

He nodded, grim. 'Your face was etched into my memory after that night. I swore if I ever saw you again you'd pay for what you did.'

Ashling felt sick as the full magnitude of what had just happened sank in. He hadn't been making love to her because he fancied her. He'd been toying with her, giving her enough rope to hang herself. And she'd been well on her way to doing just that.

Temple started to walk around her. 'Based on previous experience, I might have expected you to be waiting in my bed, naked.'

The thought of being naked in his bed made a million conflicting things rise up inside her, chief of which was a betraying surge of excitement.

He was in front of her again. She said, 'Of course I wouldn't do something like that.'

Temple arched a brow. 'Why not? When you're halfway there with this little stunt?'

'It wasn't a stunt. I really did just want to have a shower. There wasn't anything else going on.'

Until he walked into the room and told you he fancied you and you were all over him in seconds.

Ashling wanted the ground to open up beneath her feet and swallow her whole.

Temple made a dismissive sound. 'Somehow, when you've already pretended to be my jilted lover, it's not such a stretch to suspect you'd be willing to go even further,' he said. 'You cost me a lover that night, and a lucrative deal. Tell me…how much did it earn you?'

You cost me a lover. Ashling didn't like how that impacted on her, deep inside. That woman had meant something to him…

She shook her head. 'You don't know how sorry I am about what I did. I was just following instructions. I didn't even know your name. I was filling in for a friend. I never did anything like that again.'

Ashling's conscience pricked. She could remember how his rejection of her had made her go off-script, because it had impacted her on a personal level, reminding her of her father's rejection.

All she'd had to do was pretend to be his lover and then flounce out when he issued the expected denial. But she'd been caught—trapped by those dark eyes, his words of denial and rejection cutting far deeper than she'd expected.

She forced herself to ask, 'Did your lover really leave you?'

Temple's mouth was a hard line. 'What did you expect? You put on a very convincing act of knowing me intimately. Not many women would put up with public humiliation. Do you know who put you up to it?' he asked abruptly.

Ashling shook her head. 'It was a casting agency—I knew the girl who was meant to do the job because we were in an amateur dramatics group together. She was sick that evening and asked me to do it in her place at the last minute. I don't know who hired the agency.'

'I do,' Temple said tersely. 'It was someone looking to undermine my reputation and derail a deal. But until now I thought you were a call girl.'

Ashling gasped in shock. 'I am not a call girl.'

He was grim. 'Could have fooled me.'

For the first time in her life Ashling felt a surge of anger so hot it almost blinded her for a moment.

'Don't even think about it…' Temple warned.

Ashling realised her hands were clenched into fists at her sides. Shock at the very notion that she might commit violence made it drain away as quickly as it had surged.

No one had ever had this effect on her.

She felt acutely vulnerable as the memory of how he'd looked at her four years ago meshed painfully with the last few minutes. It had been a cruel lesson, designed to humiliate and punish her.

She pulled the edges of the robe together over her chest. 'Look, I'm sorry about that night. It was irresponsible of me to step into a situation that I didn't know much about. If it's any consolation I felt terrible afterwards, and I gave the money they paid me to a homeless shelter.'

Temple wasn't impressed. Or most likely didn't believe her. 'I couldn't care less what you did with the money. I want to know what you thought you were going to get out of *this* situation.'

Ashling gasped as his very clear implication sank in. '*You* came in here. *You* kissed me.'

'After making sure it was what you wanted. I wanted to see how far you would go.'

She would have gone all the way. That realisation scraped painfully along her still sensitised nerve-endings.

She said, 'I did not come here this evening for any other reason than to do a favour for my friend.'

Temple looked stern. 'How involved is Cassie in this?'

Dread gripped Ashling at the thought that her actions might have consequences for her friend. '*She's not*. She knows nothing about what happened.' She clarified. 'I mean, I told her about that night at the time, because I felt so bad about it, and I knew it wasn't right, but she never knew that you were the man involved. *I* didn't even know until she showed me your picture in the paper.'

Zach looked at the woman in front of him. Cassie was one of his most trusted employees. Right now she was in the United States, scoping out a potential investment prospect for him. The thought that he'd entrusted her with so much information and the possibility existed that she was in league with this woman would be a betrayal of the worst kind.

As if reading his mind, Ashling Doyle said, 'Please, Cassie doesn't have any idea that we've met before. She knows nothing at all.'

She looked genuinely tortured. Face pale. It was conceivable that Cassie know the extent of her friend's machinations. She was loyal. Or at least he'd always believed so. Maybe that loyalty had blinded her to her friend's true nature.

Cassie would be back from the United States in two weeks. He would have to give her the benefit of the doubt for now, but he resolved to discuss it with her on her return. First he had to deal with *this*.

Much to his intense irritation, his blood was still running too hot for him to think clearly. He'd only intended to kiss Ashling Doyle, to see how she'd react, but as soon as he'd touched his mouth to hers he'd started to lose control of the situation.

The memory of the feel of her breast in his palm, firm and plump, was still vivid enough to entice him over the edge again. As was the memory of that kiss. Her soft mouth under his had been tremulous at first, and then growing bolder.

She said she wasn't a call girl. Her faux naive ways told a different story. Gallingly, his attempt to prove how far she was willing to go had only proved to him that she still had a very unwelcome effect on him. *That he wanted her*.

Disgust at his own weakness made him feel exposed and angry. Too many revelations for one evening.

He moved back and said curtly, 'Get dressed and get out of my house, Miss Doyle.'

Ashling looked at the empty space left behind Zachary Temple for a long moment, unable to move. She had a moment of hoping that maybe she'd just experienced a very vivid hallucination. But, no, her mouth was still tingling and she could still feel his hand on her breast.

It was shocking how quickly he'd made her forget everything. Who she was. Where she was. He'd barely touched her and she'd gone up in flames.

She'd believed it was a myth that desire could consume one so utterly. She'd had two short-lived relationships and they'd only confirmed her belief that that kind of desire didn't really exist. Or didn't exist for her.

But Temple had blown that assumption out of the water. She just hadn't met *him*.

His curt dismissal hung in the air, and Ashling had a vision of him returning to find her still standing there like someone transfixed. She moved quickly, changing into the first things she could find, not caring if they matched, stuffing the rest of her clothes into her bag.

As she went downstairs she held her breath, dreading the thought of seeing Temple again. But there was no sign of him. The butler materialised, looking seriously disapproving. What was his name again? Peters? He couldn't possibly know what had happened, but she felt as if he did.

He opened the front door, saying coolly, 'Mr Temple's driver is waiting to take you home.'

Ashling's insides curdled at the thought of being any more beholden to him than she already was. 'Thank you, but I don't need a lift—'

'Mr Temple insists.' The butler's tone brooked no argument. Not unlike his boss.

Feeling shame and guilt and mortification all at once, Ashling exited the house and went down the steps. The driver was waiting by the open back door of the car. She heard the front door of the house close behind her with a distinct *click*. Another feeling joined the cauldron swirling in her gut: the all too familiar one of having trespassed where she didn't belong.

She was tempted to plead again that she didn't need a lift, but the driver looked nice and she didn't want to get him into trouble.

She thanked him as she got in, and within seconds he was executing a neat U-turn in the street and driving her away from the man she knew she'd never forget. Not now. Not now she knew how he tasted. How he felt up close. Holding her. Touching her. And it had all been a cruel act to humiliate her. To prove that she was something she wasn't.

If she'd been able to think clearly she would have pretended that she was equally unmoved. But it was too late for that now.

To try and distract herself she took out her phone and saw a message from Cassie, who must have arrived in the United States by now.

You were right about the dress, Ash. I'm not even the most naked woman here... But what happened with the tux? You had one job, Ash!!

Ashling quickly typed a perky reply.

It was a little late, sorry! Everything okay in the end. Don't worry and enjoy the wedding! Xx

She groaned and let her head fall back. She was so busted.

The following day Ashling was gritty-eyed, after a night of broken sleep dominated by scary dreams in which she'd been in a room full of people looking for someone…looking for *him*. When she'd finally found him the relief had been intense. She'd put a hand on his arm but he'd turned around and looked down at her, saying coldly, 'Take your hand off me. I would never touch a woman like you. You don't belong here.'

Now, Ashling switched the heavier shopping bag to her other hand. She didn't need to be a genius to know that meeting Temple again, and the fact that he'd recognised her, was bringing up all her insecurities and deeply buried fears. Stuff she didn't even talk to Cassie about as it felt too pathetic.

Like the fact that she'd never really felt she belonged… anywhere. Hence her very haphazard life, working at about a million different jobs to see if anything fitted. *Or felt like home.* And the fact that she wore bright, eclectic clothes as a sort of rebellion against her instinctive need to fade into the background in a bid to please her father so he might accept her. Even after all these years.

She scowled. She hated Temple even more now. For what he was. For what he'd done to her last night.

You were with him all the way…begging, reminded a little inner voice.

She scowled harder in rejection of that, even though it was true. Mostly she hated Temple for making her feel vulnerable. Exposed. For reminding her of the guilt she'd always carried since that night. Except she had no one to blame for that but herself.

She was so busy thinking about Zachary Temple that when he got out of the back of the same sleek car that had driven her home last night all she could do was blink at him. He looked completely out of place in the quiet, leafy residential street, in a steel-grey three-piece suit. No less impressive than he'd been in a tuxedo.

Ashling blinked again, sure that her too-vivid imagination was playing tricks on her. Especially after that dream. But he didn't disappear.

All she could think of to say was, 'Are you really here?'

His grim expression told her that he most likely was real. She became very aware of her pulled back hair, make-up-free face, three-quarter-length bright blue joggers, flip-flops and pink tank top. She'd been planning a yoga practice after returning from the shop.

He held something out. She looked at it. It was a shoe. One of the shoes she'd been wearing last night. She must have left it behind in her rush to change and get out of Temple's house.

Ashling cringed. She was no Cinderella, and he probably thought she'd left it behind on purpose.

She couldn't take it as her hands were full of bags of shopping. She put one down, feeling flustered. He'd hardly come just to give her a shoe. She reached out and took it, pushing it into one of the bags, uncaring if it cracked an egg.

She stood up again. 'You didn't have to come all the way here. If you'd let me know I would have picked it up.' She could imagine Peters, the butler, handing it over, pinched between his fingers, as if it smelled bad.

'It was on my way.'

Ashling looked at him, still too stunned to move, even

though they were right outside the house where she shared the ground-floor apartment with Cassie.

Temple said, 'We need to talk. We can do it here, or...?'

Ashling's pulse tripled at the thought of him in her apartment, but they couldn't stay standing in the street. She could already see curtains twitching.

She moved past him, saying reluctantly, 'Please, come in.'

She thought she heard a dry, *'I thought you'd never ask...'* from behind her, but she couldn't be sure.

She opened the front door and immediately a thin voice floated down from the floor above. 'Is that you, Ashling dear? With my shopping?'

Ashling called up, 'Yes, Mrs Whyte. I'll bring it up now.'

She looked at Temple, who had a bemused expression on his face at this little domestic exchange. Did the man ever smile? she wondered snarkily. And then she remembered him smiling seductively before he'd kissed her. Maybe it was better that he didn't smile.

She put down the bags and opened the door into her and Cassie's flat, saying, 'I need to take Mrs Whyte her shopping first. It'll just take a few minutes, if you don't mind. She gets anxious.'

Temple pushed open the door with a finger and stepped over the threshold. 'Please, don't keep Mrs Whyte waiting.'

Ashling took the stairs two at a time with the shopping for her neighbour. She took as long as she imagined would be tolerable to keep a man like Zachary Temple waiting, her insides churning as she tried to figure out why he was here.

When she returned to the apartment Temple had his back to her. He was looking at a framed photo collage that hung on the wall near the fireplace.

He pointed to a photo without turning around. 'This is you and Cassie?'

Ashling knew without checking which photo he was

looking at. A picture of her and Cassie, arms wrapped tight around each other, pulling faces.

'Yes, we were about ten.'

It was her favourite photo of them. There were also pictures of her and her mother, with her bright red dyed hair piled high on her head and heavily lashed blue eyes, wearing a kaftan and ornate earrings. Her mother's typically understated attire. *Not*. It had embarrassed Ashling as a child who had just wanted to fit in, but now she was proud of her unorthodox mother. She'd come through so much on her own.

She became very conscious of the apartment as Temple would see it. The crystals in the windows, sending out little rainbows of light across the walls and ceiling. Plants populated almost every corner. Her yoga mat was on the floor. There was a large Buddha statue in the corner, where the stick of incense that Ashling had lit earlier was almost burned through, leaving the scent of sage in the air.

Feeling panicky, Ashling said to Temple's broad back, 'What can I do for you, Mr Temple?'

He turned around, looked at her, and said, 'I want you to come to Paris with me.'

Ashling was looking at him as if he'd grown two heads. Zach kept his gaze *up*, even though he wanted to let it rove over her lithe body, where nothing much was left to the imagination, with Lycra clinging to slim curves.

The lurid clashing colours of her clothes did little to detract from her appeal. Even though her hair was pulled back and she wore no make-up, she really was extraordinarily pretty.

Last night she'd been beautiful.

And sexy.

Sexy enough to make him lose his mind for a moment.

Sexy enough to make him almost forget who she was, what she'd done, and what she owed him.

A debt.

A debt he had every intention of calling in.

He knew it wasn't entirely rational to take her to Paris with him, but his every instinct was screaming at him to keep her close. Where he could keep an eye on her. In case she ran before he felt she'd paid her due.

Not because he wanted her. He had more control than that.

That ill-judged attempt to see how far she would go if he were to push her, hadn't been enough in terms of satisfying his thirst for revenge over what she'd done.

She'd wittingly—or unwittingly, according to her— exploded a bomb in his life at a time when he'd been most vulnerable. In many respects he'd had to start over again. Prove that he was reliable. Not out of his depth, or a dilettante. Since then his liaisons with women had been carefully judged and discreet. And his work ethic left no room for error.

Eventually she said, 'Of all the things you could have said to me, that is literally the last thing I would have expected. Why on earth would you ask me to come to Paris with you?'

Yes, why would you? asked a voice that he ignored. He knew what he was doing.

'Because you owe me a debt and this is how you'll pay it off.'

Ashling went very still, and then her eyes widened and her cheeks flushed with colour. 'I told you I'm not a call girl.'

Her outrage was authentic. Zach could see that. He said coolly, 'I'm not suggesting you pay off your debt in my bed. I have an important meeting in Paris and I need someone to come with me as an assistant. As I'm without Gwen and Cassie, you can save me the trouble of going through HR to find someone else at short notice on the weekend.'

The colour had receded a little from her cheeks now. 'You want me to act as your assistant?'

'It's the least you can do.'

She started to get agitated, moving around. It only drew Zach's eye to her slim form.

'Look,' she said, 'I've said I'm sorry. That night I was doing someone a favour… I knew it was unorthodox, but I had no idea of the repercussions. I was young and naive. I should have known better. I'm sorry.' She stopped moving and looked at him, beseeching. 'But I can't just drop everything and go to another country with you because you demand it.'

Zach looked around, taking in the surprisingly homely apartment. The scene didn't entirely fit with his image of her as a con woman—or a call girl, for that matter. But then, perhaps Cassie's influence was the dominant one here.

There was a comfortable couch. A massive TV. Books on shelves. He could imagine Ashling curled up on the couch, engrossed in something. There was a yoga mat on the floor, the lingering smell of fresh coffee in the air, and something he couldn't identify. Something New Agey.

To his surprise, it caused a pang in his chest. Brought back a memory of his mother standing behind him, her hands on his shoulders as she'd said, 'Look around you, Zach. *This* is not where you belong. You belong far from here. You belong in a place that the people here will never see in their lifetimes. But you will, because it's your due.'

Zach clamped down on the memory, irritated by its resurgence. He glanced at his watch and looked at Ashling. 'You have fifteen minutes. I'll be waiting in the car. We'll return this evening.'

He was almost at the door when she said, 'Now, wait just a minute—'

He turned around. '*No*. You owe me, Miss Doyle, and I'm collecting. If what you say is true, that Cassie knows nothing of this, and you want to keep it that way, then you'll do as I say.'

She went pale. 'That's blackmail.'

'Fifteen minutes or I'll come and get you. Dress smartly.'

Ashling spent five minutes after Temple had left the apartment pacing up and down and vacillating between anger at his arrogance and fear that he would tell Cassie what she'd done.

Ashling could imagine the look of disappointment on her friend's face. Cassie had never hidden the fact that she thought Ashling had gone over a line that night, and it had only compounded Ashling's own feelings of guilt and remorse. Cassie had worked so hard to get to where she was. She had a great relationship with Temple, and Ashling would hate to damage that.

So, if anything, the fact that Temple was offering her a chance to prove that Cassie wasn't involved and redeem herself…was a good thing. They would be quits.

She cringed, though, when she thought of the first place her mind had gone when he'd mentioned Paris. *Bed. Sex.* And the rush of very conflicting reactions in her body. Shock. Relief because he did fancy her. Excitement. And only then disgust at what he was insinuating. That she could pay him back *on* her back.

But he hadn't meant that at all. Because he didn't fancy her. As if she needed reminding.

She stopped pacing. She could see the sleek car outside the window. Imagined Temple sitting in the back, growing impatient. She really didn't have a choice. She couldn't bear to see the disappointment on Cassie's face. Or, worse, get her into trouble. He was right. She did owe him. This much at least. After a day in her company no doubt he'd be only too happy to see the back of her.

When Ashling got into the back of the car approximately ten minutes later. Temple gave her a once-over and as the car pulled away from the kerb. 'What are you wearing?'

Ashling felt defensive. 'You said to dress smartly. This is smart.' *For her.* She'd even borrowed one of Cassie's cream silk shirts with a pussycat bow.

Temple was looking at her lap. 'Is that a leather mini-skirt?'

'It's fake leather,' Ashling replied, indignant that he would assume it was real.

She'd paired the skirt with black sheer tights with black dots and flat leather brogues. For her, this was positively conservative.

Temple's gaze went to her head. He said dryly, 'I'm sure my French counterparts will appreciate the authentic touch.'

Ashling resisted the urge to take off her jaunty beret. 'I'm sure they will.'

She put the briefcase she'd also borrowed out of Cassie's wardrobe on her lap. She'd stuffed in notebooks and pens, not sure what would be required of her.

In a bid to try and distract herself from the enormity of the fact that she was going to Paris for a day with Zachary Temple, Ashling asked, 'So what exactly is the meeting about?'

'You don't need to worry about the details. You'll be making sure everyone has water…that kind of thing.'

Ashling smarted at his dismissive tone—but then this was payback.

She said, 'I have the notes from last night on my phone. If you need them I can transcribe them.'

He frowned. 'Notes?'

'That's why you asked me to accompany you yesterday evening…' But then something occurred to her and she cursed her naivety. 'You didn't need notes taken at all, did you? You just wanted to watch me squirm because you knew who I was.'

Temple didn't even look remotely sorry.

At that moment his phone rang and he took it out of his inside pocket, answering and proceeding to conduct a conversation in fluent French, which made him sound even sexier than he usually did. Even when he was being hateful.

Ashling scowled and looked out of her window, willing the day to be over already.

Ashling had never been on a private jet before. She'd naively assumed they would be taking the train to Paris. But, no, they'd driven to a private airfield beside one of London's biggest airports, where a gleaming silver Learjet had been waiting.

It was seriously plush inside. Cream leather seats. Luxurious carpets. Temple settled in without a second glance, opening up his laptop. Ashling hovered, unsure what to do…totally intimidated.

Temple looked at her. 'What's wrong?'

'Nothing.' She chose a seat on its own by a window. Her phone buzzed from her—from *Cassie's*—briefcase, and Ashling took it out, relieved to have something to do with her hands. It was another text from Cassie, and Ashling's eyes widened as she read it. Cassie had apparently slept with the man she'd gone to the States to spy on.

Ashling sneaked a glance at Temple, in case he could somehow magically read the text from a few feet away—she wouldn't put it past him—but he was engrossed in his laptop. She fired back an incredulous response, telling herself that Cassie obviously had enough on her plate to be dealing with, without hearing about Ashling's temporary new job as Temple's assistant.

She put the phone away. One of the stewards came over when they were in the air. 'Would you like some champagne, Miss Doyle?'

Ashling blanched. Maybe that was what was offered to Temple's usual companions. Women he brought with him for far more recreational reasons. Not for punishment. 'Er... no, thanks. Water would be fine. Or, coffee, if you have it.'

She would need all the help she could get to stay alert around the most disturbing man she'd ever met.

CHAPTER FOUR

'HAVE YOU BEEN to Paris before, Miss Doyle?'

Ashling tensed and turned away from the car window, where she'd been sighing at the sight of the Eiffel Tower in the distance. 'You can call me Ashling. "Miss Doyle" makes me sound like a schoolteacher.'

'Very well. Ashling.'

She immediately regretted saying that. He hadn't even called her Ashling last night, when he'd been making love to her. *Humiliating her.*

But then he said, 'You can call me Zach. I don't usually stand on ceremony with employees.'

A neat reminder—as if she needed it—that her initial assumption that he meant to bring her to Paris to sleep with her was about as likely as her becoming CEO of a company some day.

'So, Ashling, have you been here before?'

She swallowed, not liking how hearing him say her name made her feel. 'Just once before, with my mother. For my eighteenth birthday.'

Her romantic mother had told her that she should see the city with someone who loved her, even if it was her mother, so that her first impression of the most beautiful city in the world would always be remembered with love.

She could be grateful of that experience now, considering she was here with someone who didn't feel remotely romantic about her.

'You've obviously been here a lot. You speak fluent French,' Ashling said.

'I have an apartment here,' he responded.

Of course, Cassie had told her. Yet he wasn't staying the night. She wondered if he had a lover at the moment.

The car pulled to a stop outside one of the world's most iconic hotels. Ashling saw glamorous women in designer dresses with sleek hair and discreet jewellery walking in. One woman led a tiny beautifully groomed poodle on a jewelled lead.

She suddenly felt self-conscious in her attempt at a 'smart' office outfit. No wonder he had looked at her the way he had. She took off the beret and stuffed it into the briefcase. She'd thought it was cute and quirky. Now she realised she looked ridiculous. All she needed was a string of onions around her neck and a stripy top.

The driver was at her door and she stepped out with as much grace as she could muster. Zach was waiting, and moved forward when she joined him. She had to almost trot to keep up with him.

A man who looked as if he must be the manager hurried over as they walked into the lobby. Zach exchanged a few words with him and then the man said to Ashling, 'Anything you need, Miss Doyle, call my personal number.'

He handed her a card and she took it. Zach was already at the lift and she ran to join him just as he stepped inside.

When the lift stopped another suited man was waiting for them as the doors opened directly into what Ashling assumed was the penthouse suite. The views were astronomical. The Eiffel Tower was so close she felt she might be able to touch it. A large boardroom table had been set up in the main living area. A group of men and women, all suited and looking very serious, were waiting for Zach.

Ashling could see that bottles of water were on another table, with glasses stacked up, so she started busying herself by putting them out. One thing she'd learnt in her years of multi-jobbing: *use your initiative and keep busy.*

Zach cast an eye around. He seemed to note what Ashling was doing and said grudgingly, 'Good. We're just waiting for a couple more people—can you make sure they know where we are?'

'Of course.' She was more than happy to escape.

She went out into the lobby area just as a man and woman were arriving. They barely glanced at her as she told them where to go. Then there was no one for a few minutes. Starting to feel bored, Ashling did a little rear-ranging of the fresh flowers in a massive vase on a round table, humming to herself.

She heard a noise behind her and turned around to see an older gentleman getting out of the lift. He'd dropped his briefcase and papers were all over the floor. With a little exclamation Ashling rushed forward and bent down, help-ing him to gather them up.

She could see that he was slightly out of breath and, worried that he might be unwell, led him over to a chair to sit down. He had a kind face and he smiled at her. She tried to communicate in broken schoolgirl French but he put up a hand.

'I speak English.'

He had an accent she couldn't quite place. European, but with a slight American twang.

Ashling smiled. 'Are you okay? Would you like some water?'

'That would be lovely. Thank you, my dear.'

When she came back he was looking much better. She handed him the water. 'Is there anything else I can get you? I presume you're here to meet Zachary Temple?'

He nodded and handed her back the empty glass. 'That's all I need.'

He looked at her and she could see the shrewd twinkle in his eye.

'Who are you? We haven't met before.'

'Oh, I'm no one—just someone filling in for Mr Tem-ple's assistants. Please, let me show you to the meeting room.' The man got up, and as Ashling led him into the penthouse she said with a little wink, 'I have the personal number of the manager, so let me know if you need anything else.'

The man grinned. 'I will do, my dear.'

Zach appeared at the door leading into the living area. He greeted the man with enough deference to make Ashling wonder who he was. But then they disappeared, and Zach closed the door behind him, leaving Ashling firmly on the other side and in no doubt as to what her position here was.

Firmly on the outside. Not that she cared.

Hours later, after the last guest had left the suite, dusk was colouring the sky outside a bruised lavender. As much as Ashling wanted to go and sigh over the view, she knew she wasn't there for that. She busied herself clearing up discarded papers and cups of coffee and plates from the snacks and food that had been delivered all day.

'You don't have to do that.'

Ashling turned around to see Zach in the doorway. By now his jacket and waistcoat had been discarded. His tie was gone and his top button was open, sleeves rolled up. His hair was mussed and stubble lined his jaw.

He looked as if he could step straight into a boxing-ring for a bare-knuckle fight and win.

She put down the plates she'd gathered. 'Um…okay.'

'Our plans have changed.'

She frowned. '*Our* plans?'

'That man—the older gentleman?'

Ashling nodded. She'd chatted to him throughout the day when they'd taken breaks between meetings. A charming man and the only one to acknowledge her. She'd gone out of her way to make sure he had everything he needed.

'Well, I don't know if you know this, but he was the

guest of honour today. The man I came to meet. All the other people were members of his and my legal teams. We're working on a top-secret deal together—hence meeting in Paris. His name is Georgios Stephanides. He owns a bank in Greece—one of the most respected in the world.'

'Oh, wow. He seemed so…unassuming.'

'He liked you. What did you do to him? Did you recognise him?'

Ashling looked at Zach and put her hands on her hips, indignant. '*Do* to him? Of course I didn't "do" anything to him, or recognise him. I wouldn't know one end of a banker from the other!'

'Yet he kept seeking you out.' Suspicion rang in Zach's tone.

Not liking how his distrust made her feel, Ashling said, 'When he arrived he dropped his papers and he looked a little shaken. I helped him—got him water…chatted to him. That was all. I had no idea who he was.'

Zach looked unconvinced. 'He wants us to go to dinner with him and his wife this evening, and the deal is too important for me to refuse.'

Ashling squeaked, '*Us?* But there is no…"us". He knows I'm just a temporary assistant.'

'Well, he's invited you too, so we're staying for the night. We'll go to my apartment now, to get ready—it's not far.'

Ashling's insides plummeted. 'But I've nothing with me.'

'My housekeeper keeps the guest suite stocked for such emergencies. I'm sure you'll find something suitable to wear.'

Zach was already turning and walking out of the room, assuming she was right behind him.

Ashling felt like stamping her foot. Instead she called after him, 'I could have plans for this evening, you know.'

He turned around. 'Do you?'

'Well…no,' she admitted reluctantly. 'But I could.'

'But you don't. We don't have much time. My driver is waiting.'

Ashling really had no choice. She could make a fuss and insist on getting the train back to London—assuming there even was one this evening. Or she could just suck this up, and hopefully Zachary Temple would be so sick of the sight of her by tomorrow that he'd consider her debt paid and she wouldn't have to see him again.

She longed to call or text Cassie, who would roll her eyes at the latest drama Ashling had become entangled in. But of course she couldn't. Because a) it sounded as if Cassie was entangled in a drama of her own, and b) her friend must never know that this particular crisis involved her boss, Zachary Temple.

Nor could she confide in her the fact that Zach evoked so many things inside her. Guilt, shame, desire…and something far more ambiguous and dangerous. A kind of yearning for him not to look at her as if she was about to put the family silver in her pockets.

He appeared at the door again, pulling on his jacket. 'Ready?'

Ashling just nodded and followed him out of the suite.

Zach's Paris apartment was at the top of one of Paris's typically elegant nineteenth-century buildings, with views no less impressive than from the suite in the hotel. The Eiffel Tower was visible from the main spacious living area.

The décor was understated and luxurious. Modern art mixed with more traditional art on the walls, showing a quirkier side to Zach than Ashling might have expected for someone so…serious.

A middle-aged lady had met them at the door. Zach had introduced her as Cécile, and she came to Ashling now, saying in accented English, 'Please, follow me, Miss Doyle. I'll show you to your room and where the clothes are.'

Ashling followed her. Zach had disappeared—presumably to his own suite—to get ready.

Ashling's jaw dropped when she walked in. The room was massive, with a huge bed in the centre. There was a terrace outside. The bathroom was sleek in black and white, with a massive modern shower and a tub big enough for more than one person. Her cheeks grew warm.

Then there was the dressing room…

Cécile pointed to some hanging dresses. 'I'm sure there will be something in your size, Miss Doyle. You will find everything you need—including fresh underwear, night-clothes, shoes and accessories. There are new toiletries in the bathroom. '

Ashling was stunned. She asked faintly, 'Does Mr Temple have many overnight guests?'

The woman smiled enigmatically. 'Mr Temple likes to be prepared for every eventuality. This is simply a courtesy for guests.'

The woman left Ashling and she revolved in a circle slowly, taking in the sheer opulence. All the dresses had tags on, so they'd never been worn. As if a man like Zachary Temple would be crass enough to reuse his lovers' dresses! Not that she was a lover… She was just a thorn in his side and he'd decided to torture her a little.

After taking a quick shower and drying her hair, Ashling put on a voluminous robe and went back into the dressing room. A shimmer of dark blue silk caught her eye and she reached in to pull out a dress looked as if it was knee-length which should be suitable for dinner.

Ashling took off the robe and slipped the dress on over brand new underwear. Sleeveless, it had a Grecian design, with a deep vee at the front and velvet bands just under her breasts. It fell to just below her knee in luxurious folds, with a slit to one side. It was simple and effortlessly elegant in the way that only designer clothes could be.

She found a pair of silver high-heeled sandals in her size, and a black clutch bag.

She did the best she could with her hair, taming it into sleek waves, tucked behind one ear and loose on the other side. There was a selection of unused make-up in the bathroom, so she aimed for a slightly dramatic look with an eye pencil, mascara and some cream blusher, a nude lipstick.

She checked her reflection one last time and, conscious that Zach would probably already be waiting, went to the door and opened it—and came to a startled halt when her vision was filled with a naked chest.

Zach's naked chest, specifically. Because he was indeed changing into his tuxedo in his own suite, which must adjoin this guest one—a detail that Ashling registered only very vaguely in that moment.

She'd never seen a naked male torso like it up close. Naturally bronzed skin over taut muscles…a sprinkling of dark hair covering his pectorals and then descending in a dark line, bisecting the ridges of muscle on either side of his hard abdomen before disappearing under the belt and waistband of the trousers sitting on slim hips.

There was not an ounce of excess flesh. He had the body of an elite athlete. Or a warrior.

She didn't even realise she was ogling until Zach cleared his throat and said, 'Lost, Ashling?'

She looked up, not able to stop her cheeks flaming. 'Sorry… I… I didn't realise the rooms were connected… the wrong door…'

He was shrugging on a pristine white shirt now, doing up the buttons, and still she felt as if she was stuck in quick-drying cement. Somehow she managed to make her limbs move, and she turned around just as Zach said, 'You found a dress, I see?'

She stopped on the threshold and turned again slowly, breathing in a sigh of both relief and regret that his shirt was now closed.

'Yes, thank you. I hope it's suitable. I'm not sure what the dress code is...'

His dark gaze felt very clinical as it moved over her. 'It's perfect. You can wait for me in the reception room. I'll be there shortly.'

Ashling turned again and fled, closing the door firmly behind her. No doubt he'd suspect that she'd done that on purpose.

When they emerged from the building a short while later, onto the street, a young man got out of a sleek low-slung silver car and threw the key to Zach, who caught it deftly. He went over and opened the passenger door.

Ashling was too stunned to move. Faintly, she said, 'That's an Aston Martin.'

'Yes, it is.'

For a blessed moment Zach was eclipsed. Ashling walked over and touched the car reverently, skimming its sinuous lines with her hand. She couldn't *not* touch it.

Zach asked, 'You know about cars?'

She looked at him, aghast. 'This is more than a mere car.'

His mouth quirked. 'I'd have to agree with that.'

She turned back to the car and shook her head. 'I've never seen one up close before.'

'We should get going.'

Zach stood by the passenger door and Ashling got in as gracefully as she could manage. The door closed, sealing her inside possibly the most luxurious and expensive confined space she'd ever been in in her life.

She breathed in with appreciation, unaware of the bemused look Zach sent her as he got into the driver's seat and started the engine.

When he'd pulled away from the kerb and into the early-evening Paris traffic, he glanced at her. 'So how did the interest in cars come about?'

'Because I'm a girl, and girls shouldn't be interested in things like cars?'

Zach was unrepentant. 'It's not that common.'

'No,' she conceded, 'I guess not. I went through a phase when I was younger. I was obsessed with cars and driving. A man we lived with taught me to drive and I got my licence. I haven't driven in a while, though, as there's no real need in London.'

'It wasn't your father who taught you?'

Ashling tensed. She had let that slip out. 'No. I didn't grow up with my father. My parents broke up soon after I was born.'

To her relief Zach didn't ask her about that. He just said, 'So, the man who taught you to drive…?'

Ashling let the tactile contours of the seat mould around her. 'He lived at the commune. He used to be a racing car driver but he got injured.'

'The *commune*?'

Ashling's mouth quirked at the tone in his voice. She glanced at him. They were stopped at a traffic light. He arched a brow, waiting for elaboration. The surreal feeling of being in this legendary car with this man, about to go around the even more iconic Arc de Triomphe, was almost too much for her to process. It made it relatively easy to tell him her colourful background story.

Zach moved smoothly with the traffic as Ashling explained.

'My mum stopped working for Cassie's father when Cassie went to boarding school. We went back to Ireland, where she's from. She had friends living in an artists' commune in the west of Ireland, so we went there.'

'I thought I detected an accent.' Zach noted.

Ashling wrinkled her nose. 'I only spent a few years in Ireland, really, before coming back to London. And "commune" makes it sounds like something from the sixties, when really it was just a kind of collective, where we all pitched in and shared and bartered goods. We grew our own vegetables. Had chickens. It's called an eco-village now. She still lives there, with her new partner Eamon. He's a sheep-farmer and a traditional Irish musician.'

'Your mother sounds…unconventional.'

Ashling hated that word. It was the word her father had used in order to dump her and her mother. Ashling's mother had been too *unconventional* for him, a successful businessman. And yet her unconventionality had been what had drawn him to her in the first place.

She pushed aside old pain and memories of her mother, hurt and diminished by rejection. Thankfully she'd moved on from that now.

A man like Zach, who came from a privileged world, would never understand the life they'd lived. That reminder of who he was made her feel disappointed and defensive all at once. And angry with herself for her helpless attraction to him.

She forced a breezy nonchalance into her voice, hiding the much stronger emotions he'd precipitated. 'Yes, my mother was unconventional, but she was also kind and loving and nurturing. I never lacked for anything. She went back to college and got a master's in Psychotherapy, and now she runs her own practice. She's amazing.'

She felt Zach glance at her. 'I didn't mean it as a criticism. Taking you to Paris for your eighteenth birthday was a pretty special thing to do.'

Ashling forced herself to relax. He couldn't know he pushed her buttons just by being…himself. 'Yes, it was.'

'Did you miss having a father?'

The question surprised Ashling. She wouldn't have expected Zach to want to pursue a personal conversation.

The sky was darkening to violet outside, heightening the sense of being in a luxurious cocoon and Ashling hesitated, thinking of all the moments when she'd seen other kids interact with their fathers and had felt that sharp pang of envy. It was one of the reasons she'd bonded so quickly with Cassie—because while Cassie's father was alive, she'd lost her mother at a young age, so they'd shared the loss of a parent on either side.

Ashling's mother had become a sort of surrogate mother to Cassie. As for Cassie's father, though, he hadn't approved of Ashling and Cassie's friendship, never missing an opportunity to remind Ashling of her rightful place.

'I can't say I didn't, because of course I did, but I wouldn't swap the upbringing I had for the world. My mother made sure I felt loved and secure in a way that most kids with two parents don't get.' She made a small face, unable to stop herself from admitting, 'That's to say that while I don't regret anything, if I had a choice I'd probably choose a more...settled life for my own family. I was always a little envious of Cassie that she had a home that didn't change and move every few years.'

'So you want a family some day?'

Ashling blanched. She'd already said too much. No way was she divulging her deeply secret daydreams of a gaggle of children who would be siblings to each other, because she'd always felt that lack in her own life.

She felt Zach glance at her and kept her answer vague? 'Well, I guess so—doesn't everyone? Don't you?' she tacked on hurriedly, hoping to deflect his attention from her.

She looked at him. If she hadn't, she might have missed the clenching of his jaw before it relaxed again.

He said, 'I expect I'll have a family one day.'

With the kind of woman Ashling had seen him with four years ago. Patrician. Beautiful. With the right bloodline.

Curious, she said, 'You don't sound too enthusiastic about it.'

He made a little shrugging movement. 'Family is about legacy and continuity.'

The faintly hollow tone in his voice made her wonder what his family was like. She imagined similarly stern parents. Nannies doing the grunt work of parenting. Boarding school? Ashling felt a pang, thinking of a young, dark-haired boy being left at the gates of a Gothic mansion. Then she cursed herself for letting her imagination run away with itself.

She said, 'For someone like you, I can see that legacy and continuity would be important. After all, what would I have to pass on to the next generation?'

Zach slid her a glance. 'A talent for amateur dramatics and causing trouble?'

CHAPTER FIVE

THEY WERE WALKING into the restaurant and Zach should have had his mind on the dinner ahead—it was a good sign that Georgios Stephanides wanted to get to know him better—but he was still thinking about the fact that he'd unwittingly brought up the subject of family with Ashling, when it was something he preferred to avoid thinking about at all costs.

The very notion of family was toxic to him. And yet he'd made a promise to his mother that he would not let the Temple name die out. That he would do her sacrifices justice by creating his own legacy. By having a family.

And, worse than that, he was distracted by Ashling's reaction to his last flippant comment about amateur dramatics. He didn't like the way it had affected his conscience.

She'd looked at him with an expression of hurt and something else on her face before she'd quickly hidden it. It reminded him uncomfortably of how she'd looked at him that night four years ago, when he'd told her he wouldn't touch a woman like her. She'd looked stricken.

Then she'd said quietly, 'I've told you I'm sorry for what happened that night. I've never done anything like that since then. I knew it was wrong. I couldn't even keep the money they paid me. I'm really not some…opportunistic con artist, but I don't know how to convince you of that if you won't give me a chance.'

The maître d' was approaching them now, an unctuous smile on his face, and Zach took Ashling's arm. She felt very slight next to him. Delicate.

He said, 'Look at me, Ashling.'

He saw the way her jaw tensed, but finally she looked

up, blue eyes huge. Her mouth was set. He wanted to see it soften. Wanted to feel it under his again, yielding...

'I'll give you a chance, okay?'

Something flared in her eyes. Her cheeks pinkened. It had a direct effect on his blood, heating it at the most inappropriate moment. He gritted his jaw.

Her mouth softened. 'Thank you, I appreciate it.'

The maître d' reached them and Zach turned his attention to the man—anything to erase that image of Ashling's soft mouth from his brain before he had to sit down and be civilised.

'So you don't work for Zach full time, then, no?'

Ashling shook her head at the very glamorous wife of Georgios Stephanides. Elena had short silver hair and beautiful features, and she was as genial as her husband.

'No. My best friend Cassie is Mr...er... Zach's executive assistant. She's in the States for a couple of weeks, and Cassie's own assistant is out sick, so Zach needed help at the last minute.'

Or, more accurately, needed vengeance.

The older woman's dark eyes were as shrewd as her husband's. She looked from Ashling to Zach, who was deep in conversation with her husband, and then she said, 'So tell me, dear, what do you normally do?'

Ashling smiled, glad of the change of subject away from Zach and her role. 'I'm a yoga teacher, mainly, but I dabble in a few other things as well.'

The woman's face lit up. 'Yoga saved my life after I had a back operation. Now, tell me which kind you practice...'

'They're a lovely couple.'

Zach looked at Ashling. Her skin was lustrous in the dim light of the car. 'That's one way of putting it. You do realise that Stephanides is one of the most powerful men in Europe, if not the world?'

Ashling shrugged. 'I don't care about any of that. He's down to earth. Nice. They both are.'

Zach made a sound. He'd seen Georgios Stephanides's less genial side. But he had to admit that Ashling was right. Georgios was no push-over, but he was a rare thing: a humble billionaire.

'So what's the deal you're working on? Or is it too top secret to divulge?'

Every instinct within Zach screamed at him not to say a word. After all, that was how he'd achieved the success he had. By trusting no one. It was lesson he'd learnt at an early age, when he'd tried to make friends at a new school. A boarding school in the middle of nowhere. He'd been twelve years old.

They hadn't been interested in making friends though. Only giving him a lesson in knowing his place. They'd given him a bloody nose and then sneered at him. 'Listen up, Temple. You are not one of us and you never will be, so let's not pretend otherwise, hmm? You're only here because you're a box-ticking exercise in showing charity to the underprivileged. No matter where you end up, you'll never be one of us.'

One of the boys had punctuated that speech by spitting on him where he'd lain on the ground. That had been Zach's first lesson in learning control. Stopping himself from going after them and punching and kicking until the humiliation went away.

And then—many years later—this very woman beside him, in a cheap red wig and a tarty dress, had given him a refresher lesson in not letting his guard drop. Ever.

Now she cut into the slew of unwelcome memories, saying quickly, 'Actually, of course you can't say anything.'

But, perversely, in spite of the memories and his better instincts, Zach felt a strong compulsion to speak. Before he could overthink it, he was saying, 'Georgios and his wife never had children. So he's looking for someone who can take the reins of his bank. He wants to retire and move into philanthropy.'

Ashling looked at him, compassion all over her face. 'Oh, no, that's awful. Elena never mentioned anything… they would have made great parents too.'

Zach had never considered that, because his own view of family was so ambivalent. It was slightly jarring to think of his business acquaintance as someone who might have felt the lack of a family.

And he noted uncomfortably that Ashling's first reaction hadn't been to comment on the fact that he'd just revealed he was in line to take over one of the world's oldest and most respected financial institutions.

Feeling a little bemused, Zach said, 'Elena seemed to like you.'

'Not everyone has the worst impression of me. She's interested in yoga—we talked about that.'

He had to admit—reluctantly—that Ashling had been a good foil this evening. Easy company. He thought of the hurt look on her face when he'd made that comment about amateur dramatics.

Maybe he was being unfair to judge her wholly based on one incident four years ago. She was either telling the truth about it being a one-off, and she really was just a scatty friend of Cassie's. Or she was lying through her teeth and still angling to make the most of this opportunity.

Had she really grown up on a commune with a mother who sounded like the ultimate hippy? He felt something reckless move through him. He wanted her to prove that he was wrong to give her a chance. That she wasn't innocent of trying to seduce him in his own home.

On the spur of the moment Zach pulled in at the side of the road.

She looked at him. 'What are you doing?'

He got out of the car and went around to open Ashling's door.

He said, 'Do you want to have a go?'

She looked up at him, comprehension dawning on her face. 'You mean the car? Drive the car?'

He shrugged. 'Sure—why not? I'm not precious about things like that.'

'But…but I haven't driven in a while. It's an Aston Martin!' she spluttered.

'You know how to drive, don't you?'

'Yes, but this is the other side of the road. I mean, it's not even a road—it's the Champs-élysées!'

'It's just a road. My apartment isn't far from here. I'll direct you.'

A mixture of excitement and shock warred on Ashling's expressive face.

He half expected her to confess that she didn't actually know how to drive, but then she scrambled out of the car, the slit in the dress showing one very taut and toned thigh.

She was breathless. 'Okay, I'll give it a go.'

Zach realised that what he was doing was madness. They were on one of the world's most famous roads. If anything happened it would be splashed all over the papers. But that uncustomary reckless spirit moved through him again.

He watched Ashling walk around and get into the driver's seat. He got into the car.

Ashling wondered if she was having an out-of-body experience. She felt the steering wheel under her hands, the leather warm from Zach's touch. Looked at the lit-up dashboard with its iconic design. Heard the low, throaty purr of the engine.

It was automatic, so she didn't have to worry about the gearstick, and Zach pointed out a few things. When there was a lull in the traffic, she followed Zach's instructions to move out into the road, the car throbbing with barely leashed power underneath her. To her intense embarrassment it made her think of Zach and how he might feel if he was under her...

'Red light,' Zach said.

Ashling pulled to a smooth stop, breathing deep to try and calm her racing heart. Awe and excitement flooded her blood. 'It feels amazing. So light, but powerful at the same time.'

'I wanted an Aston Martin ever since I saw my first Bond movie as a kid.'

Ashling hit the accelerator again when the light went green. The car surged forward with the barest tap. When she felt she had it under control, she sneaked a quick glance at Zach. 'You were a Bond fan?'

'Still am.'

'I loved them too,' she admitted. 'Even though my mother could never understand my obsession. I think it was the cars and gadgets I loved more than anything else.'

'Not the wealth? The glamour?'

Ashling was barely aware of Zach's question as she concentrated on not crashing the car. 'No, I was never into those things. My favourite gadget was the rocket belt Sean Connery wore in *Thunderball*.'

'Take the next left.'

Ashling was both relieved and disappointed to see the concierge step out of Zach's building onto the quiet street as she came to a stop outside. She was still reeling from the shock of him letting her do this.

She looked at Zach, feeling shy. 'Thank you. This was... amazing.'

'You're a good driver. Next time we should go somewhere you can really let her run.'

Ashling blanched a little. *Next time?*

As if he'd just realised what he'd said, Zach's face shuttered. He got out of the car and came around to help her out. The concierge took care of parking the car. Ashling told herself that what Zach had just said was a slip of the tongue. He obviously didn't mean it.

In the lift on the way up, she studiously avoided looking at him. There was tension in the air, though, something hot and restless.

When the doors opened he let her step out first. She turned around and a wave of gratitude for the experience he'd just given her made her act on impulse. She stepped forward and reached up, pressing a kiss to his jaw in almost exactly the same spot she'd kissed him that night four years ago.

His scent hit her, hurtling her back in time. She regretted it as soon as it had happened. She stepped back, her face flaming. His was unreadable. *Oh, God.* He'd think she was trying to seduce him again.

'Sorry, I just… I didn't mean to do that. I just wanted to say thanks…that was an amazing thing to do… I'm quite tired now. I'll go to bed. Night, Zach.'

And she fled.

Zach watched Ashling disappear. Almost absently he touched his jaw, as if expecting to feel some kind of a mark. She'd barely pressed her lips there, but it burned.

Cursing himself, and the reckless urge that he'd given in to—the same urge that now made him want to follow her to her room and crush her mouth under his, punish her for appearing in his life again and for making him want her—Zach turned and went into the reception room.

It was vast and silent. He stopped on the threshold,

struck by that fact. He'd never really noticed it before, but he realised now that he usually didn't let the silence in.

For his whole life he'd been alone to a lesser or greater extent. An only child. And then, at school, once his aptitude had become apparent, he'd been put under a punishing regime by his mother to succeed at all costs. There'd been no room for friends. For frivolous pursuits.

He'd soon learnt to stay apart. Not only to focus, but also because he knew he wasn't welcome. It had become like a second skin—the fact that he didn't need anyone else. And if he had ever felt the lack he'd shut it out with work. Or, later, with sex.

But here, now, after Ashling's disappearance, he could feel the void. The absence of her bright presence. She had an effervescence that drew people to her. He'd seen it in the way Georgios and his wife had reacted to her.

The fact that Ashling tapped into Zach's sense of isolation wasn't welcome. Was that what had prompted him to suggest another outing in the car before he'd even realised what he was saying? He was usually so careful around women, never putting himself in any position that might lead them to think he wanted more than a finite affair.

Zach heard a noise behind him and turned around.

Ashling was standing in the doorway. Barefoot.

The introspection of moments before dissolved in her presence. He instantly felt warmer. *Less isolated.*

She looked hesitant. 'I just… I just wanted to say I really hope you don't think that when I kissed you just now it was because I was trying to do anything…because I really wasn't. And last night too. I wasn't trying to seduce you.' She gave a little laugh that sounded strained. 'I've had two boyfriends and neither lasted very long. I'm really not that…experienced.'

Her face went crimson. She half turned away.

Zach heard her say, almost to herself, 'I can't believe I

just said that...' She looked back. 'Forget I said anything. I'll leave you—'

'Don't.'

Zach knew he should resist, but in actuality he couldn't. He needed something from her in that moment. Something he'd never needed from another woman because no other woman had impacted him the way she did. *Connection.*

The sharp tone of Zach's voice stopped Ashling in her tracks. She looked at him. He dominated the vast space around him. The Eiffel Tower glittered like a bauble through the window behind him.

Ashling forced her voice to work. 'Don't...what?'

'Don't leave.' His voice sounded rough.

Ashling's heart hitched. Her skin prickled all over. The air was thick. Heavy with a tension she could feel coiling tight in her lower body.

Zach walked towards her, shucking off his jacket as he did so, dropping it on a chair. He stopped a few inches away, his gaze roving over her face.

He said, 'I gave you the impression last night that I didn't want you. But that wasn't entirely fair. And neither was what I said four years ago—that you were the last woman I would touch. You made an impression on me. That's why I recognised you. I never forgot your face. The truth is from the moment I saw you, I wanted you.'

Ashling swallowed. *He did fancy her.* It was too much to absorb for a second.

'The woman you were with that night...'

'She dumped me—like I told you. But I didn't care. I was angry at first, but then I realised that I didn't even want her any more.'

Because he'd wanted her...?

Ashling shook her head. 'You're just saying this. Teasing me. More punishment for what I did.'

She turned to go but Zach caught her hand, lacing his fingers through hers. It felt shockingly intimate.

'I'm not teasing. I don't tease women. It tends to send out the wrong message.'

Ashling could believe that. He was far too serious. She wondered what he would be like if he laughed. Properly laughed. Out loud. Smiled.

'So what…?' *What happens now?* She couldn't say the words out loud.

Zach tugged her closer. He lifted their entwined hands against his chest and curled his other hand around her neck. Just before his mouth descended on hers, Ashling realised he wasn't asking her permission because she'd made it all too painfully obvious that she wanted him. For a second she wanted to pull back, disconcert him as he did her, so easily, but then his mouth touched hers and the world went on fire.

Ashling could feel the press of Zach's arousal against her belly. She strained closer, seeking friction to assuage the ache building between her legs, sharp and urgent.

Zach pushed the strap of her dress off one shoulder. He untwined his fingers from hers and Ashling's hand slid over his chest, revelling in the sheer breadth and strength of him. He was tugging her head back, deepening the kiss, drugging her, pulling her deeper and deeper into a carnal spell where the whole world, her very existence, was reduced to this moment, with her heart beating and the delicious tug and pull of Zach's tongue against hers.

And then he broke the kiss, trailing his mouth down over her shoulder. She realised through a hot haze that he was resting back on the arm of a couch and had spread his legs either side of her thighs, so that he could trap here there. It placed his erection closer to the apex of her legs, and Ashling bit her tongue at the sharp tug of need.

He pulled down the strap of the dress further, until one side of her dress was peeled away from her bare breast. He looked up at her for a moment, dark eyes hooded and full of something that made her shake. She'd never known she could have such an effect on a man. Or a man on her. Her previous experiences hadn't prepared her remotely for this rush of sensations and desires piling up inside her, stealing her sanity and her wits and—

Ashling let out a low moan when Zach's mouth surrounded the peak of her breast in hot, sucking heat.

Her hands clasped his head. She was torn between pulling him back from torturing her and keeping him there for ever. He laved the hard peak with his tongue, teeth nipping gently, before sucking so hard that Ashling saw stars. She didn't even know if she was still standing. Every nerve cell was straining towards a release that shimmered just out of reach...

And then his other hand was under her dress, reaching up to find her thigh, caressing her there, moving higher, fingers sliding under silk underwear to cup her bottom.

Ashling couldn't think or breathe, but something was struggling to reach her through the fog. A small voice. A warning. She didn't really know this man. He was Cassie's *boss*! She'd done something awful to him in the past and he hated her for it. So how could he now—?

Ashling tensed and pushed back, dislodging Zach's mouth from her breast. She pulled the dress back up over her throbbing breast, securing the strap on her shoulder again with shaking fingers. Her blood was pounding. Her body crying out for fulfilment.

But she wasn't even sure if she liked this man, and yet he'd connected with her on a level so deep and intimate that it made her head spin.

She took a step back and said shakily, 'I don't think this is a good idea. You're Cassie's boss. She's my friend. You don't even like me. You don't trust me.'

Zach's hair was mussed. *She'd done that, grabbing his*

head to keep his mouth on her breast. She could still feel the delicious tugging—

She closed her eyes in a bid to stop her imagination.

'I don't trust anyone.'

Ashling's eyes snapped open again. Zach stood up and went over to a drinks cabinet. He poured himself a measure of golden liquid, asked, 'Do you want a drink?'

Ashling shook her head. Then said, 'No, thank you.'

I don't trust anyone.

He looked very remote at that moment, his back to her. Ashling wanted to go and put her arms around him from behind, press close. The men she'd been with before— sweet and kind and ultimately dull—would have let her do that. But this man…he would resist. And the fact that she knew that and yet still wanted to do it told her she was doing the right thing.

Zachary Temple was not looking for comfort. He was not even someone she thought she could admire. He shouldn't be having this effect on her. It made her wonder about the rock-solid values she'd taken for granted her whole life, having been taught that things like compassion, wellbeing, happiness and good health were more important than wealth and ambition.

This just proved to Ashling that passion was dangerous. It scrambled your brain cells. Made you fall for the wrong person. Made you trust in something that wasn't there. Like her mother and her father.

Something struck her. Maybe the men she'd been with before had been attractive to her precisely because she'd known they wouldn't push her to the edge of her boundaries and over. It wasn't a welcome revelation.

She wondered if she really knew herself at all. How could someone like Zach fascinate her so much when he'd just been handed everything his whole life? When he was so ambitious—pursuing a deal to gain control of one of Europe's biggest banks just to add it to his portfolio?

She backed away to the door even as her body still ached for satisfaction. 'This isn't a good idea. I'll go.'

Zach didn't turn around. He just took a swig of the drink and said, 'That's probably a good idea.'

Ashling turned and left on very shaky limbs. It was as if an earthquake had just exploded inside her and her cells had been rearranged. She knew that on some fundamental level Zach had triggered a response that she would never be able to bury or deny again. He'd changed her, whether she liked to admit it or not. In spite of who he was.

Zach knew that no amount of alcohol burning its way down his throat would extinguish the desire that had just knocked him off his feet. He'd felt it last night, but he'd not given it full rein. Just now, though…it had almost overwhelmed him. The feel of Ashling's mouth under his…her tongue shyly touching his…her slender limbs that belied the strength he'd felt in her muscles…soft breasts, filling his hand and his mouth.

No woman had ever made him lose it. He'd seen his peers fall by the wayside, seemingly driven mad with lust they couldn't control…he'd pitied them.

But just now he'd been afraid to turn around in case Ashling saw the extent of the need still burning him up inside written all over his face. He felt feral. Animalistic.

He should be secretly thankful that she'd pulled them back from the brink. She was right. They shouldn't be doing this—for many reasons. Not least of which was because she was not his type at all. And he suspected she'd tell him that he wasn't hers.

But instead of feeling thankful, all he felt was seriously unsatisfied. And angry with himself for his serious lapse in judgement. He'd shared top secret information with her, and now he had to face the prospect that letting her go was not an option.

The following morning Ashling felt heavy-headed after a restless night. She'd been too keyed-up to sleep. Too full of aches and wants.

Zach, on the other hand, when she met him in the dining room for breakfast, looked as pristine as if he'd just spent a weekend at a spa resort. Clean-shaven. Hair damp from a shower. Smelling delicious. The worst thing was that she could imagine only too well the power behind his civilised clothes. The warm silky skin over steel muscles.

He looked at her when she sat down at the table, not a hint of what had happened the previous evening in his expression or his eyes. It was disconcerting.

But then Ashling had to remind herself that Zach was far more used to this kind of thing than she was. And in a way she should be thankful they hadn't slept together, because there was no way she knew how to navigate a morning-after situation with a man like him.

He poured her a cup of coffee. There were delicious-looking pastries and fluffy croissants laid out on trays.

'What are your plans this week?' he asked.

Ashling picked up the cup, hoping the coffee might make her feel half as put-together as he looked.

She stared at him. 'Plans?'

He nodded.

Feeling a little nonplussed, Ashling said, 'I have yoga classes to teach, and I care for Mrs Whyte—'

'Mrs Whyte?'

'The woman whose shopping I buy. I delivered it to her yesterday…when you came to my apartment?'

Zach nodded. 'Yes, go on, what else?'

Ashling put down the cup. 'Apart from the yoga and

Mrs Whyte I have a couple of shifts at the cafe… I think that's it. Why?'

'I need you to work for me this week.'

'You…what?'

'I'm still without assistants. Gwen will be out for another week at least. Cassie isn't due back until the end of the week after next. And Georgios Stephanides wants to move ahead with this deal. I'm hosting an event at my Somerset house at the end of next week and he's coming with his wife to talk over final details. I've told you this deal is top secret. I don't want anyone else to know what's going on until contracts are signed. You and my legal team are the only ones in the loop. And Georgios has met you. He thinks you're part of my team. He likes you. He sent a message this morning saying that he hoped you'd be there, which is as good as an order.'

'But you don't trust me.'

Because he didn't trust anyone.

Had her actions four years ago had this effect on his outlook? Ashling told herself she was being ridiculous. She might have caused him some embarrassment, but she'd hardly have enough influence to cause him to become less trusting. He moved in a world where cynicism pervaded everything.

Zach countered with, 'Precisely. Not only do I need to keep Georgios Stephanides happy, I also want you where I can see you.'

Ashling chafed at that. 'I'm not a child.'

Something flared in his eyes. 'No, you're not…'

Ashling flushed. 'I can't just drop everything at the last minute. What I do might not seem consequential to you, but I can assure you that—'

'I'm sure your neighbour would appreciate full-time care, no?'

Ashling's mouth stayed open. 'What are you saying?'

'That if you work for me for the week I'll ensure that she has help for as long as she needs it.'

Ashling struggled to take this in. 'But that's…that's like winning the lottery.'

Zach shrugged minutely.

Anger at his cavalier attitude to something potentially life-changing flared up inside Ashling. 'People are just pawns to you, aren't they? You're angry with me so you've moved me around to teach me a lesson. And now you think you can just click your fingers and change someone's life just because it's expedient for *you*.'

'I don't let things stand in my way.'

'Because you don't have to.'

'Because I've worked for it.'

'I doubt that,' she scoffed. 'Someone like you was born with a golden ticket into the arena.'

Zach's face tightened. 'You know this because…?'

A prickle of unease skated down Ashling's spine. 'Because it's obvious.'

Was it, though? a little voice prompted. It wasn't like her to judge. But Zach oozed privilege. To get to his level of success demanded entry at the very top levels of society from birth. She pushed aside her conscience.

'You'd really set up care for Mrs Whyte for as long as she needs it?'

'Consider it done.'

'I'd have to talk to her…see if it's something she wants. She's very private.'

'I can offer her more consistent care than you ever could. With the best will in the world.'

That stung. But Ashling knew it was true. She couldn't guarantee that she'd always be there, and Mrs Whyte had grown quite dependent on her.

Zach said, 'You still owe me, Ashling. There is a deal

here that I want very badly. If you can help me close it then we really will be quits.'

Ashling squirmed inwardly at the thought of causing him to lose a deal four years before. The guilt was still fresh. 'I'd have to sort out my other commitments. My yoga classes. The café."

'Whatever you need to do—do it.'

In other words this was a fait accompli and Ashling was being sucked into Zach's orbit whether she liked it or not.

Much to her disgust, her prevailing reaction was one of illicit excitement, not outright rejection of this turn of events. And, even worse, she realised that her anger had flared so quickly not just because of his arrogance in knowing that he would prevail no matter what, but because just a few hours ago she'd been a very willing pawn in his arms.

Nevertheless, she forced herself to say, 'What about... what happened last night?'

Zach's jaw clenched. 'That was a mistake. It won't happen again.'

CHAPTER SIX

ZACH BLINKED. LESS than twenty-four hours later, Ashling stood in the doorway to his office wearing a blue silk sleeveless jumpsuit. A yellow belt cinched her waist and a yellow neckerchief adorned her throat. She wore yellow wedge sandals. A jaunty cross-over pink bag rested at her hip.

She looked bright and fresh. And totally out of place. And yet something perverse inside him made him resist his reflex to instruct HR to discreetly let her know there was a dress code. After all, this was just a temporary arrangement.

You could have let her go.

He *should* have let her go.

Especially after what had happened the night before last.

Especially because the lust she'd awakened inside him was snapping back to life now.

He ignored his libido and stood up. 'Come in, Ashling.'

She looked nervous and that caught at him. He told himself he was being ridiculous. She was street-smart and savvy.

But she must have seen his look and she said, a little defensively, 'I'm not used to this kind of environment.'

'And you're really not that interested, are you?' Zach noted dryly.

She flushed. Looked behind him. 'The views are amazing.'

Zach rested back on the side of his desk. 'So is the wealth I generate for my clients.'

'You hardly need my approval for that.'

Zach cocked his head. 'You really expect me to believe that wealth, success, means nothing to you?'

'Oh, it means everything—I just measure wealth and success differently.'

'Says the woman who loves an Aston Martin, one of the most expensive cars in the world.'

She flushed again. It was fascinating to watch her react to things.

'I can appreciate a beautiful car without wanting to acquire it as a trophy.'

Zach made a wincing face. 'Ouch.'

Now she looked contrite. 'I'm sorry, that wasn't fair—especially after you let me drive yours.'

Zach stood up, realising he was indulging in exactly the kind of chatter he expressly forbade among his employees. 'I'll have HR send someone up to show you how to navigate the computer system. Essentially, though, your job is just about running interference. They'll explain everything. You can use the desk in the office next door.'

Ashling took a deep breath after she had put a closed door between her and Zach. She'd only realised when she'd got to his office that morning and seen him in a dark grey three-piece suit that everyone in the building was similarly attired in monochrome colours. Even the decor was muted. No doubt to minimise distraction.

No wonder people had given her second and third glances on her way up here. A familiar sensation washed over her—she didn't belong here. But she pushed it aside. She hadn't *asked* to be here after all. She'd been *instructed* to be here.

It was as if the universe had conspired with Zach to leave her no option but to do his bidding. Since she'd seen him last Mrs Whyte had met and approved someone from an agency who would help her until such time that she decided she didn't need it any longer. And Ashling had asked a friend to cover her yoga classes, half hoping there might be a problem. But he'd been delighted at the prospect of extra cash.

Similarly, a friend at the café had jumped at the chance of more shifts because she was saving for her wedding.

So now she was here, her heart still palpitating in her chest.

She had the strong impression that, in spite of Zach's justification for asking her to work for him, he was just doing it for his own amusement…stringing her torture out for a bit longer. He probably had a personal bet on how long she would last, so she resolved right then to do everything in her power to confound his expectations.

Except one thing.

She refused to dress to fit in with the crowd.

Two days later, Ashling was making coffee for Zach, expecting his arrival at any moment. She was not a morning person at the best of times, and the effort it had taken for the past two days to be on time—early, in fact—and bright-eyed and bushy-tailed was not inconsequential. But it had been worth it for the look of sheer surprise on Zach's face the first morning and then, yesterday, his look of disbelief.

The fact that he'd evidently expected her to bail within twenty-four hours only spurred her on. With a little judicious borrowing from Cassie's wardrobe Ashling had managed to pull together something resembling a corporate uniform each day. Albeit her kind of corporate uniform… about as far from monochrome as one could get.

She heard a noise in the outer office and her heart thumped. Zach seemed to have had no problem moving on from the other night—as he'd called it, *a mistake*—but for her it wasn't so easy. The tension she felt in his presence coiled tight inside her now, as she anticipated seeing him.

He appeared in the doorway to little kitchen that led into a private dressing room and bathroom. Ashling handed the cup of coffee over carefully, avoiding looking directly at his face. She didn't want to see the cool appraisal he subjected her to every morning.

But then he said, 'Pink today?'

She forced herself to meet his eyes. 'Is that a problem?'

He took a sip of coffee as that dark gaze drifted down from the pussycat bow at her throat—the pink silky shirt had been an impulse buy on her way home the previous day—to the wide-legged three-quarter-length trousers dotted with a variety of colourful flowers and the blue suede high heels. She had to admit that, even for her, there was a lot going on. But in her defence, bleary-eyed that morning, she'd thought the shoes were black.

He raised his gaze again. By now Ashling's pulse was hectic.

He just said, 'Not a problem at all.'

He was turning away, and then he stopped, turned back. 'By the way, I should have mentioned it before, but we have to go to a function this evening. A garden party.'

'I didn't bring anything to change into.'

Zach gestured with his free hand towards the dressing room. 'Cassie usually leaves a selection of outfits here in case of last-minute events. I'm sure you'll find something. If not, just order in.'

Order in. Like a Chinese takeaway.

Ashling felt slightly hysterical at the thought of appearing in public officially as Zach's assistant. What if someone spoke to her and expected her to say something knowledgeable? In Paris she'd been winging it. And that had been a punishment for her transgression. This was… She wasn't even sure what this was. Only that Zach wasn't done with punishing her and that he stirred up so many things inside her that even if he told her she could walk away right now she wasn't sure she'd want to.

At that moment he appeared in the doorway again, without his coffee. He was holding up an object shaped like an egg. 'What is this?'

'Oh, that's just an aromatherapy oil diffuser.' She gestured to the matching device on her desk. 'Mine is a mixture of sage and peppermint. Sage to clear the energy and peppermint to keep things fresh. Raise the vibration.'

He arched a brow. '"Raise the vibration"? "Clear the energy"?'

She nodded. 'It's quite dense in here—but no wonder, considering the stress of your employees.'

'They're stressed?'

She made a face. 'Not in a bad way…just working hard to keep up with your…er…pace. Yours is bergamot, to stay focused and grounded…' Ashling trailed off, sensing she'd lost him as soon as she'd said *energy*.

He just looked at the diffuser in his hand and then walked back into his office with a bemused expression on his face.

Much later that day, after everyone else had left Temple Corp, Zach was escorting Ashling out of the building, across the carefully landscaped concourse, to where his chauffeur-driven car was waiting.

Ashling was self-conscious in the only suitable dress of Cassie's that she'd been able to find in the dressing room. A deep royal blue colour, it matched her shoes. It was a very simple silk shift dress, with thin straps. It reached to the knee. Or just below, in Ashling's case, as she was shorter than Cassie.

Zach was dressed in a tuxedo, and when Ashling had seen him she'd said in dismay, 'I should be wearing a full-length gown… But all of Cassie's are too long on me.'

He'd looked her over. 'You'll be fine—you'll be there as my guest.'

In other words, Ashling had surmised on their short

journey down to ground level, it would be obvious that she wasn't Zach's date. It made her wonder if he'd prefer to be taking a woman who *was* a date. Who he wouldn't have to stop kissing because there was just too much baggage between them...

From what Cassie had told her over the years, Zach was discreet to the point of obsession when it came to his personal life. Rarely did any picture surface online of him with a woman, and if it did she was always a perfect foil. Tall, sleek, beautiful... There were no kiss-and-tells.

Ashling's conscience pricked. Had what she'd done to him ended up in the papers? She didn't even know because she'd felt so humiliated and guilty. She hadn't looked.

In the back of the car now, heading for central London, Ashling bit her lip, the urge to know trembling on her tongue. But before she could let it out, Zach spoke.

'You've done well these past few days.'

Ashling looked at him, surprised. She knew after only a few days of observing him that he didn't hand out platitudes or compliments. 'Thank you.'

'You're not as ditsy or flaky as Cassie has suggested over the years. Or as you yourself would have people believe, I think.'

Surprise rendered Ashling speechless. No one had ever really taken the time to look past the persona she projected, of a free spirit pinballing her way through life. She knew she used it as a device to protect herself from deeper scrutiny—something her mother had pointed out when she'd been dissecting everyone around her during her Psychotherapy master's degree. The fact that it appeared as if this man—of all people—could see right through her was very exposing.

Telling herself she was silly to feel exposed—after all, Zach wasn't interested in who she really was—she said lightly, 'Who knew that a career spanning everything from waiting tables to teaching yoga would prepare me for one day working for you?'

Zach frowned. 'You didn't go to university?'

Ashling shook her head and forced down the ingrained reflex of feeling inadequate. It had taken her a long time not to feel insecure about her lack of higher education. Even though Cassie had often said to her, *'Ash, I work with people who have degrees coming out their eyeballs and you're smarter than them.'*

She said, 'I'm a little dyslexic, so I was never very academic. I prefer to learn on the job.'

Something else that distanced her from her father, who couldn't be more different, having come from a solidly middle-class academic background.

Zach looked at her for a long moment and she felt like squirming under that dark unreadable gaze. She said, 'I presume you were top of your class?'

His expression was shuttered. 'Something like that.'

Ashling was intrigued. She wanted to know more. She had to concede that this man she'd dismissed for years as arrogant and snobbish was a lot more complex than she'd expected.

And that was her cue to divert the conversation away from personal topics. 'What do you expect me to do at the event?' she asked.

He looked at her. 'Just stay by my side and be a second set of eyes and ears.'

He turned away again, and Ashling curbed the urge to salute and say, *Aye-aye, sir.*

The gardens attached to the American Ambassador's residence were beautiful and pristinely ornate. Personally, Ashling preferred something a little wilder. Black-clothed staff moved gracefully between the guests, handing out delicious canapés and vintage champagne. Classical music drifted from a gazebo where a small band were playing.

The man Zach had been talking to walked away and Zach turned to Ashling. 'What did you make of him?'

Thankfully, she'd studied the other man, while also being preoccupied by her surroundings. And Zach. A skill she obviously needed.

'Too desperate for your attention. Fake laugh. Untrustworthy.'

She spoke automatically, without thinking, and nearly choked on her wine when Zach threw back his head and laughed out loud. People turned to look, and a very dangerous warmth bloomed in Ashling's chest.

Zach looked down at her, a smile transforming his face from merely gorgeous to savagely beautiful. He looked younger. She couldn't breathe.

'That's certainly one way of putting it—and very accurate,' he said.

Damn him. He was totally irresistible when his stern facade cracked a little. And when she was the cause.

He gestured for her to follow him further into the crowd. Ashling picked her way carefully behind him in her heels, acutely conscious of the fact that most of the other women were wearing long dresses. Not that she needed more help to feel out of place in a situation like this.

A charity auction was taking place in another part of the garden, with cheers going up every now and then as someone bid successfully on something spectacular.

When there was a brief lull in the steady stream of gushing people seeking an audience with Zach, Ashling said, 'You're not bidding on any of the lots?'

He looked at her. 'I've already given a healthy donation. I don't need to make a public spectacle of myself.'

Ashling's conscience pricked. As if she needed a reminder... Forgetting all about keeping things impersonal, she blurted out, 'Was it very bad? After that night? I mean, I know you told me you lost a deal, and the woman you were with dumped you…'

He arched a brow. 'That wasn't bad enough?'

Ashling regretted her runaway mouth now. But she'd started… 'Did it get into the papers?'

Zach sighed. 'Yes—but thankfully only the gossip section of a couple of rags. It didn't last beyond a couple of weeks. It was the rumours and word of mouth among my peers that did the most damage. People weren't sure if they could trust me. Which was the intention of the person who initiated the whole thing—to destabilise my success.'

'You know who it was?'

'I do.'

It was said with such finality that Ashling didn't dare probe further. The smile was long gone. He was back to being stern.

Someone else approached them and Ashling cursed inwardly. She wanted to ask why people hadn't trusted him when he came from their world. But he looked about as likely to tell her that as he was to tell her that all was forgiven and he trusted her implicitly.

She kicked herself for having mentioned anything. This…this truce, or whatever it was between them, wouldn't last long if she kept bringing up the past.

Zach was aware of Ashling beside him, swaying to the music. When he glanced at her she had a dreamy look on her face, which completely threw him off the thread of the very boring conversation going on around him.

Her question about what had happened four years ago had brought back unwelcome reminders of a sense of betrayal that still had the power to sting.

Not hurt.

He had to concede now that no one could sustain this

level of acting in order to convince him that she really wasn't interested in this world. She wasn't trying to talk to the A-list celebrities. She wasn't goggle-eyed at the fact that a very recent and popular ex-American President was just yards away, holding court with a rapt crowd.

The dreamy look on her face made him feel something completely alien. *Jealous.* He found himself asking something he'd never have asked another woman, 'What are you thinking about?'

The dreamy look disappeared, to be replaced with a sheepish one. 'Sorry—was I meant to be listening in to your conversation? When I heard you talking about stocks and shares I zoned out.'

Zach shook his head. 'No, it's fine.'

Now she looked embarrassed. 'It's this song…it's one of my favourites.'

Zach hadn't even noticed it. But he heard it now. Slow and jazzy. He could imagine Ashling dancing to it, laughing up at someone. A perverse impulse gripped him and he grabbed her hand, tugging her towards the dance floor set up under a canopy of trees full of twinkling lights. He didn't notice them. All he noticed was how small Ashling's hand felt in his. And how he wanted to snarl at anyone who looked at her.

Usually it gave Zach a kind of detached pleasure to know he was with a woman other men coveted. As if it was confirmation that he was *one of them.* But not this time.

Ashling hissed at him. 'What are you doing?'

Zach stepped onto the dance floor and pulled Ashling into his arms. She was so much smaller than him, but she fitted in a way that reminded him all too vividly of how she'd felt in his arms the other night. His blood sizzled.

She was looking up at him. He raised a brow.

She said, 'I didn't have you down as a dancer.'

He wasn't. Not naturally. But in her quest to furnish him

with all the skills he'd need to navigate the upper echelons of society his mother had ensured he'd taken lessons long ago. Not that he needed a lesson to hold this woman close and move around the floor with her. She was as light as a feather. But supple. Strong.

'You think I'm dull? Boring?'

Pink tinged Ashling's cheeks. 'Not dull. Or boring. Just…serious.'

A memory came back into Zach's head. A teacher. One of the nice ones. She'd stopped him one day after class and said, 'You don't have to take everything so seriously, Zach. The world won't fall in if you have some fun.'

But he'd never had the freedom that others had to have fun. To fail.

He shoved aside the memories. 'What do you do to have fun?' he asked her.

Ashling bit her lip and Zach's body tightened with need. He gritted his jaw to curb his response. Next to impossible.

'I read,' Ashling said, 'but quite slowly because of my dyslexia. I like cooking… I practise yoga. I love going out and dancing to loud music—the louder the better. Wild swimming…'

'Wild swimming?'

She wrinkled her nose. 'A fancy way of saying swimming outside. Lakes, rivers, the sea… My favourite is to swim in the Atlantic, off the west coast of Ireland. It's wild and magical.'

How was it that Zach, who literally had everything he could possibly want, was feeling jealous again—this time for a life he'd never even imagined existed?

Ashling felt exposed. And acutely aware of how her body was responding to Zach's. She realised she'd not listed one sophisticated pursuit. She sounded like a teenager.

Desperately wanting to deflect Zach's attention from her, she asked abruptly, 'What do *you* do to relax?'

An image popped into her head of Zach in a heaving nightclub, his eyes focused on her as the music pounded like waves around them. He'd be in a T-shirt and worn jeans... the material clinging to his taut muscles. His hands would reach for her, lifting her so that she could wrap her legs around his waist, and he'd be kissing her so deeply that she'd feel it in the centre of her body—

Zach's voice broke through the fever haze in Ashling's mind. 'I go to the gym. I run. I like good whisky. I have a motorbike...but I can't remember the last time I took it out.'

Now the image of him in worn jeans in a nightclub was replaced by an image of Zach on a motorbike, dressed in worn leathers...a white T-shirt. Stubble on his chin. That brooding look on his face.

Ashling swallowed. 'Maybe you should take it out soon.'

He looked at her, and for a second she thought she saw something wistful in his expression before it disappeared. 'Maybe I will.'

Terrified that Zach would see how much he was affecting her, Ashling muttered something about the bathroom and pulled free of his embrace to leave the dance floor, her limbs shaky with need.

When she returned she expected Zach to be surrounded again, but he stood a little way off to the side of the crowd. Ashling's heart squeezed. He looked very...alone.

And then she castigated herself for being so soft. Zach was not someone who invited sympathy. If he was alone it was because he chose to be—because he was brilliant and ruthless and intolerant of anyone who couldn't keep up with him. And yet she knew it wasn't that simple...

He was far too enigmatic. That was the problem.

As if hearing her thoughts, he turned around in that moment. She picked her way carefully over to him. High heels and grass didn't really mix. When she was about a foot away her heel caught and she pitched forward with a little cry. Landing straight into Zach's arms.

A spark of electricity zinged between them. Ashling's breath stopped. For an infinitesimal moment the possibility that Zach would pull her closer, lower his head, seemed to hang in the air… But even as Ashling made a telling movement towards him he was pushing her back, steadying her.

Her face burned and she was glad they were somewhat in the shadows, which were disguising her humiliation. There might be an attraction between them, but it wasn't so overpowering that Zach couldn't resist it. And it would only be because she was a novelty to someone who came from this world.

Exactly as her mother had been to her father. Until he'd realised that her zest for life and her hippyish tendencies wouldn't fit into his world.

Ashling felt ridiculously vulnerable. She'd talked too much about herself this evening. She was out of her depth in this place where women's faces didn't emote and the men all had cynical sharp edges like Zach.

She avoided his eye, not wanting him to see the conflicting emotions she was feeling right now.

And then he said, 'Ready to go?'

She nodded, feeling a mixture of relief and disappointment.

When they were in the back of Zach's car, Ashling said, 'Your driver can drop me off at the nearest tube.'

'No way. He's driving you home.'

'But I—'

'No arguments. I'd do the same for Cassie.'

That stopped Ashling protesting further. She knew very well that Zach's driver often dropped Cassie home after-hours.

She was glad her friend wasn't around at the moment.

The last thing she needed was to have her be witness to the ridiculous crush she'd developed on her boss. Especially when he was a man she'd judged so vociferously in the past, shamefully driven by her guilt about what she'd done when she'd first met him.

Just as they were turning into his street, Zach said, 'I have to go to Madrid tomorrow for twenty-four hours. I don't need you to come with me.'

For a second all Ashling was aware of was a rushing sound in her head and the plummeting of her stomach. He was letting her go. He'd seen how much she wanted him and it had embarrassed him. He hadn't really needed her to work for him except to humiliate her, and now her humiliation was complete—

'…hold the fort at the office…call me if there's anything urgent. And don't forget to pack a bag, Gerard will pick us up from the office at lunchtime on Thursday.'

Zach had been speaking all the time, but she hadn't heard him. The car had stopped now. He was looking at her.

'What did you say?' she asked.

'The event at my house in Somerset at the weekend. We leave on Thursday. We'll be back on Saturday.'

Ashling had forgotten. The event at which Georgios Stephanides and his wife were to be the guests of honour. The top secret deal. He wasn't letting her go. He was just going to Madrid.

'I… Of course…okay. I'll be ready.'

Zach got out of the car and walked up the steps. Ashling saw the door open. He disappeared. The car moved off again.

She tried to deny it, but she couldn't. The relief coursing through her blood was humiliatingly heady.

CHAPTER SEVEN

THE FOLLOWING MORNING—early—Zach's plane took off from the small airfield. His sleep last night had been broken by dreams of dancing with a woman. Of how her body felt against his. Lithe and supple and soft and tempting. With a lush mouth that smiled readily. And huge blue eyes that looked at him as if she genuinely wanted to know what was going on in his head and even deeper. Where he kept things hidden.

At first her hair had been blonde in the dream—a familiar blonde bob—but then he'd realised it was a wig when she'd pulled it off to reveal long red hair underneath, and her smile had turned sly and calculating as everyone around them had stopped to look and laugh.

Zach scowled as the ground dropped away beneath him. He'd made a last-minute decision not to bring Ashling with him to Madrid. But maybe it was a wasted opportunity to seduce her and be done with her. Because no woman ever held any allure for him beyond the conquest.

Ashling might appeal to a different side of him, but once he'd had her she would cease to intrigue him. Cease to have the uncanny ability she seemed to have to be able to tap into his psyche in a way that he really didn't appreciate.

Zach thought ahead to the weekend. Ostensibly Ashling was going to be there to keep Georgios Stephanides happy. The man seemed to find Zach more trustworthy with Ashling around.

Whatever… Zach didn't like feeling as if he was depending on anyone else for success, but Ashling owed him a deal at the very least. After the one she'd been instrumental in ruining four years ago, undoing years of hard work.

But the deal had only been part of it. The rest had been ritual humiliation and the erosion of the respect he'd built up.

Ashling wouldn't really have paid off her debt in full until he had her underneath him, begging for mercy.

Anticipation fired along all his nerve-endings and into his blood as he contemplated the weekend ahead. By the time it was over he would have closed the biggest deal of his life to date and Ashling would have paid her debt to him in full.

Two days later, Ashling was delivered to the private airfield where she'd taken the plane with Zach to Paris. Thankfully she saw him before he saw her, so she had a minute to compose herself. He'd stayed in Madrid longer than he'd intended, but an absence of some thirty-six hours had done nothing to inure her to his effect. There was a helicopter a little bit away from where Zach was talking to a man who looked like a pilot in uniform. And then she realised what Zach was wearing and her brain went into meltdown.

Faded jeans and a dark short-sleeved polo shirt. Aviator sunglasses. Her imaginings of how he would look in faded jeans could never have come close to the reality. The material cupped his buttocks and his thighs with such indecency that it felt voyeuristic just to look at him.

His arms were crossed over his wide chest and his biceps muscles bulged. The car came to a stop and Zach turned around. Ashling instantly felt she'd chosen the wrong outfit to wear—a short, multi-coloured sleeveless sundress and gladiator sandals. Suddenly she longed to be in one of Cassie's structured suits.

The driver opened her door and helped her out. Butterflies zoomed and collided in her gut as she walked towards Zach. She was glad of her own sunglasses. Two could play the game of hiding.

She saw the driver giving her luggage and what must be

Zach's to one of the airport staff. The man Zach had been talking to melted away.

'How was Madrid?' she asked.

'Good.'

Ashling couldn't help wondering if he'd been with a woman. There was a faintly smug—*or satisfied?*—air to his demeanour. Maybe he had a lover there. A sultry Spanish siren with the kind of curves Ashling had longed for ever since she'd started developing. Maybe she'd enticed him to stay. Maybe she'd made him laugh. Made him forget to be serious. Made him kiss her as passionately as he'd kissed Ashling.

Ugh. She was pathetic. And, even more disturbingly, she was *jealous.* Sure now that he must have been with a woman, and that he was probably laughing at her, Ashling all but stomped towards the small private jet.

No man had made her jealous before. Not even her ex-boyfriends when she'd seen them with new girlfriends. She'd felt relieved!

'Where are you going?' Zach asked from behind her.

She turned around, feeling disorientated for a moment.

He pointed to the helicopter. 'We're going in this.'

Ashling blanched.

'You've never been in a helicopter before?'

She shook her head, both terrified and exhilarated at the thought, all thoughts of Zach in bed with another woman forgotten for a second.

'Come on.' He held out a hand.

Ashling looked at it suspiciously. Then she told herself she was being ridiculous. She put her hand in his and let him lead her over to the small sleek craft. He stowed her bag and helped her up, showing her how to buckle herself in, helping fasten the belt across her chest when she was all fingers and thumbs.

He was so close she could smell him. Remember how he'd tasted. An awful yearning aching settled inside her.

Before he moved away and before she could stop herself Ashling blurted out, 'Were you with someone in Madrid?'

He stopped. Looked at her. She was glad she couldn't see his eyes. Or he hers. After a long moment that had Ashling's nerves screaming, he shook his head.

'No—not unless you count a bunch of fellow financiers.'

The relief was so immense she almost felt dizzy. Which was crazy because she had no jurisdiction over this man. And was it her imagination or was there the tiniest smile playing around the corner of his mouth as he walked away? *Damn.* If she hadn't exposed herself before now, she just done it spectacularly.

'You're the pilot?' Ashling squeaked a few minutes later, when Zach got into the front right-hand seat.

The other man got in on the left-hand side and Zach looked back at Ashling. There was a definite small smile playing around his mouth now, not helping to settle her nerves much at all.

'I only have a few hours left to log to get my pilot's licence. This is Steve, my instructor. He'll bring the helicopter back.'

Ashling smiled weakly at the other man. Then she was being instructed to put on her headphones, and they were lifting into the air with a little wobble.

Zach was obviously a bit of an adrenalin junkie—the Aston Martin, the motorbike, now the helicopter. Ashling didn't like the way this intrigued her more than it should. She couldn't just roll her eyes and pass it off as a rich man's playthings, because she had a very real sense that he didn't take any of this for granted—and that didn't fit with the man she'd believed him to be.

* * *

Ashling had been blown away by the view of London from the air, with the Thames snaking between iconic landmarks that had looked like toys far down below. But now they were in lush green countryside and she noticed that they were circling over an area with a grand house in the centre of some woodland and a garden. It was possibly one of the most idyllic scenes Ashling had ever seen.

As the helicopter descended she could see that the house was a classic redbrick Georgian manor, surrounded by bucolic countryside as far as the eye could see. There was a lake near the house, beyond the trees, and a walled garden and an orchard. A marquee was obviously being set up for the function. People were milling about.

And then she spotted an outdoor swimming pool with a pool house, tucked away in another corner of the garden.

To Ashling's shock and surprise, a well of emotion caught her off-guard. She'd dreamed of a forever-house like this ever since she was a little girl, living in the basement of Cassie's father's grand house in Belgravia.

They landed in an empty field just a little way off from the house, where a staff member met them with a golf buggy.

Ashling was very aware of Zach's hard body next to hers as the small vehicle went over the bumpy ground, knocking them off-balance and into each other.

When they approached the back of the majestic house the full impact of the grounds and the level of work going into the function that would take place the following night was apparent.

They got out of the golf buggy and walked along a winding path towards the house through the garden.

Finishing touches were being put to an area that looked as if it would be a dance floor. Ashling caught a glimpse inside the marquee, where it looked as if an army of interior decorators were hanging up swathes of material and putting out tables and chairs.

There was a huge expanse of garden blooming with flowers of every colour from the rainbow. The scents, even from a distance, were heady. This was exactly the kind of garden she adored. A little bit wild. Unstructured. And a terrace ran the length of the back of the house, where gardeners were artfully twining foliage and flowers along a wall to create a backdrop.

'Wow,' Ashling said. 'I didn't realise this would be so elaborate.'

An attractive slim woman with short silver-grey hair, who looked to be in her sixties, approached them from a back door. Zach embraced her easily and smiled.

'Diana, everything seems to be in order.'

The woman smiled back. 'Exactly as a Zachary Temple event should be.'

Zach turned to Ashling. who'd come to a stop beside him. 'Ashling, this is Diana, my housekeeper. She and her husband Rob take care of pretty much everything here for me.'

As Ashling smiled and shook the woman's hand Zach was saying, 'Ashling is a friend of Cassie's who has kindly stepped in temporarily while Cassie is abroad and her PA is out of the office.'

'Nice to meet you, Ashling.'

Ashling liked the woman on sight. 'You too, Diana.'

Zach said, 'Diana will show you to your room. I'll take a quick look around while you're settling in. This afternoon I have a meeting with Georgios, and this evening we'll have dinner with him and Elena.'

'They've arrived and had lunch,' Diana told Zach. 'They're resting in their suite now.'

Diana led Ashling into the house. She wasn't sure what she'd expected, but the manor's interiors were open and airy, with polished parquet floors and elegant soft furnishings. Tasteful antiques dotted the downstairs reception rooms and bold modern art popped from the walls, providing a contrast.

The décor reminded her of the apartment in Paris. *Where she could have slept with Zach if she hadn't had a fit of sanity.* She couldn't seem to recall why it had been a bad idea. But the moment was gone now. All she'd done was remind Zach that he didn't really want her.

Diana took Ashling up to the first floor and stopped outside a door, opening it. 'These are your rooms, my dear.'

Ashling walked into the plushest, most luxurious bedroom she'd ever seen. A massive four poster bed dominated the room, dressed in soft blues and greys. Her feet almost disappeared into the carpet, it was so thick. There was an ottoman at the end of the bed, and through a doorway was an en suite bathroom that took her breath away. A romantic rolltop bath, and a marble floor matched with marble sinks and discreet silver fittings. Modern elegance in a house that had to be two hundred years old at least.

And there was a dressing room.

After the Paris apartment, Ashling wasn't all that surprised to see a selection of clothes hanging up. Dresses, men's shirts and suits. Also casual wear. She saw brand-new jeans and women's shirts and cashmere sweaters. Even raincoats.

Diana said, 'Zach employs a local boutique to keep a stock of clothes at the house, in case a guest stays over, or there is a mishap at one of his parties and someone needs to change. We keep them in this dressing room—I hope that's not an issue?'

Cassie shook her head. 'No, of course not.'

'Feel free to help yourself if you need something to wear this evening.'

Ashling saw long shimmering gowns in bright hues and

her fingers itched to explore, but she said almost reluctantly, 'I've got everything I need with me, but thank you.'

Unable to resist, when Diana had left Ashling explored a little more. She guessed this floor was where the guest bedrooms were. There was a set of stairs at the end of the corridor and she went up them, finding that they led into another corridor.

From a window up there she could see the outdoor pool, its water shimmering under the afternoon sun. The blue mosaic tiles glistening under the water made it look very enticing. Diana had told her that she should feel free to use it and to help herself to swimwear from the dressing room at the pool house.

The sheer luxury of this place was truly intimidating— and this was after she'd seen Zach's London townhouse and his Paris apartment.

She heard a sound from behind a doorway—the low rumble of a voice. She walked closer. The voice stopped. She moved and a board under her foot creaked. The door opened. Zach.

'Sorry, I was being nosy.'

He stood back. 'Come in.'

Ashling went in, curious, and saw that it must be Zach's office. Actually, it was a suite of rooms. It was a masculine space. Dark furniture. Floor-to-ceiling shelves. She could see through to what looked like a boardroom with a big table, and there was another room with a couch and armchairs. A TV with the news on mute.

'You could run an industry from here,' Ashling noted.

'I do.'

Zach was leaning back against his desk, arms folded. Watching her. She felt self-conscious. 'Sorry, you're busy. Is there anything I can do? Check on the event plans?'

'I have an event manager, and Diana is pretty much in control of everything else.'

'Okay...do you need me to do anything for your meeting with Mr Stephanides?'

Zach shook his head. 'No, it's very informal—just he and I, here in my office.'

Ashling felt as if Zach knew something she didn't. It made her nervous. 'I don't think you really need me here at all. Maybe I should go.'

'You're here because Mr Stephanides requested that you be here.'

And because he didn't trust her.

The thought that those were the only reasons she was here made her feel prickly now more than nervous. 'But I don't even work for you—not really. I think you just enjoy watching me dance to your tune. Anyone could have done what I've done these past few days.'

'We haven't lied to Georgios. He knows you're only a temporary employee... But you have a point. I don't think we need to fool ourselves any longer.'

'Fool ourselves about what? The fact that I'm not really an employee at all and the only reason I'm here is because you want to punish me and you don't trust me?'

He inclined his head slightly. 'All of that—and the fact that we're ignoring the elephant in the room. The only way your debt will be fully paid to both our satisfaction.'

The last time Zach had said something like this she'd misinterpreted him, but this time she didn't think she had it wrong. And this time she wasn't indignant...she was something much more ambiguous.

'What exactly are you saying, Zach? Why am I here?'

'Because I need you for this deal and because I want you.'

Heat bloomed in her belly. Between her legs. Under her skin. 'I thought we discussed this. You agreed it wasn't a good idea... Cassie—'

'Cassie has nothing to do with this. We're two adults

who have insane chemistry. We don't have to answer to anyone.'

Ashling lifted her chin. 'You think I still owe you a debt.'

Zach pushed off the desk and started to walk around her. She held herself very still, even though every cell seemed to have developed a magnetic urge to go towards him.

'What I think is that there's a certain karmic beauty to the fact that you will help me achieve a deal now when you helped me lose one four years ago. And, even though it's four years too late, you'll take the place of the lover you also helped me lose.'

'I'm sure you've had many replacements since then.' Ashling was surprised at the caustic tone in her voice.

He stood in front of her. 'Of course…but none I've wanted as much as I want you.'

Ashling desperately wished those words didn't have any effect on her. But they did.

She wanted to dent that insufferable arrogance. 'What if I don't want you?'

'You really want to go there? Make me show you up as a liar?' He glanced at his watch. 'Georgios is on his way up here right now. We can either give him a show or you can stop playing games. We both feel it, Ashling, as inconvenient as it is and as much as we might not even like each other.'

He took a step closer. Ashling could smell him. Musky and masculine. Could see stubble on his jaw. That hard mouth with its sensual lower lip. Her heart beat fast. If he kissed her now he would prove her resistance to be the sham it was.

She heard voices outside.

Zach arched a brow. 'What's it to be?'

The voices were closer now. Ashling recognised Diana's voice and a much lower, accented one. Georgios Stephanides. Feeling a sense of panic and desperation mixed with excitement, she said, 'Okay, fine. I admit it. I want you too. But I can't just… How would this work…? For how long…?'

Zach put a hand around her neck, under her hair, and tugged her close. He pressed a swift hot kiss to her mouth and pulled back. 'Don't overthink it, hmm? This lasts as long as it takes to burn out. I predict it'll be short and hot.'

He took his hand away as his words sank in and her mouth burned. And at that moment Diana showed Mr Stephanides into the room.

He saw Ashling. 'My dear! How lovely to see you again. I'm so glad you're here. I warn you that my wife is going to beg for a private yoga lesson.'

Ashling greeted the older man, genuinely pleased to see him in spite of the undercurrents flowing between her and Zach. And that incendiary kiss. What she'd just agreed to.

'Of course your wife can have a yoga lesson. I'll go and chat with her now.' She was eager to put some space between her and Zach so she could fully absorb what had just happened.

Mr Stephanides looked at Zach. 'I'm not taking her away from doing anything important for you, am I?'

Zach smiled at Ashling and it was wicked. 'Oh, no, Ashling is fully briefed. She knows exactly what I need her to do.'

CHAPTER EIGHT

THAT EVENING, ASHLING was still rattled—even though she'd done a yoga practice with Elena Stephanides. She hadn't seen Zach again. He'd been in his office with Georgios for the rest of the day.

She looked at herself in the mirror. She looked flushed. Bright-eyed. *Was she really going to do this? Embark on an affair with Zachary Temple?* What had he said? That it would be short and hot…

Maybe that was what she needed after two earnest but admittedly dull relationships that had been based on all the things she'd thought were important. Like mutual respect. Compatibility. Things in common.

Maybe those things didn't matter for a short and hot affair.

After all, as Zach had said, they didn't even have to like each other. There was something very freeing about that. Even if Ashling had to admit uncomfortably that her feelings for Zach were a lot more ambiguous than they had been before.

She looked at herself in the mirror. The cocktail dress was cream silk and chiffon with a ruched and sweetheart-edged bodice, it fell in chiffon folds to just below her knees. The halter neck straps were encrusted with pearls and crossed over her bare back. The only jewellery she wore was a necklace her mother had given her. An Algerian love knot.

She slipped on a pair of black high heels and before she could lose her nerve—or, as Zach had warned her, *overthink it*—Ashling took a deep breath and left the room.

Zach couldn't remember the last time he'd felt such a sense of anticipation. It was even eclipsing the fact that Georgios

Stephanides had finally agreed to do the deal. Their legal teams were going to travel down from London first thing tomorrow and contracts would be signed.

The old man had looked at him earlier, after their last intense round of negotiations, and he'd said to Zach, 'I'm glad I've seen you here, in this place. To be perfectly frank, I've been reluctant to sign a deal till now because I didn't really think you could understand the importance of the legacy I'm handing you... To put it bluntly, you're a lone wolf, Zach. And lone wolves are dangerous. They're unpredictable. But you were smart to invite me here,' he'd continued. 'This house...is a home. Or it will be one day. I feel that very much. And Ashling—'

Zach had cut in, in shock at Georgios's blunt insight. 'Ashling is just—'

The man had put a hand up. 'I might be old, Zach, but I'm not blind yet. I can see the passion between you.'

A familiar but for the first time unsavoury ruthlessness had urged Zach to stay quiet in that moment. After all, the man was right. There was something between him and Ashling. He just didn't know how finite it would be.

And as for this place being a *home* some day... That concept made Zach feel a little winded. And yet he couldn't deny the irrational desire he'd had when he'd seen this house. To buy it even though it stuck out of his property portfolio like a sore thumb.

Georgios had continued. 'I've seen here that the lone wolf can be tamed, and *that* is why I will do the deal with you.'

Ridiculous, Zach thought to himself now, as he waited for his guests to arrive for dinner. *Georgios Stephanides is a romantic old fool. That's all.*

He poured himself an aperitif and just then heard a sound from behind him. Even before he turned he knew it was her.

She was standing in the doorway. Hesitant. Before, he'd suspected it was artifice, but he recognised it now. Because for a long time he'd had to consciously battle his own feelings of inadequacy. Of feeling that he didn't belong in places like this. She had it too.

She looked like a vision in cream and silk, her skin lightly golden. Absurdly, an urge to protect rose up in him. To reassure. Zach shoved it down. There was no place for that here.

'Would you like a drink?' he asked.

She stepped over the threshold, her legs slim and shapely. Bare. Lust surged, hot and uncontrollable, at the thought of those legs wrapped around him, her body milking—

'White wine would be nice, thank you.'

Even her voice, soft and husky, caught at him. It was as if now that he'd decided to give free rein to his desire it was morphing out of his control. Almost.

He poured her a drink and told himself to get it together. He was more sophisticated than this.

When he'd handed her the drink he said, 'You look beautiful.'

Her cheeks pinkened. 'Thank you.'

She seemed skittish. Avoiding his eye. Zach was used to women being forward, confident. Especially if they knew he wanted them. But Ashling wasn't emboldened by the knowledge that Zach had exhibited his weakness for her. In his world, any kind of vulnerability was ruthlessly exploited. He wanted her to look at him, wanted to see her eyes.

'Ash—'

'Good evening. I hope we haven't kept you waiting?'

Zach cursed silently as the Stephanides made their appearance.

Ashling sent up silent thanks when the other couple arrived. She'd watched Zach for an unguarded moment before he'd turned around to see her. Hovering on the threshold…beset for a moment by old insecurities. It had been a reminder that she didn't belong in a world like this. That she didn't fit…

Unwelcome memories had come…one in particular.

She'd been waiting for Cassie to come home from school one day, and when she'd heard the car arrive back at house in Belgravia she'd run upstairs, excited to see her friend. She'd burst into the hall as Cassie had arrived—only to be hauled backwards by the rough hand of Cassie's father, whom she hadn't seen emerging from the library.

He'd loomed over her, a powerful, intimidating man. 'Who said you could come into this part of the house?'

Cassie had cut in plaintively, 'But, Dad—'

He'd looked at his daughter, 'Upstairs, Cassandra. Now. I've told you that if you want to see Ashling you can play in the garden or in her quarters.'

The embarrassment was still vivid. She'd laughed about it afterwards with Cassie, but she'd never forgotten the awful feeling of shame. Of feeling that she didn't belong.

Elena Stephanides gasped, bringing Ashling back from the lingering wisps of the past. 'My dear girl, is that a Chanel dress?'

Ashling smiled. 'Yes, it is. It's vintage. I found it in a charity shop in Mayfair.'

The other woman sighed theatrically. 'I don't even want to know how much you paid for it, because I can still remember the original price when it was brand-new!'

Ashling laughed, grateful for this buffer between her and the brooding intensity coming from Zach. She knew it was too late to resist what was inevitable. *She didn't want to resist.* But that didn't stop her from being very afraid that he would consume her utterly and reveal just how flimsy her defences really were.

Because the truth was she'd never risked her heart before—even if she'd fooled herself into thinking she had.

And to risk her heart was to risk being humiliated, like her mother had been. Humiliated and rejected. Cast aside because she didn't belong. She'd prided herself on being more savvy. But she hadn't been tested. Until now.

'Come here.'

A delicious shiver skated over Ashling's skin at Zach's request. Dinner was over. Their digestif drinks in the sitting room were finished. The Stephanides had just retired.

Over the course of the evening Ashling's concerns had faded more and more into the background, replaced by growing heat and tension. She'd never been so conscious of another human being before. She was aware of every tiny gesture Zach made. The way he sat back in his chair and lazily held his wine glass. The way he smiled. The way his eyes slid to her when the other couple were talking to one another.

She'd felt herself blooming more and more under each successive glance and look. Like a flower opening up to the sun. It was heady.

Seeing him interact with Georgios and Elena, relaxed and charming, showed Ashling just how devastatingly irresistible he could be. She didn't have a hope. And he hadn't even had to seduce her. He'd had her from the moment she'd stood in front of him four years ago and set in train this chain of events.

She sat in a chair at right angles to the couch where the older couple had sat. Zach was in a chair at the other end. She felt a need to resist, even though she knew it was futile. Zach was just too…assured.

As if sensing her resistance, he sat forward, relaxed and yet primed. She could sense his tension. It mirrored hers.

'Come here, Ashling.'

She'd never been so conscious of her name and how it sounded.

'Why should I come to you?'

Zach arched a brow. He stood up, uncoiling his tall body. He closed the distance and stood in front of her. And then, to her surprise, he went down on his knees before her.

'Better?' he asked.

Suddenly she couldn't breathe. Zach put his hands on her knees, watching her.

He pushed her knees apart slightly. 'Okay?'

Something about his solicitude relaxed the knot inside her. She nodded.

He pushed her knees apart more and moved forward, coming between her thighs. He ran his hands up her bare thighs under her dress. Every nerve-ending screamed with tension.

He said, 'I want to see you.'

Ashling lifted trembling hands and undid the tiny hooks that held the pearl-encrusted straps to the bodice of the dress at the front. The bodice sagged, and after another explicit look from Zach Ashling nodded.

Zach took his hands off her thighs and lifted them to the dress. He slowly pulled down the bodice, exposing her to his dark gaze. She'd never been more conscious of her modest-sized breasts. They felt heavy, the nipples tightening to sharp points of need.

He spread his hands around her back, urging her forward slightly so that she sat down in the cradle of the chair. And then he bent forward, placing his mouth first on one breast and then the other. His tongue laved the peaks, his teeth tugging gently on skin so sensitised that Ashling bit her lip to stop crying out.

Her hands were in Zach's hair, holding tight. She was torn between pushing him away when it got too much and never letting him go.

He left her breasts and Ashling's blurry eyes focused. His face was flushed. Eyes glittering. He moved back, but not far, and pushed the skirt of her dress up. He pushed her thighs apart even more and sat back on his haunches, looking at her.

The only thing stopping her from trying to close her legs was the naked hunger in Zach's gaze. She'd never seen anything like it.

He reached forward and pulled her underwear to one side. Every drop of heat in Ashling's body migrated to that spot.

She could only watch as Zach's dark head moved down and she felt his breath feather along her inner thigh, his mouth pressing open-mouthed kisses to skin she'd never thought of as sensitive before.

She was squirming as he came closer and closer to the centre of her body. He put a hand on her belly, holding her still, as he all but lifted her with his other hand and placed his mouth right between her legs.

Ashling was barely aware of his hand moving up to cup her breast, kneading her flesh, trapping a nipple between his fingers, as his mouth and tongue explored her secret folds of flesh with a thoroughness that left her shaking.

She put a fist to her mouth to try and stop the sounds leaking out…hoarse screams. Tension spiralled deep inside her and she tried desperately to cling on, not to let herself shatter, because it seemed very important to avoid shattering at all costs.

But it was impossible. With one flick of Zach's tongue Ashling's world exploded into a million pieces and she was undone.

She was vaguely aware of Zach pulling her dress back up over her breasts. She looked at him as he stood up. She felt dizzy. Waves of pleasure throbbed under her skin.

He reached for her hands, tugging her up and out of the chair. Much to her mortification, her legs wobbled. He immediately scooped her up into his arms as if she weighed nothing.

He took her into the dimly lit hallway. All was quiet. Preparations for the event had stopped hours before. Ashling felt deliciously lethargic. She knew she should probably object to being carried in Zach's arms, but his chest was so solid and her arms fitted around his neck as if they'd always been there.

He climbed the stairs with ease, bringing Ashling down to the end of the hall, past her bedroom and others.

He opened a door and Ashling had the impression of a corner suite…windows overlooking the property on two sides…a massive bed dressed in dark colours.

Zach put her down. Her shoes were…somewhere. She vaguely remembered kicking them off after dinner, having a conversation with Elena about the discomfort of high heels.

Her dress was still loose around her chest and Zach moved behind her, carefully lowering the zip. The dress fell down under its own weight, around her feet.

Now she wore nothing but her underwear.

Zach came back in front of her and his eyes were heavy-lidded. He trailed a finger across one shoulder and down her arm. Traced the side of one breast. 'You are beautiful.'

Ashling ducked her head, her hair falling forward. He put a finger under her chin and urged her to look up. He seemed to want to say something, but then he just cupped her face in his hands, and his mouth was covering hers, and a new hunger licked at her blood, seeking more. Much more.

She felt Zach shed his clothes, cursing against her mouth when a button wouldn't open. She heard it *pop* and land somewhere. She felt like giggling.

But she didn't feel like giggling when Zach stood in front of her naked.

He was majestic. All the way from the corded muscles of his shoulders, down to his chest and his slim hips, where his erection was long and thick and hard.

Ashling's mouth dried.

His thighs were powerful. Long legs planted like a warrior. He was completely unashamed. And why shouldn't he be? He was exquisite.

Overcome with a feeling of awe and curiosity, Ashling whispered, 'Can I touch you?'

His jaw clenched. He nodded.

Ashling tentatively put out a hand to his chest, exploring the warm skin over steely muscles, the curve of his pectoral muscles and the ridges that ran below. The dark line of hair that dissected his lower belly.

She moved around to his back, broad and strong. His taut buttocks. And then returned to his front. She looked at him. At the evidence of how much he wanted her. Instinctively, she reached out and wrapped her hand around him lightly. Veins ran under the delicate skin. Moisture beaded at the head.

'Ash...if you keep touching me like that this will be over very quickly. And I have no intention of letting that happen.' Zach sounded tortured.

Ash.

Her heart beat faster. She took her hand away and Zach led her over to the bed.

She lay down and watched him looking at her. She felt a heady rush of feminine power. And then he came down on his hands over her and showed her all too easily who really held the power here.

He explored her body like a man discovering new territory. Every dip and hollow was traced. He paid homage to her breasts for long, luxurious minutes. He dispensed with her underwear, delved back between her legs, exploring with his fingers this time.

Her back was arching off the bed. His mouth was on hers, his fingers pushing her to the edge of her control, but it wasn't enough.

She pulled back. Zach looked at her. 'Please,' she said, 'I want *you*.'

His eyes glittered. For a second she thought she saw something like a flash of triumph, but she couldn't decipher the enigmatic look. She was too needy right now. She'd never known it could be like this. All-consuming. Desperate.

Zach reached for something and she heard foil rip. He smoothed protection onto his erection and moved over her, nudging her legs apart.

Ashling sucked in a breath when Zach breached her body.

He stopped. 'We'll take this slow, okay?'

She nodded, once again disconcerted by his consideration. She didn't know what she'd expected, but in her limited experience of lovemaking she had felt as if it was a man's journey, not necessarily a mutual one, or even hers. But this was a world apart.

Zach joined their bodies with a slow, deliberate movement, giving her time to adjust. He was big. He took her breath away. For a moment the sensation almost bordered on painful, but as if sensing that Zach pulled out and then eased back in again. And this time Ashling breathed out.

It was amazing.

An instinct as old as time took over as Ashling's body adjusted to Zach's and she moved beneath him, wordlessly telling him he could go faster, be less gentle.

A big hand caught her thigh, lifting it up. He went deeper and Ashling made a helpless sound of pleasure. Perspiration covered her skin as her entire being became consumed with this moment, this man, and the storm of sensation gathering inside her, coiling tighter and tighter as Zach's movements became less considered and more elemental.

She was climbing and climbing, begging incoherently, pleading...

Zach pulled out and she looked up at him, half-crazed. 'Please, Zach...'

He surged back into her body and Ashling tipped over into a place of such extreme pleasure she blacked out for a second.

When she became aware of her surroundings again, Ashling felt Zach pulling something over her—a soft, light cover. She was so stunned by what had just happened, and by the waves of pleasure that still pulsed inside her, that she couldn't help confiding, 'I didn't know it could be like that...'

Zach went still. He was leaning on his elbow beside Ashling. Her eyes were closed. Her words had been almost slurred, as if she was drunk. But he'd heard her. Her body was covered now, but he knew that after what had just happened every line of her physique would be burnt onto his brain.

The truth was, he hadn't known that it could be like that either. His body was still humming with an overload of pleasure. He was still—after what had felt like the most intense orgasm of his life—semi-aroused.

He waited for a sense satisfaction to hit, recalling how she'd been completely at his mercy, begging for release. And she had begged. Her eyes had been wide and desperate, breath coming fast. She had been totally at his mercy. But any sense of satisfaction was elusive.

And at the time of her capitulation, Zach had barely noticed.

Because the edges of his own control had been badly fraying. The moment had come and gone before he'd even really realised its significance, drowned out in the desperate pursuit of a pleasure so mind-altering that he could only put it down to an anomalous freak of chemistry.

Short and hot. That was what he'd told Ashling.

It had definitely been hot. The only problem was that right now Zach couldn't foresee just how short it might be. He had an uncomfortable feeling that he'd just unleashed a hunger that wouldn't be easily sated.

When Ashling woke there were pink tendrils kissing the sky outside. Dawn. She was disorientated. Her body felt… different. *Good.* Heavy… Hungry, yet sated. A strange contrast.

And then there was a movement in the bed beside her and it all came flooding back in glorious Technicolor. She held her breath and turned her head. Zach was on his back asleep, an arm thrown over his head. His chest was bare, and a sheet rode strategically low on his hips, showing the start of dark curling hair where the sheet tented over an impressive bulge, even at rest.

Heat curled into Ashling's belly and between her legs, where she felt tender.

She looked at his face. He looked younger in sleep. Lashes long and dark. Those dark, watchful eyes hidden. She imagined him waking and finding her looking at him. That galvanised her to steal from the bed as quietly as she could.

She pulled on her dress, just to cover up, and picked up her underwear. Back in her own room, she slumped against the closed door. The full magnitude of what had happened sank in. How amazing it had been. How considerate Zach had been. How she did have a capacity for pleasure—extreme pleasure.

She thought of Zach's prediction that this would be *short and hot.* She almost hoped that Zach was right. Last night had been so intense, and totally unexpected. Surely, she thought a little desperately, that had been a one-off. Not every time would be like that? It had been a culmination of everything between them since they'd met again…that was all.

The thought of sleeping with Zach again, now that she knew what to expect, alternately excited and terrified her. She'd been so exposed. So needy. So ravenous. It was a side to her that she hadn't known existed and it scared her slightly, because it hinted at a level of passion in which she could lose herself. Forget to protect herself. Forget the lessons she'd learnt about not falling for the wrong person.

In all honesty, she didn't know if she could withstand a prolonged period of Zach's seduction. She had a very real fear that she would be incinerated in the process.

Zach couldn't quite believe his eyes. At the end of the garden, tucked away from prying eyes, well away from the hubbub of people preparing for the party that night, Ashling was giving a yoga class to Elena Stephanides. They both had yoga mats and Ashling was standing on one leg now, with the other one bent, her foot tucked against her inner thigh, arms outstretched.

Elena was mirroring her pose. But all Zach could see was Ashling. Every lithe and toned inch of her petite body. He'd felt her strength last night. The power in her thighs, clamped around his waist as the inner muscles of her body had contracted around his so forcibly that he'd—

'Zach?'

It was as if someone had dumped a bucket of cold water over his head. What on earth was he doing?

He turned around. Georgios Stephanides was looking at him with a far too knowing twinkle in his eye. He was holding out a heavy silver ink pen.

'Time to sign—unless, that is, you've changed your mind?'

No way, thought Zach, pushing all thoughts of a lithe temptress out of his mind.

He sat down and took the pen, and scrawled his name beside Georgios's. He waited for the surge of satisfaction to come. After all, this deal blew everything else out of the water, and after this there would be no doubt that Zach had taken his place among his ancestors, whether his family liked to admit it or not. They wouldn't be able to deny it—or deny him his rightful place.

Satisfaction was there. But it was hollow. Almost an anti-climax. Which made him think of another climax. One a few hours before, that had almost seared his brain clear of everything he'd ever known.

Georgios clapped him on the shoulder. Zach looked up.

'Take care of my legacy, Zach,' the man said. 'Don't make me regret what I've done here today.'

Before, Zach would have spoken some platitude. He'd done it a million times before in similar situations. But for the first time he felt an echoing of the older man's emotion inside him. Georgios Stephanides didn't really know Zach. They shared no blood. And yet he'd shown a level of trust in Zach that his own flesh and blood never had.

He stood up, shook Georgios's hand, feeling surprisingly humbled. 'Thank you. I will.'

Georgios and the rest of their teams left the boardroom attached to his study. Zach took a breath. He was losing it. Going soft. Great sex had never had this effect on him before. He'd also never woken in his bed after a woman had left it. Usually he was the one to put very clear boundaries in place. He was the one to leave.

A sense of foreboding prickled over his skin.

He went back to the window and looked out. Ashling was bent like a triangle now, with her Lycra-clad bottom in the air. And just like that, any sense of foreboding melted into a haze of heat.

The first piece of karma had just been served. The second piece was *her*. In his bed again. For as long as this heat continued. And then he would be free to move on, unencumbered by any ghosts from the past.

Maybe Georgios Stephanides was right, and this house would be a home one day. But it would not be a home for the type of family that had shunned Zach since he was born. It would be for a family that would cement Zach's legacy in society, and make all the sacrifices that had led to this moment, worth it.

CHAPTER NINE

IT WAS HER dream dress. A fairy-tale concoction of cream silk, lace and tulle, covered with huge embroidered gorgeous colourful flowers in reds and pinks and dark mulberry. Loose sleeves came down to her elbows, with lace trims. A layer of dark pink tulle also covered in appliquéd flowers fell to the ground.

It was breathtaking.

And Ashling couldn't resist it.

She'd never seen anything so whimsical and romantic in her life. She felt like a princess.

The dress was one that had been sent over from the boutique. It had caught her eye a few times, so she'd pulled it out, and before she'd been able to stop herself she'd been trying it on. Just to see...

And now it was on and it was as if it had been made especially for her. The temptation to wear it was huge, and yet she felt guilty. Even though Diana had told her to help herself to anything.

The dress she'd been planning on wearing was the black silk one she'd worn the previous weekend. Normally Ashling would take pride in reusing clothes, not sniffy about being judged. But now it looked drab and cheap.

A voice whispered to her. *You want to wear this because you feel romantic after last night. Because you want romance...with Zach Temple.*

Immediately Ashling went to open the catch at the back of the dress, to take it off, but then something rebellious flamed to life in her belly. Was it so bad to feel romantic? To want romance?

She found Zach more and more intriguing. They'd slept

together. And that had been…earth-shattering. Yet she wasn't deluding herself for a second that there was anything beyond the purely physical happening here. So was it so bad to want to indulge in this moment? To feel beautiful? Desired?

Ashling made a face at herself. She was being ridiculous. It was just a dress. And after looking out of the window and seeing the guests start to arrive she needed all the glamorous armour she could get.

She hadn't seen Zach all day. He'd been in his office suite with Georgios Stephanides and their legal teams. She looked out of the window one more time to see if she could see him.

The garden had been transformed into a wonderland. It was a gorgeous summer's evening. The sky was vast and turning to dusk. Fairy lights in trees and flaming lanterns illuminated the darkening space. Small tables and chairs were dotted around. She could see the dance floor. A canopy of lights was strung from the trees to cover the space. It was like the setting for a Shakespeare play, or a film set.

Then she saw him, and her heart hitched before she could stop it. He was wearing a white dinner jacket and black bow-tie. He stood out, and once again Ashling felt a little pang at seeing him look somehow…isolated, even though he was surrounded by people.

As if sensing her regard, he turned his head and looked up, directly at her window. Ashling shrank back, heart thumping. But she couldn't hide up here for ever.

She found a pair of pink silk high-heeled sandals, and at the last minute picked up a yellow silk flower and pinned it in her hair on one side, where she'd gathered it up into a rough low bun. And then, steeling herself to see Zach for the first time since she'd left his bed that morning, she made her way to the party.

* * *

Where the hell was she?

The need to see Ashling gnawed at Zach like a physical craving. People were arriving. Surrounding him with their fake smiles and the sycophancy which he'd become inured to over the years...

And then, just when he was about to go in search of her, he saw her on the terrace, near the French doors. She was talking to Diana. Her hair was pulled back, showing off her delicate bone structure. And her dress...

Her dress stood out among all the monochrome, the blacks and greys and whites, in a riotous profusion of colours. He saw a flower in her hair. He found himself smiling. He shouldn't have expected anything less.

She turned and looked and found him. At the moment their eyes met Zach felt for a second as if he was losing his footing. She picked up the dress, so it wouldn't trail on the ground, and walked towards him across the lawn. The disconcerting sensation of something shifting underneath him, around him, lingered.

He shook his head. It was Georgios's mention of *home* that was messing with his head.

She reached him and her scent tickled his nostrils. Sweet and musky. It reminded him of how she'd smelt when he'd tasted her—

'You look beautiful.' He forced the words out in a bid to regain some semblance of control.

He noticed she wore no jewellery apart from the necklace she'd worn the previous night. A kind of love knot. Clearly of sentimental value. That snagged in his brain, but he pushed it aside for now.

'Thank you.' She looked shy. Then she gestured to the dress. 'It's one of yours.'

Zach arched a brow. 'Really? I didn't know tulle was my thing.'

She realised what she'd said, and laughed. Zach was aware of people turning to look. He wanted to snatch her away.

'No, sorry—not like that. I mean, it's one of the dresses you have sent from the boutique. For guests.'

For his lover.

The dress could have been made for her. Impulsively, because he wasn't usually inclined to give gifts to lovers in case they got the wrong idea, he said, 'Keep it. It suits you.'

Her eyes widened, and then some expression that Zach couldn't decipher crossed her face. She shuttered it quickly.

'No…but thank you. I'll arrange to have it cleaned… after…'

Zach shied away from trying to figure out what that expression had meant. He privately thought it would be a miracle if the dress survived intact. He couldn't see any obvious fastenings, and anticipation was already firing his blood. He remembered waking and finding her gone that morning and that prickle of exposure.

'You were gone this morning.'

She looked contrite. 'I woke and… The truth is that I didn't know if you'd appreciate waking and finding me still there. I wasn't sure what you'd expect. I thought you'd want your space.'

It was the first time a lover had wanted to give him space. The irony that he hadn't appreciated it wasn't lost on him.

He said, 'What I wanted was *you*.'

'Still?'

He almost didn't hear it, her voice was so low. He looked at her, wondering if she was fishing for reassurance. But she looked genuinely uncertain.

'Yes, still.' The fact that it wasn't patently obvious how much he hungered for her was comforting.

A waiter stopped beside them and Zach took two glasses

of champagne, handing her one. If she was reacting to him telling her explicitly that he still wanted her, it wasn't evident on her face.

He said, 'I'm celebrating.'

She looked at him, comprehension dawning. 'The deal? With Georgios Stephanides?'

He nodded, feeling a mixture of exposure and pride. Usually these victories were solo affairs. For the first time he felt the need to share it.

She took his hand, moved closer. 'Zach, that's amazing. Congratulations.'

He gave in to an urge too powerful to ignore. He bent down and covered her mouth with his. She was tense.

He pulled back. He saw the desire in her eyes, but she said, 'I thought you wouldn't want people to see…to know…'

He shook his head. 'Come here.'

Something flared in her eyes and her cheeks grew pink. He put an arm around her waist, pulling her into him. This time when he kissed her she didn't tense. She melted against him. It took all his restraint to stop the kiss. Pull back. When he did, her eyes stayed closed for a second. He uttered a silent oath.

'Zach, there you are. Mr Carmichael has just arrived. He's looking for you.'

It was Diana's voice that broke Ashling out of the lust haze in her brain. Zach still wanted her. He hadn't wanted her to leave his bed. He'd just kissed her in front of everyone.

He said, 'I'll be right there.'

Diana melted away discreetly. Ashling took a step back from Zach in a bid to try and clear her head. But he took her hand and led her with him into the crowd. She took a sip of sparkling wine, as if that might fortify her.

It only made things worse.

Zach introduced her to his guests, but he was their main focus. They simply looked at Ashling with naked curiosity.

She saw the Stephanides arrive and gestured to tell him that she would go to them, welcoming a chance to get her breath back. Zach nodded and let her go. She felt a prickle between her shoulder blades as if he was watching her leave but then she told herself she was being ridiculous.

About an hour later Zach was growing impatient again. *Where was she now?*

He'd watched her meet the Stephanides, and then a small crowd had formed around them, as if Ashling were attracting people to her by her sheer open demeanour.

He'd never been with anyone like her before. He was used to people who wouldn't dream of emoting or talking with unguarded abandon. But she literally had no agenda. Or appeared not to.

She also didn't appear to need to plaster herself to his side at all times, which was irritating. And irritating for being irritating.

He saw Georgios and Elena and extricated himself from his group of guests and went over. Elena said something about an emergency in the kitchen, and that Ashling had gone to see if she could help.

As Zach was walking to the kitchen he met Diana, who looked flustered. 'Oh, Zach, the chef has been taken to hospital with a suspected heart attack. Rob has gone with him. He'll let me know what happens, but we think he'll be okay.'

Zach said, 'Call my physician and have him on standby in case he's needed.'

'Of course.'

'Have you seen Ashling?'

Diana looked sheepish. 'She's in the kitchen.'

Zach frowned. And then he followed Diana to the kitchen—where he was greeted by the sight of organised chaos as everyone worked—with Ashling slap-bang in the middle of the confusion, wearing an apron over her dress. She was taking a tray out of the oven.

'What the hell…?'

He hadn't even realised he'd spoken out loud until Diana said, 'Ashling was with me when Rob told me what was happening and she came straight in and took over. She's amazing, Zach. Did you know she trained as a chef?'

Zach felt a mixture of shock, frustration and pride. 'She might have mentioned it at some point.'

He went over to her and she looked up, cheeks pink, distracted.

'What are you doing?'

She was unfazed. 'Keeping your guests supplied with canapés.'

He looked around at the hive of activity. 'No one else here can do that?'

'They got a fright when Marcel collapsed, and they needed someone to take over.'

'You have fifteen minutes to reassure the assistant chef that he is capable of the job and come back to the party.'

'Is that an order or a request?'

Desire twisted inside Zach at her cheeky expression. No one spoke to him like this. It was exhilarating.

He reached out and put a hand behind her neck, caressing. Suddenly she didn't look so cheeky. She was looking at his mouth.

'It's an order.'

Ashling sneaked into the back of the marquee just as Zach was delivering his speech before the charity auction. Money would be raised for local charities—chief of which was a cancer charity which, she'd discovered, he'd set up himself.

Ashling was shocked to hear him reveal now that he'd set up the cancer charity after his mother had died of a rare form of cancer. He was also involved in the local hospice, after they'd provided care for her at the end of her life.

Everyone was rapt as he spoke. And she couldn't blame them. He was mesmerising and not remotely sentimental, even though he was talking about something that was obviously deeply personal.

Ashling realised that she knew next to nothing about Zach's family. She wondered if his father was still alive. If he had siblings. He'd very skilfully deflected any focus on his personal life—which Ashling could understand, coming from her own less than conventional background.

At that moment his dark gaze pinpointed her, standing at the back of the crowd. She told herself a little desperately that Zach's family was none of her business. She didn't care about what had shaped him. She only cared about the very explicit promise in those eyes.

'Finished saving the world?'

'One canapé at a time,' Ashling quipped, her response hiding how unsettled she'd felt after hearing him talk about his mother.

After he'd delivered his speech Zach had come straight to where Ashling was standing and taken her hand, leading her out of the marquee.

She heard them start the bidding for the charity auction. 'Don't you need to be in there for that?'

He shook his head. 'It's all under control.'

She looked up at him. His face was half in shadow in the dusky light. 'I'm sorry about your mother…you must have been close.'

'We were.'

'Your father…?'

Zach's jaw tensed. 'He's not in my life.'

Ashling guessed his parents must have divorced. Some of the guests who weren't bidding in the auction had spilled out into the garden and were taking to the dance floor, dancing to the slow, sensual rhythm of the jazz coming from the band. She spotted Georgios and Elena, looking very much in love.

Zach said, 'Thank you for helping Diana to cope with the emergency. You didn't have to do that.'

Ashling shrugged a shoulder, embarrassed. 'It was nothing.'

'Dance?'

She looked up. 'Okay.'

Zach led her over to the dance floor and swept her into his arms. Ashling caught Elena's eye and the older woman smiled indulgently. She felt like a fraud, though, next to their very obvious absorption in each other.

What she and Zach had was...*short and hot*. Not long-lasting. Enduring.

'Is that a love knot?'

Ashling looked up to see Zach was looking at her necklace. 'Yes, it's an Algerian love knot.'

'Given to you by a lover?'

Ashling was tempted to be blasé and say yes. To try and even out the inequality she felt next to this man who must have handed over hundreds of trinkets to his lovers.

But she couldn't. 'No, it was a gift from my mother. For my twenty-first birthday.'

Zach said, 'Good. I'm glad.'

Ashling couldn't stop her silly heart pounding faster at that response.

The canopy of golden lights twinkled overhead and out of the corner of her eye she could see the tulle of her dress swirling around her as Zach twirled her away from his body and then back in. She felt herself being sucked into the fantasy of believing in the romance of the moment.

But when Zach pulled her close again, and she felt her body respond helplessly to his whipcord strength, she had to remind herself that any sense of romance was fleeting and an illusion. What was happening here was purely physical.

As if to make sure she understood that, Zach pulled her even closer, and Ashling's breath stopped when she felt the press of his arousal against her belly. Desire, sharp and urgent, licked at her lower belly.

He stopped moving. She looked up at him, caught by the intensity of his gaze. The air thickened between them, tension rising. And urgency.

He caught her hand in his and was leading her off the dance floor before she could take another breath. With single-minded focus, not stopping for anyone, he led her onto the terrace and through the French doors.

It was quiet in the house, because everyone was outside in the humid summer evening.

'Zach…where are we going?'

Ashling was afraid to articulate the need building inside her. Surely it was the same for him and they had the same goal. *Now.*

He took her through one of the formal reception rooms and then through a secret door, camouflaged because it was wallpapered the same as the wall. The room he took her into was a library, with floor-to-ceiling shelves and worn leather furniture. He closed the door behind them and, still holding Ashling's hand, went and sat down on one of the big leather chairs, pulling her down onto his lap.

She landed with a flurry of silk and tulle billowing around them. Within seconds their mouths were fused, and Zach's hands were moving from Ashling's waist to her bottom. She could feel him underneath her, hard, and she moved against him.

He pulled back. 'Witch.' Then he put his hands on her waist, lifting her. 'Straddle me.'

Ashling lifted up the material of the dress and came up on her knees, either side of his thighs.

Zach put his hands on her thighs under the dress. She looked down at him. His expression was hidden in the dim light. She reached for his bow-tie, undoing it, opening his top button. She bent down, pressed a kiss to his jaw, feeling the stubble tickle her mouth. She was trying to ignore the welling of dangerous emotion.

Zach's hands left her thighs and she heard him undo his belt. There was the snap of a button, the tug of a zip.

She pulled back and came up on her knees. She could feel the heat of Zach's body. He reached between them, rubbing the silk of her underwear where it covered the centre of her.

Ashling groaned softly. The sounds of the party drifted in from outside. Laughter, music… She put her hands on his shoulders.

He tugged her underwear to one side, the movement causing delicious friction along her sensitised skin.

He asked, 'Are you tender? After last night?'

Ashling could feel herself blushing. 'A little, but it's okay.'

She heard foil rip as Zach protected himself, and then he was taking himself in his hand and nudging the head of his erection along her folds. Ashling met him, taking in a breath as she sank down. He impaled her. Slowly. Deliciously. Until she was so full she could barely breathe.

Then, with his hands on her hips, he urged her to move up and down, taking his time, setting the rhythm, letting her get used to him.

Until her own instincts took over and the need inside her grew. Her movements became faster, more urgent. Her skin grew damp, and every cell in her body strained for release. But she was afraid of the oncoming storm.

'Let go, Ash. I've got you.'

Zach reached up and tugged her head down, claiming her mouth just as the storm broke. He captured her breathy groan of release as his other hand clamped to her waist and held her still while his own body found its release inside her embrace.

The shock waves ebbed slowly. The perspiration on their skin cooled. Ashling's face was embedded on Zach's shoulder, her mouth touching his neck. She flicked out her tongue to taste his skin and, incredibly, his body jerked in response.

He huffed a laugh. Ashling smiled against his skin, a wave of satisfied exhaustion claiming her before she could stop it.

When Zach went back out to the party he felt drunk. Drunk on sex. He'd lain Ashling down on the couch in the library, covered her with a throw. It had taken all his willpower not to just carry her up to the nearest bedroom.

He'd never behaved so spontaneously. But no other woman had ever precipitated such a visceral hunger in him. A hunger that had to be assuaged immediately.

It wasn't just desire, though, a little voice reminded him uncomfortably.

No. There had been an expression in her eyes when they'd danced. Open, unguarded. Wistful. He'd acted on a powerful instinct to do whatever it took to turn that expression into something much earthier. Base.

The women he'd chosen as lovers up to now had been pragmatic. Ambitious. Well-connected. They hadn't looked at him as if they could see right into him. Or as if he was promising them something beyond a mutually satisfying liaison.

If he ever was going to settle down, then it would be with one of those women. Women who didn't stir his emotions. Women who didn't rouse old fantasies of a different life. The kind of life that had been snatched out of his grasp the moment he'd been born.

This weekend with Ashling…getting her out of his system and settling old scores...was all he needed to move forward with the next phase of his life. The deal with Georgios Stephanides was done. It was time to take his rightful place among his peers and prove to the family who'd rejected him that he was their equal.

Ashling felt disorientated when she woke the following morning. She was alone in Zach's bed.

She saw two empty champagne glasses on the bedside table and pieced together the events... After the library, she'd woken in Zach's arms last night as he'd carried her up to bed. She'd protested, saying, 'Shouldn't we get back to the party?'

He'd replied dryly, 'Most people have left...it's just a few stragglers.'

Ashling had buried her head in his chest. 'I'm sorry. I didn't mean to fall asleep like that.'

He'd brought her here, to his room. By the time she'd stood in front of him she'd been wide awake again. His bow-tie had been hanging rakishly loose. Jacket gone.

Ashling could see her dress now. The swathe of romantic silk, lace and flowers trailed over the bottom of the bed like a glorious stain of rich colours.

They'd made love again, as hungrily as if they hadn't just made love a short time before. It had scared Ashling slightly...this ravenous craving he'd awoken in her.

They'd woken during the night, ravenous again except this time for food. They'd gone down to the kitchen and eaten leftovers from the party. Zach had given Ashling a pair of his sweatpants and a T-shirt. She'd rolled the pants up and tied the T-shirt into a knot at her midriff.

They'd come back to the bedroom as dawn was breaking, with two glasses of champagne. And then made love again.

Ashling's body felt deliciously heavy. Sated. Tender. She

was just wondering where Zach might be when she heard a noise and looked up, to see him walking out of the bathroom with nothing but a towel hitched around his waist.

Her mouth dried. His skin was gleaming, muscles bunching as he rubbed his hair with a smaller towel. Ashling's belly tightened. Again.

He saw her. Took the towel from his head. He was clean-shaven again. 'Morning...'

'Hi.' Ashling felt ridiculously shy, considering the fact that this man knew her more intimately than anyone else in the world. Even her previous boyfriends. Safe to say that Zach's very thorough brand of lovemaking meant that he'd touched, caressed, kissed, licked, nipped every part of her body.

He stood at the end of the bed. 'I've decided to stay for the weekend.'

Ashling's insides contracted. *It was over.* Already. She shouldn't be surprised, really. Even though every successive time they'd made love it had just got better and better.

For her.

She had to remember that she was a novice compared to Zach. He was probably bored already.

She saw the discarded T-shirt nearby and reached for it, pulling it on back to front. She didn't care. She felt a bit panicky now.

'Okay, that's cool. I can get a train from the nearest village—or maybe one of the event people will be going back into town. I can get a lift with—'

He frowned. 'What are you talking about?'

'You said you're staying for the weekend. I presumed...' She trailed off, and watched as he dropped the smaller towel and stalked around the side of the bed.

'What I should have said was that I've decided to stay and would like you to stay too. Otherwise it's a pointless exercise.'

Because he wanted to be here with her.

Ashling felt light-headed.

'Don't you normally stay for the weekend if you're here?'

He shook his head and moved over her on the bed, leaning on his hands. 'No, usually I leave again straight away.'

'Oh.'

'But this time I'm inspired to stay.'

That implied—far too dangerously for Ashling's liking—that he hadn't done this before.

Ashling lay back. Zach loomed over her, bronzed skin tight over taut muscles, more tempting than anything she'd ever known before. She knew that it would be cooler to try and not appear too available, but she was afraid that horse had bolted long ago.

'Well?'

'Okay… I'll stay.'

A bubble of excitement rose up inside her. She reached down and twitched open Zach's towel. It fell from his hips to the bed, exposing every inch of his masculinity.

She met his eye. 'Oops…'

He smiled and came down over her, crushing her deliciously to the bed. '*Oops*, indeed.'

CHAPTER TEN

WHEN ASHLING WOKE again it was much later. A throbbing noise had woken her but she couldn't place it. She was alone in Zach's bedroom and she stretched luxuriously under the sheet, feeling thoroughly decadent.

She got up and put on the sweatpants and T-shirt again to go to her own room, wincing a little as she moved, her muscles aching.

She didn't see anyone on her way. When she got there she looked out of the window and saw that most of the event decorations were already down. The marquee was half dismantled. She realised then that it was after lunch.

She went into her bathroom and looked at herself, eyes widening. Tousled hair, pink cheeks, a little bit of red on her jaw—a slight irritation from Zach's stubble. She almost didn't recognise herself.

She took off his clothes and dived into her shower, before he would come looking for her and find her documenting every bit of evidence of his lovemaking on her body.

When she was out and freshened up she felt slightly less dreamy, a little more in control again. Which she knew would probably last for about a second in Zach's company.

She weakly pushed aside the clamour of her conscience, demanding to know if she had really thought this through. Zach epitomised everything she disdained, and yet all that felt hollow now. It wasn't that black and white. He was a complex man. Surely, she thought a little desperately, she wouldn't be attracted to him if he was driven purely by blind, greedy ambition? Surely she was attracted to him because she saw something more…layers…contradictions.

The realisation that she was trying to justify her decision to stay and indulge in an affair with a man who was entirely wrong for her drove Ashling from her room.

She was wearing the only other piece of clothing she'd brought, not having expected to stay beyond today. It was a yellow sundress, with wide straps over her shoulders and little buttons all the way down the front.

When she got to the reception hall she saw Diana, placing a big vase of blooming flowers on the centre table.

The woman looked up and saw her, smiled. 'You'll be pleased to hear that the chef, Marcel, is fine. They think it was some kind of a panic attack.'

To Ashling's mortification, she realised she'd forgotten about the chef. Zach's form of distraction was too potent. Genuinely relieved, she said, 'That's good news.'

'I believe you and Zach are staying for the rest of the weekend?'

Ashling couldn't help blushing. 'Yes... I hope that doesn't put you out too much?'

The woman smiled wider and said, *sotto voce*, 'Not at all, my dear. I'm delighted to see him actually using the house for once. It's a crying shame to use it as little as he does, and I know he enjoys it here.'

More evidence that this wasn't usual for him, which made Ashling's heart speed up.

Diana said, 'He told me that if I saw you to tell you he's making some calls in his study. You're to have some lunch on the terrace and make yourself at home—he'll come and find you when he's finished.' The housekeeper winked at her. 'If I were you, on a beautiful day like this, I'd use the pool. Or even the lake—it's deep and perfectly safe for swimming.'

The thought of a swim in either the pool or the lake was definitely appealing. But as Diana was walking away Ashling thought of something. 'The Stephanides...do you know where they are? Maybe Elena would like another yoga lesson.'

Diana turned around, 'Oh, they left a little while ago in the helicopter. They were sorry not to see you, but Zach didn't want to disturb you.'

That must have been what had woken her. Their helicopter leaving. Ashling was disappointed not to have been able to say goodbye. She probably wouldn't see them again and she'd liked them.

'Okay, thanks.'

Ashling had a light salad on the terrace. She saw the garden was miraculously almost back to its original state, thanks to the hive of workers clearing everything. Not used to feeling redundant, when she was finished she took her lunch things into the kitchen, but was quickly shooed out by Diana.

She explored the gardens a little more, walked down to the lake. It was utterly idyllic. A beautiful summer's day. Just a small breeze. The water looked seriously tempting. Ashling looked back towards the house. She couldn't see a thing—the foliage shielded the lake from view.

Before she could think about it too much—*'Don't over-think it, hmm?'*—she scowled at Zach's voice intruding in her head and undid the buttons on her dress, letting it drop to the wooden jetty. She slipped off her underwear. She wasn't wearing a bra.

Before she lost her nerve entirely, she dived into the lake.

Zach had looked all over for Ashling. No sign. The last of the event staff were leaving, and he thought of Ashling mentioning getting a lift because she'd assumed he'd meant her to leave so that he could stay here on his own.

It was something he'd never done. Instinctively he'd shied away from owning the space completely. Avoided thinking about what it meant.

He was down at the end of the garden now, near the trees that bordered the lake. He heard a sound.

He walked through the trees and emerged near the jetty. The first thing he saw was a splash of yellow. A discarded dress. He scanned the lake. Then he saw her. She was on her back, floating, her arms outstretched. Limbs pale. The twin mounds of her breasts were visible above the water line…the small pebbles of her nipples. He could see her belly, and the dark blonde cluster of curls that hid the moist and hot evidence of how much she wanted him.

Zach's body jerked in response. He shed his own clothes and executed a near-soundless dive into the water, coming up for air just as Ashling turned her head. She squealed and lost her balance, sinking under the water. Zach reached for her, tugging her up again.

She came up gasping, hair slicked back, her body lithe and smooth. 'What the…? I didn't even hear you…'

Zach pulled her into him and she put her arms around his neck. The sharp points of her breasts against his chest sent blood rushing to his head and groin.

'Put your legs around me.'

She did it wordlessly.

He covered her mouth with his, relishing that sweet, cushiony softness, then giving way to something deeper and more erotic when she opened up to him.

She squirmed in his arms and he reached between them to where she was exposed, sliding his fingers along the slick folds of flesh before exploring deeper, sliding in one finger, then two. She tensed against him and he felt her shudders of release, the contractions around his fingers.

He pulled back. She looked at him, shocked.

'You're so responsive…'

It was beyond gratifying to have this effect on her. Gratifying enough to almost take the edge off his own sharp need. But then the dreamy soft-focus look faded from her face and she reached for him, circling his length with her hand, stroking his flesh until he was the one losing control and shuddering into her hand.

Breathless at the speed with which they'd responded to each other, Zach didn't try to hold her when she pushed back a little. He watched her tread water, a little bit away. His body felt languorous.

He said, 'If I'd known the lake was this much fun I would have used it long before now.'

Ashling trod water. 'You haven't used it before? But it's amazing. If I lived here I'd never leave and I'd swim here every day.'

Colour poured into her cheek—which was astounding given what they'd just done.

'That is… I don't mean I want to live here. I mean, I would, who wouldn't? But that's not what I—'

Zach took pity on her, reaching for her again, pulling her into his rapidly recovering body. 'Don't overthink it, Ash.'

She rolled her eyes and pushed free of his embrace again. She smiled at him cheekily and said, 'Race you to the jetty.'

'What does the winner get?'

'To have their wicked way with the loser.'

'I thought I just did that?'

Ashling splashed water at him, and then turned and struck out with a graceful crawl to the jetty.

Zach had no problem losing this game. He just watched her, an alien sensation of lightness filling his chest. Then he struck out after her to avoid deciphering what that sensation was.

'I've given Diana and Rob the rest of the weekend off, so they can go and visit their grandkids. Diana has left meals in the fridge, so we won't starve.'

So they were here alone now.

The prospect of that sent more than a tremor of awareness and anticipation through Ashling. She was still reeling from the aftermath of Zach joining her in the lake a few hours ago. From watching him pull his sleek body out of the water and the fact that he'd revealed that he'd never swum in the lake before.

They'd walked back up to the house, their clothes pulled on over damp bodies. Zach had had to go and make a few calls, and Ashling had taken the opportunity to have another shower and try to gather her wits again. Except she had a feeling that as long as she spent time with Zach any sense of equilibrium or control would be elusive.

She wondered if it would ever come back.

'What would you like to drink?'

Ashling had joined Zach on the terrace for an aperitif. The evening was humid. The sky was turning a bruised colour. 'White wine, please.'

He came out with their drinks. He was wearing dark trousers and a dark polo shirt. He looked vital and sexy.

He observed, 'You like colour, don't you?'

Ashling made a face. 'I had to borrow some more clothes. I didn't bring enough with me for the weekend.'

She wore a strapless black silk jumpsuit, with splashes of vivid colour.

He said, 'It suits you.'

'I didn't always like colour,' Ashling admitted. 'I used to prefer to fade into the background.'

Zach affected a look of shock. 'Not possible.'

Ashling bit back a smile. Like this, he was…irresistible. And she didn't have to resist him.

The thought was heady. Intoxicating.

'Why did you want to fade into the background?' he asked.

Ashling gave a little shrug. 'My mum was a single parent. We were living in a posh area, albeit very much downstairs. My school was conservative. Most other kids had two parents. My mum was…not afraid to express herself. She wore her red hair piled up. Big jewellery. Trendy clothes. And Cassie's dad never let me forget where I belonged.'

'How?'

Ashling told him the story of Cassie's father not allowing her in the main part of the house. 'It's silly, and it was a long time ago, but I still feel intimidated sometimes. Especially in places like this. As if someone is going to come along and accuse me of trespassing.'

She looked at Zach, where he stood near her by the terrace wall. His face was in shadow, which made it easier for her to say, 'That night of the party four years ago… I only realised when I was walking up to you that they'd totally set me up to look as out of place as possible. To make it even worse…for you.'

'But it affected you too?'

'Yes—if that's any consolation.'

'It's in the past now.'

'Is it?' Ashling almost whispered, afraid to ask. 'Am I still being punished?'

Zach put his glass down and took hers, setting it aside. He came close and cupped her face in his hands. Ashling felt vulnerable. There were moments like these when she felt so exposed, and it would take nothing much at all for Zach to capitalise on her vulnerability and crush her. She held her breath.

He said, 'No more punishment. Now it's just about pleasure.'

Ashling released her breath, shakily, and it mingled with Zach's as he covered her mouth with his and showed her exactly the difference between punishment and pleasure.

To say that Ashling felt as if she was in a bubble outside of time was an understatement. She lay on a sunbed in a swimsuit she'd borrowed from the pool house and wasn't even sure what time of day it was, never mind what day.

The last twenty-four hours had been spent mainly in bed, punctuated by trips to the kitchen. And once to the lake again, as dawn had risen. That swim had been magical…magical enough to make Ashling very afraid that she was fast losing any grip on remembering what this weekend was about.

Short and hot.

Weakly, she felt she could happily live in this dreamlike state and never go back to the real world again. She'd never felt so at peace. Which was disconcerting when she was in a milieu that she'd always found a little uncomfortable.

She heard the sound of someone emerging from the pool and opened her eyes, squinting up at a six-foot-plus embodiment of masculine perfection, with water sluicing down over his hard muscles. Short swim-trunks left little to the imagination.

'Sure you don't want to swim?'

Ashling feigned a level of nonchalance she really wasn't feeling. 'I'm happy to take in the view.'

She squealed when he came down over her, showering her with droplets of water. This relaxed version of Zach Temple was more than a revelation. He was fatally seductive.

He kissed her, and any hope of pretending to be nonchalant melted. The craving he woke in her with just a look, a kiss, was seriously addictive. Ashling had heard people talk about sex as if it was a drug and she'd never understood it. Till now…

When Zach pulled back she went with him, loath to break the contact. He lay down on the sunbed beside hers.

Ashling turned on her side to look at him. 'This house must have been amazing for a child.'

'I'm sure it was,' Zach said lazily.

Ashling was surprised. 'It wasn't in your family?'

He shook his head, eyes closed. 'I bought it a few years ago.'

Ashling recalled what he'd said about his father. 'You said your father's not in your life…were your parents divorced?'

For a long moment Zach said nothing, and then, 'My mother was a single parent. I grew up in a tower block in one of the roughest parts of London.'

It took a long moment for that to sink in. When it did, Ashling sat up on the sunbed, shocked.

Zach turned his head and looked at her. Mocking. 'Weren't expecting that, were you?'

No. Not in a million years. She was speechless as she absorbed this. Finally she said faintly, 'But you went to boarding school… Oxbridge…'

'Scholarships.'

Suddenly Ashling felt cold, in spite of the heat. 'Your father…'

'He wanted nothing to do with me. He has his own family, who were all bred with the right woman.'

This was all too sickeningly familiar. 'You have half-siblings?'

'Yes.'

Ashling wrapped her arms around her knees. 'I just assumed you came from that world.'

'Rich. Entitled.' He stated the words.

She nodded. Zach was expressionless, but she could see the tension in his form. She felt defensive, because she hated it that she'd misjudged him so badly. 'You let me assume…'

He shrugged. 'I find that people don't really like to have their assumptions disproved.'

That hurt. But he was right.

She said, 'I pride myself on not judging people, but I judged you.'

Because it had kept him at arm's length.

'You saw what you wanted to see.'

Ashling swung her legs around to the side of the sunbed. She felt agitated. 'Zach…we've had the same experience. More or less.'

'It's a small world.'

He sounded blasé, but Ashling wasn't fooled. 'Have you ever met your father?'

Zach sat up and reached for her, tugging her up from her sunbed and over to his. She landed in an inelegant sprawl across his chest, her breasts crushed against warm, damp skin.

He said, 'Funnily enough, I can think of better things to do than talk about my father.'

He trailed his hands up along her waist, across the bare skin of her back, and then traced the side of her breast, exposed by the far too daringly cut swimsuit that she hadn't been able to resist choosing earlier. Now she regretted it.

He took his hands away and looked at her. 'But if you'd prefer to talk…'

Ashling wanted to scowl. He knew exactly how he affected her. The inevitable fire lit up her blood and turned it molten in seconds. And she of all people could understand his need to deflect.

What he'd just revealed was huge. Maybe she wasn't ready to pursue that line of conversation either…afraid of what it would change between them.

Weakly, she put her hands on either side of his head, and just before touching her mouth to his she said, 'You win… I vote we go with this…'

'You don't have to cook.'

'I like cooking. Just sit there and look pretty.'

Ashling pushed a glass of wine towards Zach, who was sitting on the other side of the island. What she didn't mention was that she found cooking therapeutic—especially when she needed to think stuff over in her head. Like the bombshell Zach had dropped earlier about his background...

He'd managed to keep her pretty distracted for the rest of the afternoon, until she'd left him sleeping in bed, had a shower and come downstairs. She'd been inspired to cook when she'd seen Diana's well-stocked larder and fridge.

The fly in the ointment was that the object of her ruminations was sitting a few feet away, looking far too distracting in a dark T-shirt. She didn't have to see his bottom half, because the image of him appearing in the kitchen in worn denims a short time before was seared on to her brain.

'What are you cooking?'

'Seafood risotto.'

'Tell me how you ended up doing a cordon bleu course.'

Ashling added onion, garlic and some other ingredients to a heavy pan. 'It was the year my mother took me to Paris for my birthday.'

'You were eighteen.'

Ashling looked at him, hating the spurt of warmth in her chest because he remembered. 'Yes. Well, I fell in love with the food, so when I'd saved up enough money to do a basic course I went back. I waitressed to make money while doing it.'

Zach took a sip of wine. 'So why didn't you become a chef?'

Ashling added rice to the pan, stirring with a wooden spoon. 'I knew from early on that I wasn't really cut out to be a chef. I don't have the temperament.'

'You're too nice.'

Ashling smiled sweetly and added white wine to the mixture, and more stock. She'd found a white off-the-shoulder peasant-style dress in the dressing room. She was aware of

Zach's eyes on her, but she was still not quite believing that she could be that enticing to him.

Short and hot. That was why. Tomorrow was Monday. They'd go back to London…and that would be that.

'Did you ever meet *your* father?'

Zach's question took her off-guard. She looked at him, and deflected for a moment by saying, 'It's okay for you to ask me, but not for me to ask you?'

He was unrepentant. 'Absolutely.'

Ashling hated talking about her father. Even though her mother had done her best to try and help Ashling not to feel bitter about him. But bitterness and anger at being rejected lingered. Especially after that last time.

'I've met him three times. When I was four—too young to really remember much, except him and my mother fighting. And then when I was nine. It was a disaster.'

'Why?'

Ashling focused on stirring the rice. 'He took me to an expensive toyshop and couldn't understand why I wouldn't pick a toy. I wanted to talk to him, but he just wanted to fob me off with *stuff.* I wasn't into toys. He didn't understand me—I'd worn a bright red dress and he made a comment about me attracting attention. He was probably terrified someone would recognise him. And I cried because I'd made him angry, attracting even more attention. For years after that I refused to wear anything too bright or outlandish, because I thought if I faded into the background then he might come back…give me another chance.'

'And now you wear bright colours to show him you don't care?'

Emotion at Zach's far too incisive remark almost closed Ashling's throat. When she felt she could speak again she said lightly, 'Maybe you should have gone into therapy. You could give my mother a run for her money.'

'You said there were three times you'd met him. What was the third?'

Ashling wanted to scowl at Zach, but she was afraid of the emotion bubbling under the surface. 'The third time wasn't long before that night...*the* night...' She sneaked him a look.

He raised a brow, 'Go on.'

'I was at the theatre with Cassie and I saw him in the crowd. I got such a shock. I acted without thinking. Cassie tried to stop me, but I went over and tapped him on the shoulder. He didn't even recognise me. I had to tell him who I was.'

Ashling rubbed her arm as if she could still feel the pain of his hand gripping her, hauling her to one side.

'What happened?'

Again, Ashling forced a lightness into her voice that she wasn't feeling. 'Let's just say that he made it clear I wasn't welcome in his milieu. I hadn't realised it, but he was with his family. He was afraid I'd cause a scene.'

Zach sounded disgusted. '*His* milieu? You had as much of a right to be there as he did.'

'That's what Cassie said.'

'Some people aren't fit to be parents.' Zach's tone was stark.

Ashling forced a smile, wanting to banish the toxic memories. 'My mum is amazing. I'm lucky to have her. What was your mum like?'

Zach got up and took his glass to stand at the open French doors that led out to a kitchen garden full of plants and herbs. Ashling could still smell the thyme she'd picked earlier for the risotto.

She thought for a second that he was going to ignore her, but then he said, 'She was driven.'

Ashling carefully added the prepared seafood to the rice mixture. 'What do you mean? She was ambitious?'

Zach let out a short, harsh laugh. 'No! As she liked to tell me often, she didn't have the luxury of being ambitious because she was a single parent.'

Ashling's heart clenched. She'd witnessed how tough it was for single parents. 'She couldn't afford to get qualifications?'

'She was intelligent. Intelligent enough to get a place at university. She would have been the first in her family. She came from a working-class town in the north of England. She had plans to go. She was working three different jobs to make enough money. That's how she met my father. She was a cleaner at the House of Commons.'

Ashling stopped stirring the risotto. 'Your father is a politician?'

'He's retired now. A peer of the realm.' The sneer in Zach's voice was unmistakable.

Ashling put down the spoon. 'That's why he didn't want anything to do with you?'

'He didn't want an illegitimate child messing up his very public life. He gave my mother money to get rid of me, but she was too proud. She sent the money back to him, told him she'd be keeping me.'

The risotto started hissing, Ashling stirred it again.

Zach said, 'I grew up very aware of the fact that I had to justify my existence. To prove myself. To pay her back for her sacrifice. She didn't have a life because of me.'

Ashling bit her lip. Then she said, 'You were her life. She must have been so proud of you.'

Zach's mouth compressed. 'I don't think she ever saw much past the fact that I'd sent my father a message that I'd thrived in spite of his rejection. That he hadn't broken her with his treatment of her. She was obsessed with the fact that I'd succeeded enough to be accepted into his world. My "rightful world", according to her.'

'Did you ever meet him?'

Zach walked away from the open door and put his glass of wine down on the island. He avoided her eyes.

It was so unlike him not to look her in the eye that she said, 'Zach…?'

He looked at her. She couldn't read the expression on his face, but something sent a shiver down her spine.

He said, 'We've moved in the same circles for some time now…we tend to avoid each other.'

'But…' Ashling trailed off as something occurred to her. She felt sick. 'He was there that night, wasn't he? Four years ago? He was there and he saw the whole thing and…' Ashling stopped stirring and sat on a stool, feeling weak at the thought.

Zach nodded. Grim. 'He wasn't just there—he was the one who set me up.'

She looked at Zach, horrified. But it made a kind of sick sense. Humiliate your illegitimate son to send him a lesson. And she'd played a role in that lesson.

Ashling shook her head, 'Zach, I'm so sorry. I had no idea.'

'How could you? I only found out after the fact. If I'd seriously suspected that you knew any of this we wouldn't be having this conversation.'

A smell of burning tickled Ashling's nostrils. She gave a gasp of dismay and turned off the heat, reaching for the pan handle before stopping to think.

The pain of the burn registered at about the same time as Zach moved like lightning and had her hand under the running cold water tap.

'It's fine…honestly.'

But Zach kept her hand there, numbing the pain.

Emotion welled inside Ashling before she could stop it. Emotion at the thought of Zach overcoming serious adversity to achieve above and beyond what anyone could have imagined. The thought of his mother…giving up her life for her son, but also sending him a toxic message about revenge and retribution.

And Ashling's own part in it all. And, even worse, her quick and easy judgement of him. Assuming the worst. Because it had been easier than believing things might be more complex—that he might be more complex. Because that would make him...so dangerous.

He turned off the water and wrapped Ashling's palm in a damp towel. She was embarrassed now, and feeling intensely vulnerable. 'That's really not necessary.'

He tipped up her chin. She blinked back the emotion, drowning in his dark eyes. She had no defences left.

His mouth quirked. 'See what happens when we talk? It's dangerous.'

She smiled, but it felt wobbly. And then Zach led her over to the dining table and sat her down. He went back over to the stove, dumped the burnt risotto in the bin, making Ashling wince, and then she watched, fascinated, as he tied an apron over his jeans and expertly rustled up a fluffy cheese and mushroom omelette served with warm crusty bread and wine.

By the time he sat down she was very afraid that the revelations of the evening and Zach's easy charm had left her no place to hide from the truth. The truth that she was falling in love with him. With a man who had just told her in no uncertain terms that he might come from her world, but he had no intention of going back there again.

And she couldn't even blame him, after what he'd told her.

CHAPTER ELEVEN

THE FOLLOWING MORNING Ashling made an unintelligible grunting sound at the persistent calling of her name. She felt so deliciously lethargic and relaxed, and she squealed when the sheet was ripped off her body, leaving her naked and exposed. The fact that the culprit was very much responsible for her exposed and naked state wasn't much comfort.

Zach was standing at the end of the bed in jeans and a long-sleeved polo shirt, hair damp from a shower. 'Come on.'

Ashling squinted. 'It's not even light outside.' A thought struck her. Her heart sank. 'We're leaving for London already?'

Zach must have early meetings lined up.

But he said, 'Not quite yet. We're doing something first.'

He pointed to the end of the bed. 'I've laid out some clothes. Get dressed and meet me downstairs in fifteen minutes.'

Ashling came up on one elbow. 'Where are we going?'

'You'll see. Hurry up.'

Ashling hauled herself out of bed and had a quick shower, relishing the smell of Zach's spicy gel. Wrapped in a towel, she looked at the clothes he'd laid out. They were from the dressing room. Jeans and a stripy Breton top...sneakers.

Ashling got dressed and went downstairs. Zach greeted her with a cup of coffee and a croissant. He said, 'I'll be outside when you're ready.'

Intrigued, Ashling gulped down some coffee and a couple of bites of croissant, then went outside—and nearly tripped over her own feet. Zach was shrugging on a leather jacket and standing beside a beast of a motorbike. Dawn was just starting to appear in the sky.

He handed her a leather jacket. 'It's probably a bit big, but it'll do.'

Ashling took it. She was wide awake now, and speechless. She'd imagined Zach on a motorbike, but nothing could have prepared her for the reality when he zipped up the jacket and swung a leg over to straddle the machine.

He handed her a helmet and showed her where to step to help her hitch a leg over so she could sit behind him. She put a hand on his shoulder. When she was behind him her body naturally slid down right behind his. Her pelvis tucked against his backside. She automatically put her hands around his waist.

He put a hand on her thigh and turned to look at her, straightened her helmet. 'Okay?'

She nodded. She was exhilarated, and they hadn't even started moving yet. He started the bike and the engine roared to life underneath her. Between her legs where she was still tender.

They drove out of the estate and onto the empty main road. As Zach drove the sky lightened more and more. Ashling felt as if they were the only people in the world.

After about fifteen minutes Zach drove the bike through a gate where there was a huge hangar and a small plane in a huge field. He stopped the bike. They got off. He took off her helmet. She felt a little wobbly after the adrenalin of the bike-ride. He took her hand and led her over to where a man was waiting by the plane. Zach introduced him as the tow pilot.

Ashling was beginning to wonder if this was a dream. 'Tow pilot?'

Zach took her around to the other side of the plane, where she saw the most delicate flimsy-looking glider.

She looked from it to Zach. 'No way...'

He said, 'Do you trust me?'

Ashling wished she didn't. She wished she still had some tiny bit of distrust left. But he'd eroded it. The problem was that she didn't believe for a second that he trusted *her*. He wanted her. But that was it. And today they'd go back to London and this would be over.

Short and hot and over.

She nodded. 'Yes—yes, I do.' He didn't have to know that she meant it in a deeper sense. That she trusted him with her life. *With her heart.*

He helped her into the glider. which looked like a toy. She sat in the back seat and he got into the front. She watched, struck dumb, as the tow pilot got into the small plane and another man did something with the rope attached to their glider.

Then the other plane was moving, tugging their glider plane along behind it, and then suddenly they were off the ground, soaring into the sky behind the plane. And then the rope must have been detached, because the plane was banking left and they were going straight on, gliding higher and higher.

The thing that struck Ashling was the silence. All she could hear was the pounding of her heart. She was too afraid to move for a moment, and then she took in her surroundings, the countryside around them, as dawn broke over the horizon bathing everything pink and golden.

'Okay?' Zach half turned his head.

Euphoria gripped Ashling as the shock of what they were doing wore off. She nodded, emotion gripping her throat. 'Yes—yes! It's amazing.'

It was like nothing she'd ever experienced. Transcendental.

Ashling had no idea how long they stayed in the air… only that she would have happily stayed up there for ever.

When they got back to the field and landed, Ashling was

mortified to find tears on her cheeks. She quickly wiped at them as Zach undid his seatbelt and got out.

He turned around and reached for her. He saw her face and frowned. 'Hey, are you okay?'

Ashling nodded and stood beside him on rubbery legs. Lingering emotion made her voice husky. 'I've never experienced anything like that…it was beautiful. Thank you.'

She reached up and put her mouth to his jaw. Disconcertingly, she was reminded of that fateful night, of kissing him in the same spot. Zach pulled back. A shiver of foreboding went down her spine. She told herself she was being ridiculous. Paranoid.

After a quick chat with the pilots who ran the company, Zach led her back over to the motorbike. She couldn't explain it, but something had shifted between them since they'd landed. Zach didn't meet her eye as he put on her helmet, made sure she was secure. His touch was brisk. Impersonal.

She clung to him on the way back to the house, but she couldn't escape the feeling that Zach was regretting that impetuous move.

It had been impossibly romantic. And this wasn't about romance.

In the end, no amount of premonition could have warned Ashling just how brutally efficient Zach could be when dispensing with a lover.

The beautiful glider experience had obviously been a goodbye gift. As soon as they'd got back to the house Zach had turned distant in a way that he hadn't been since that night four years ago. Because since she'd met him again he'd been far too vengeful to be distant and then…then it had turned into something else.

Diana had been back at the house when they'd returned from their glider experience. Had it been Ashling's imagination or had she taken one look at Zach and Ashling and then looked at Ashling with sympathy? As if she had intuited exactly what was happening.

Zach had said, 'We'll be leaving within the hour. You should pack and get ready.'

And now they were in the back of his chauffeur driven car returning to London. No helicopter this time. Zach was in a three-piece suit. Ashling was in the laundered clothes she'd worn on her arrival.

He was on his phone now, speaking in French. It made her think of how far he'd come. From nothing. And how much it must mean to him to be considered equal by his peers and, more importantly, his father who'd rejected him.

To her surprise she felt her phone vibrate in her bag. She took it out. It was just a random text from her phone provider about billing. She read the last text exchange she'd had with Cassie over the weekend, when she'd last checked her phone.

Cassie had been wondering how she was, and Ashling—feeling inordinately guilty—had mentioned something vague about doing errands for Zach while Gwen was still away. Cassie had rung her then, and Ashling had tried to ascertain what was going on with Luke, the guy she was sleeping with, but her friend had been unusually elusive.

But then, Ashling hadn't been able to speak either, and she'd been equally elusive about what was really going on with her and Zach. She longed to talk to her friend now, though. But she'd have to wait.

Cassie would be back soon. Order would be restored.

For Zach, it would be as if nothing had happened—except for the fact that he'd settled an old score.

For Ashling, though… She couldn't even go there.

'I can get the tube.'

'Gerard will drop you home. No argument.'

The driver caught Ashling's eye in the mirror. 'No problem, miss.'

Weakly, Ashling smiled, 'Thanks, Gerard.'

They were almost at Zach's Mayfair townhouse. The city looked busy and intimidating to Ashling after the last few days in a bucolic paradise. She felt as if a layer of skin had been removed.

Zach pushed a button and the privacy partition went up between them and Gerard. He turned to her. She noticed that he must have shaved since they'd taken the glider flight that morning. It struck her then, in a moment of insight, that Zach must love the rush of adrenalin because he'd had to be so careful for his whole life not to make waves. To succeed and excel.

The fact that she'd recognised that only made this moment even harder.

She spoke first, to stall whatever it was he was going to say. 'Thank you… This morning was amazing. The whole weekend…'

'Thank you for being there. The deal with Georgios Stephanides… I don't know if it would have happened without you.'

'I'm sure that's not true, but it was the least I could do, considering the destruction I caused in the past.'

He shook his head. 'That's in the past. Gone.'

The car pulled to a stop outside Zach's house. He said, 'Look, Ashling, this was—'

She put up a hand, her chest tight. 'You really don't have to say anything, Zach. We both know what this is. Was. It's cool.'

If he mentioned *short and hot* she might hit him.

His jaw was tight. Eventually he said, 'After this morning I was afraid that—'

Ashling shook her head so forcibly she was afraid it

might fall off. 'No. It was lovely—and thank you again. Now I should really get going. I have tons to catch up on.'

'Of course. Goodbye, Ashling.'

'Bye, Zach.'

He got out of the car, took a bag out of the boot, and Ashling watched him go up the steps to the house. The door opened before he reached it and she caught a glimpse of the taciturn Peters.

Vengeance meted out. Order restored. Interlude over.

Ashling was glad the driver left the privacy partition up for the duration of the journey back to her and Cassie's apartment. Because she cried like a baby the whole way.

Zach lasted until lunchtime.

He'd thought he was doing the right thing. Seeing Ashling's tears that morning had been the biggest wake-up call of his life. They'd reminded him of the emotion he'd seen in her eyes the previous evening, when he'd all but spilled every gut he had at her feet. And her too. When she'd told him about her father he'd felt violent.

And had that made him run? Or send her packing? No, they'd eaten, drunk wine, made love. And then he'd woken her up this morning and taken her out on a glider—one of the most transcendental experiences of his life, shared with no one else before.

What the hell are you doing?

The words had resounded in his head like a klaxon when he'd seen her tears. In that split second he'd realised how far off-track the weekend had veered. At what point had *short and hot* turned into deep and meaningful?

An image formed in Zach's head. Heat pulsed into his blood.

It had happened right about when he'd found Ashling floating in his lake like a sexy water nymph.

He still wanted her.

It had taken all his restraint not to kiss her in the car. But she'd been looking at him with those huge eyes. Full of an emotion that convinced him he was doing the right thing.

But maybe he'd underestimated her. After all, she'd had a couple of relationships. She was savvy. Smart. Maybe he was doing them both a disservice by ending things so abruptly...

He assured himself that he was moving on to the next chapter of his life, and that he'd never been clearer about where he wanted to go—thanks in a large part to the person who had almost helped derail it four years ago.

But maybe the next chapter didn't have to start today.

Ashling had put on a pair of old cut-off shorts and a crocheted wrap-over top. She was attempting to take her mind off things by doing a bit of gardening in the small patch she and Cassie had outside their apartment at the back. But it wasn't doing much to ease the ache in her chest.

When the door buzzer rang she welcomed the distraction, dusting off her hands. Expecting to see her neighbour, or a delivery person, Ashling opened the door and blinked stupidly up at Zachary Temple.

He was halfway through saying something but Ashling was already in his arms, legs around his waist, mouth clamped to his. He walked them back into her apartment and kicked the door shut behind him.

Much later, in Ashling's bed, with the sounds of children playing on the street outside and sirens in the distance, they had a conversation.

Zach. 'This doesn't mean...'

Ashling.'I know.'

'What we said at the start—'

'What *you* said.'

'That this would be—'

'*Don't* say it now. It doesn't need to be said again. I know what this is.'

'You do?'

'Yes. And that's okay.' *Liar.*

'Okay. Good.'

'Good.'

'We're clear…?'

Ashling turned to Zach in the bed and twined her bare legs with his, relishing the feel of his body responding to hers. 'Clear as crystal.'

She kissed him then, to stop him saying anything else. She didn't need to be reminded of her weakness. Or that this was just a stay of execution.

Thirty-six hours later Ashling was on the other side of London in Zach's townhouse. She adjusted the pearl-encrusted collar that tied at the back of her neck. The dress was sleeveless, held up by the collar, with a line of pearls running from the collar on either side of the edge of the bodice of the dress, under her arms and around to the back. The rest of the dress was black, with a nipped-in waist, and it fell to the floor in a single elegant fall of material.

It was classic and…conservative. Her overriding instinct was to add a bit of colour. But she told herself it wasn't appropriate.

She'd come to Zach's house yesterday, after he'd spent the day and the night at her apartment. She hadn't expected anything social. But he'd asked her to come to a charity event this evening.

She'd said, 'Is that a good idea? People might start to ask questions…wonder who I am…'

Cassie, for starters. Her friend was due to arrive home any day now, and Ashling had no idea how she was going to begin explaining what had happened.

But Zach had brushed it off. 'It's a private event…tight security. It shouldn't attract too much attention.'

Then she'd said, 'I don't have anything to wear to an event.'

He'd said, 'Leave it with me. I'll arrange it.'

And this was the dress that had been delivered. Obviously to his specifications.

She'd put her hair up, to try and look as sophisticated as the dress.

Zach appeared in the doorway, wearing a tuxedo and carrying a box. He said, 'You look…stunning.'

A part of Ashling was a little disappointed with Zach's obvious approval. Especially after what he'd intuited the other night at his country house—that she wore colour to rebel against her father's lack of interest. It might have started like that, but now it was her. Who she was. Her essence.

Right now, though, she didn't really feel like *her*. Not like she had in that glorious dress at the weekend. She felt she was betraying herself a little.

But then she told herself she was being ridiculous. It was one night. One dress. These moments with Zach were finite.

'Thank you.' She affected a little curtsey.

Zach came into the room and opened the box, saying, 'I thought you might need something to go with the dress.'

Ashling looked inside and gasped. There was a pearl bracelet, with what looked like a diamond catch, and pearl drop earrings.

She looked at Zach. 'Are these real?'

'Of course.'

Ashling shook her head. 'Zach, I can't. They're too valuable. What if I lose an earring or the bracelet falls—?'

'They're yours. A gift.'

Her mouth dropped. A veritable tsunami of conflicting

emotions swirled in her belly. When she could move her jaw again she said, 'I can't…really. It's too much.'

But Zach was already taking out the bracelet and fastening it around her wrist, saying, 'Just try them on, hmm…?'

He handed her the earrings. She wasn't even sure why she was so reluctant, or why there was a feeling of gathering dread in her belly, so she put them on. They swung from her ears, their lustrous sheen catching the light.

Zach put his hands on her shoulders. He towered above her. They matched. Her black dress and pearls with his classic black and white tuxedo. And yet something jarred inside Ashling.

But then he was taking her hand and leading her out, downstairs to his car. They passed Peters on the way, and if Ashling wasn't mistaken the man gave her a sliver of a smile.

Now she was even more freaked out.

It took Zach a minute to realise why he couldn't find Ashling in the crowd. Because she looked like everyone else in their tones of black, grey, white and not many variations on those themes.

He pushed aside the niggle of his conscience. He'd deliberately instructed the boutique to deliver a dress that he knew Ashling wouldn't choose for herself. Obeying some very nebulous desire to see her in another environment. *His* environment. Because he needed to know if—

'Sorry. I got lost coming back from the ladies.'

Zach looked at Ashling. His eye was drawn to the splash of colour just above one ear. Delicate pink flowers tucked artfully into her hair.

'What's that?'

She touched the flowers. 'Is it too much? I spotted the hotel florists changing the flower display. They were going to end up in a bin, so I took a few.'

Zach shook his head, biting back a smile. 'No, it's not too much. It's pretty.'

He took her hand, feeling something inside him ease—just before he looked across the room and saw something, *someone*, and any sense of ease dissolved in a rush of hot emotion.

'What is it?' Ashling had clearly noticed the change in him immediately.

'My father.' He bit the words out.

He barely heard Ashling's intake of breath or felt her hand tightening around his.

'Where is he?'

'Talking to his wife. The mother of my half-brothers and sisters.'

Ashling followed Zach's eyeline to a tall man in the crowd. Distinguished. The woman beside him was also tall and elegant. The perfect couple. Ashling felt sick for Zach. She could imagine only too well how he must be feeling. Betrayed and rejected all over again.

A surge of protectiveness rose up inside her—and a need to right the wrong she'd done four years before. Zach's father had used her as an unwitting tool to hurt his own son.

Before she could think it through, Ashling had pulled her hand free of Zach's and was marching through the crowd towards his father, borne aloft on a wave of righteous anger.

She wasn't even aware of the sense of déjà-vu: walking through a crowd towards a tall man…walking around to stand in front of him.

This time she wasn't nervous, though. She was livid.

Zach's father looked her up and down. His eyes were blue. Not dark. Cold.

'Yes? Can I help you?'

'Don't you recognise me?'

The man immediately looked discomfited and guilty, more than hinting at a lifetime of behaviour similar to what he'd subjected Zach's mother to.

Ashling was disgusted. 'No, I don't mean like that. I mean from four years ago, when you hired an actor to publicly humiliate your own son.'

The man's eyes narrowed and comprehension dawned. 'You had red hair. A short dress.'

'So you do remember?'

He hissed at her. 'Get out of here now or I'll call the police.'

The women beside him spoke sharply. 'Henry, what is going on?'

The man looked at Ashling, up and down. 'Nothing, darling. This tart is just some opportunist. She shouldn't be here.'

Those words made a red mist descend over Ashling's vision. Her voice rang out. 'Zachary Temple is more of a son than you could ever deserve. You're not fit to clean his shoes. You're a disgrace.'

Before Ashling knew what was happening Zach's father had lifted his hand, as if to strike her, but someone stood in front of her before he could.

Zach. His voice was ice-cold. 'Don't even think about it. I'll have you flat on your back with a broken jaw and the police will be here so quickly your head will be spinning for a year.'

Ashling took a step to the side, to see Zach's father's hand still raised. The look in his eyes was one of pure and utter hatred. His face was mottled. There was a deadly silence. And then a flash of light.

Zach turned, took Ashling's hand, and then everything was a blur until they were outside the venue and Zach was bundling her into the back of his car. Ashling realised she was trembling all over from the overload of adrenalin and emotion. She could still feel herself flinching in anticipation of a physical blow.

Zach was like a statue next to her. The journey back to his house was made in tense silence. As the shock wore off, though, dread settled in Ashling's belly. She'd overstepped the mark—spectacularly. He'd never forgive her for this.

When they got back to the house Zach went straight into the reception room. Ashling followed him. He poured himself a drink and threw it back.

He turned around. 'What the hell were you thinking, Ashling?'

She swallowed. 'I'm sorry. I just… I saw him and I got so angry when I thought of everything…'

Zach started to pace. 'He could have hurt you. He nearly did!'

Ashling almost flinched again at the memory. 'You stopped him.'

Zach kept pacing. 'Four years ago was bad. It was embarrassing and it cost me. But I managed to overcome the talk and the reputational damage. I worked hard to restore confidence and faith. But now… I have so much more to lose.' He stopped, looked at Ashling. 'The one thing I had going for me was the fact that no one knew who my father was. There were rumours, but that was all. At first I hated it that he didn't acknowledge me. Then I didn't want to be associated with him. But now that's all gone. It'll be all over the papers that I'm Henry Field's son. There'll be constant speculation as to whether or not he influenced my success in any way. My reputation will come under scrutiny all over again.' Zach gestured to Ashling. 'You might look the part this evening, but you've just proved that you really don't belong in this world.'

If he'd slapped her across the face it wouldn't have had the same impact. He might as well have taken out a knife and sliced her heart wide open.

Ashling couldn't breathe for a long moment, so sharp was the pain. Then she said shakily, 'I knew it. You got this dress on purpose, to try and see if I could fit in. Was it some kind of an audition to see if I was suitable for a wider public audience?'

'Well, if it was, you failed.'

Ashling shook her head. 'I didn't ask for this, Zach. I thought we were done.'

He closed the distance between them so fast, she took a step back.

'Don't make me prove you a liar, Ashling. When I turned up at your door you were with me all the way.'

She really didn't need to be reminded of the relief she'd felt right now. 'I meant I didn't ask to be a part of your world. I know it would never work.'

Zach made a rude sound. 'The innocent ingénue is back, I see.'

'What's that supposed to mean?'

'Elena Stephanides has been in touch, looking for your contact details. Apparently you were discussing her investing in a business, the setting up of a yoga studio?'

Ashling's mind was blank for a moment—and then she remembered. It had been a very innocent conversation that she'd passed off as nonsense at the time. Flattered but embarrassed.

She shook her head. 'That was nothing. *Is* nothing. She was complimentary about my yoga teaching. I told her I had a pipedream to one day own my own studio... I had no idea she'd actually follow up on it.'

Zach made another sound. 'Kind of convenient to have a conversation about *"nothing"* with one of the wealthiest women in Europe, though.'

The pain deepened and spread throughout Ashling's body, turning her blood cold. 'I knew you were cynical, Zach, but that is...beyond...'

Zach tugged at his bow-tie, undid his top button. Even now, in the midst of all this, Ashling could still be aware of him. Those long fingers.

'It's not cynical. It's how the world works.'

'Your world. Not mine.'

Zach took down his hand, leaving the bow-tie rakishly undone. 'Oh, yes—because your world is so much more worthy. Because you get enjoyment out of earthy, basic pleasures. Because you're not corrupted by ambition and success and wealth.'

Before she could respond he went on.

'And yet you took to the billionaire lifestyle without too much of a struggle.' He put his hands out, 'Now that we know where we both stand, maybe we can revisit that audition to be my mistress. After all, I don't think we're quite done, are we?'

Ashling was so angry and hurt she was dizzy with it. 'Whatever I felt for you is dead, Zach. I could never want someone so cruel, so cynical—'

She was in his arms and his mouth was on hers before she had time to take another breath.

Ashling managed to resist for about one second, while the anger raged, but then Zach's mouth softened, his arm relaxed infinitesimally, and desire overtook the rage, blazing up in a storm of want and need and hurt and anger. Because even in the midst of her pain she understood his.

Her arms climbed around his neck, her body straining against his, and then he pulled back. He put his hands on her arms, held her away from him. She could feel her hair unravelling. The flowers lay at her feet, wilted. Mocking.

She pulled back too, with a jerky move. 'I think we are done, actually. Goodbye, Zach.'

Ashling turned and walked from the room on very wobbly legs. She went upstairs, changed into her own clothes. Left the dress and the jewellery behind.

This time when she went downstairs there was no disapproving Peters, no sign of Zach.

She opened the door and walked to the nearest tube station and went home.

Zach heard the front door opening and closing. He knew she was gone.

It was only now that the volatile mix of inarticulate rage and lust was finally clearing from his brain. Except when he thought of seeing his father raise his hand to strike Ashling he felt the anger rise again. Not even anger. Murderous rage.

His insides turned to ice. *No.* Not going there.

And then all he could see was Ashling standing in front of him just now. Looking pale. Stricken. Mouth swollen from his kiss. He'd had to put her away from him. He'd been afraid that he wouldn't be able to stop kissing her, and that was all he had intended. To make a point. It had been very important not to expose himself.

There was a bitter taste in his mouth. Four years ago he'd stood in a room and felt the judgement and condemnation of his peers. He'd thought he might never recover. It had happened again this evening. With possibly worse repercussions. He had more to lose now. A lot more.

But instead of *that* being his focus all he could feel were the four walls of the empty room closing in around him and the sensation that, whatever damage had been done in that ballroom full of his peers this evening, somehow the real damage had been done here in this room.

And then he told himself he was being ridiculous. The only damage he needed to worry about was damage limitation. Putting Ashling out of his head once and for all. She was right—they were done. He didn't need a lover who tied him up in so many knots he couldn't think straight. Or a lover who waded in to fight battles he'd been fighting on his own for years.

He didn't need any of that.

He didn't need her.

He didn't need anyone.

In a bid to prove something to himself, Zach went upstairs, taking the stairs two at a time. He found the dress Ashling had been wearing hanging up in the wardrobe. Something about that detail irritated him intensely.

And then he looked around for the sheen of cool, pale pearls. He saw the box and picked it up, opening it. It was empty.

Annoyingly, his first reaction wasn't a sense of vindication because she'd taken the jewellery—after all, he'd told her it was a gift. But he was disappointed.

He was almost out of the room before something caught the corner of his eye. He stopped. The bracelet and earrings were on the top of a chest of drawers, neatly lined up. She hadn't taken them.

CHAPTER TWELVE

THREE DAYS LATER, and back in his office, Zach was in a foul humour. Suddenly he became aware of a commotion coming from the other side of his door and heard Gwen's slightly raised voice.

Zach's heart thumped. *Could it—?*

But before he could finish that thought the door burst open and a man strode in. He looked vaguely familiar, but Zach couldn't place him.

Before he could say anything, the man said, 'I need to know where Cassandra James is.'

'Who the hell are you and how did you get into my office?' Zach shouted to Gwen. "Gwen, get in here."

Gwen appeared at the door, looking concerned. 'I'm so sorry, Mr Temple. He said he had an appointment.'

'Like hell he—'

'I'm Luke Broussard of Broussard Tech.'

Now Zach recognised him. This was the man he'd sent Cassie to suss out in America. He felt anger that it wasn't Ashling—that he'd even wanted it to be *her*—but he cut off that direction of thinking. Focused on the other very valid reason for his anger.

He narrowed his gaze on the man in front of him, who almost as tall as he was. 'Terrific. The man who managed to lose me the best executive assistant I've ever had. What are you doing here? Have you come to gloat?'

'What do you mean "lose you"? Where is Cassandra?'

'I expect she's at home, being head-hunted by one of my rivals. So thanks for that.'

'She's resigned?'

Broussard looked genuinely shocked.

Then he said, 'You need to give me her address. Please, man, I need to talk to her… To explain.'

Zach put up a hand. 'What the hell makes you think I'd give you my executive assistant's address? Why should I? Not only is it unethical, but it's also quite possibly illegal. And I really could not care less if—'

'Because…' the man cut him off, and stopped.

Zach was getting seriously irritated now. 'Because *what*?'

Broussard ran a hand through his hair. 'Because I know why she resigned her position here. You want her back? You need to let me speak to her—so I can explain.'

Something about the man's demeanour caught at Zach's gut. He recognised it. He looked as tortured as Zach felt.

Muttering about ethics, and threatening to do him serious damage if he did anything to hurt or upset Cassandra, Zach scribbled her address on a piece of paper and handed it over. The fact that it was also Ashling's address…that she might be there…was something that stuck under his skin like a thorn.

Broussard left.

Zach put his hands on his table and dropped his head. Damn. Ashling was even managing to eclipse the fact that his best assistant had resigned for no apparent reason.

The sense that things were beginning to fray badly at the edges of his life was not welcome.

And it only got worse.

After one of the most tumultuous weeks of his life, Zach walked into another exclusive society gathering with a beautiful woman on his arm. The fact that she'd agreed to come with him—she was closely related to the royal family—was proof positive that he'd survived the storm unscathed.

It should be a moment of triumph. But it felt unbelievably hollow—like a lot of other momentous occasions recently.

He couldn't stop his eyes scanning the room. Looking for a splash of colour. A bright blonde head. A flower in hair. A huge open smile.

A stricken, pale face.

The woman beside him tucked her arm into his. He felt like recoiling. He forced a smile. She'd already irritated him by asking him about Ashling—about the identity of the mystery woman who had confronted Henry Field—but thankfully the photographer hadn't caught her face because Zach had stepped in front of her.

It was still all anyone could talk about, though. And it appeared his date wasn't willing to let it go.

She said now, with a little pout that really didn't suit her, 'Honestly, I won't tell a soul. Who was she?'

'She was—' Zach stopped. He'd been about to say *no one*, but the words wouldn't form on his tongue. He literally could not voice the lie.

He looked at the woman on his arm. This was it. She was stunning. Perfect. He was on the threshold of everything his mother had wanted for him. The culmination of all the years of work that had precluded his making friends. Having fun. Because it had all been about reaching the ultimate goal.

Walking into a room with the right woman on his arm and being accepted by the very people who would have ground him to dust before he had a chance to speak. The illegitimate son of a cleaning lady.

His mother had been the *wrong* woman, and all she'd wanted for him was *this*. To be standing here with the *right* woman, who would make everything worthwhile.

But he realised now that had been his mother's fight. She'd lived her life through him, bitter and vengeful. She'd blamed Zach for the fact that no man would want to take on a child that wasn't his. But the truth was that she'd never even looked.

'Zach?'

He looked at his date. She was perfect. The right woman. And so wrong.

He extricated her arm from his, said, 'I'm sorry,' and turned and walked out.

'Are you sure you're okay, love? You say those are happy tears, but I know there's something else going on.'

Ashling forced a smile. Of course she couldn't fool her mother, but she really didn't want to distract her today of all days. 'I'm fine, honestly. It's nothing.'

Just a shattered heart.

She pushed her pain aside and hugged her mother. 'I'm so happy for you and Eamon. You deserve this happiness so much. He's so in love with you, it's just…' More tears welled and Ashling had to clamp her mouth shut.

Her mother's partner had rung Ashling during the week, to remind her that it was her mother's fiftieth birthday that weekend and also to ask for Ashling's blessing in his asking for her mother's hand in marriage.

So this evening, while her mother had been celebrating what she'd thought was just a surprise party for her fiftieth, Eamon had got down on one knee and proposed.

Her mother had said yes even before he'd finished speaking.

The surroundings couldn't be more romantic. It was a beautiful garden in the middle of the eco village, just yards from a sandy beach and the wild Atlantic Ocean. Poles had been set around a central area and there were flaming lanterns and fairy lights imbuing the space with a golden glow as the dusk drew in on a long late summer evening.

Children were running free. People were laughing and

chatting. Teenagers were building a bonfire on the beach.
Music came from the traditional Irish musicians on a makeshift stage. At some point the younger people would moan
and complain and start playing more modern music, but
not yet.

'Are you sure you're okay?'

Ashling nodded, wiping at her cheeks. She'd tell her
mother another time. 'I'm fine. Now, would you please go
and celebrate with your fiancé? He's looking lonely over
there, surrounded by a hundred people.'

Ashling's mother laughed and went back to Eamon, both
of them beaming so hard with happiness they could probably power the national grid. Ashling sighed. She was happy
for her mother, truly, she just—

'I have no idea who that man is, but if he's a lost tourist then I am first in line to give him directions. Straight
to my bedroom.'

One of Ashling's old schoolfriends, Dervla, had come
to stand beside her. She was looking towards the entrance
into the village off the main road.

Ashling turned around. And her heart stopped. A man
was climbing off a motorbike. He was wearing worn jeans
and a leather jacket. Even before he took off his helmet she
knew exactly who he was. Her whole body did.

And her heart. That stupid, weak muscle.

Zach was looking around. Bemused. And then he saw
her. *Zing.*

Ashling watched him put down the helmet and walk
over. He should look ridiculous. A billionaire in an eco-
village. Even if he was wearing jeans and a battered leather
jacket.

He walked over and stopped in front of her. 'Here you
are,' he said, as if it was entirely normal for him to just turn
up in the west of Ireland.

Ashling sensed her friend melting away. She barely

heard the music and the noise around her. There was a dull roaring in her ears. Blood. Anger. *Desire.*

'Zach.'

His name felt rusty on her tongue. But it had only been a week or so. The longest week of her life. It was as if she had to say his name to make sure this wasn't a hallucination.

'What are you doing here?' She shook her head. 'Did you ride the bike all the way from Dublin?'

'From Dublin Port. Yes.'

That was literally cross-country, about three and a half hours.

His dark gaze swept her up and down, taking in the sundress with its purples and pinks and reds, over which she wore a yellow cardigan, and then all the way down to her yellow wedge sandals.

'You look…colourful.'

Ashling tensed. 'If you've come here just to remind us both how unsuitable I am then—'

He caught her hand. She heard him curse under his breath. He had a look on his face she'd never seen before. Sheepish.

'I'm sorry.'

Ashling pulled her hand back, afraid to have him touch her for fear she'd end up twined around him like a monkey.

'How did you know where to find me?' Her phone had been switched off for days now.

'I went to your apartment. Saw Cassie. She told me— but only after I begged.'

'You begged?'

He nodded. 'I was desperate.'

Ashling's conscience pricked. 'How is Cassie? I left her a phone message, but I didn't see her before I left. I just couldn't…' She trailed off.

She hadn't been able to contemplate seeing her friend

and explaining everything that had happened, so she'd left before Cassie had come home.

'She's fine. She's a little preoccupied herself.' Zach's tone was dry.

'With what?'

'The man who followed her to London—Luke Broussard. And the fact that she's resigned.'

'Resigned?'

Zach nodded. He seemed remarkably sanguine about it. 'She said to say that she's sorry she missed the party, but she'll make it up to you and your mother, and that you need to call her ASAP. But you're not to worry and she's fine. And really happy. But she might be moving to America. She'll explain everything when you call.'

Ashling absorbed all that. She was delighted for her friend if everything Zach said was true.

Zach said now, 'Can we go somewhere a little more private to talk?'

Ashling looked around. Dervla and a large contingent of the party guests were subjecting them to serious scrutiny. Ashling didn't want her mother to notice and come over. If she guessed that Zach was the reason behind her tears it wouldn't be pretty.

Ashling led him away from the party to a quieter part of the garden. She faced him. 'What do you want, Zach? Why did you come all the way here?'

'Because I want you.'

Her heart leapt and every cell in her body sizzled with awareness. But she clamped down on her reaction. Wanting wasn't enough. It was temporary. She knew how persuasive Zach could be, so she had to nip this in the bud. Now.

She forced herself to look at him. 'I want you too, Zach. I wanted you from the moment we met four years ago. When you rejected me that evening I took it so personally that I went off-script, which I know probably had a lot to do with my last interaction with my father. But I wouldn't have re-acted like that in the first place if I hadn't felt a connection. I've never felt that connection with anyone else,' she went on. 'And I don't think I will, ever again. The thing is, Zach, it's more than just physical for me. It's—'

'I love you.'

'I—' Ashling's mouth shut. She opened it. Shut it again. Opened it. 'What did you say?'

'I said I love you. You say you wanted me four years ago? Well, I think I fell in love with you four years ago. You turned my life upside down in less than two minutes and, as much as I'd have loved to dismiss you, I knew there was more to you than that. That's why I reacted so strongly. Then I couldn't get your face out of my head. I think I looked for you everywhere. And when you arrived that evening, with my tux…' He shook his head. 'You set something alight in me four years ago. You made me ques-tion everything I was striving for, even though I wouldn't admit it at the time. It was only when we met again that I had to confront it.'

'Confront what?' Ashling felt as if she was in a dream.

'Confront the fact that I'd been living out my mother's ambition for revenge. She sacrificed her life for me and never let me forget it. She loved me, but she also resented me. Blamed me for a lost life. Look at your mother…get-ting engaged…finding happiness. She hasn't let bitterness blight her life. Or yours.' Zach shook his head. 'When you stood in front of my father—' He stopped, the colour leach-ing from his cheeks. 'I've had nightmares about him hit-ting you, Ash. If he had…he could have—'

Ashling caught Zach's hand. Lifted it up. 'He didn't be-cause you stopped him. I'm sorry again about that…'

Zach shook his head. 'Don't be. You were fearless. I've never seen anything like it.'

'Did it come out in the papers?' Zach nodded and Ashling winced. 'I'm so sorry.'

'Don't be. It was the best thing. Not for him, though. His life has unravelled spectacularly. His wife has accused him of domestic abuse. A legion of women have come out of the woodwork claiming that he fathered their children and paid them off. He's been accused of violence by more than just his wife. His reputation is ruined. But in all honesty I don't even take any pleasure in it. I'm ashamed he's my father, but I feel I can move on now and live my life for *me*. Not to get back at him and not to avenge my mother.'

Emotion made Ashling's chest tight. 'I'm really glad, Zach. You deserve that peace of mind.'

Zach looked serious. 'And you deserve an apology. I'm so sorry for the things I said that evening. For making you wear that dress.'

Ashling let his hand go. 'It was a beautiful dress…just a bit…black and conservative.'

He shook his head. 'It wasn't you. You are not conservative or monochrome.'

There was a beat, and then he said, 'You need to know something. I went to an event last night. I took a woman.'

Ashling went very still.

Zach caught her hands. 'A woman who made me realise that the only woman I wanted with me is *you*. The first thing I did when we arrived was look for you. For some colour—anywhere. There wasn't any. So I left pretty much as soon as we'd arrived. And now I'm here. Because I want you, Ash. I want colour and I want to live in a world where cynicism isn't the norm.'

'That thing with Elena—'

He put a finger to her mouth. 'Not my business. *Your* business—with her. And if some day it happens that you do something together I'll be there to support you in any way I can.'

Ashling's heart beat fast. 'Some day…? You mean… like in the future?'

Zach smiled. 'I mean…like for the rest of our lives. If you'll have me.'

'Have you as in…?'

'Lover, friend, life partner… Husband. And maybe… when we figure out how we feel about it after our own experiences…children?'

Ashling's head was spinning. She took a breath. 'Zachary Temple, are you telling me that you love me and that you want to marry me and have a family?'

'I actually told you I loved you a couple of minutes ago, but maybe that got lost in—'

Ashling hit him on the arm. She felt suddenly shy. 'I heard you. I just don't think I believed what I was hearing.'

'You heard me right. So now there's only one more thing to ascertain…'

She looked at Zach's mouth, wondering what it would take to get him to stop talking and kiss her.

'Eyes up, Ash.'

She looked at him.

'Do you love me?'

She looked at him in disbelief. Was he completely blind? 'Of course I do. I love you so much but I didn't say it because I thought you just wanted a relationship until things fizzled out, and I knew I couldn't cope with that ultimate rejection and then watch you go on to marry some perfect corporate wife. Because that's what my father did and I just…' She stopped. Sucked in a breath. Then she put her arms around Zach's neck. 'Yes, I love you, Zach Temple. And yes to everything. For ever. *Yes.*'

And then, finally, he kissed her, and didn't stop for a very long time.

EPILOGUE

Five years later, Somerset

'THIS PLACE IS so idyllic, Ash. How can you ever bear to go back to London?'

Ashling grinned at her best friend Cassie, who was sitting on the other side of the table on the terrace. They'd just finished a long, leisurely lunch.

She threw a napkin at her friend, 'Says the woman who has a freaking island!'

Cassie smiled smugly. 'Well, yes, there is that...'

Cassie and her husband Luke Broussard, tech zillionaire, lived mostly on an island off the coast of Oregon in the United States. The place where they'd first fallen in love. They also had a townhouse in San Francisco, for when they needed to attend to their extremely successful corporate lives, not to mention homes in pretty much every other major city in the world, so their family could always have a settled base when they needed to travel.

Just then a mewling sound came from Ashling's breast. She looked down and stroked the downy cheek of her baby girl, Georgie, and helped her to latch on again.

Opposite, her friend was similarly engaged. Except *her* baby girl—Celestine—was a month older. Ashling was already having visions of them being best friends, living together and having adventures...

'You know that Zach thinks we deliberately contrived to have babies at the same time?' Ashling commented wryly.

Cassie laughed. 'Luke may have said something similar.'

'It's not still weird for you, is it? Me and Zach?'

It had taken Cassie a little while to get used to seeing her best friend with her old boss. But she rolled her eyes now.

'Ash, I think I got over it as soon as I saw you together. If ever there was a case of opposites attracting… The thing that freaked me out most was him turning into a man who had actual feelings! Although hearing you call him by his first name for the first time was also a bit of a shock…'

Ashling laughed. She missed her life with her best friend, especially as they lived so far apart now, but they saw each other as much as possible. Each summer here at the country house, for Zach's annual party, and many more times during the year.

Cassie asked now, 'How's the newest studio going?'

Pride filled Ashling. She'd just opened another yoga studio, here in the local village. Elena Stephanides had championed and invested in Ashling's pipedream to open her own business, and her first studio had opened on the ground floor of the Temple Corp headquarters, along with a crèche for its employees.

She had other studios in London now, and one in Athens too. The Stephanides were close, valued friends and godparents to Georgie.

'It's amazing,' she said. 'The locals have really embraced it—' She broke off when she heard shouts from the other end of the garden.

'There goes our peace,' Cassie observed dryly.

Ashling took in the scene. Zach and Luke were walking back from the lake with two small boys on their shoulders—Devin and Louis, their respective sons. The men were dripping wet after their swim in the lake, wearing nothing but board shorts. A view that both women took in with a sigh of very feminine appreciation.

Orla, Devin's non-identical twin sister, ran ahead, holding something small and furry and distinctly wet, that was wriggling in her arms. 'Mum!' she shouted, 'Ziggy had his first swim and he didn't drown!'

Ashling smiled. There went their peace, indeed. But what was coming in its place was so much more satisfying.

Just before the chaos reached her and Cassie they shared a private look. They might relish their moments of peace, but they both relished *this* so much more. It was a life and existence beyond anything either of them could ever have imagined, filled with infinite love.

* * * * *

THE ITALIAN'S DOORSTEP SURPRISE

JENNIE LUCAS

MILLS & BOON

CHAPTER ONE

A FIERCE SUMMER storm was raging off the Atlantic coast, pummeling his sprawling oceanfront mansion. Nico Ferraro stared out the open window, his mood as dark as the crashing surf below.

Rain blew inside his study, running down the inside wall to the hardwood floor as bright lightning crackled across the sky. He took another sip of Scotch. Thunder shook the house, rattling the windows. Nico remained unmoving, staring broodingly into the night.

He'd lost the thing that mattered most. All the billions he'd accumulated, his fame, his romantic conquests, meant *nothing*. He'd lost his chance at vengeance, had it ripped from his grasp at the very moment of his triumph.

Nico heard a loud bang from the other side of the house. Not thunder this time. Someone was banging at his front door.

"Please," a woman's voice screamed into the storm. "Please, Mr. Ferraro, you have to let me in."

Nico took another sip of the forty-year-old Scotch. His butler would handle the intruder, assisted by his security team if necessary. He was in no mood to see anyone tonight.

"If you don't, someone will die," she cried.

Now *that* piqued his curiosity. He suddenly wanted to at least hear the woman's story before he tossed her back into the rain. He started to turn from the open window, hesitated, then closed the glass window behind him. He didn't give a damn about this place—just another anonymous fifty-million-dollar Hamptons beach house—but he'd be putting it on the market tomorrow. This estate was useless to him now it could no longer be the scene of his revenge.

Going down the wide hallway to the foyer, he saw three men gathered in a semicircle around the front door. Behind them, Nico saw the smaller shape of a young woman, soaking wet, with her hair plastered to her skin and her clothes stuck to her body…

Nico sucked in his breath as he realized two things.

First, the young woman, beautiful and dark-haired, was pregnant. Beneath the light on the front porch, her white sundress revealed every luscious outline of her body, her full breasts and heavily pregnant belly.

Second, *he knew her.*

"Stop," Nico said, coming forward. "Let her come inside."

His head of security frowned back at him. "I don't know if that's such a good idea, boss. She's been talking wild—"

"Let her in," he cut him off, and his henchman reluctantly stepped aside.

"Thank you, oh, thank you," the young woman cried, though it was hard to tell if those were tears streaming down her cheeks or rain. She grabbed at Nico's hand urgently. "I was so scared you wouldn't…when I have to tell you—"

"It's all right." Nico tried to remember how to be polite. His skills were a little rusty. "You're safe now, Miss—" Then he realized that he'd forgotten her name, which of course was embarrassing and damnable, since her grandfather was the longtime gardener at his Manhattan penthouse. To cover, he said sharply, "Your hands are like ice." He turned to a bodyguard. "Get her a blanket."

"Of course, Mr. Ferraro."

Her teeth were chattering with cold. "But I have—have to tell you—"

"Whatever it is, it can wait until you're not freezing to death." He started to offer her the half-empty glass of Scotch still in his hand, but then stopped as he remembered pregnant women generally avoided such things. "Perhaps a warm drink?"

"No, really," she croaked, "if you'll just listen—"

Nico turned to his butler. "Find her some hot cocoa."

Sebastian looked rather doubtful. "Cocoa, sir? I'm not sure—"

"Wake the cook," he bit out, and the man scurried off.

It occurred to Nico that his staff had gone to seed. Once, it would have been unnecessary for him to repeat any order—ever. All of his houses, like his international real estate conglomerate, had run like well-oiled machines. Though of course, that was before. How long ago had that been, when Nico had still cared so desperately to make his life appear perfect?

Christmas. It had been Christmas Day. And now it was—

"What day is it?" he barked at his security chief. The man looked at him like he was mad.

"It's the first of July, Mr. Ferraro."

Six months. And he could barely recall any of it, though he'd obviously continued to buy properties and run his company from Rome. He clawed his hand through his dark hair. Was he losing his mind?

"Nico. *Please.*"

Hearing his gardener's granddaughter call him by his first name drew Nico's attention as nothing else had. He looked at her.

The young woman gripped his hand, looking up at him pleadingly, and he had a strange stirring of memory. But of what?

He barely knew her. He'd seen her occasionally over the years, of course, as she'd grown up amid the rooftop gardens of Nico's Manhattan penthouse, a few hours from here. She had to be in her midtwenties now. Perhaps he'd said hello once or twice, or wished her happy holidays, that sort of thing, but nothing more. Nothing to warrant her suddenly calling him *Nico*, as if they were friends. As if they were lovers.

He withdrew his hand, folding his arms. "Why are you here? Why have you made such a scene?"

As a bodyguard wrapped a warm blanket over her slender shoulders, she nearly sobbed, "Just *listen*."

"I'm listening," he said. "Tell me."

Her eyes were an uncanny green in her pale complexion, beneath striking dark eyebrows that matched her wild, dark hair. She took a deep breath. "My grandfather is coming here to shoot you."

Nico frowned. "Your grandfather? Why?" He could think of no complaint the gardener might have against him. To his best memory, he hadn't even spoken to the man since before Christmas, when he'd given him exact instructions about the holiday lighting for the pergola and trees on the penthouse terrace. Back when Nico had cared about such things. Back before—

He pushed the thought away. "Is this some kind of joke?"

"Why would I joke about that!"

He saw the terror in her eyes. However ridiculous it sounded, clearly the woman believed her story. So it was either true, or she was having some kind of psychotic breakdown. He could hardly judge her for that, after his six months of near-fugue state as CEO of Ferraro Developments Inc. He knew he'd made multimillion-dollar deals, but he could hardly remember a single one. "Why would he want to kill me, Miss…uh…?"

Damn it. Too late, he remembered *again* that he didn't

know. Glaring at the Scotch, which he held entirely to blame, he set the half-empty crystal glass on the hallway table.

The woman's expression changed as she stared up at him with big eyes. She said slowly, "You don't remember my name?"

There was no point in pretending.

"No. I'm sorry. I mean no disrespect to you or your grandfather. Even if he's trying to kill me." He smiled grimly, and when she didn't return the smile, he sobered and said, "Tell me your name."

There. He'd said *I'm sorry*, which he rarely did.

But she didn't seem particularly impressed. She lifted her chin, her green eyes shooting emerald sparks in the light of the foyer.

"My name is Honora Callahan, my grandfather is Patrick Burke and he thinks you've disrespected both of us. That's why he's on his way here right now with his old hunting rifle, intending to shoot your head off."

Nico almost laughed at the image. He stopped himself just in time. "Why would he?"

She stared at him, her pretty face bewildered. He shifted his feet, growing uncomfortable beneath her searching gaze.

"I'm sure you can guess," she said finally.

He snorted. "How would I know?"

She licked her lips, glancing nervously at Frank Bauer, his security chief, and the other bodyguard still standing by the front door. Both men were pretending not to hear, though they'd moved their hands to their holsters when Honora mentioned her grandfather's rifle.

"Fine," she said. "If that's how you want to play it. But when Granddad gets here, he'll be waving his rifle and shouting crazy threats. Just tell your bodyguards to ignore him. Don't let them hurt him."

"What would you prefer? That I just let your grandfather kill me?" he said acidly. "Burke is a good gardener, but there are limits to what I'll do for employee morale."

"As soon as he gets here, I'll go outside and calm him down. Just stay in here, and tell your men not to pull out their guns. That's all."

"Hide like a coward in my own home?"

"Oh, for the love of—" Honora stamped her small foot. As she did so, Nico's gaze fell unwillingly on the bounce of her full breasts. He could even see— His mouth went dry. The shape of her hard nipples were clearly visible beneath the wet, thin fabric. "Just stay inside and don't respond." Her voice changed. "Should be easy for you."

There was some criticism there he didn't understand. Forcing his gaze upward, he said, "You still haven't explained why Burke would do this. I haven't spoken to the man for months."

Honora's pale cheeks seemed to burn. Ducking her head, she glanced down at her belly and mumbled, "You know why."

Nico's heart dropped to the floor, as if somehow his body knew what she was about to say, even though his brain protested it was impossible. "No."

Honora huffed with a flare of nostrils. "I'm pregnant, Nico. With your baby."

Lightning flashed, flooding the foyer with brief white light as Honora stared up at Nico's handsome face, her heart pounding. Thunder followed, rattling the windows of the oceanfront mansion. Her whole body was shivering. Not from cold, but from fear.

She'd spent six months dreading the thought of seeing Nico Ferraro again. But she'd never imagined it could be as bad as this.

It shocked her now to remember the schoolgirl crush

she'd once had on her grandfather's boss. Her infatuation had lasted throughout her teenage years, all those afternoons she'd helped Granddad after school, or done homework sitting at a bench in the far corner of the penthouse terrace.

She'd been in awe of Nico Ferraro, billionaire real estate tycoon, watching him with big eyes every time he came or went—equally handsome whether wearing a tuxedo with a beautiful woman on his arm as they left for some glamorous ball, or in a black leather jacket, going motorcycle racing; or even in casual khaki shorts, flying off to the Maldives in his private jet. It was a world that Honora couldn't even imagine, even though she'd spent her entire childhood adjacent to it. And now, at thirty-six, he was the most gorgeous man she'd ever seen, a James Bond of the society set.

While Honora often felt invisible. When Granddad was done with his work tending the enormous rooftop garden, treating every plant and flower with loving care, they would head home on the subway to their two-bedroom walk-up in Queens. He'd raised Honora since she was eleven, after her parents had died. He'd been patient, gruffly kind and dutiful in his care of her.

But he saved his true devotion for his plants. Sometimes, Honora had wished she might have been a rhododendron bush, or perhaps a cypress or juniper, in order to get more of his warmth and attention. He seemed to save all of his true love, and most of his conversation, for them. He could chat and coax and croon to his plants in a way he never did to Honora.

But when she felt unloved, she told herself she was lucky her grandfather had taken her in and given her a home. She had no right to ask for more. Patrick Burke had always put duty ahead of all else. Honor was important in their family. So important her mother had named her for it.

That had made it all the more shocking and painful when

Honora had had to tell her old-fashioned grandfather that she was pregnant—pregnant and unwed.

She'd known he would find out sooner or later. She'd hidden her pregnancy with loose clothing as long as she could, hoping with increasing desperation that Nico Ferraro would either answer her messages, or return to New York City. But he'd done neither. Which was really all the answer she needed, and it broke her heart.

As spring had turned to summer, it had become increasingly difficult to come up with good excuses to wear oversize hoodies. When New York City suffered its first blast of sticky humid heat in June, she was already so hot in her pregnant state, and their Queens apartment had no air-conditioning. Her grandfather caught her standing in front of the open refrigerator, gasping the cool air in her T-shirt and shorts. His eyes had gone to her belly.

"Oh, no," he'd gasped, and for the first time since her parents' funeral thirteen years before, he'd cried in front of her. Then his tears had turned to rage. "Who is the bastard who did this to you?"

Honora had refused to reveal the father's identity, even to her friends. The chauffeur at the penthouse, Benny Rossini, an Italian American from the Bronx, had offered to marry her, which was very kind. *Too* kind, in fact. She'd thanked him, but couldn't take advantage of their friendship. For a month, she'd held her breath, hoping somehow it would all blow over.

Then today, while she was helping her grandfather tend the rooftop garden, the housekeeper told them that after six months away, Nico Ferraro had finally returned to the US. His private jet had just landed in the Hamptons, a three-hour drive from New York City.

After more than a decade of working for him, Patrick Burke knew his employer's playboy ways. He'd taken one look at Honora's stricken face and dropped his shovel, muttering that he was going to their apartment to get his antique hunting rifle.

Honora had been terrified, imagining Nico Ferraro's security team would take one look at her gray-haired grandfather waving his rifle like a maniac, and shoot the old man down immediately in an act they could reasonably claim was self-defense. Her only hope had been to get there first and reason with her grandfather's employer.

It had taken all of Honora's efforts to talk the older man out of his lunatic plan of jumping on an eastbound train with the big rifle slung openly over his shoulder. "At least have Benny take you," she'd said desperately. "It will be faster than the train."

When her grandfather grudgingly agreed, she'd rushed downstairs to ask the young chauffeur for help with her plan.

Benny had been shocked, then angry, to learn the identity of her baby's father. But he'd recovered quickly and agreed to give her grandfather a ride to the Hamptons in the boss's Bentley, and "accidentally" get lost on the way. He'd added with a nervous laugh, "Just make sure they don't shoot us when we get there."

But her drive had taken longer than she expected. She'd borrowed Benny's personal car, a vintage Beetle, and it had broken down three miles from the house. Terrified of arriving too late, she'd run here. At six months pregnant. In a sleeveless stretchy dress and strappy sandals, in a rain storm with the wind pushing against her every step.

Now, Honora looked between Nico and his bodyguards anxiously. "So you agree? When my grandfather gets here, you'll keep your guns down and let me go out there alone?"

Nico came closer to her in the foyer. "You can't be serious."

She looked up at him, the billionaire playboy she'd once thought so exotic and wonderful. Her hands tightened at her sides. "I told you, this is no joke. Granddad's already on the way, but they're taking the long route—"

"I can't possibly be your baby's father," he interrupted. "I never touched you."

Honora's mouth fell open. Never touched her?

It was one possibility she'd never considered. For him to deny he'd made love to her! As if she were lying about their night together. As if she were some gold digger trying to trap him into marriage under false pretenses!

In February, after she'd discovered she was pregnant, she'd tried to do the right thing and let him know, but he'd ignored all the messages she'd left at his office in Rome and his villa on the Amalfi Coast. Resigned, she'd known she'd have to raise this child alone. If Nico wouldn't take responsibility, so be it. She was a grown-up. She'd known the risks of sex.

But hearing him deny their night together, she realized Nico Ferraro had taken full advantage of her schoolgirl crush. He'd helped himself to her virginity, then meant to toss her and the baby—*his* baby—aside like trash.

It was the final straw.

Fury filled her, rushing like fire all the way to her fingertips and toes, burning her heart to ash.

"How dare you," she said in a low, trembling voice. She clenched her hands into fists. "I have been nothing but honorable—unlike you—and this is how you treat me? By calling me a liar?"

Nico's forehead furrowed, his expression turning perplexed as he stared down at her. "If I'd slept with you, I would remember."

He was tall and broad-shouldered and so handsome, in spite of—or perhaps even because of—his dark hair being uncombed and wild. His tailored white shirt and black trousers were unkempt and wrinkled. He smelled of Scotch and leather and smoke from the fire and rain, everything masculine and untamed. She breathed it in and yearned for him, still, in spite of everything.

She hated herself for that, but not as much as she hated him. She'd never let herself want him again. Never, ever.

"So you don't remember my name and you don't remember our night," she choked out. "How can you be so heartless and cold?"

His dark eyes narrowed as he said acidly, "And when do you claim you conceived this miracle baby?"

"Christmas night."

He snorted. "Christmas—" Then his expression changed. His forehead furrowed, as if straining to remember a half-forgotten dream. For a moment, he looked bewildered. Then he lifted his chin defiantly. "Even if it happened, which I'm not saying it did, how could you be sure I'm the father?"

She looked at him, nearly speechless with anger. "You think I slept with other men the same week?"

"It's the twenty-first century, and you're a free woman..."

"You know I came to your bed a virgin!" She knew his men were listening, but she was too enraged to care. Her cheeks burned. "How dare you!"

Then their eyes widened at the noise of a car outside, and doors slamming.

"Get out here, Ferraro!" she heard her grandfather's voice holler above the wind and rain. "Get out here right now so I can shoot you right between the eyes!"

She looked at the two bodyguards by the door, who'd already put their hands on their holsters.

"Please, don't hurt him," she pleaded. "I told you. I'll go out and talk to him."

The older bodyguard stared at her, then glanced at his boss. She saw Nico Ferraro give him a tiny nod, and she hated him for that. How awful to have to ask him for favors!

"Keep him outside," the head bodyguard said. "If he doesn't shoot at us, we won't shoot back."

"Thank you," Honora said, but fear caught at her throat. How could she guarantee Patrick wouldn't start taking potshots at the house in his current emotional state? Trembling, she hurried to the front door.

Then she suddenly stopped, whirling back to face Nico.

"I'm doing this to protect Granddad, not you," she said. "Personally, I think I'd be happy to see you shot."

And opening the door, she ran out into the dark summer storm, beneath the torrent of rain and howling wind on the wild Atlantic shore.

CHAPTER TWO

PERSONALLY, I THINK I'd be happy to see you shot.

As Honora disappeared out the beach house's front door into the storm, Nico stared after her in shock. Standing in the foyer, he felt his men's gaze on him, before they discreetly turned away. He felt a twist in his solar plexus.

So you don't remember my name and you don't remember our night. How can you be so heartless and cold?

Her scornful words made him feel hollow inside, reminding him of similar words from Lana when he'd called her film set in Paris on Christmas Eve to end their engagement.

You heartless bastard. You never loved me at all, did you? Lana had yelled into the phone.

No, he'd replied shortly. *Sorry.*

Being woken earlier that morning with news of his estranged father's death had felt like being submerged in ice water. Prince Arnaldo Caracciola had dropped dead of a heart attack in Rome, right before he would have been forced to fly to the Hamptons to beg for Nico's mercy.

What point was there in being engaged to a movie star if he couldn't rub the old man's face in it?

After hanging up with Lana, Nico had tried to go to work as if nothing had happened, but he'd found himself shouting at, even firing, several of his most valued employees. "It's Christmas Eve. Go home before you ruin us," his vice president of operations had said quietly, then handed him two sleeping pills. "Get some rest. You look like you haven't slept in days."

It was true; he'd barely slept all week in anticipation of his father's visit. But Nico didn't need sleep. He was fine. Never better. To prove it, he'd gone to his gritty downtown gym and sparred against a former heavyweight boxing champion. Nico had pushed himself in the ring, insulting his bigger, better-skilled opponent, until he'd gotten himself knocked out twice. The second time, when he sat up, he hadn't been able to see anything for nearly three minutes. But as soon as his sight returned, he'd started to get back in the ring.

The owner of the gym would not allow it. "You want to destroy your brain, Mr. Ferraro, go do it somewhere else. I'm not running a morgue. And get a doctor to look at that concussion!"

Doctor. Nico had sneered at the idea, but his head had ached as he walked back the long city blocks to his midtown penthouse.

Late afternoon on Christmas Eve, his home had been deserted, all the employees gone home to spend the holiday with their families. The dark, empty rooms had echoed inside him. He'd reached for a bottle of Scotch, sent to him by a rival congratulating him on his recent acquisition of beachfront land in Rio, which would soon be developed into a world-class hotel. He'd paced all Christmas Eve night, looking out at the city lights, his soul howling with fury.

He didn't remember much after that. He'd started to hallucinate and imagine things. At some point, he must have taken the two sleeping pills and washed them down with Scotch, because when his housekeeper arrived early the day after Christmas, she'd found him collapsed in the hallway with a smashed bottle of Scotch on the floor. Alarmed, she'd called an ambulance.

Nico had woken up in the hospital to see his doctor standing over him with worried eyes. "You need to take better care of yourself, Mr. Ferraro. You've had a severe concussion, which was not helped by alcohol and sleeping pills." He'd paused delicately. "Perhaps you'd find it beneficial to talk to someone. Or I could recommend a residential facility that would help you rest and work through whatever you're—"

"I'm fine," Nico had said, detaching himself from the monitors. Against medical advice, he'd checked himself out of the hospital and rolled onto his private jet, just in time to make it to the old man's funeral in Rome.

His father, who'd denied him everything all his life, couldn't stop him from doing it, now he was dead. Nico had had the last word. But as his evil stepmother glared at him with tearful, accusatory eyes over the grave, Nico had felt otherwise. He'd felt heartsick that wintry day in Rome, as if his father had won, contriving to die of a heart attack just when Nico finally had him by the throat.

Now, Arnaldo would never be forced to admit that his abandoned son had surpassed him, or to say that he was desperately sorry for seducing his maid, Nico's mother, then tossing her out like trash. The married prince had known Maria Ferraro was pregnant, but he'd still refused to take responsibility. He'd left her and Nico to starve. The man deserved to be punished for—

Personally, I think I'd be happy to see you shot.

Nico sucked in his breath. Was it possible that he was doing the same thing as the man he'd despised?

Could Nico have fathered a child with—well, not a maid, but with his gardener's granddaughter? Could Honora Callahan be telling the truth?

No. He would remember!

He'd never had an affair with an employee. He preferred the women he slept with to have power that matched his own. His mistresses before Lana Lee had been supermodels. Heiresses. A chemist. A makeup millionaire. They were women who wanted hot sex, who wanted to see and be seen, but who wouldn't demand emotional intimacy he couldn't give. For the entirety of their six-month engagement, he'd never felt emotionally close to Lana; he'd assumed she preferred it that way, too.

The idea of anyone sacrificing their own self-interest for the sake of someone else seemed like total insanity to Nico.

Like when Patrick Burke became guardian to his orphaned granddaughter thirteen years before. Nico had thought it was sheer lunacy for an elderly widower to raise an eleven-year-old child. But it didn't affect the man's work, so Nico had never said so. He had no right to an opinion.

But the old man sure seemed to have an opinion about his employer, coming here with a hunting rifle.

Going to the window, Nico looked past the silk curtains. In the dim light from the windows, he saw Honora talking to her grandfather some distance from the house, beneath the lightning and rain. There was another dark figure hovering nearby. What the hell? Was that his chauffeur, who'd apparently driven the murderous old gardener here to kill him, in Nico's own Bentley?

He saw the old man waving the rifle around, seeming to point it toward the house. He couldn't hear his words.

There was another flash of lightning, and he saw Honora's pleading face before she turned away, trying to block her grandfather from approaching the house.

Patrick Burke seemed very sure that Nico was the father. Honora had seemed so, too. *You know I came to your bed a virgin.*

But he would remember sleeping with her, wouldn't he? Yes, he'd slept with many beautiful women, and some people called him a player. But even with a bad concussion, even hallucinating from insomnia, even on sleeping pills washed down with Scotch, he'd remember—

Her long, dark hair spread across his pillow. Her emerald eyes glowing up at him as she whispered, *I can't believe this is happening...* The softness of her skin as he slowly stroked down her naked body, cupping her breasts, then moving down farther still, as he lowered his mouth to taste her sweetness...

Oh, my God. Nico's eyes went wide.

Turning abruptly from the window, he pushed open the door and went out into the dark, wind and rain.

Behind him, he heard Bauer shouting, "Sir?"

The Bentley was parked in the circular driveway, with his chauffeur standing behind it. Nico went straight to where the old man stood with Honora.

The old gardener sobered when he saw Nico. He quit waving the rifle around, even as he lifted his chin defiantly.

"You think you can just take whatever you want, Mr. Ferraro?" His voice broke. "Even seduce an innocent girl, and then toss her callously aside, when she's pregnant with your child?"

"I didn't know," Nico ground out. "She never told me."

Her eyes narrowed. "I tried."

"Well, now that you know," Patrick Burke said pointedly, "what are you going to do about it?"

Honora nervously placed herself between the two men, as if she were afraid of what they might do. "I don't need him to do anything, Granddad. He made it clear he's not interested in being a father. I can raise my baby alone."

Not interested in being a father. It was jarring. He had a sudden flash of a memory of his own mother holding him tight when he was a boy, and they were evicted from their tiny apartment outside Rome.

Why won't your father pay for you? Why doesn't he want you? How does he expect me to do this on my own?

Now, Nico felt oddly suspended in time as the storm pelted him with rain and lightning flashed across the wide dark sky. In the distance, he could hear the roar of the ocean against the shore.

For six months, he'd been lost, even to himself, after the failure of a lifetime's worth of plans. Just when ultimate triumph had been within his grasp, he'd lost his last chance at victory. His father was dead, and would never recognize Nico's right to exist, much less claim him as his son.

Nico couldn't inflict the same pain his father had. He could claim his own child.

If this baby was his, he had the opportunity to be better than his father ever was.

Nico could never inherit the title of prince, or the aristocratic Caracciola name. But he could sire his own dynasty. Build his own legacy. And make sure that his own children never felt as he had—rejected, adrift, alone.

"You *will* do something about it," Patrick Burke told him fiercely, his whiskers shaking beneath the rain as he shook his rifle in Nico's direction. "You'll take responsibility for what you've done! Or meet the short end of this stick!"

Reaching out, Nico yanked the rifle away in a swift, easy movement. For a moment, the old man stared at him, shocked and outraged.

Backing up a step, Nico held the rifle almost casually, pointing it upward. "I take your point, Mr. Burke. I believe we can come to some arrangement."

"Arrangement?" Those bushy gray eyebrows shook. But it wasn't just his eyebrows, Nico realized. The man's hands were shaking, as well. He was upset. And why shouldn't he be if he truly believed his boss had coldly taken Honora's virginity and then refused to take responsibility? "What kind of arrangement?"

Nico looked at Honora, who was watching with big eyes as rain fell, all of them so wet they might as well have been swimming in the sea. "Why don't you come inside where it's warm, and we can discuss it."

The old man scowled. "If you think my granddaughter will ever accept a payoff…"

"No. If she is pregnant with my baby, there can be only one answer." Lifting his chin, Nico looked straight at Honora's lovely, worried face. "I will marry her."

Honora's jaw fell open. She felt dizzy.

Behind her, Benny Rossini, the young chauffeur, said harshly, "You don't have to do that, Mr. Ferraro…"

But her grandfather was staring only at Nico. "Do you give me your word, sir?"

Nico Ferraro's handsome face was deadly serious. "I do."

"Well, then!" Her grandfather was suddenly beaming. A flash of lightning crackled in a sizzling line above them, cracking the sky. He came toward Nico, holding out his hand. "Welcome to the family."

"Thank you," said Nico, shaking his hand gravely, still holding the rifle upright with the other.

And just like that, it seemed, Honora's fate was sealed.

Was she losing her mind?

"What century are we living in?" she said incredulously. She looked at Nico. "I'm not going to marry you!"

Her grandfather, whom she'd always trusted and obeyed, turned to her almost chidingly. "That's no way to talk to your husband, little one…"

"My *future* husband. Which he isn't!"

Patrick waved his hand airily. "You two kids have a lot to talk about." Turning to Benny, he said, "We should give the happy couple time to discuss wedding plans."

"Wedding plans?" she sputtered.

"But there's no reason to remain out here in the cold and rain." Nico nodded toward his sprawling Hamptons beach house. "Come inside."

As Benny started to step forward, Patrick stopped him with his hand on his arm.

"No." Her grandfather's shoulders sagged in his old coat, as if he'd just aged twenty years in five seconds. "I'm exhausted, as only an old man can be. Please, Benny." He looked at the young chauffeur plaintively. "Just take me home."

Honora looked at her grandfather sharply. Other than a touch of arthritis, Patrick Burke was more energetic than some men half his age. Was he up to something? Or had the worry of her unwed pregnancy truly exhausted him?

"All right," Benny said grudgingly. Turning to Honora, he said, "You coming?"

She bit her lip. She was grateful the young driver had helped her keep Granddad from harm, but she was afraid Benny felt more for her than friendship. And she'd never love him back, no matter how many times he offered to run down to the local bodega to buy her ice cream and pickles. No matter how many times he tenderly offered to marry her and be the father her baby "obviously needed."

It annoyed her. Why was it that everyone seemed to think that just because Honora was pregnant, she was desperate for a husband? They didn't seem to realize, as Nico had said earlier, that it was the twenty-first century!

But at least Benny's proposal had been real. Unlike Nico's. Setting her jaw, she tossed a glare at her baby's father.

"Please take Granddad home, Benny. I want to stay and have a little chat with my *future husband* here."

"Honora," her grandfather said quietly, "be nice."

Be nice.

He rarely spoke those words to her, but they always made her shrink back in shame. Had she been unkind? Rude? Selfish? Had she acted in a way that meant she didn't deserve to be loved—didn't even deserve a home? *Be nice* made her try harder to be good, to be helpful, to be no trouble to anyone.

But this time, the unfairness of it made her catch her breath.

Turning in amazement, she glanced pointedly at the old hunting rifle. Patrick had the grace to blush.

"That's different," he said with dignity. "I was just doing a grandfather's duty."

"You're right. We do have a great deal to discuss." Nico gave her a calm smile. "It's late. I'll take you back to the city first thing in the morning."

"Honora?" Benny demanded.

"Go. I'll be fine." Her eyes narrowed. But she wouldn't say as much for Nico.

Nico gave the rifle back to Patrick, who pointed the muzzle at the ground, looking a little embarrassed.

"Oh, Benny." She suddenly remembered. "Your car broke down a few miles up the road."

"Then how did you get here?"

She shrugged beneath the rain. "I ran." She felt, rather than saw, all three men look at her belly, as if judging her ability to run by her condition, and felt irritated. "It was fine. I'm fine."

"You need to be careful," her grandfather began.

"I'm so sorry," Benny said at the same time. "I thought the engine was okay. I'll have it towed tomorrow."

"My men will handle it," Nico said coolly. "I'll have it repaired and brought to you. No charge of course." He glanced at Honora. "Not when your car brought me such happy news."

Benny ground his teeth into a smile at his boss. Then

he turned and said reluctantly, "All right, Mr. Burke. I'll take you home."

"Great." Her grandfather turned and leaped back to the Bentley like a teenager running a hundred-meter dash. Honora's throat caught. So much for him being exhausted. She'd spent her whole life trying to be helpful and sweet and no trouble at all, either to her parents or, later, to her grandfather. Was she really such a burden that Granddad seemed so eager to be free of her?

"And this time, take the interstate," the old man called to Benny. "I have no idea where you thought you were going, driving in loops all over Long Island. I'd expect a chauffeur to have a better sense of direction."

Honora watched as the Bentley pulled away into the stormy night. Then she exhaled and turned to her grandfather's boss.

"You have some nerve."

"Say it inside."

Taking her hand, Nico pulled her toward the house, out of the rain. She felt the warmth and strength of his palm against hers, and even hating him as she did, she shivered a little.

Once inside the grand foyer, as the front door closed behind them with a bang, she felt how much warmer it was, and realized that she was soaked to the bone.

"You need to warm up." He glanced at his butler. "Where's her cocoa?"

She had her anger to keep her warm. "I don't need cocoa."

"Cook had to send out for chocolate, sir. She's warming the milk—"

"Tell her to hurry," Nico said. "But first take Miss Callahan upstairs to the rose room. She'll be staying the night."

Was no one listening to her? Honora lifted her chin. "I have not agreed to—"

"Make sure she has everything she might require for her stay," Nico said, ignoring her as he seemed to ignore anything contrary to his will.

"Of course," the butler intoned. "Miss Callahan, if you'll just come this way…"

"I can't sleep here," she said to Nico. "Unless you expect me to sleep naked."

All four men in the foyer stared at her, startled. It took several seconds before any of them recovered. The butler was the first to clear his throat.

"We have ladies' pajamas," he ventured, "clean and never worn that I believe might fit." Honora looked incredulously at Nico. Ladies' pajamas! Did he bring lovers here on a regular basis? The butler continued, "And if you'll just leave your clothes outside your door tonight, they'll be washed, pressed and ready in the morning."

"You don't need to fuss over me," she told the butler. "My grandfather's a member of staff. I can catch a train back later tonight."

Nico said sharply, "Don't be ridiculous. You're cold and wet, and clearly you've had a difficult night. If you're the mother of my unborn child—"

"If?"

"Then I must insist you take care of yourself. Go take a hot shower. We can speak after you're warm."

"You'd like that, wouldn't you?"

"Yes," Nico growled, moving closer. "I would. And if you don't go with Sebastian right now, I'll take you upstairs myself."

Honora's eyes went wide at his threat. The two of them, alone in a bedroom? Even if he couldn't remember their night together, she did. Every moment of shocking pleasure would be forever burned on her skin, on her body, on her soul. Even if the secret sensual dreams she still had of him made her hate herself. She'd never forget. Especially not now that she was carrying his baby inside her.

"Fine," she bit out. Following the butler, Sebastian—she wondered whether it was his first name, or his last—she went up the sweeping staircase and was escorted to an elegant, feminine room all in pink, where she found a brand-new, freshly laundered white silk nightgown and robe, as well as men's pajamas and a white cotton bathrobe. The soaps and shampoos were Italian and imported.

This guest room had been meant for someone, she thought. But who?

The shower warmed her up and made her feel human again, as well as sleepy and comfortable. Suddenly, the idea of sleeping here rather than shivering on a rattling, cold train through all hours of the night seemed like an excellent plan. Which made her mad. She didn't want Nico to make her feel good. She hated him for what he'd done, for what he was continuing to do.

I will marry her, indeed! She ground her teeth. Saying that to her *grandfather*! How could he!

Going downstairs in the soft silk nightgown and matching white robe that she was amazed fit her pregnant body so well, she found Nico in the grand living room off the stairs, beneath the wall of tall, curved windows overlooking the dark night. He was sitting in a sleek sofa beside a roaring fire.

For a moment, Honora hesitated, her gaze tracing over him unwillingly. It looked as if he'd had a shower, too. His dark hair was just long enough to be wavy, which looked impossibly sexy and Italian over his high chiseled cheekbones. He'd changed into comfortable clothes. A thin white T-shirt clung to his hard-muscled torso and low-slung sweatpants hung over his powerful thighs. His aquiline profile was facing the fire. His mood seemed pensive, even sad. She felt instinctive sympathy rise inside her.

She fought it with fury. Nicolo Ferraro feel sad? Not about anything but a dip in the stock market or a sudden drop in commercial rental rates!

Still. Best to get this conversation over with so they could move on with their lives. And she could go to bed. Striding forward purposefully, Honora sat next to him on the sofa. She was careful not to touch him.

"Look, I know you were trying to help," she started, "but you've only made it worse with your lie."

Nico looked at her, his handsome face bemused. "What lie?"

"Telling Granddad you wanted to marry me. Sure, that solved today's problem, but long term it will be ten times worse. Do you think he won't notice when you swan through the penthouse a week from now with some Instagram model?"

"I wasn't lying," he said, sipping a glass of amber liquid. "I'm going to marry you."

She stared at him. "You can't be serious."

"Why?" He turned when Sebastian brought in a white ceramic mug on a silver tray.

"I apologize it took so long, Mr. Ferraro. Apparently the grocer had to be awoken to find and deliver the chocolate."

"It's fine." But as Nico reached for the mug, he drew his hand back in irritation. "But it's cold."

The man bit his lip. "It was ready some moments ago, but as the young lady was upstairs—"

"Make another," Nico said impatiently, leaving the mug on the tray.

"I don't actually like cocoa," Honora said.

Nico turned to her. "What do you want? Herbal tea? Hot apple cider?"

She could only imagine how much trouble that would make for the poor cook. Poor woman would probably be forced to go out and pick apples in the rain. "I want you to leave me alone."

He said to his butler, "Herbal tea. With organic milk." Turning to Honora, he confided, "Calcium is good for the baby."

"Oh, is it now." As if she hadn't just spent the last six months reading every baby book and going to doctor's appointments, while he'd only known about it for, like, ten minutes and already considered himself the expert. She couldn't keep the sarcasm out of her voice as she added, "Tell me more about what my baby needs."

As the butler disappeared, Nico looked at her calmly. The firelight flickered over the hard, handsome planes of his face and the five-o'clock shadow over his square jawline. "A father, for a start. Why didn't you tell me?"

"I did! I told you that I tried. I sent multiple messages to your office in Rome in February."

"Saying you were pregnant?"

"Just saying it was personal, urgently asking you to return my call."

He stroked his chin. "I don't answer desperate messages from women I don't know. Since I didn't remember our night together, or your name…"

Irritated, she set her jaw. "I also left messages with the housekeeper at your new villa, since I heard you'd sold your apartment in Rome. I asked you to call me back as soon as you arrived."

"The Amalfi Coast is hours from Rome. I never stayed there. I slept at the office."

"What?" That explained why Luisa had sounded so doubtful every time Honora called.

"I have a sofa in my private office. A shower. There was no need for me to leave."

"You slept at the office? For six months?"

"I was working," he bit out. His handsome face was full of shadows. "I was fine."

It sounded awful. When had Nico become a workaholic without a soul? He'd always been intensely focused on work, but in the past, he'd at least found *some* time for fun, whether that meant extreme sports or getting himself engaged to world-famous movie star Lana Lee.

Honora told herself she didn't care. The state of his soul wasn't her problem. "The point is, I did try to tell you. When I never heard a response, I realized you weren't interested in anything I might say to you. So I decided to raise this baby on my own."

His eyes narrowed. "Now that I know, I will give you and the baby everything. Including my name."

"It's not necessary. We're good."

"Good? Good how?"

It was a question Honora had often asked herself in the middle of the night when she couldn't sleep for worrying. Her cheeks went hot. "I have a job."

"Doing what?"

"I work in a flower shop. People need flowers," she added defensively at his incredulous look.

"I'm sure they do, but I can't imagine it's enough to support you and the baby."

"I'm also working my way through community college."

"Studying what?"

She looked at the floor. "General education courses." It was a sore point. Honora still hadn't figured out what she wanted to do as a long-term career. She'd been unable to convince herself to study something she hated, just because it would pay, as her accountant friend Emmie had. "I'll figure something out."

Nico let that pass. "Does your current job even have maternity leave? Benefits?"

Honora bit her lip. Her boss, Phyllis Kowalczyk, was a

retiree with few employees. The flower shop seemed more like a labor of love than a growing, profitable business. "Um. I'm not sure…"

"You're probably still living with your grandfather."

Guilt flashed through her. As if she needed to be reminded that she already felt like a burden to him. "So?"

"You deserve more." He lifted an arrogant dark eyebrow. "I will take care of you and the baby."

His tone got her hackles up. "No, thanks."

"Why? Are you in love with someone else? Rossini?"

"Benny?" Frowning, she shook her head. "We're friends."

He relaxed. "Well, then. Shall we say next week for the ceremony?"

Ceremony? "But I don't love you!"

He shrugged. "*Love*. A momentary feeling that makes people do things they regret once the madness passes. A make-believe notion. An illusion. I'm grateful that I'm immune."

Honora stared at him. Was there no getting through?

"I'm not going to marry you." She enunciated the words, trying to drive them into his arrogant brain. "I'd be a horrible wife for you. And *you*…you would be a disaster."

Nico looked at her, his handsome face impassive.

"Why did you sleep with me, then?" he asked quietly. "Was it so horrible? Was it such a disaster?"

Everything she'd been about to say got caught in her throat. *Yes*, she wanted to tell him, *it was a mistake*. But then that would mean her baby was a mistake, and she wasn't. She was precious.

As for that night… Honora remembered the sparkling Christmas lights glowing every color in the frosty night. The scent of pine from the enormous, decorated tree in the penthouse with two-story windows overlooking all of glittering Manhattan.

And Nico, taking her in his powerful arms. The taste

of his kiss, sweetness and Scotch, savage and tender all at once. The feel of his body against hers as he'd made her feel pleasure she'd never imagined.

Honora couldn't lie. She took a deep breath. Looking up at him with tears in her eyes, she whispered, "It was the most beautiful night of my life."

CHAPTER THREE

NICO STARED AT HER in the enormous living room, as the warm fire flickered over her lovely face. Outside, he could still dimly hear the wind and rain and the crashing surf. But in his heart, something tight…loosened, and he could breathe again.

"I wish I could remember." His voice was quiet. "As you can."

Honora gave a smile that seemed sad. "And I wish I could forget. Like you."

He looked at her sitting at the other end of the sleek new sofa, wrapped in the white robe. Her dark hair was still damp, tumbling over her shoulders in a way that was much too sexy for comfort. And if she leaned forward, the robe fell open a little, revealing the neckline of the silk nightgown. Modest as it was, her full, pregnancy breasts strained against the silk. Swallowing hard, he forced himself to look only at her eyes. "If it was the best night of your life, why do you want to forget?"

She looked away. "Because…because it hurts to remember what a fool I was. Imagining I was in love with you. Imagining I even *knew* you."

Nico had sudden disjointed flashes of memory, the feeling of holding her in his arms in the penthouse, kissing her passionately against the window with all of Manhattan's skyscrapers sparkling behind her. Taking off her clothes

piece by piece, pulling her down on the soft rug beneath
the Christmas tree… Later, he'd thought it was a hallucination, a dream of a sexy dark-haired woman whose exact
features he could not recall.

*I love you, Nico. I wasn't brave enough to say it before.
I love you.*

Abruptly, he stood up and went to the wet bar. Pulling
a crystal lowball glass from the shelf, he dumped in two
cubes of ice. He opened a new bottle of Scotch and poured a
generous amount over the ice. He swallowed the first sweet
sip, trying to control the pounding of his heart.

Lifting her gaze, Honora said quietly, "You were drunk
the night we slept together, weren't you? That's why you
don't remember. You were drunk."

A thousand excuses poured into his mind. Evade, deny,
don't say anything that could be used against him, either
in a court of law or in the much rougher court of public
opinion.

But as Nico looked into her face, he thought how easy
it would have been for her to lie and say that their night together had been awful, a tragedy, that she regretted it and
hated him. She'd certainly proven that she had no problems
insulting him to his face. But she hadn't.

She'd been brave enough to tell the truth. He could at
least tell her something that wasn't a lie. "It's more com-
plicated than that."

"Tell me."

"I had…some problems. I hadn't been sleeping, and I
took pills for a…bad headache. Janet—" that was the penthouse's housekeeper "—found me collapsed on the hallway
floor the next morning and called an ambulance," he said
bluntly. "You didn't know?"

She shook her head, wide-eyed.

"Good." He was relieved his housekeeper was discreet
and not spreading rumors. He felt foolish enough to imagine

himself insensate and drooling on the floor when she'd discovered him. It was horrible to imagine he'd made a fool of himself in front of Honora, slurring his words or stumbling around. "I didn't seem…off to you on Christmas Day?"

"You did seem a little…different. You had some bruises, but you laughed it off and said it was just from boxing in the gym."

So he'd told her that much. "It was."

"I knew you'd broken up with your fiancée the day before." She looked at her hands. "I thought I was so lucky, like you'd suddenly realized I was the one you'd wanted all that time." She looked up. "But I was just a booty call, wasn't I? No, worse, I was a booty *delivery*—I just happened to be there."

It hadn't been breaking up with Lana that had crushed him, but losing the dream of revenge that had poured rocket fuel on his whole life. But he could hardly explain, since only one other living person even knew that Prince Arnaldo Caracciola was his biological father. "I'm sorry."

It was the second time he'd said that to her. It was starting to become a habit.

"Me too." Her eyes met his. "I was so sure I loved you. Then, when you disappeared and never even bothered to contact me again, I realized I'd loved a dream."

Nico hated imagining that he'd caused her pain. He didn't know her very well, but the more he knew, the more he thought that she was like her name: honorable. And also loving and kind. Perhaps too much of those things—because how could she ever have looked at Nico, with his tattered soul and empty heart, and imagined in her innocence that she saw something worthy of love?

"Honora," he said in a low voice, "you must know I never meant to—"

He stopped as the butler came in with a mug on a tray.

"Your tea with milk, madam." He sounded faintly disapproving. "We had to send out for organic milk."

Honora's cheeks turned rosy. "I never asked for—" But when the butler continued to hold out the tray, she took the mug with a sigh. "Thank you. I'm sorry I was so much trouble."

"My pleasure, madam." The butler turned toward Nico. "Anything else, sir?"

"No, nothing," he said coolly, not even looking at him.

After the butler left, she took a small exploratory sip. She looked very cozy on the sofa in the flickering shadows of firelight. Still holding his barely tasted Scotch, he went to sit beside her, a little closer than he'd been before.

After another sip of tea, she looked at him. "It's not bad." She tilted her head. "You aren't very worried about your employees' feelings though, are you?"

"What?" Frowning, he said, "They should be worried about *mine*. It seems ridiculous that we'd be out of milk and chocolate, even if I arrived with no warning."

"Do you usually require organic milk and cocoa powder?"

"No, I never touch the stuff." Her lips lifted on the edges, and he realized her point. So he changed the subject. "I didn't like Sebastian's tone with you."

"Since your bodyguards didn't shoot Granddad, I'm happy for your staff to talk in any tone they want." She tilted her head. "Two bodyguards? Is that really necessary? Is there so much crime in the Hamptons?"

"Any self-made man makes enemies," he said shortly. He didn't want to talk about his employees. He moved toward her on the sofa. "So is that why you don't want to marry me? Because I hurt you when I ignored your messages in Rome? I told you, I had no idea—"

"It's not just that," she said in a small voice. Looking down at the mug in her hands, she bit her full, tender pink lower lip. "You're very rich, Nico," she said finally. "Incredibly powerful. And as handsome as the devil himself."

He knew she didn't mean it as a compliment. "But?"

She looked up. "A relationship has to be more. There has to be respect on both sides. Trust."

"And you think you can't trust me."

Honora shook her head. "We have nothing in common."

He looked at her baby bump.

"Obviously that's not true," he said quietly.

She looked sad. "It's not enough."

What she meant was that *Nico* wasn't enough. And how could he argue with that? He had secrets he would never share. Not with anyone. Especially not her.

Because he suddenly realized he cared about her opinion. The thought shocked him. For the first time since Christmas, he wanted to make an effort. He wanted someone to think better of him.

Looking up, she threw him a tentative smile. "I'm curious. Why do you believe me now about the baby? What changed your mind enough to make you suddenly propose to me?" She shook her head. "I thought you were just trying to placate Granddad. But you actually meant it."

"Yes."

"Without so much as a DNA test?"

How could he explain what he himself did not really understand? Had he decided to believe her out of pure instinct, based on his perception of her honor and honesty? Or was it because, after months of working sixteen-hour days on projects he could not remember and barely cared about, he grasped at one final chance to prove to his dead father, and himself, that he was a better man than Arnaldo ever was?

And what do you know about being a father? a voice said mockingly inside him. He squelched it coldly. He'd show up, for a start. That would be more than Arnaldo had ever done. "I suppose I could ask for a paternity test…"

"After the baby is born, I guess." She seemed doubtful. "But I'm not going to risk my baby's health on an intrusive test just to convince you."

"After," he agreed. He wasn't worried about it. He already knew this baby was his, in the same way he knew when an undeveloped plot of land would pay off. In the same way he'd known since he was twelve years old that someday he'd *be* somebody, that he'd put his boot against the throat of the world to prove his worth.

Honora tilted her head. In an uncertain voice, she said, "You really want to be a father?"

"How much clearer can I make it?"

"You've never shown the slightest interest in children."

"I've never had one."

"Or commitment. Except for Lana Lee. And even with her, you were only together a few months…"

He gave a crooked half smile. "You were paying attention?"

Her cheeks burned. She set down her empty mug on the end table. "You always changed the color of roses you wished grown in the greenhouse based on the woman you were giving them to."

She must have helped her grandfather with the gardening more than he'd realized. It was strange to realize that Honora knew him so well, when he knew so little about her. Strange and disconcerting.

Her tender pink lips twisted. "Are you still in love with Lana?"

Nico wondered what it had cost her pride to ask. With anyone else, he might have refused to answer. But he didn't want to do that. Not when the stakes were so high. And anyway, in this case honesty cost him nothing. "No."

"You can tell me the truth. You must have been heartbroken on Christmas Day, otherwise you wouldn't have been drinking so much."

"I told you, it wasn't my drinking that was the problem. At least—" he flinched a little "—not the only problem."

"Right. You also said you hadn't slept in days and took pills for a horrible headache." She tilted her head. "Sure sounds like a broken heart to me."

"The headache was a concussion from picking a fight with a world heavyweight champ at my gym."

Her pretty face was tranquil. "And that level of pure stupidity could only come from a broken heart."

He shook his head with a snort. "I told you, I don't *do* love. So my heart can never be broken, as you so romantically describe." He took a deep breath, then said, "I'd just found out my father died."

It was the first time he'd said those words to anyone.

Honora's eyes went wide. "Oh, no! I'm so sorry." Reaching out, she put her hand on his, seeking to offer comfort. "I didn't know…"

"We were…estranged." That was the understatement of the century. "But I'd expected my father and his wife to come here the day after Christmas."

"So that's why you had my room ready for guests." Her eyes glistened with sympathetic tears. "How awful. I'm so sorry. I… I know what it feels like to lose your parents. I know how badly it hurts."

"Yes," he said, feeling like a fraud. Honora had clearly loved her own parents. If she knew the real reason he was upset…

Honora glanced at his half-empty glass of Scotch. "But you have to learn other ways to deal with your grief. Or it will eat you alive."

Her hand felt soft and warm on his own. She was so close on the sofa, almost touching him, that he could feel the warmth of her, the heat of her body. She was so beautiful, with those haunting green eyes, and the massive amounts of damp, dark hair tumbling over her shoulders, leaving traces of wet on the white silk robe that barely contained her lush body. As he looked down at her, he felt an unbearable surge of desire. His gaze fell to her mouth.

Her lips parted as he heard her intake of breath.

Nico didn't think. He didn't hesitate.

Cupping her face with both his hands, he lowered his head and kissed her.

Honora's lips parted in a gasp as his mouth seared hers.

His kiss was sweet, so sweet. For a moment, in her surprise, she was lost in a sensual haze. Her hands moved to his hair.

His embrace, which had started out so exploratory, so tender, turned hungry. He reached inside her silk robe—

Wrenching away, she stood up from the sofa. "No."

Nico looked up at her. His hair was tousled, his dark eyes hazy with desire. His forehead furrowed as he stared up at her, as if he didn't understand.

But Honora still remembered how lonely and cheap she'd felt after their night together, when she'd discovered Nico had left for Italy without a word. When she'd discovered she was pregnant. When he ignored her messages.

She had changed her life forever in that one night, just by loving the wrong man. She wouldn't make that mistake again.

"Maybe you're accustomed to women falling at your feet," she said coldly, wrapping the robe around her pregnant belly more firmly, "but I won't be one of them. So if you were trying to lure me into bed by pretending to have a heart, don't bother."

She started to turn to go, but as she did, he said in a low voice, "Don't make it seem like I'm using you. I felt how you just kissed me. You want me, too."

Honora could hardly deny it. She ground her teeth.

"Even if that's true, I'm not going to do anything about it. You're not the right man for me."

He didn't move from the sofa. "How do you know?" He lifted his chin. "From the moment I learned you were pregnant, I've tried to take responsibility. I proposed marriage. I made you tea."

"And am I supposed to be grateful?"

"I even told you about my father, something I've shared with no one else on earth." His dark eyes glittered in the flickering firelight of the salon. "What more do you want?"

What more did Honora want?

So many things.

She wanted to be the naive twenty-four-year-old she'd been, with her whole life ahead of her and no need to rush to make plans or decisions. She wanted her grandfather to be happy, and to know that she wasn't a burden to him. She wanted to have a college degree and a lucrative career so she could get her own apartment and provide for her baby and pay her bills without worry.

She wanted to fall in love, really in love, with a man who would love her back with his whole heart. She wanted him to propose because he loved her—not out of sense of duty, which was the unromantic reason her own parents had married, and her grandparents, too.

She wanted a joyous wedding attended by their friends and family, who were all ecstatic because they thought the two of them so perfect together. She wanted a happy family for her daughter in a real home, where she'd never feel like Honora had, like a burden no one truly wanted.

With an intake of breath, she whispered, "I want more than you can ever give me."

Never taking his eyes from her, Nico rose to his feet. He towered over her, making her feel delicate and petite, even at six months pregnant. He stood close, without touching her, and as their eyes met in the flickering red shadows, he made her feel so *alive*. He said in a low voice, "You don't know that."

"Wrong. I do." Her teeth were chattering with the effort it took not to lean forward, to be closer to him, to be embraced in the circle of his warmth and power.

"Let me tell you what I know, *cara*," he said softly. His hand tucked back a long tendril of her hair and she nearly shuddered, just from that small touch. "I know that I've felt half dead for the last six months, and getting the news you've given me today has brought me back to life."

"It's just an emotion. Like you said." She tried to smile. "Don't let a fleeting emotion make you do something you'll regret…"

Nico pulled her into his arms, his dark eyes piercing her soul.

"I want to be your husband. And I am our baby's father. That is not emotion. That is fact." He nuzzled her as he whispered, "And I want to be your lover…"

With his arms around her, it was so hard to resist. Her body was already galloping ahead, coming up with a million excuses that would lead to another spectacular night upstairs, and the promise of a lifetime more.

And yet… That was the mistake she'd made at Christmas. Letting her body and heart do the thinking, instead of her brain. And that one simple choice had ended so many of her dreams.

Honora had to be smart now. She wasn't an innocent, careless girl anymore. In less than three months, she'd be a mother. At twenty-four, she didn't feel remotely ready for such an enormous responsibility. But it was hers regardless.

She pulled away from him.

"We both know you're not the type to commit to forever," she said quietly. At his startled look, she shook her head ruefully. "I don't mean any insult. But whatever you might be thinking now, we both know who you are. You're a player, Nico. You'll never settle down—especially with a woman you don't love."

"Perhaps this is my moment," Nico said. "Finding out I'm going to be a father has changed me. That could change anyone."

"But it won't."

His expression hardened. "Why else would I marry you, except out of duty?"

"For love." She felt an ache in her throat. How different it would have been if he'd loved her! If they'd already been married. How happy they might have been together, expecting their first baby!

"Then marry me for love," he said. "You said you loved me the night we conceived our baby."

How could he throw that in her face? Swallowing hard, she shook her head. "Those were the romantic dreams of a girl. Growing up, I watched you from a distance and you seemed so handsome and powerful, building skyscrapers and traveling the world. But that wasn't love."

"What was it, then?"

"Illusion."

"Fine." He set his jaw. "How about our child? Doesn't he or she need a father?"

"Why does everyone keep saying that?"

"They keep saying it because it's true," he said coldly. "Hate me if you must, for not being the man you wish I could be. But don't punish our child for it."

Honora sucked in her breath. Was that what she'd been doing? Punishing him? She hated the thought.

She bit her lip. "If you really want to be part of her life—"

"Her?" Nico's eyes lit up. "We're having a girl?"

She nodded. It might have made her happy, seeing the delight on his face, if it hadn't made her so sad. "Due in mid-September."

"A daughter," he whispered. "A child of my own."

"You don't have any other children? You're sure?"

He shook his head. "I've always been careful. I've always made utterly certain… I must have been careless that night." He gave a crooked smile. "Obviously."

Careless. That was one way of putting it. The lump in her throat became a razor blade. "Me too," she said in a low voice. "I blamed you…but I made my own choices. I could have insisted you use a condom. I could have chosen not to sleep with you at all." She lifted her gaze. "I took the risk. My choice. And I'll have to live with that for the rest of my life. But I won't let our baby pay the price."

"Does that mean you'll marry me?"

Honora held desperately to the last shreds of her dignity, and her hope for a family created out of love, not cold obligation. She shook her head. "But if you can really be a good father, then I'll let you share custody."

"*Let* me?" The satisfaction in his handsome face faded to anger. "*If* I can be a good father?"

She felt his coldness and raised her chin. "If you can cut back on the Scotch and come back to the world of the living. If you can actually be good to her."

"I already gave your grandfather my word I'd marry you."

She shrugged. "You should have asked me first. I have something else in mind."

"My chauffeur?"

Was he jealous? No, surely not. Nico Ferraro dated women by the score and tired of them quickly. If even a world-famous beauty like Lana Lee couldn't keep him, what chance did an ordinary girl like Honora have? She knew, to her core, that if she married him, he'd only break her heart.

"If you truly want to be a father, I will do everything I can to support that." She turned toward the beachfront mansion's windows. The storm had abated, and she could see silvery moonlight frosting the clouds scattered across the ocean's horizon. She said in a small voice, "But I can't marry you. I want to be loved."

Nico stared at her for a long moment.

"Maybe you're right," he said suddenly.

She blinked. "What?"

"It's clear nothing I say tonight will convince you."

Honora had been about to list more reasons why she could never, ever marry him. She felt strangely off-kilter by his sudden surrender. She told herself she was relieved. Wasn't she? "Oh. Good. How will we explain it to Granddad?"

"I'll talk to him. I owe him that much."

"Right now?"

"It's almost midnight." Nico went to the wet bar. For a moment, she thought he was going to pour more Scotch into his half-empty glass. Instead, he dumped it all down the sink and turned to her with a charming smile. "I'll take you back home in the morning. Until then, I bid you good night."

"Good night," she said faintly, her lips slightly parted as he turned and left the room without a word.

As she followed him up the sweeping staircase of the beach house, she could hardly believe it. She'd won. She'd actually won. Nico Ferraro had given up his desire to marry her.

So why didn't she feel more joyful about it?

CHAPTER FOUR

WAKING UP THE NEXT morning in the master bedroom of the Hamptons beach house, Nico smiled to himself, amazed at how well he'd slept. Getting out of bed, he stretched in his silk boxers, then went out on his balcony to breathe the fresh ocean air.

The summer storm had cleared out, leaving only beauty behind. Wispy clouds of pink and magenta and peach traced the eastern horizon in the vivid colors of dawn. The deep blue sky, growing lighter by the second, stretched as wide as the Atlantic. He felt like his future, too, was wide open. Nothing but blue skies and blue ocean, ripe with possibility.

First on his agenda: making Honora his wife.

He felt a zing of nervous energy at the thought, and decided to go for a run on the beach. He had to dig in the closet for exercise clothes because he hadn't brought any in his suitcase from Rome. The realization shocked him.

Before Christmas, he'd been very disciplined about intense daily exercise, as he was about everything. But since then, his only real exercise had been sparring in a boxing gym in Rome—and even that he'd only done out of self-preservation after an altercation with a random lawyer who'd tried to get his clients out of a real estate deal. Nico didn't remember much about the work he'd sunk himself into over the last six months, but he did remember the moment he'd lunged across the boardroom table and punched the man in the face.

He'd paid for it, of course. He'd settled out of court for a million euros. Pretty expensive way to let off steam. After that, he'd started expending his dark energy at the gym. Better to vent his anger wearing gloves and face guards fighting willing participants or, better yet, a gym bag. Other than that, he'd just worked all day, every day, until he collapsed with exhaustion on the sofa in his private office.

Last night was the first time in months that Nico had slept the whole night through. He marveled at how much better he felt. He hadn't known it was even possible for him to sleep ten hours.

He'd only had one drink last night—he'd thrown the rest down the sink. He'd wanted to prove a point to Honora, but he knew that wasn't the only reason he felt better.

He had a mission again. A totally impossible mission, just like when, as a penniless teenager, he'd vowed to be rich.

He would convince Honora Callahan to marry him.

True, he couldn't give her the romantic love she dreamed of. But he could offer so much more, more than enough to compensate. His fortune, of course. His name. Clearly, the marks of status that would appeal to most women didn't hold much weight with her. So he'd offer more.

He'd lure her with passion, and a partnership based on mutual respect, even friendship. He had to convince her that she could trust him to cherish and provide for them always. That was the most important thing. She had to know their daughter would be raised in a stable home and would always know she was adored, wanted and welcomed by both parents.

Compared to all that, what was some paltry thing like romantic love? Nothing but sickly sweet love poems and wilting roses.

As soon as he could prove to Honora that he'd never break his commitment to them, he knew she'd fall into his arms.

Thinking of it, Nico smiled to himself and ran a little faster on the edges of the white sandy beach, running on the packed wet section close to the blue-gray surf. The sea air felt fresh and new in the dawn. And that was how he felt. Fresh and new.

He'd changed tactics last night when he'd realized his heavy-handed marriage demand wasn't working. The more he'd insisted he wanted to marry her and that he intended to be a good husband and father, the more she'd argued with him. So he'd backed off. Insinuated he'd changed his mind about marriage.

He hadn't.

But he'd learned that in business, the most desirable acquisitions usually took extra time and care. It was her own free choice. She had to *want* to marry him.

So he would convince her.

Nico picked up the pace to a flat-out run, wet sand flying behind him on the beach in the early-morning light.

All he had to do was become the man she needed. A man who was ready to be a good husband, a good father.

He'd already stopped drinking. Next he would cut back on his working hours and return to a healthier lifestyle of exercise and sleeping in a proper bed. It was horrifying to Nico now, in the cold light of dawn, to realize how lost he'd been the last six months. Yes, he'd added millions to his company's bottom line by working with such monomaniacal focus. But he'd done that only out of desperate need for distraction. Other than the fistfight with the lawyer, he hardly remembered any of it. Because none of it mattered.

What difference did it make if Nico's net worth went up another hundred million? His father was dead. He'd never have the satisfaction of seeing the old man weep his regret that he'd rejected Nico as a boy, believing him unworthy of being his son.

He'd never been Nico's family. Honora, their daughter, their other children yet to come—they would be.

He just had to convince Honora he was worthy of her. And since their baby was due in around two and a half months, he was on the clock.

Checking his smartwatch, Nico saw he'd run five miles. He looked at his speed. Not bad, considering that yesterday he'd been a numb, pathetic workaholic without a reason to live. Now he was getting back to life, to his old discipline, he'd soon improve. With his new focus, he'd springboard to even greater wealth, greater power. Only now, instead of rubbing it in the face of that aristocratic bastard, Nico would bask in the glow of a loving wife and adoring children. He would be happy, damn it.

And hopefully *that* would leave his dead father spinning in his grave.

Turning around, he started running back toward his house five miles down the shore. He wouldn't put the mansion up for sale after all, he decided. They'd make memories here. Fill those bedrooms with children.

Just thinking of Honora, he felt his blood grow hot. He could hardly wait to have her in his bed. And this time, he'd make sure he remembered every delicious moment of touching her. He could hardly wait.

Maybe tonight. Or tomorrow. How long did it usually take for a man to prove himself worthy of a woman?

Whatever the usual time was, Nico would do it faster. And better.

Honora Callahan didn't stand a chance.

Was it hot in here, or was it just her?

"Thank you for the ride," Honora said, resisting the urge

to fan herself. She felt a bead of sweat forming between her breasts. Because she was pregnant, she told herself fiercely. Not because she wanted him.

"My pleasure." Nico's voice was a low purr beside her. His hands were casual on the wheel as he wove the Lamborghini through highway traffic with confidence and grace. His dark eyes gleamed as he gave her a sensual smile. She gritted her teeth. Damn the man.

The morning after she'd refused his marriage proposal, it seemed cruel that he looked even more handsome and desirable than ever, in a white collared shirt that hugged his muscular torso and flat belly, the top two buttons undone around his thick neck, and wearing trim-fitting dark trousers over his powerful thighs.

He gave her a wicked grin. Realizing she was fanning herself, she stopped with a blush and clasped her hands firmly in her lap.

"It's July," she said sharply. "Aren't you hot?"

He shrugged. "I'm used to it."

His Italian leather shoe pressed on the gas. He looked relaxed, as if he'd had an amazing night's sleep and plenty of fresh air and exercise.

While Honora had just had the worst night she could remember. She'd felt anxious and tense in the beautiful guest room, staring up at the ceiling, questioning the choice she'd just made. Had she been utterly selfish, holding out for love instead of marrying the father of her baby?

Nico had offered her everything. Except his heart.

And after a lifetime of trying to make herself sweet and helpful and small, to take up as little space as possible, to feel less like a burden to the people she loved, she didn't think she could bear to live like that for the rest of her life. Was it selfish to want to be loved?

Honora finally fell asleep a few hours before dawn. When she'd woken up, it was midmorning, and the slant of warm golden light flooded the wide windows overlooking the Atlantic. Anxiety rushed through her as she glanced at the clock over the fireplace. She was going to be late!

Peeking into the hallway, she'd found her white sundress, folded with her white cotton bra and panties, clean and pressed as promised. She couldn't stand tight clothes anymore. This dress was stretchy, and with its spaghetti straps helped her stay cool in the summer heat. After getting dressed and putting on her sandals, she paused just long enough to brush her teeth and run a comb through her hair before she hurried downstairs.

She found Nico in the breakfast room, his dark hair still wet from the shower, drinking black coffee as he perused the morning's news. When she rushed in like a madwoman with her hair on fire, he looked up in surprise.

"Good morning." His voice was husky, his dark eyes glowing. "I trust you slept well."

Honora could hardly admit otherwise without revealing the emotional tumult inside her. "Yes. Thank you." She cleared her throat. "But I overslept. I need to leave now, if I'm going to get the train on time."

"The train?" Folding his paper, he looked bemused. "I told you I'd take you back to the city. You have an appointment?"

"At my doctor's. In three hours."

"Then we have plenty of time. Sit down." His dark eyes caressed her, making her feel shivery inside. "What would you like for breakfast?"

You, she thought, then kicked herself for even thinking such a traitorous thing. "Um…buttered toast?"

"We can do better than that."

Sitting at the farthest edge of the long table, she was soon tucking into a big plate of fruit, eggs and buttered toast, served by Sebastian the butler, who seemed to have warmed to her. Nico smiled when, blushing a little, she asked for tea with milk.

"So you like it," he said.

"I never thought of putting milk in herbal tea."

His smile widened to a wicked grin. "So I showed you something new."

Honora had bitten her lip as she remembered how he'd shown her all kinds of new things on Christmas night, things that made her shiver whenever she allowed them in her memory, kisses and touches and nibbles that would forever be imprinted on her skin.

Sitting beside him in the Lamborghini as they sped toward the city, Honora caught her breath. She had to get ahold of herself!

As they crossed the Queensboro Bridge, she looked out at the Manhattan skyline. Skyscrapers reached into the blue sky in a city that hummed like the buzzing center of the world. Or was it just the rush of blood through her own heart?

They arrived at her obstetrician's office on the West Side in record time.

"You can drop me off at the curb," she said quickly.

"I'd like to come."

Honora looked at him in surprise. "You want to go to my doctor's appointment?"

"I want to hear our daughter's heartbeat. I don't want to miss a thing."

"Okay. If you really want," she said, but as Nico looked for a place to park, she could barely contain her shock. Never, in all the years she'd known him as her grandfather's boss, had she ever seen Nico Ferraro give away his time to anyone.

He gave people money, of course. He paid his employees well and donated large sums to charities, gifts that were always splashed in the news as PR for Ferraro Developments Inc. And Nico had occasionally given her grandfather praise, or gifts arranged by one of his personal assistants. But spend an hour of his precious time on something that was not for his own direct benefit? Never.

And yet Nico was patient and attentive during the doctor's appointment, asking lots of questions. He squeezed Honora's hand during the ultrasound, and when he saw the outline of their baby on the screen, the small head, fingers and toes, Nico's handsome face filled with emotion.

"That's our baby," he whispered, and he lowered his head to kiss her.

It was barely a peck, just a friendly kiss. But still. It reminded her of the kiss he'd given her last night, a kiss that had made her want to forget every warning of self-preservation and fall into his arms.

But Honora had learned her lesson. No matter how interested and patient he seemed now, she knew his attention would wane. He wasn't the kind of man who would ever settle down—especially not with someone as average as Honora.

As they left the doctor's office, Nico held her hand, and in his other he clutched the ultrasound image of their baby. He kept smiling down at it. And it made hope rise unbidden inside her.

Did he really want to be a father? Did he mean it? Would it last?

Honora's phone rang.

"Are you back in the city?" Her grandfather's voice sounded odd.

"Yes, we're coming from my checkup."

"*We*? Your fiancé is with you?"

"Granddad, he's not—"

"When is he bringing you home?"

"Now." The sooner the better. Being with Nico was starting to make her want things she shouldn't.

"Good. Your doc's in midtown, right?"

"Near Lincoln Center—"

"See you soon." And her grandfather hung up. She stared at the phone with a frown, wondering why he was acting so weird. He'd acted weird last night, too. Not the bit with the rifle but afterward, when he'd pretended to be old and tired so he could return to the city immediately.

Had it just been an excuse to leave Honora and Nico alone, so they'd pick a wedding date? Or was it something else?

As she walked down the sidewalk in the bright July sunshine, a wave of foreboding went through her.

Nico said suddenly, "What do fathers usually drive? Minivans?"

"What?" She looked up, confused.

Seeing her face, Nico gave a low laugh. "I must sound like an idiot," he said ruefully as he opened the passenger door of the Lamborghini. She climbed in, carefully lowering herself into the low-slung seat. "I just don't know much about them."

"Babies?"

"Fathers."

Had he spent no time with his father at all growing up? "You don't need to rush out and buy a minivan. You already have tons of cars," she told him when he got in the driver's seat. "Just choose one with a back seat. An SUV is fine, or even a sedan like the Bentley."

She regretted mentioning the Bentley almost immediately. As he started the engine, he shot her a questioning glance.

"Rossini's in love with you, you know."

Honora looked out the window as they drove down the street. "Are you sure you don't mind driving all the way to Queens? I could take the subway."

"Of course I don't mind, and don't change the subject."

She gave a regretful sigh. "I know he is," she said in a small voice. "But I'm not sure what to do about it." She tilted her head. "What do *you* do? You must have lots of women fall in love with you."

Nico snorted. "No."

"How is that possible?"

He gave a shrug. "If any woman starts acting like she's in love with me, I'm extremely rude until she changes her mind."

She gave a low laugh, then grew thoughtful. "What about Lana Lee? She must have loved you to want to marry you."

Staring at the road, he said quietly, "I doubt it. She liked the press attention and lifestyle I could provide."

"Wasn't she already rich, as a movie star?"

"There's rich, and then there's *rich*," he pointed out. "But you're right. She didn't need me. She was just surprised when I broke up with her. She isn't used to it."

"Why did you propose to her in the first place if you didn't love her? I mean, *she* wasn't pregnant, was she?"

Nico shot her a sharp glance, and she felt her cheeks go hot. "Of course not. I told you. You're the first and only." His hands tightened on his steering wheel. "The reason I proposed to Lana is no longer relevant."

Honora waited, but he didn't explain his clear nonanswer. She tried to think of a way to ask probing questions without it being obvious. She couldn't.

"Was it because she was so famous and beautiful?" she said finally.

"You could say it was a mark of success. At least to a certain type of person."

As marrying Honora wouldn't be. The thought made her feel small.

"But still—" she tried to keep her voice casual "—you've dated lots of other women since we were together."

His forehead creased as he glanced at her in surprise. "Why do you think that?"

"Because you're so handsome and..." She caught herself, biting her lip hard. She couldn't seem to stop making a fool of herself. "Are you saying you haven't?"

Nico gave a low laugh. "I told you how I spent my time in Rome. Dating was the furthest thing from my mind. All I did was work." Changing gears, he looked at her. "Until you told me you were pregnant, and changed my life."

As they came out of the Midtown Tunnel into Queens, she gave him her grandfather's address. Heads turned as the Lamborghini passed by. Millionaires didn't live here in their sterile high-rises, like in Manhattan. Instead, this neighborhood was filled with small businesses and interesting neighbors, with streets rich with color and life. Before her parents had died, she'd lived in a small apartment around the block.

When he found a place to park along the street, four children, playing nearby on their scooters, came closer with big eyes.

"Keep an eye on my car, will you?" As Nico got out of the vehicle, he gave the little girl in front a friendly smile. "I'll pay you twenty dollars."

"Each?" demanded the lead kid, folding her arms. Nico gave a single nod, one CEO to another.

"You got it."

"Oh, hey, Honora," the girl said as Nico helped her out of the passenger seat.

"Hey, Luna."

"This guy your friend?"

Honora glanced at Nico. *Friend* seemed much nicer than *baby daddy.* "Yes, my friend."

"Hang on." The little girl huddled up with her friends, and then announced to Nico grandly, "We'll watch your car for free."

"Thanks," he said, amused. As the two of them walked down the sidewalk, he looked at Honora. "They think highly of you."

She gave a shrug. "I help them with homework. Buy them Popsicles when it's hot. Last month, I helped Luna find her lost cat." She smiled at the memory. "We looked for hours, then found her hiding in a tree across the street."

Nico looked at her gravely. "Your friendship is a good thing to have."

She felt her cheeks go hot. "It's no big deal. Anyone would have done it." She cleared her throat. "The apartment's just up here."

Her grandfather's two-bedroom apartment was above a pizza shop on the avenue. She punched in the code, and once inside, they went up the stairs.

As she reached into her purse to get out the key, the apartment door suddenly opened in front of her. Her gray-bearded grandfather stood inside the doorway. He was still in his morning robe, though it was late afternoon.

And he wasn't alone.

"Mrs. Kowalczyk?" Honora gasped at sight of the sweet widowed lady who owned the flower shop where Honora worked part-time. "What are you doing here? Er…?"

Even to her innocent mind, it was obvious what Phyllis Kowalczyk had been doing. The plump, white-haired woman looked flushed and disheveled, as if she'd dressed in a hurry, with the buttons of her yellow blouse done up in the wrong places. The older couple stared back at them in shock, their cheeks red.

"How did you get here so fast?" her grandfather demanded indignantly. "You must have broken the speed limit!"

"Patrick," Phyllis said quietly, "you might as well tell them."

Her grandfather sighed. "Fine." Waving them inside, he

led them into the tiny living room, with a window directly over the pizza shop's neon sign. "You should sit down."

Staring at her grandfather, Honora thought she had better. She fell heavily into the small, slightly saggy sofa. Nico sat beside her, neither of them touching.

Across from them, Patrick sat in his old chair and Phyllis in the chair beside him. They glanced at each other, smiling tenderly.

Holding her breath, Honora looked between them. "Are the two of you…?"

Patrick Burke looked proud and shy all at once, puffing out his chest like a teenager. "I've asked Phyllis to marry me."

Honora blinked, feeling dizzy. "I didn't even know you were dating."

"We weren't," Phyllis said. "We met sometimes in the shop, and around the neighborhood over the years. I fell hard." She looked at him. "But he wasn't free to be in a relationship. Not when you needed him."

Honora turned to her grandfather, flabbergasted. "I did?"

Patrick looked embarrassed. "My duty was to you, Honora. You'd already been through so much. I couldn't bring someone else into our apartment, into our lives. I couldn't be in a relationship. Especially when you were pregnant and alone." His wrinkled face lit up. "But when Nico agreed to take responsibility last night, and with the two of you starting a family of your own…" His eyes looked dreamy as he turned to Phyllis. "Now I'm free."

Honora felt an ache in her throat. It was just as she'd thought. She'd been a burden, keeping her grandfather from living the life he wanted. "I never meant to…"

"First thing I did when I got back here last night was tell Phyllis I loved her." Patrick looked at Phyllis. "I'd wanted to say it for so long."

"I know," Phyllis said, reaching out for his hand. "I know."

Honora stared at the grandfather who'd raised her. She barely recognized him in this moment.

"You love her?" she whispered. Granddad had never said those words to her, not once, not even when she was a child. She felt suddenly more alone than she ever had. Taking a deep breath, she pasted a happy smile on her face. "So you're moving in together?"

"Moving in?" Patrick looked shocked. "Like a couple of hippies? My intentions are honorable!" he protested, then gave Phyllis a sly glance. "Though last night, one thing led to another. This afternoon, too…"

"Patrick!" Phyllis was blushing. "Stop!"

"Anyways…" He cleared his throat with a *harrumph*. "We got the license this morning. We're getting married tomorrow."

"Tomorrow?"

"Don't worry, dear," Phyllis said kindly. "We won't steal your thunder. We're going down to city hall. No big ceremony or fuss. Just a couple of witnesses, then we'll leave on our honeymoon."

"Which is more to the point." Patrick grinned. She gave him a mock glare.

"I'd signed up for a horticulture cruise," Phyllis rushed to explain. "Two weeks down the coast, and it leaves tomorrow night. We're going to take it together, as a honeymoon."

"It all seems so fast." Honora's voice was a little hoarse.

"Not fast enough." Her grandfather looked at Phyllis. "We'd be married already if it weren't for the twenty-four-hour waiting period."

The older woman turned to Honora. "But listen to us going on and on about ourselves. I haven't congratulated you on your engagement, dear." She smiled broadly. "Such happy news. And don't worry—" she held up her hand "—I've already replaced you at the store."

"I told her I'll work for free," Patrick chortled.

Honora stared at him in shock. "You're leaving the roof-top garden? But it's your passion!"

He shook his head. "Honestly, the way my arthritis has been acting up in winter, I was ready to try something new. Besides, *Phyllis* is my passion now, and she says life begins at seventy."

"It does," she agreed. He looked at her.

"Letting myself love you has already changed me," he said quietly. "It's let the light in."

He suddenly seemed younger than Honora, in spite of all his gray hair. And she saw it all clearly.

For thirteen years, he'd given up his own dreams to take care of his grandchild. Even after Honora had become an adult, he'd still had to put her first. After being widowed for decades, he'd pushed away the woman he loved. He'd obviously thought he had no choice, since Honora had only had a part-time job, no apartment of her own, and then to top it off, she'd accidentally gotten pregnant.

She'd known she was a burden. She just hadn't realized how much of one. She felt sick with shame.

"I guess I'll need a new gardener," Nico said dryly.

"Yup."

"Probably for the best," he responded. "Though I'll never find another gardener who can coax daffodils so well."

Patrick grinned. "No, that you won't."

"Darling," Phyllis said, "I need to go check on the shop—"

"Right." He abruptly stood up. "And I'm sure you two have places to be." Tilting his head, Patrick said to Honora, "So did you set a date?"

Rising in his turn, Nico cleared his throat. "Actually, I should tell you, we—"

Grabbing his hand, Honora squeezed it. "We'll wait to get married until you return from your honeymoon."

She stared hard at Nico, willing him to play along.

"Yes," he said. "In two weeks."

"Perfect." The older couple beamed at them.

"I'll say goodbye, then," Nico said to Honora, and started to leave. But as he did, Phyllis elbowed her grandfather in the ribs.

"Right. The thing is," Patrick said, "Phyllis is having her apartment painted, so she'll be staying here tonight. Even though it's not strictly proper." His cheeks were pink as he cleared his throat. "You're very welcome to stay too, of course, Honora. At least until you move in with Nico after your marriage."

It was like being a deer and seeing the approaching headlights of the car that was about to hit you. She stared at her grandfather, frozen.

He smiled. "But I thought…why make you pretend? I'm sure you'd rather stay at the penthouse immediately. I can't fool myself that you're not sleeping together, not when…" His eyes fell briefly on Honora's belly. "So if you'd rather…"

"But of course, you'll always be welcome here, dear," Phyllis added. "It's your home."

"Thanks." This place *had* been Honora's home, but it suddenly wasn't anymore. The thought of staying here, butting in on their love affair, being a burden, feeling like an outsider…

"You're right, Granddad." She forced herself to smile. "The truth is, if you don't mind, I'd rather stay with Nico tonight."

The other couple looked relieved.

"I figured. And I can hardly criticize you for impropriety, can I?" her grandfather said with a sheepish grin. Then he blinked, reaching to squeeze her hand. "I'm so happy for both of us, Honora." His eyes wandered to his fiancée. "Have you ever felt this way before?"

Honora looked up at Nico, who was watching her with dark, inscrutable eyes.

"Never," she whispered.

CHAPTER FIVE

"THANKS FOR NOT blowing my cover," Honora said as he packed her small overnight bag into the Lamborghini, then helped her into the car. "I'll tell them the truth after they're back from the honeymoon."

"I'm glad to have you stay with me tonight," Nico said honestly. It had been a lucky break, he thought. And with a little more luck, by the time Patrick and Phyllis returned from their honeymoon, the fake engagement would be a real one.

"Do you mind dropping me off at a hotel?" she asked as he got into the driver's seat.

He looked at her. "Hotel?"

"Just for one night, until they're safely married and away." Her green eyes looked sad. "Otherwise he might cancel his wedding if he thinks he's still stuck with me."

He frowned. What a strange way to put it. "*Stuck* with you?"

She looked out the window at the dark city, lights sparkling hollowly against the glass. "I'll figure something out by the time they're back. Find a new place to live."

"Or come live with me."

"And I'll need a new job," she said, as if she hadn't heard. She gave him a crooked smile. "You need a new gardener for your rooftop terrace."

He snorted. "You're the mother of my child. I'm not hiring you as a gardener."

Honora looked at him, then sighed. "I guess you're right. It would be awkward. But I need to do something. Two weeks isn't very long."

"I'll always provide for you, Honora. You and the baby both."

Her green eyes looked sad. "Thank you, but the last thing I want to be is a burden."

Was she serious? "You're not—"

"And I know you promised Granddad you'd come tomorrow and be a witness at their wedding, but you don't have to. I can ask Benny instead."

Nico's hands tightened on the steering wheel. "Rossini?"

"He's a friend," she said, a little defensively.

Friend or not, Nico made a mental note to tell his residential staffing manager, Sergio, to reassign the young chauffeur to a different job on the other side of the world. He didn't care what or where, as long as he wasn't around Honora.

Nico protected what was his. And she was his.

He just needed more time to convince her of that.

"Are you hungry?" he suggested suddenly.

She grinned. "I'm pregnant. I'm *always* hungry."

"How about Au Poivre?"

She looked at him incredulously. "That fancy place downtown?"

"They make a good steak."

Honora snorted. "Sure, if you don't mind paying two hundred bucks for it. And don't you have to book a table six months in advance?"

"What sounds good to you, if not steak?"

She pondered. "Chicken potpie?"

"The owner's a friend of mine." He pulled out his phone. "I'll tell him we're on the way."

Thirty minutes later, as a valet whisked away the Lamborghini, Nico escorted her into the restaurant, which was decorated in an old French country style, with worn brick walls and heavy timber braces across the ceiling. The owner himself escorted them to a prime table beside the tall, rustic French fireplace, which, since it was July, was filled with a cluster of lit candles instead of a roaring fire.

"I am glad to see you again, Mr. Ferraro," the man said warmly. "I'll never forget how you moved heaven and earth to settle our real estate dispute."

Nico felt embarrassed. "I pointed you in the right direction, that's all. The right lawyer…"

"Not only that, you paid for it. We never would have survived lockdown if not for your investment."

Honora was looking between them with big eyes. Nico was ready for this conversation to be over. He cleared his throat. "You make the best steak in New York."

"Thank you." The owner beamed at him, then turned to Honora. "My chef is already preparing your chicken pot-pie, *madame*."

"You're too kind." Now she was the one to look embarrassed. "I'm sorry to be so much trouble."

"No trouble, no trouble at all, *madame*. For a friend of Mr. Ferraro, our menu has no end. But I fear it will take a bit of time to prepare. I am so sorry. I'll bring an appetizer while you wait." He bowed, then turned to Nico. "Your usual Scotch?"

"I'll have sparkling water tonight."

"Of course. And the lady?"

"The same," she said, surprised. The man departed with another bow. She looked at Nico. "Are you trying to impress me? If you are, it's working."

He shrugged. "I did the restaurant a very small service, and invested a little money. It was nothing…"

"I mean that you've stopped drinking." Their eyes met across the small candlelit table.

"You suggested I stop," he said gruffly. "I was smart enough to take that advice."

"Why would you care what I think?"

His voice was quiet. "Your opinion matters a great deal."

Honora's eyes were wide as waiters brought sparkling water to the table, along with an *amuse-bouche* of fig, walnut and goat cheese wrapped with prosciutto.

As Nico sipped the water, Honora reached for one of the appetizers, then froze. Leaning forward across the table, she whispered, "People are staring at us."

Looking around, he saw well-heeled patrons at the other tables watching them, some surreptitiously, others openly. Turning back to Honora, he shrugged. "It happens. Don't worry about it."

She looked down at her white sundress and sandals in dismay. "Is it because I'm not dressed up?"

"People are always interested in the women I date," he said matter-of-factly.

Her blush deepened as her lips parted. "But you and I… we're not dating!"

"They don't know that." Looking at her in the candlelight, he added quietly, "And neither do I."

Biting her lip, she looked up at him with big eyes, her lovely face stricken. She leaned back in her chair. Her hand seemed to tremble as she reached for her water glass and took a long drink.

"This place is beautiful inside," she said finally. "It feels almost medieval."

"Not quite. That wall over there—" he nodded towards an exposed brick wall "—dates back to when the city was New Amsterdam. I celebrated making my first million here, after I moved to New York. The architecture reminded me of Europe. I liked it."

"Because you were born there?" At his surprised look,

she smiled. "The housekeeper told me. I *have* been in your life for over ten years, even if you didn't notice."

Nico wondered now how it was possible that he'd never noticed his gardener's granddaughter. Looking at Honora now, here, in the body-skimming sundress with thin straps that revealed her full pregnant glory, she looked intoxicatingly beautiful, her dark hair tumbling over bare shoulders. Her big eyes shone in the candlelight.

"I lived in Rome till I was eight," he said. "Then my mother married an American and moved us to Chicago."

"Does your family still live there?"

He blinked at the word *family*. Was that what they'd been? "My mother died when I was seventeen. My stepfather last year."

"I'm sorry." Honora put her hand over his on the wooden table. Her hand was soft, comforting, warm. "Were you close?"

Close. His throat closed. He still couldn't bear to remember his mother's death, the silent cancer that had showed no symptoms until it was too late. There had been an experimental treatment that might have saved her, if they'd had three hundred thousand dollars to pay for it. Desperate, Nico had buried his pride and phoned Prince Arnaldo. It was the first and only time he'd ever spoken directly to his father. "Please," he'd choked out in Italian, "help her. And I'll never ask you for anything again."

"Why would I give you so much money?" the man had replied coldly. "I'm not some fool to throw away my fortune on quack treatments with no chance of success."

"But you owe her. You owe us."

"Maria is nothing to me, and neither are you." And he'd hung up.

Arnaldo had been right about one thing—the experimental treatment had turned out to be a mirage. But it might have saved her, Nico told himself stubbornly. His mother might have been the exception. After her death, Nico had taken his hurt and rage and thrown himself into working around the clock. Starting at eighteen, he'd bought his first Chicago property with credit, using his beat-up Mustang as collateral. He'd gotten lucky when a car wash chain had offered to buy the land from him at nearly double the price. He'd taken that profit and moved to New York, determined to make himself so rich and powerful that he could never be hurt again.

But after he'd become rich, he'd found he still felt an overwhelming restlessness inside.

That was when he'd decided to make Prince Arnaldo Caracciola pay—for everything.

"No," Nico said in a low voice. "We weren't close. But she was still my mother."

Honora didn't move her hand from his. "I'm sorry," she said quietly. "Like I said. I know how it feels."

She couldn't possibly know how he felt. But as she pulled her hand away, he thought how pretty she was, how enticing, with her pink lips and warm green eyes, as alive as a sunlit forest.

Nico changed the conversation to lighter things, to a project he was building in London that he knew would interest her, because it was surrounded by five acres of green space. It seemed like mere minutes before their dinners were served, chicken potpie for her, and his usual steak in peppercorn sauce. As they ate, he enjoyed listening to her talk, her brightness, her cheerful optimism, her kindness—all so different from the entitled world-weariness and humblebragging he was accustomed to hearing from mistresses. Honora Callahan was honest and enthusiastic and lovely. She was a breath of fresh air. Any man would be lucky to have her in his life, he thought suddenly.

"This potpie was amazing." Setting her fork down on her empty plate, she sighed in pleasure. Her full breasts and baby bump pressed against the small table as she leaned forward. "By the way, thanks for being with me at Granddad's today. I'm not sure I would have survived otherwise…"

He forced himself to lift his gaze from her curves. "I'm glad I could help."

Honora shook her head wryly. "He actually said he loved her. *Aloud.* I can hardly believe it." She gave a wistful smile. "He's never said that to me, not once."

Her tone was cheerful, but he could feel an ocean of sadness beneath it. He recognized that ocean. Everything he'd done as a man had been in order to leave that sad, lonely boy behind and become powerful, and impervious to hurt. He shrugged.

"My mother used to say it to me all the time." He took a drink of the sparkling water. "She never meant it."

"I'm sure she loved you." But her voice was uncertain.

He gave a small smile. "It's hard to love the person who blows up your life and forces you to give up your dreams and live in poverty."

"Your father didn't help?"

He shook his head. "He was a married aristocrat. She was a maid in his palace. The last thing he was going to do was recognize me as his own."

The words hung in the air like a toxic cloud. He'd never said them to anyone before.

"Oh, Nico, how could he?" she said softly. "He didn't even pay child support?"

He realized his hand was clenching the edge of the oak table so tightly that it hurt. Strange. One might think he was still angry about it. But he felt nothing. "My mother tried, but she was young, without family, and no one to give her advice. And he was powerful, untouchable, behind guarded palace walls." He took a deep breath. "She worked three jobs to support us. Then she met my stepfather, who worked in the American base. He told her loved her and swore he'd take care of her."

"What happened?"

"She married him and we moved to the States. She thought her life would be easier, but it wasn't. She never felt at home in Chicago. Then Joe started complaining that she wasn't the same girl he'd fallen in love with." He gave a hard smile. "He complained about me, too."

"Why? What did you do?"

"I loved reminding him he wasn't my father, and had no right to tell me what to do. Even at age eight, I hated him. I felt like an outsider in my own home. Then he told my mother he'd fallen in love with someone else, and I hated him even more for making her cry. They didn't have any assets. After the divorce, we were even poorer than before."

Twilight was falling outside the lead glass windows, leaving a trail of violet across her bare shoulders. "I'm sorry…"

"He told her he loved her all the time, at the beginning. My father apparently said it to her, too, during their affair. They both told her they felt true love that would last forever."

Honora looked at him in the flickering candlelit restaurant. "No wonder you think so little of love."

Nico shrugged. "It's a momentary emotion at best. At worst, it's manipulation. A way to trick people into surrendering their lives."

"My grandfather used to say feelings didn't matter," she said in a small voice. "What was important was family, duty, being true to one's word."

"He's right." But she looked sad, so he changed the subject. "I'm getting some coffee. Would you like dessert? Chocolate cake with raspberries? Strawberry tart?"

She took a deep breath, then tried to smile. "The tart, please."

Turning away, he gave a small gesture to a waiter.

When they finally left the restaurant, Nico realized they were the last guests there, and had been talking for hours. To make amends to the waiters for keeping the table, he quietly left a five-thousand-dollar tip.

"Thank you for a lovely evening." Honora took his arm as they walked out into the moonlight. "And the food! I'm afraid it's spoiled me for all other chicken potpie. And strawberry tarts."

His glance lingered on her as the valet collected the Lamborghini. The summer night was warm as city lights sparkled in the skyscrapers looming above the slender lane.

"But now it's over." Honora looked wistful again. "Is there an affordable hotel nearby?"

"There's no reason to stay in a hotel."

"I told you I couldn't possibly go back home tonight, with Granddad and Phyllis there."

"Stay with me."

"With you?" She swallowed, then shook her head. "Thank you, but I couldn't possibly."

"No strings. You can stay in the guest room. I promise I won't touch you, Honora, for as long as you're staying with me. Not unless you ask." His gaze fell to her lips as he added huskily, "No matter how much I want to."

Staying with Nico would be a big mistake. Honora knew it before the valet even pulled the Lamborghini up in front of the restaurant.

"Guest room?" she repeated, then shook her head. "I couldn't impose."

"You keep using words like *burden* and *imposition*— words that make no sense to me. How much clearer can I be that I want you?"

She bit her lip. "But—"

His eyes gleamed. "It's just a night in my guest room, Honora. Not marriage vows."

She hesitated. What was she afraid of? That she'd fall into bed with him? No. Of course she wouldn't. She told herself she'd learned that lesson. And as he said, it was just crashing at his place for a night, not marriage vows. She exhaled. "All right. Thank you."

Nico gave her a small smile as he opened her car door, helping her inside.

They drove north to midtown. Pulling into his residential building's parking garage, he punched in his code, which lifted the gate into his exclusive parking area. He parked near his Mercedes G-Wagen, Tesla and the Bentley.

Lifting her overnight bag onto his shoulder, he helped her out of the low-slung car. He didn't drop her hand as they took the elevator to Nico's penthouse on the skyscraper's top two floors.

Nico's hand felt so good in her own. She shivered. He was so powerful, so broad-shouldered, towering over her. She wondered what the penthouse staff, who'd all watched Honora grow up, would think if they saw their billionaire boss holding her hand like this.

But by now they already knew about her pregnancy. Her grandfather hadn't exactly been discreet, and Benny knew too, as well as the staff at the Hamptons house. There'd likely be general gossip about Nico's pregnant date at Au Poivre, too. Soon, everyone would know she was Nico Ferraro's unwed baby mama.

She glanced at him out of the corner of her eye. He'd wanted to marry her, and she'd refused him. No one would ever believe *that*.

The elevator doors opened directly into the penthouse with its wide, sparsely decorated spaces and hard, modern furniture that seemed designed to impress, rather than be comfortable. But she'd always loved the big windows with the views of Manhattan, and the rooftop garden on the terrace was filled with flowers for nine months of the year.

Nico followed her gaze to the hard-edged furniture. "It doesn't look very baby-friendly, does it?"

"No," she agreed.

"You can help me figure out how to change it. And turn the guest room into a warm, cozy nursery." He grimaced. "Obviously my usual interior designer doesn't do warm and cozy."

"You want a nursery?"

"Sure. If we're sharing custody, sometimes the baby will be here. She'll need a place to stay."

Honora stared at him in dismay. Her mind hadn't gotten that far—imagining what would happen as they raised the baby separately. But of course Nico was right. Sometimes he and their daughter would have joys and make memories that Honora wouldn't share, because she wouldn't be with them.

And someday, when Nico got married, he'd have a family. And if Honora was very lucky, she would someday do the same. But their daughter would always go back and forth between them, never really at home anywhere.

"I wish this all could be different," she whispered.

Nico looked at her. "Why did you sleep with me at Christmas, Honora?" he said suddenly. "You weren't drunk."

She looked down at her sandals. "I told you." She spoke quietly. "I thought I was in love with you."

"And now?"

"Now…" She looked away. "I hate the thought of you raising our baby here without me. Each of us someday marrying someone else, starting a new family."

His voice was low. "You said that was what you wanted."

"None of this is what I wanted," she choked out, then turned away. Grabbing her overnight bag, she fled for the guest room before he could see the tears in her eyes. "I'm going to bed…"

Climbing into the big, empty bed of the penthouse guest room, Honora looked out the windows. Stretching up into the inky black sky, skyscrapers glittered like stars.

Why had she slept with Nico?

Why had she taken the subway to his penthouse on Christmas Day, telling her grandfather she urgently had to pick up a book she'd left there—for a homework assignment that wasn't even due till January? And why, when she'd found Nico brooding and alone, had she decided to stay?

Closing her eyes, she remembered that darkening afternoon, when she'd found him sitting alone on the hard furniture, staring at the flickering fire, beneath the wan lights of the Christmas tree. She'd hoped for a glimpse of him, that was all. Nico Ferraro was always surrounded by beautiful women, or friends as ruthless and powerful as himself.

She'd been shocked to find him alone. He'd looked at her, and the expression on his handsome face had starkly mirrored her own loneliness.

Her whole life, she'd felt like she had to earn her right to exist. By being cheerful. By being helpful. No one liked a girl who was selfish. Selfish girls caused parents to die in car crashes. If her grandfather hadn't taken her in, Honora would have gone to foster care. In the back of her mind, she'd always feared that if she were ever too much trouble, then perhaps he might send her away.

So seeing her same loneliness reflected in Nico's dark eyes, Honora had felt so drawn to him that she forgot to be afraid. She'd sat beside him on the sofa.

"I know how you feel," she'd whispered, as the firelight flickered in the room.

"How can you?" His expression had been blank as he took another sip of the drink in his hand. She saw a half-empty bottle of Scotch on the end table. But his words weren't slurred. He seemed in perfect command of his senses, only sad.

With a deep breath, she'd said quietly, "For most of my life, I've felt alone, too."

Nico had turned to her. His dark eyes seemed to devour her whole, as if he were truly seeing her for the first time. And then, leaning forward, he'd suddenly taken her in his arms and kissed her.

Their passion had been a revelation. The happiest night of her life—cut short because she'd had to slip away at midnight, while Nico was still sleeping, to take the subway back home, so her old-fashioned grandfather wouldn't worry, or know what she'd been up to.

But the next morning, Honora had been tired but shyly happy as she accompanied Patrick to work at the penthouse. She'd wondered how Nico would greet her, if he'd take her in his arms and immediately make his claim. She dreamed about him telling her grandfather straight out that they were in love, about him asking for her grandfather's permission to court her. It had been a delicious fantasy.

But Nico hadn't been there. The housekeeper, Janet, had crisply informed them that their boss had already left for Rome, with no immediate plans to return.

Honora had felt like a fool. How could she have ever dared hope that she'd meant anything to him at all?

But yesterday, Nico had asked her to marry him. He wanted her. And she'd refused him. Her brain, her heart couldn't quite believe it.

She slept hard, in a dreamless sleep, and even when she woke, she felt like she was in a strange dream all day. She showered and put on sandals and a knit purple sundress with spaghetti straps. She went to the courthouse with Nico, who was wearing a white shirt and dark trousers. He drove the Bentley himself, since Benny Rossini had been suddenly and inexplicably transferred to another job.

She watched her grandfather, grinning and obviously beside himself with joy in his coat and tie, speaking marriage vows in front of a judge, before he kissed his new bride, who was wearing a simple white dress. Nico insisted on taking them all out for a late lunch, and then drove them to the docks to board their cruise ship.

Her grandfather seemed to shine with some brilliant inner light. Was that what love was? Should Honora hold out for the thing that everyone said made life worthwhile?

Or was it all just an illusion, as Nico had said? She thought of his mother and love that promised to last forever but swiftly died. Even her own parents, hadn't they both believed, at least when they were dating, that they were in love?

"Do you want me to take you home?" Nico asked quietly as he drove her away from the docks.

She thought of the small Queens apartment. Somehow it no longer felt like home. Even with it empty, she would feel like an interloper in a space that now belonged to the married couple.

"No," she said in a low voice. She looked at him. "Can I stay with you tonight?"

Nico's dark eyes widened but he didn't ask questions, only stepped on the gas.

When they arrived back at the penthouse, it was just past sunset. Honora went straight out to the terrace garden.

Outside, the rising moon traced lines of silver over the ivy climbing the walls of the garden, and lights dangled from every trellis, making it look like a fairyland.

She took a deep breath of the cooling air, breathing in the scent of honeysuckle, rose, gardenia. After so many hours spent here, this garden had always felt like home, even more than the tiny Queens walk-up apartment. It was her home. Her heart.

Which suddenly felt like it was breaking.

"Honora." Nico's voice was husky behind her. "What is it?"

She turned to face him, fighting back tears. "I don't want you to have your own nursery."

Nico came closer, towering over her, making her feel petite and feminine by comparison. He started to reach for her, then stopped himself, dropping his hands. "This pregnancy wasn't planned, by either of us," he said quietly. "But maybe it's fate. The start of something wonderful, for both of us. You know I want to be our baby's father, Honora. I want to be your husband." Looking down at her without touching, he whispered, "Whatever your dreams are, let me try to make them come true."

Honora's heart was pounding as she looked up at him.

Nico was so handsome, so broad-shouldered and powerful, standing in the rooftop garden in the moonlight. It seemed like a scene out of a movie, in which he'd start suddenly waltzing with her beneath the sea of lights sparkling in the velvety black sky with the glass and steel skyscrapers all around them.

Whatever your dreams are, let me try to make them come true.

But her greatest dream had always been to be loved.

"I don't want to feel like a burden. Never again..."

"A burden?" He looked incredulous. "Are you insane? Don't you understand how much I want you?"

"Because of the baby..."

"You're right. What do I know about children? I need you to teach me how to be the parent I want to be. But it's more than that. I *like* you, Honora. I respect you. I want you as my partner. My friend. I want you at my side." He whispered, "I want you in my bed."

She wanted all those things, too. But if it meant she'd never be loved, would the exchange be worth it?

Was it possible that Nico was right? That the dream

Honora had hungered for all her life—love—was at best a passing emotion and at worst a manipulation?

Maybe there were more important things. Like kindness. Trust. Family. Loyalty. Friendship. *Passion.*

Her gaze fell to his lips, and she yearned for his touch. She knew he wanted her, too.

But she also knew he would keep his promise.

All around them on the terrace, skyscrapers stretched up into the night, their windows sparkling bigger and brighter than the stars.

She trusted him, Honora suddenly realized. She believed he would keep his word. That one simple fact changed everything.

He wouldn't touch her.

But there was nothing to stop *her* from touching him...

With an intake of breath, Honora threw her arms around him and lifted her lips passionately to his.

He froze in surprise, then as her mouth claimed his, he wrapped his powerful arms around her and kissed her back hungrily.

"Thank heaven," he whispered against her skin when they finally pulled apart. "Not being able to touch you was killing me."

"We can't have that." She looked up at him. "If you can commit to a lifetime," she said in a small voice, "if you're sure, I'll marry you, Nico."

His dark eyes lit up. "You won't regret it," he said huskily. "I'll make you happy. You and the child both. I swear it."

Honora prayed he was right and tried not to hear the desperate howl of her heart. She didn't need him to love her, she told herself. Just giving their baby a loving, secure home, being friends, being lovers, would be enough. It *would.*

And now, it would have to be.

CHAPTER SIX

WINNING WAS TORTURE.

Being kissed by Honora was paradise. Nico gloried in the feel of her petite, lush body in his arms. Her baby bump and full breasts pushed against his flat belly. Her lips were soft and warm, and as they parted for his, a small sigh came from the back of her throat.

Standing on the penthouse terrace in the cooling summer night, after she'd agreed to marry him, he'd felt the wind blow against his skin like the promise of a new life. For a moment he'd felt dizzy as he held her tight. He'd wanted that moment to last forever.

And he'd also wanted it to end immediately, by lifting her in his arms and carrying her inside, to his bed.

But no. Honora wanted to wait for their wedding night. So the next two weeks—filled with agonizingly delicious kisses, but no sex—were agony for Nico.

"I want it to be special," she said quietly. "This time, I want it to feel real."

He then tried to persuade Honora to wed immediately, elope to Las Vegas on his private jet. But she'd held firm, wanting to wait and have a real wedding after her grandfather returned from his honeymoon.

"All right." Nico had sighed, giving in with all the grace he could muster. "I did promise to fulfill all your dreams. You should have the wedding you want."

She'd looked startled. "It's not for me. Weddings are for family and friends. For our baby. For the *community*."

Which was so opposite to Nico's usual way of thinking that he hadn't even known how to argue. To his own mind, all he wanted to do was marry her and start the honeymoon today. She was living in the guest room of his penthouse. So close! But so far away!

They kissed, of course. Constantly. He would grab her in the hallway, at breakfast, at dinner, and lean her against the wall, against the sofa, holding her tight and ravishing her with kisses until they both went weak in the embrace. He felt like an unsatisfied teenage virgin, voracious in his hunger and need.

Two weeks seemed like torture. He felt like he'd never waited for anything so long.

But apparently two weeks was lightning fast for wedding planning. When Honora had suggested that they simply order a cake, hire some friends of hers who were musicians and buy a bouquet ready-made from Phyllis's shop, he'd wanted to make the ceremony more special for her, so he'd convinced her to hire a wedding planner.

"That would leave me more time to decorate the nursery," she'd said, stroking her cheek thoughtfully. "Although it seems like a silly thing to hire out."

"I just want to make your life easier."

"Fine," she'd said with a sigh. He'd had the feeling she was indulging him, but he wanted to take care of her. When he'd found her pulling weeds in the rooftop garden, he'd quickly arranged for Sergio to hire new gardeners, a talented middle-aged couple who worked as a team. Honora had liked them immediately, but she couldn't resist pointing out smugly, "See? It took *two people* to replace Granddad!"

Even with a wedding planner, she was very busy, bustling around to help the man select flowers, food, colors. She and Nico spent one obligatory afternoon with his lawyers, signing the prenup that his phalanx of attorneys had insisted was necessary. Honora rolled her eyes at the mention of settlements, seeming not to care. But in this, as in everything, he made sure his terms were generous. The longer they were married, the more alimony she would receive if they ever divorced.

But Nico didn't like to even think of her leaving. He knew their marriage would last.

He loved seeing her joy as she decorated their baby's nursery in soft pink and cream, filling it with books and a crib, buying tiny little clothes that seemed doll-sized to his eyes. Nico, for his part, contributed a six-foot-tall white teddy bear selected by Giles, his assistant at the New York office. Gifts weren't Nico's thing. Anyway, at the moment he was so distracted by lust that he could barely even pretend to work, or care about the land his company was trying to procure in Dubai. It felt like their wedding day would never come.

Then, suddenly, it did.

They'd decided on a beachside wedding at his home in the Hamptons. The weather dawned clear and bright, the previous day's mugginess swept away by the fresh Atlantic breeze.

Around them, tufts of long grass laced gently rolling sand dunes. The chairs faced a wedding arch laced with white and pink flowers, on the edge of the grassy bluff overlooking the blue ocean.

The guest list was small, only about a hundred people, as Honora had wanted only close friends and family. "Just people we truly love, who love us, people we want to support our marriage." Honora, of course, had many such people. Nico had struggled to come up with anyone who fit that description. So much of his life before now had been about climbing the ladder, about becoming rich and powerful, all to try to punish and impress someone who was now dead.

Did he really care about any of the people he called friends? Or was he just using them—as they used him?

But that had reminded him of one person he felt a little guilty about. He gave her name to the wedding planner, wondering if Lana Lee would even show, and half hoping she wouldn't, so he could tell himself he'd done what he could and forget about it.

Other than his ex-fiancée, he only managed to think of one true friend, who was more than a business rival or colleague. Theo Katrakis was a fellow self-made billionaire, an outsider like Nico—and a notorious womanizer who had similarly reached the age of thirty-six without a wife. But they'd watched a few football games together, done some race car driving on a lark, and once had actually had a personal conversation in which they'd discovered they'd both been educated in hard luck streets—Nico in Rome, Theo in Athens.

But now, Nico was wondering about the rightness of choosing him as his best man.

"No sight of the bride yet," Theo said in a low voice. The two men, dressed in sleek tuxedos, stood beneath the vivid pink roses in the wedding arch, watching as the guests arrived for the late-morning beachside ceremony. "You can still make a run for it."

Nico looked at his friend and was amazed to see he was serious. The Greek really thought Nico might desert Honora at the altar, in front of all her friends, after he'd given his promise to marry her. "You're my best man, Theo," he bit out. "You're supposed to be supportive."

"I *am* being supportive," he said cheerfully. "Run while you can."

Nico scowled. "You suck at being a best man."

"*You* suck at being a groom, since you wouldn't even let me throw you a bachelor party, which is really the whole point."

Nico was irritated. "Hey, anytime you want to leave…"

"Before I see if the maid of honor is worth seducing? Not on your life."

Baring his teeth in a smile for the benefit of the arriving guests, he said, "Maybe you just shouldn't talk."

"Nico," a woman's voice said behind him.

Whirling around, Nico saw Lana Lee coming across the grass from the house.

"Lana," he said in a low voice. He took a deep breath as he looked at his former fiancée. "I didn't think you would come."

"Didn't you want me to?" She looked elegant as always, with her glossy black hair tied back in a long ponytail, wearing a chic dark dress that draped perfectly over her model-thin body. Her sunglasses were movie-star-big, and no wonder. She was one of the most famous actresses in the world, specializing in blockbuster action films. "I was close by, shooting a film in New York."

"It's good to see you."

"Let's cut the crap." She tilted her head. "Why did you invite me?"

Yes, why? "I thought that things ended…badly between us."

"So you thought inviting me to your quickie wedding to some new girlfriend would make it better?" She took off her sunglasses. Her lovely face was blank. "My therapist said I'd get closure by seeing you. That's the only reason I'm here."

"Closure?"

"You used me," she said. "You made me think you loved me, proposed marriage, then dumped me without any reason." She gave a humorless smile. "I'm curious to see if you'll do the same thing to your new fiancée. Is it true what I heard? You knocked up your maid?"

"Honora was never my maid." Nico set his jaw. He

was starting to feel seriously annoyed. Why had he ever thought it was a good idea to invite his ex to his wedding? Maybe Theo was right when he'd said weddings were an unnecessary evil. He took a deep breath. "I wanted to tell you I was sorry. I never meant to hurt you."

Lana stared at him then said, "You never thought of me at all. If I were a good person, I'd warn your bride about how selfish you are."

He set his jaw. "Oh, come on, Lana. Don't try to pretend we were some great love affair. I wasn't *using* you. We were using each other. You enjoyed the lifestyle, the extra attention right before awards season. Don't make it out to be something it wasn't. I only hurt your pride, not your heart."

She glared at him, clearly not listening. "How pregnant is she?"

"Seven months."

"Seven! You must have gotten her pregnant just days after you dumped me."

He forced himself to be honest. "Hours."

She looked at him with loathing. "Heaven help this girl if she ever loves you."

"She won't. She's too smart."

His ex-fiancée gave a low laugh. "That's the best news I've heard all day. In that case, I hope you fall in love with her, Nico. Wildly and desperately." She spoke the words as a curse. Lana's dark eyes glittered. "And I hope you'll suffer for the rest of your life when she never, ever loves you back."

"I'm so happy for you, Honora." Her maid of honor's voice was strangely wooden as she spoke the words.

Honora turned from the three-way mirror, where she stood in her simple strapless wedding dress in cream silk, which went to midcalf, and pretty sandals on her feet. Her toenail polish matched the bright pink roses in her long dark hair. A twenty-carat diamond—Nico had picked it out—was on her left hand.

She was standing with Emmie in a sunlit room inside Nico's Hamptons mansion. It was strange to Honora now, remembering how just a few weeks before she had rushed here on a stormy summer night, desperate to keep either Nico or her grandfather from being shot by his hunting rifle.

And now, Granddad had just returned from his honeymoon cruise with Phyllis yesterday, deliriously happy, and she herself was Nico's bride. She never could have imagined any of it.

With her grandfather so focused on his new wife, Honora had been glad that her best childhood friend, Emmie Swenson, had been able to take the weekend off to be here with her.

Unlike Honora, Emmie came from a large family. She'd grown up with her parents and four brothers, crammed into a tiny three-bedroom apartment on the same street. Also unlike Honora, Emmie had already worked her way through community college, sensibly ignoring her interest in baking to major in accounting. At twenty-five, her friend always looked exhausted, working long hours as an underpaid junior accountant on Wall Street, even on weekends.

And now, Emmie's round, pretty face looked more pinched than ever.

"You don't seem very happy," Honora said quietly.

Emmie took a deep breath. Her blond hair was tucked back in a chignon, and she was wearing the strapless pink silk gown in a flattering bias cut that the wedding planner had arranged. "You're right." She rubbed her eyes. "I'm a lousy friend and I'm sorry." She looked at the door. "It's time to start. Your grandfather is probably waiting…"

"Wait." Honora looked at her friend anxiously. "Tell me what's bothering you."

Emmie paced a few steps, then stopped. "Look at how big this room is. And it's just a vacation home. For two people."

"Three, once we have the baby." Feeling guilty, Honora decided not to mention Nico's island in the Caribbean, his chalet in St. Moritz, or his recently acquired, but never lived in, villa on the Amalfi Coast, for which they'd leave tonight on their honeymoon.

Emmie looked out at the ocean through the wall of windows. "This is going to sound awful, but…for all these years, I've worked so hard." She sounded as if she were about to cry. "I've worked myself to the bone, doing a job I hate, with people who treat me like dirt. But I've done it because I want my family to have a better life."

"I understand, Emmie."

"How can you?" She looked from Honora, in her strapless silk wedding gown, to the bouquet of pink roses and the big diamond on her hand. "You didn't have to work for it. You're just *marrying* it."

Honora's cheeks went hot with shame as she looked down at her bouquet of pink roses. She couldn't answer because she knew everything her friend said was true. A lump rose in her throat.

"Damn it. I'm sorry." Emmie reached for her hand, tears streaming down her cheeks. "I hate myself for saying such awful things. And on your wedding day! I know you're not marrying Nico for his money. You love him." Her friend wiped her eyes. "You're lucky, that's all. And I'm hideously jealous and you should just smash cake in my face. I deserve it. Please forget everything I said and forgive me."

"There's nothing to forgive."

The two friends hugged each other, but as the wedding planner knocked on the door and said, "It's time," Honora still felt the distance between them. As they went into the hall, she felt like she was leaving the world she'd grown up in behind, the world where things made sense. Because Emmie was right. In what world was it fair that Honora was suddenly rich, just because she'd slept with Nico, while Emmie, who'd worked all these years at a job she hated, still had so little?

Things could have gone differently, Honora knew. If Nico hadn't insisted on taking responsibility, she'd be raising the baby alone, with very little income. In fact, that had been the most likely outcome. So Honora was lucky.

Just not lucky in love.

No, she wouldn't think about that. She'd just be grateful for what she had and not let herself feel sad about what she'd lost forever—the chance of loving someone, and being truly loved in return...

"Are you ready?" the wedding planner asked brightly. Without waiting for an answer, the man turned to Emmie. "Now, you have to pay attention, when the music starts..."

"You look beautiful, Honora."

Turning, she saw her grandfather behind her in the hallway. He was dressed in a tuxedo, waiting to walk her down the makeshift aisle on the bluff outside.

"You clean up pretty well yourself." She was relieved to see him. Her grandfather would help steady her nerves, reassure her about the lifetime commitment she was about to make.

To her shock, she saw tears in his eyes. "I just wish your mother could be here."

Her mother. Honora had a sudden flash of memory of the day before the crash. Her red-haired mother, Bridget, hugging her tight. Holding her close.

I love you, Honora. You're all that matters. The light of my life. I love you.

It had been the last time she'd heard those words from anyone.

"No, don't," Honora gasped. She felt an ache in her throat that was as sharp as a knife. "Don't…don't make me cry. It'll…it'll wreck my makeup, and…the planner will yell and there will be a delay and cause everyone trouble."

Patrick glanced toward the wedding planner scornfully. "Huh. Let them wait." He leaned in close to his granddaughter and whispered, "Are you sure about this?"

She blinked hard to kill the tears and smoothed her face in a smile. "About what?"

"Do you love him, Honora? Nico? Your fella? Does he love you?"

Her smile dropped. She stared at him in shock. These were not questions she'd ever imagined her grandfather would ask. "You ask me this now? Right before the ceremony? After you were ready to shoot him with your rifle if he didn't marry me?"

Patrick shook his head, his bushy gray eyebrows furrowing. "I didn't understand it then." He ran a hand over his forehead. "After seventy-odd years on this earth, I didn't understand till now, how wonderful it can be to love the person you're married to. I didn't know." He looked up, his eyes gleaming with unshed tears. "Life's not just about duty, Honora. At least, it shouldn't be."

What? "But you said…"

"The last two weeks have been the best of my life. Don't wait until you're my age to learn about love. Don't make my mistake." He put his hand over hers. "If you don't love Nico Ferraro, if he doesn't love you, then don't do it. You can come live with Phyllis and me. You and the baby both. As long as you need. It's your home, too."

Honora stared at him, stricken.

"It's time," the wedding planner trilled. "Maid of honor, go!"

"Honora?" her grandfather said urgently.

"Of course Nico loves me," she lied. "And I love him." She tried to smile. "Let's do this."

But as she held her grandfather's arm, and they went outside into the bright summer sunlight, she was suddenly afraid. Her grandfather's change of heart troubled her more than she'd thought possible.

Life's not just about duty, Honora. At least, it shouldn't be.

As they walked down the makeshift aisle between the folding chairs, on the grassy bluff overlooking the wide blue sea, she saw her friends and neighbors, the people she'd looked up to and loved her whole life. She saw Emmie's parents and her four strapping younger brothers crammed together, their shoulders overflowing the width of the folding chairs. She saw Phyllis beaming at Patrick, whose shoulders straightened a little as he walked by where his new bride was seated, and became visibly younger just at the sight of her.

Honora's footsteps faltered when she saw someone she hadn't expected—Lana Lee, Nico's famous movie-star ex, looking glamorous and insanely beautiful, and wearing big sunglasses in the back row.

You're so ordinary in comparison, her insecurity whispered. *Why would he ever love you if he couldn't even love her?*

"Steady," her grandfather said, holding her arm as he smiled at her. "We're almost there."

And then Honora saw Nico, standing beside a minister and his best man, whom she didn't know, beneath an arch of white and pink flowers. She felt the warm sea breeze and breathed in the scent of salt and green grass.

Her fiancé's dark eyes met hers. Above his sleek tuxedo, Nico's handsome face was shining, as if he'd never been happier. As if she were the most beautiful woman in the world. When she reached him, he took her hand.

Ten minutes later, he was kissing her as the minister presented them as husband and wife, to the guests' approving murmurs and applause.

Nico's kiss burned through her. And as Honora looked up into her husband's eyes, all her doubts were caught by the wind and blew out to sea. There was only him. Them. Forever.

CHAPTER SEVEN

WOULD THIS DAMNED reception ever end?

Nico didn't care about the wedding toasts—neither Emmie Swenson's sweet, tender good wishes, nor Theo Katrakis's surprisingly classy tribute.

"My assistant wrote it!" the Greek confided later, with a grin.

Nico wasn't hungry for the elegant beachside luncheon of lobster and asparagus in hollandaise sauce. He didn't want white wedding cake with raspberry filling. And the one thing that might have been palatable, the chilled champagne, he didn't touch, since Honora couldn't.

There was only one thing he actually wanted. And every minute he had to wait was agony.

Tables had been spread across the lawn with a view of the ocean. The July afternoon was bright, the sky a perfect blue. With only a hundred guests, the reception was intimate.

But not nearly intimate enough for him.

He looked down hungrily at Honora sitting beside him at the head table. Honora. Mrs. Ferraro. His wife.

She was leaning back against him in her wedding dress, her green eyes sparkling as she laughed at some joke Theo had made. The Greek was being his usual charming self, likely for the benefit of her maid of honor sitting on Honora's other side. But even still. Nico didn't like it, all that joy in her face, caused by another man.

He wanted his bride all to himself.

He'd never forget the moment he'd first seen her at the end of the aisle, in her strapless wedding dress, perfectly formfitting around her full breasts and baby bump, holding a small bouquet of pink roses. Her dark hair was falling free over her shoulders, and she had matching pink roses in her hair. Her green eyes had glowed as she walked toward him, holding her grandfather's arm.

Nico's knees had actually gone weak. He'd heard the thundering roar of the surf behind him as his blood rushed through his veins.

In that moment, everything else had fallen away. And he'd known she was the solution to that nameless emptiness, the anger, the restlessness he'd felt all his life. Once he possessed her, he would be whole.

Nico's voice had been calm and confident as he'd spoken his vows. Honora's had been quieter, seeming to hesitate, to tremble on the edges. But as the minister pronounced them husband and wife, and Nico took her in his arms and kissed her, he almost hated the applauding guests. He wished them a million miles away. He'd already waited weeks. Months. Years. In some ways, he'd waited his whole life. Now the hours of the obligatory wedding reception seemed unendurable.

The only good thing was that at least they didn't have to worry about an all-night spree of dancing and drinking, which the wedding planner had suggested but which he'd flatly refused, both because he'd promised Honora he wouldn't drink for the rest of her pregnancy, and because he thought he would explode if he had to wait to be alone with his bride until people toddled off drunk at two in the morning.

And they didn't have to worry about wedding presents, either. Honora had suggested that in lieu of gifts, guests could donate to their favorite charity. He'd been relieved.

Nico hated receiving gifts—having to pretend to be grateful and indebted and say thank you and on and on, usually for some trinket he didn't value and had no use for. Charity was a fantastic idea.

Nico ground his teeth, trying his best to make it a smile as he looked around him at all the round tables filled with people who loved his wife. Why were they still here? It had been hours. The luncheon had been eaten, the cake served, the toasts given.

Too bad he didn't have the old man's hunting rifle. *That* would have encouraged their guests to leave right quick. His lips curved at the pleasant thought.

Then he sighed. As sensible a course as that seemed in his current state, he didn't think his wife would approve. Honora seemed to place a lot of importance on family, friends and community. Far too much.

But he wanted her to be happy. His arm tightened around her shoulders as she sat beside him at the head table. And soon, she'd make him very happy, too.

Honora looked up at him and smiled. "Don't you think?"

"He'll never admit it," Theo said.

He focused on them abruptly. "What?"

His new bride gave a dreamy smile. "I said I've never been so happy. I think we were meant to be. Soulmates. It was fate."

Nico blinked, then felt a sudden shock of panic that he couldn't explain. Just a moment before, he'd been thinking how contented he felt to be wed to her, how proud. But now he saw something in Honora's shining eyes, some overwhelming emotion that scared him. And he imagined he saw a question in her lovely face, wordlessly asking if he felt the same.

He didn't. His heart was a stone, had been since childhood. The only emotions he could still feel were anger and satisfaction and…anger. He felt satisfaction at the thought of possessing her, and winning his point, and bedding her, and starting a family with her.

But somehow he didn't think she would be flattered if he told her what was in his shallow heart.

Cover, block, hide.

Lifting her hand to his lips, he kissed it. "I think," he said huskily, "it is time for our guests to leave."

"Nico!" Honora blushed, but he saw how she hid a smile and felt the tremble of her hand in his own. That was enough. He rose to his feet.

"Thank you all so much for coming to our wedding," he said loudly, over the roar of the waves against the sand dunes. "But my wife..." *My wife!* What delicious words! "...is very tired, and so I'd like to invite you all to leave."

"Oh..." Honora moaned softly, covering her pink face with her hands. For a moment, the guests were silent. Then he received help from an unexpected source.

"Quite right," Patrick Burke said loudly, rising to his feet from the nearest table. The old man looked around at all the guests, almost entirely his and Honora's friends. "If we leave now, we can beat the traffic back to the city!"

Beat the traffic. Those were magic words. Everyone looked at each other with alarm and, as if of one accord, rose to their feet.

"May I take you back in my Bugatti, Miss Swenson?" Theo asked the maid of honor, Emmie.

"Not a chance," she responded crisply, then turned to hug Honora one last time. "Congratulations and good luck. You deserve everything good." She bit her lip. "And I'm sorry for...for what I said before."

"Nothing that wasn't true," Honora said, smiling, then handed her the bouquet of pink roses. "You're a good friend. The best. Thanks for being here for me."

"What was that all about?" Nico asked, as the guests

crossed the grassy bluff back toward the sprawling mansion, back toward valet parking.

Honora watched them go, including her grandfather, who was holding Phyllis's hand tightly as they departed, and Emmie stumbling over the dunes with her family, and Theo, now flirting with Lana Lee.

Now *there* was an interesting idea for a couple, Nico thought. Though they were so similar in their selfishness that they might kill each other.

"I feel bad…" Honora whispered, watching her maid of honor.

"About what?"

She turned back with a small smile. "Nothing."

"Good," he said, because the last thing he wanted to do was talk. Standing together on the grassy bluff, beside the flower-strewn wedding arch overlooking the vast blue-gray Atlantic, Nico pulled her into his arms.

"Kiss me, Mrs. Ferraro," he whispered.

Reaching up, she stood on her tiptoes and pressed her lips to his.

At her touch, something in his heart unfolded. His body relaxed and grew tight all at once. His hands moved in her dark hair, and pink rose petals whirled around them in the soft ocean breeze as she wrapped her arms around him, holding him close.

With an intake of breath, he lifted her up into his arms to carry her back to the house. Even at seven months pregnant, her weight felt negligible, as she pressed herself against him, so soft and warm. In this moment, he would have killed anyone who tried to take her away from him. Their eyes locked with wordless hunger as he carried her inside the sprawling beachside mansion.

Inside, the back foyer was empty, deserted. The staff was gone. She looked around.

"Where is everyone?"

"I told Sebastian we wanted to be alone after the reception…to pack for the honeymoon. Bauer is waiting at the car." The Rolls-Royce had been festooned with flowers to take them to the airport. "We're due to leave in an hour."

"I'm so excited. I've never been to Italy." She gave a crooked smile. "The farthest I've ever traveled is New Jersey."

Nico wished she hadn't chosen the Amalfi Coast for their honeymoon. She'd said she wanted to see the country where he'd been born, but it only reminded him of unfinished business there.

Or maybe that was a good thing. Maybe this was fate, telling him to finally take what was rightfully his, the one thing his father had managed to keep from him: the palace where Nico's mother had once worked as a maid. His father's ancestral home, passed from generation to generation.

He'd tried to play nice. He'd offered to buy it from the widow for more it was worth. His evil stepmother had turned him down flat.

Maybe it was time to play hardball.

"Nico?" She was looking at him with concern. "You were a million miles away."

Still holding her in his arms, he looked down with a reassuring smile. "It's nothing."

Honora looked around the enormous room with its tall windows overlooking the Atlantic. "All this space. Just for the two of us."

"Yes." He looked down at her in his arms. "I bought it hoping I'd someday have a family here. You've made that dream come true."

He felt her melt a little in his arms. Honora didn't know that when he'd bought this house he'd imagined he'd have

Lana Lee at his side, and he'd rub his success in the face of the man who'd callously let his mother die. The aristocratic father and stepmother who'd thought Nico wasn't *good enough* to be their son.

No. He didn't want to remember. That was all in the past. Stopping in the grand main room, he looked down at his wife, heavily pregnant, cradled in his arms. Honora was the future.

Standing in front of the tall, open windows, he felt the soft summer sea breeze coming up from the beach, swirling the long translucent curtains that were pushed back to the edges of the windows.

Kissing her, he gently set her down on her feet. She returned his embrace passionately. His hands roamed over her creamy wedding dress, cupping her breasts, her hips, her backside.

She drew back. "We can't," she breathed against his lips. "People will be waiting for us."

"We own the plane. Let the pilots wait."

"We could get caught, here in the living room…"

"The servants are gone. The house is all mine. Which means—" he kissed down her throat "—it's all yours…"

He heard the softness of her gasp as she leaned back to brace herself against a wall. She tilted back her head, her dark hair tumbling down her back in another flurry of pink petals.

He yanked off his tuxedo jacket, ripping off half the buttons of his white shirt in his desperation to remove it. She stroked the taut muscles of his bare chest, which was laced with dark hair. The feel of her hands on his skin made him ache with need.

She was pregnant with his child, and yet he felt as if he were touching her for the first time. As if this were his first time making love to anyone…

Reaching around her, he unzipped her wedding dress, and it fell to a heap at her feet. She stood before him like a goddess, her pregnant curves barely contained by a white demi-bra and tiny white panties. He swallowed.

"You're so beautiful," he whispered, touching her, stroking her. "I can't believe you're mine…"

He felt her shiver beneath his fingertips as he ran his hands over her arms, her shoulders, cupping her face as he kissed her hungrily, deeply. Her pregnant belly pressed against him. He wanted to ravish her, but he felt strangely uncertain.

He breathed against her skin, "I don't want to hurt you…"

She gave a shy smile that was the most seductive thing he'd ever seen. "You won't. Let me show you…"

She pushed him back against the sectional sofa in soft cream leather, at the center of the room. Climbing on top of him, she lowered her head to kiss him.

He felt the veil of her dark hair fall softly against his skin. Her hips swayed over his, causing his desire to spike higher still. With her on top, she was the one in control. He felt as if he were completely in her power.

It was a new sensation for him, and almost unbearably erotic.

Her full breasts overflowed the tiny silk bra. Reaching around her, he unhooked the fabric, allowing her swollen breasts to spring free. He gasped, then leaned up to suckle her, cupping both mounds with his hands. His hard shaft strained against his trousers as she straddled his hips.

She sucked in her breath, closing her eyes. For a moment she held still. Then her hips started to sway instinctively. The pleasure was too much. Ripping his mouth away from her swollen pink nipple, he gripped her wrists.

"No—stop," he gasped. "It's too much… I can't control…"

Her eyes flew open. She looked at him, her lovely face surprised. Then she smiled a small, feminine smile. In this moment she seemed far more experienced than he; she at least remembered the night they'd conceived their child. While he felt like a damned virgin, helpless, lost in his desire for her, this intoxicating woman who was now his wife.

Rising to her feet, she reached down and slowly unzipped his trousers, careful not to touch the part of him that most strained for her. She pulled the fabric, along with his silk boxer shorts, slowly down his legs.

Then, standing in front of him, she took off her white lace panties.

He closed his eyes, his breathing shallow and quick. Through the tall windows, the sea breeze blew against his hot skin as he felt her climb back over his naked body on the leather sofa. Naked.

He couldn't look. He was afraid if he did, he would explode. And he wanted to last for her. He should be able to last, damn it. With any other woman in his past, he'd always been able to last as long as he wanted. His sexual stamina was legendary.

But with Honora, he'd lost his power. He could not resist her. At any moment he knew he would surrender...

She lowered her soft naked body over his. She leaned forward to kiss his lips, and he felt the press of her pregnant belly, her full breasts against his chest, felt the whispered caress of her long hair. As she kissed him, a sigh came from the back of her throat.

And moving down, she lowered her naked hips to his, pulling him slowly, slowly inside her.

His lips parted in a silent gasp as his hands gripped the leather cushion beneath his body. He felt like he was hanging on by a thread.

Making love to Honora...

This woman he'd wanted for so long…

Pregnant with his child.

His wife.

All he could think of was her; he had to please her, to pleasure her.

His whole body was tense, on a razor's edge of desire.

Honora had never felt so wicked.

She was naked, in the middle of a grand room in a beach house, totally unprivate, where anyone in the open hallway could walk by—or someone outside could peer right into the enormous windows and see them, if they wanted.

But here she was, like a shameless wanton. It was only the second sexual experience of her life, but somehow, it felt different, as if their roles were reversed. She felt powerful, alive, with this billionaire playboy tycoon beneath her thighs, under her control.

Why did she feel this way? Because they were married? Because she was pregnant with his child? Or some other reason?

Her heart raced as she looked down at Nico's darkly handsome face, at his closed eyes, his rapt expression, as if what they were experiencing together was something wholly new, something holy.

And it was.

When they'd first slept together last Christmas, she'd been an untried girl, dreaming of a powerful man. Now she felt like she'd come into her own. She was a wife. A mother-to-be.

She was a woman.

Feeling him inside her, she felt pleasure burn through her body, from her scalp to her toes and everywhere in between. Gripping his powerful shoulders with her hands to support her weight, she lifted her hips, then lowered them again, drawing him inside her, deep, deeper still. His shaft was so wide, so hard and thick. He filled her deeper than she'd imagined. But he could not break her.

She heard him gasp, and he gripped her hips, stilling them.

"I can't, Honora. For the love of heaven—"

But seeing her power over him only increased her desire. When had she become so wicked? Was it the moment they were wed? Or had this passion always been inside her, waiting for the right moment—the right man—to set it free?

Leaning down, she kissed his mouth, licking his upper lip with a small flick of her tongue as he gasped her name.

Still gripping his shoulders, she slowly began to ride him. She closed her eyes as pleasure coiled deep inside her, tighter and tighter as her breasts bounced softly against her pregnant belly with each thrust. She held her breath as the tension built inside her, higher and higher. She dug her fingernails into his skin, going harder, faster, letting him stretch her wide, filling her to the hilt as her movements grew rough—

He gave a strangled curse and said her name as a prayer. "Honora!"

She exploded, soaring into the sky with a joyful cry, just as he poured into her with a guttural shout.

Afterward, she collapsed over him. They held each other, naked, on the white leather sectional, surrounded by tall windows, as the warm summer breeze oscillated the translucent curtains, caressing their skin.

Turning to her side, Honora rested her head on her husband's chest, listening to the beat of his heart as he softly stroked her hair, both of them sweaty and tangled in each other, the only sound the distant plaintive call of seagulls.

And it was in listening to his heart that she finally knew her own.

Her eyes flew open.

She was in love with him. Utterly, completely in love with the man in her arms. The man who'd promised to be hers forever. The man who wanted to give her everything. His name. His fortune. His honor. His life.

Everything. Except his heart.

CHAPTER EIGHT

Nico had flown the transatlantic route many times since he'd moved to New York and created his real estate development firm. He'd justified the expense of the state-of-the-art Gulfstream G650 because it gave him space and privacy, either to work in the sitting area, or to sleep in the private stateroom. Time was money.

The New York–Rome route had been the most frequent for the last two years, as he'd quietly bought everything his estranged father possessed, both assets and debts. After his father's death, he'd remained in Rome to distract himself with multiple billion-dollar deals, a new resort on the Costa Smeralda in Sardinia and other projects that were a quick flight away—Dubai, Athens, Barcelona.

He'd told himself there was no longer any point in trying to acquire his father's ancestral home, the Villa Caracciola, in the quaint village of Trevello on the Amalfi Coast. The former palace was decrepit, barely clinging to the rocky hillside. When his father's elderly widow, Princess Egidia, had still refused to sell it, even at top dollar, he'd let it go. Fine. Let her live there without staff and barely enough money to pay the electric bills. It seemed a just punishment.

But as he traveled back to the Amalfi Coast with his new bride, Nico found he'd changed his mind. Perhaps taking possession of the villa where his young mother had been seduced and betrayed would finally exorcise the ghosts of the past.

It wouldn't be the main goal of his honeymoon, of course. As they boarded the private jet in New York, all Nico could think about was making love to his wife. After their time together at the Hamptons house, he should have been satiated. Instead, he desired her even more. He was bewitched. *Obsessed.* Honora would be the main focus of this vacation.

But in spare moments, he would set his lawyers loose on his widowed stepmother, and force her to sell the Villa Caracciola. How hard could it be?

Once the jet was in the air, the smiling flight attendant served them a light meal of fruit and freshly baked crusty bread, cheese and ham, and sparkling water. As Nico and Honora ate, they looked at each other over the glossy oak table, and he felt shivery inside. By her dazzled expression, the way she bit her passion-bruised lips, he thought she must feel the same.

It was only the presence of the flight attendant, flirting with his security chief on the other side of the cabin, that kept Nico from sweeping all the food off the table and taking Honora right there. As it was, he barely tasted the food, and as soon as Honora was done their eyes met, and without a word, they rose and went to the private stateroom in the back.

Locking the door behind them, he kissed her passionately and drew her down to the bed. They remained there for the entire transatlantic flight, making love, sharing a shower in the tiny en suite bathroom—laughing at the tight squeeze of space. Holding each other quietly in bed afterward, they whispered the secrets of their hearts into the darkness.

At least, *Honora* whispered the secrets of her heart. How

lonely she'd been as a child, how she'd never felt smart in school, how she'd always felt like a burden to her family.

Nico didn't answer. He just listened. Listened? He devoured and consumed her secrets like a miser tucking away pieces of gold. But he himself did not share. He'd learned long ago that being vulnerable was just offering rope for someone else to hang him with.

So he marveled at her fearlessness, as she confided that she'd never thought she deserved to be this happy, not after the way her parents had died in a car crash when she was a child. Somehow she seemed to think it was her fault—he didn't understand why, but he assumed she had her reasons. And he promised himself that he would never, ever use any of it against her.

Nico was her husband now. Her protector. If he could not love her, or feel emotions as she did, he could at least do one thing: keep her secrets as closely as he kept his own.

By the time the jet was preparing to land at a small airport near the Amalfi Coast, Nico was nearly licking his lips in anticipation of their honeymoon—two weeks of nothing to do but make love to his beautiful, sensual wife, showing her the pleasures of Italy, the delicious pasta and fresh seafood, and swim in the Tyrrhenian Sea.

And then, to cap it all off, in his spare time, he'd toss his wicked stepmother out of her rathole and raze the Villa Caracciola to the ground. In its place, he'd build a brand-new modern mansion in which to start his new dynasty.

He might have no idea how to be a parent, but he could for damn sure build his daughter a palace to live in. Whenever he felt anxious, wondering how on earth he would make his child feel loved when he himself had never known what that felt like, he reassured himself with the thought that his wife could be in charge of nurturing and loving.

Nico would be in charge of building an empire. He would

protect and provide for them in a new ancestral home. The Villa Ferraro.

As he and Honora descended the steps of his private jet to the tarmac, it was full morning. The sun was warm, perfectly suited to his white collared shirt and dark trousers, and Honora's red cotton maternity sundress and sandals. Nico felt tired, having gotten very little sleep on the flight, but happy. What was it that made his wife so addictive, like a drug he could not resist?

And how was it possible that he'd barely noticed her for all those years? How had he never truly seen her until he'd been exhausted and drunk with a bad concussion last Christmas?

"We're here," Honora said, gripping the handrail as she stood at the top of the steps, looking out rapturously at the tiny airport nestled behind the hills. *"Italy."*

He smiled down at her. It gave him so much pleasure to see the joy in her eyes. And at such a small thing—a honeymoon on the Amalfi Coast. He looked forward to a lifetime of seeing her lovely face light up with delight, knowing he was the one who'd put it there.

Not to mention a lifetime of nights where he made sure her full lips were bruised from the passion of his kisses.

As they came down the steps to the tarmac, with his security chief following, Nico saw Gianni, his personal assistant from the Rome office, holding a briefcase. Behind him, he saw a large SUV and a driver... Nico's mouth fell open.

"Welcome to Italy, sir." Benny Rossini, the young chauffeur he'd banished from New York City, smiled at Nico's new bride. "Honora."

Her face lit up. "Benny! You're here now?"

"Yes." He smiled. "I'm managing the new villa." He puffed up his chest a little. "A promotion. But I can still be your driver wherever you need to go." He gave a low laugh. "Driving along the Amalfi Coast is not for the faint-hearted."

Nico scowled. When he'd told his residential staffing manager to move the young driver to another job, he'd never imagined he'd move Rossini *here*. He felt irritated. Really, Sergio should have known. He paid his staff well enough to expect them to read his mind.

It didn't matter, Nico told himself firmly. Honora was his wife now. Besides, they'd be at his estate for only two weeks. Surely he could endure his employee's presence for such a short time. And it wasn't like Rossini and Honora would be spending time alone together.

"Good to see you, Rossini," he said coldly, taking Honora's hand. As he helped her into the back of the luxury SUV, Nico added, without looking back, "Gianni, with me."

While his security chief, Frank Bauer, followed with their luggage in a separate vehicle, his assistant accompanied Nico into the back of the SUV, which had been fitted with two facing rows. Before the chauffeur even started the engine, Nico was speaking to his assistant in rapid Italian, telling him he wished to restart legal efforts to force the Villa Caracciola from the elderly widow's possession. Gianni seemed surprised, then moved forward, pulling up legal documents on his tablet.

Glancing up toward Benny Rossini, sitting in the driver's seat, Nico wondered whether he was listening. He didn't trust the young man, and the last thing he wanted was for his stepmother to be forewarned—or, for that matter, for Honora to hear a version of the story that might make Nico look like he was somehow the villain in this. Pressing the button to lift the privacy shield, he turned back to his assistant with a scowl, and told him in the same language that any delay was unacceptable. He wanted the Caracciola property *now*.

"Oh." Honora looked between the two men in dismay.

"Are you planning to discuss business on the drive? In Italian?"

He saw how tired she looked, and was worried about her and the baby. "Feel free to rest. The drive to my villa will take an hour."

She stared at him for a moment, then produced a sudden cheerful smile. "Don't worry. I'll just go sit in the front with Benny."

And before Nico could stop her, she hopped out of the back seat and went to sit with the young, handsome driver on the other side of the privacy screen.

As the SUV pulled away from the airport ten seconds later, Nico's assistant prattled on about how they could get around a governmental delay, which apparently was based on some claim that the widow's villa, two hundred years old, had "historical and architectural significance"—a classic stunt.

But he was distracted now. All he could think about was his wife, on the other side of the privacy screen, sitting beside Rossini, who was clearly infatuated with her, and though he had little money, perhaps the young man could offer her things Nico couldn't. Like emotion. Like vulnerability. Like love.

A curse went through Nico's mind.

"Sir? What do you think?" his assistant said in Italian into the sudden awkward silence.

Nico bared his teeth in a grin. "Just do whatever it takes to win."

His eyes strayed toward the closed privacy screen. He wondered what they were talking about. He wanted to lower the screen, but that would be an admission of jealousy, which he didn't want to make. He couldn't show Honora how important she was to him. That would give her too much power and make him feel…weak.

He had nothing to worry about, he told himself firmly.

After all, it wasn't like his employee would be stupid enough to make a pass at his wife, with Nico himself sitting in the back of the SUV.

"I'm telling you, I'm in love with you!"

Sitting in the front seat, Honora drew back from the young driver, scandalized. "How can you say such a thing! I'm Nico's wife. I'm pregnant with his baby!"

Benny looked mournful, in a handsome, pudding-cheeked sort of way. He reminded her of a particularly forlorn basset hound. "I wish I'd only been brave enough to tell you before he seduced you…"

"Stop it!" As he started to reach his hand toward her, she slapped it away. "Watch the road!"

He did as he was told, gripping the steering wheel with both hands as they went around a taut hairpin curve on the cliff, practically dangling off the edge. It was a little terrifying, especially with her longtime phobia about car crashes. But not as awful as being pestered like this.

"And for your information," she added tartly, "Nico didn't seduce me. If anything, I seduced him!"

"No, that can't be…"

"It is," Honora said, exasperated. "He was drunk on Christmas Day, he'd just broken up with his girlfriend, and I took heartless advantage. So there!"

That wasn't exactly how it had happened, but she was fed up with Benny mooning after her.

The truth was, she'd been a little relieved when he'd been transferred to a different position in the Ferraro business empire. She felt sorry for him, and a little guilty, but she wanted him to be happy. When she'd come up here to sit beside him, she'd hoped to discover that the weeks and miles of distance, not to mention the fact of her marriage, had helped him gain a little perspective. She'd thought they could have a short private discussion that would put them both at ease.

But it had only made things worse. So much worse.

He was pale. "You're telling me I no longer have a chance?"

Honora wanted to scream. "You never had a chance with me! Never!"

He narrowed his eyes as he stared forward at the road. His expression was surly. "Because he's so rich, right?"

Her sympathy was disappearing. She was getting tired of friends, people who should have been on her side, implying she was some kind of gold digger.

"Because I'm in love with him." It was strange to realize that she was saying the words for the first time aloud, and not to Nico but to some other man who was stupidly making a pass at her.

His jaw dropped. "You can't!" He stared stonily at the road. "Nico Ferraro is a selfish bastard. He doesn't care for anyone but himself. And sooner or later—" he glanced at her "—he's going to hurt you. A man like that can do nothing else."

Honora felt a shiver of fear. Was Benny right? Would Nico break her heart and leave her crying and alone?

No. Impossible. He wouldn't leave her. He was the one who'd first wanted marriage, not her.

But you love him now, and he'll never love you back, whispered a small voice.

Setting her jaw, she pushed the painful thought away. "If this is how you show loyalty to Nico as your employer, and to me as a friend, I think you should seriously consider finding another job."

His lips twisted. "Way ahead of you."

Benny didn't speak to her again on the drive. Honora sat in the front seat, gripping the handle over her head as the big SUV swayed sharply around the turns of the narrow coastal road, passing within inches of tour buses flying in the opposite direction.

She felt sick from the twisty roads, exhausted by jet lag and lack of sleep, and horrified by his words.

But as the SUV finally entered through a guarded gate into a beautiful estate filled with lemon trees, Honora thought of how lucky she was: a newlywed, expecting a baby, in love with her husband. Surely she could be kind to Benny and not ruin his life just because of some ridiculous infatuation.

With a deep breath, she turned to him. "Look, I'm sorry. I don't want you to lose your job—"

"Don't worry about it." Pulling up in front of a grand, classical villa, he faced her. "I'll be fine. I already know someone looking for a driver. She lives in Hollywood." He gave a sharp smile. "I'll be a movie star within a year. I would have left a long time ago if you'd just been honest with me."

"When was I not honest?"

"Every time I flirted with you, showed you how much I liked you, bought you pickles. I believed you when you said you couldn't date because your grandfather needed you. But it was just an excuse. The second Ferraro crooked his finger, you couldn't wait to fling yourself into his bed. The second he bought that ring—" he eyeballed the huge diamond on her left hand "—you couldn't wait to say your vows."

Her cheeks went hot. "I didn't want to hurt your feelings…"

Benny gave a harsh laugh. "So you kept me around for years in hope, rather than telling a single hard truth to set me free."

"I never meant to—"

"Save it." Getting out of the SUV, Benny came around to her side and opened her door, his expression hard. He didn't look at her. Honora got out slowly, feeling bewildered by his sudden anger.

Wrenching open the rear passenger door, Benny waited stone-faced as Nico got out, his Italian assistant trailing behind him. Her husband looked between the driver and Honora sharply. He seemed to sense something was wrong.

As Frank Bauer got out of the second car, he called, "Hey, Benny, mind helping me with the bags?"

"Screw you, Bauer. And as for you—" Turning to Nico, Benny said something in Italian, complete with a gesture that even Honora knew was vulgar.

Nico's jaw dropped a little, but he responded with a cool smile, "Thanks for making this easy, Rossini."

"Same to you." Dropping the car key onto the gravel driveway, Benny stomped into the large, imposing villa, surrounded by gardens and overlooking the blue sea from a rocky cliff.

"Follow him," Nico drawled to his employees. "I imagine he's packing his things, but make sure he doesn't run off with the silver."

His security chief and assistant nodded, then hurried into the looming white villa with its elegant columns and statuary.

Nico's pretense of impassivity dropped as he went to Honora.

"What happened on the drive?" he demanded, looking down at her. "What did he say? Did he hurt you?"

"No, he just…he said he loved me. And he's angry because he thinks I led him on, but I didn't!"

"Of course not," he said soothingly. He gave a crooked grin. "You can't help it if you're desirable."

Honora choked out a laugh, but it sounded like a sob. "He'll be happier now. He's off for some new job, working for some woman in Hollywood." She tilted her head. "Do you think he's talking about Lana Lee?" Now *that* was a woman every man desired!

"Probably. I don't give a damn." His hands tightened at his sides. He turned grimly toward his villa. "I can't believe he tried to seduce you while I was in the same car. I'm going to go in there and—"

"No." Frightened by the look on Nico's face, she put her hand over his. "He didn't try to seduce me, not like you mean. And maybe he had a point."

"What do you mean?"

"All these years, I pretended not to notice how he was always flirting with me, asking me out to dinner."

"You should have just punched him in the face," Nico said darkly. She laughed, then saw he was serious. She shook her head.

"That probably would have hurt him less. I should have been brave enough to tell him the truth." Trying to change the subject and take away the scowl on her husband's face, Honora looked up at the enormous villa. "Wow. It's a palace."

Nico looked up at it. "It's not a palace. But it will do." His lips curved at the edges. "Until I get the one I *really* want."

"There's a villa nicer than this?"

"No. It's a ruin. And I'm going to knock it down and build something beautiful and new."

Shaking her head, she smiled. "You're never satisfied, are you?"

"No," he said huskily, drawing closer. "Especially not where you are concerned. I'll never get enough of you."

Her heart lifted, helping to dispel the dark clouds caused by Benny's words. *Sooner or later he's going to hurt you.* Glancing past his ear, she gave him a tentative smile. "Is that a garden?"

"Yes. I think you'll like it."

"Will I?" Holding his hand, Honora tugged him around

the edge of the villa. She stopped, her mouth agape when she saw the formal garden with roses and palm trees surrounding marble fountains, and past that, groves of lemon trees with the biggest lemons she'd ever seen. Beyond the grand villa, she could see the turquoise sea crashing against the rocky cliffs. The soft Italian wind, redolent of oranges and spice, blew against her skin.

Nico looked down at her with a frown. "Are you crying?"

"I've never seen anything so beautiful," she whispered. She looked up at him. "I can't believe all this is yours."

He looked at her and his harsh expression changed, became almost tender, as a light entered his dark eyes. *"Ours."*

"Ours?" she breathed. "Even the garden?"

"No." He smiled. "The garden is just yours."

She danced on the spot. "I love you!"

Nico gave a surprised, joyful laugh as she threw her arms around him. He hugged her back.

Then she looked up at him, trembling with fear, and it felt as if time stopped. But she'd learned her lesson. It was better to reveal the truth, come what may.

"I mean it." With a deep breath, she looked straight into his eyes and said in a totally different tone, "I love you, Nico."

CHAPTER NINE

"I LOVE YOU."

Nico felt the words like a blow, as if she'd punched him in the throat.

I love you.

Those words had been said to him before, by overeager girlfriends trying to take the sexual affair to the next level, to tie him down, to get him to put a ring on it. He'd seen them for the manipulations they were.

This was different.

Nico looked down at his beautiful pregnant wife in his arms. *Honora.* So beautiful inside and out. She meant the words. He saw emotion shining in her big green eyes. *Love.* What did that even mean?

Her heart-shaped face was filled with adoration—adoration Nico knew he didn't deserve. He knew he was selfish and ruthless and cold.

How had Honora convinced herself to see something else? Had he been complicit in her self-deception?

He also saw her unspoken longing for him to return her love.

Why? His demons reared their ugly heads. So she could possess and control him? He would never allow himself to be so weak, so vulnerable, so helpless, giving his soul up into the power of another. As a boy, he'd always yearned desperately for attention, to feel like he belonged, like he was valuable. Instead, he'd been neglected, heartsick and alone, always wondering what was wrong with him that even his own mother seemed to regret his existence. *Never again.*

But as Honora looked up at him, as her soft body pressed against his, he looked down at her full breasts, pushing up against the thin straps of her red cotton sundress, and felt a different emotion. The only one he could allow himself to safely feel.

Desire.

Even after hours of making love to her—in the Hamptons, on the private jet—Nico suddenly wanted her more than ever.

She loved him. He'd never asked for her love, but now he possessed her, body and soul.

And if he couldn't love her back, he could at least give her his body, because it was utterly and completely hers…

The sky above the villa was bright blue, and a warm wind blew in from the azure sea as he held her amid the lemon groves. Nico saw the growing question in her beautiful face: Did he love her, too? He could not break her heart with the truth.

So he kissed her.

She felt warm in his arms, her baby bump pressed against him in her red sundress, as he stroked her bare arms. Her hands reached up to pull his head down to deepen the kiss, which made him ache for her even more. It was as close as he could get to love.

He ran his hands through her long dark hair, which swept loose and long over her bare shoulders. Her fingertips stroked lightly through his short black waves, then down over his shirt. Around them, he could smell the scent of lemons, of Italy, of the sea. He smelled roses and vanilla—the scent of his wife's perfume. He kissed her passionately, holding her close.

Cupping his unshaven cheek, she whispered against his lips, "I love you, Nico."

Again. He shuddered from a mixture of desire and dread. He liked her loving him, he realized. But if she knew he could never return her feelings...

He had to make sure she never realized that. For her sake. He had to protect his wife's feelings, to make sure she never knew his heart felt nothing.

But his body—

"I want you," he whispered huskily. He kissed her again and felt the sweet pleasure of her lips drawing him down, down into an intoxication more thrilling and mind-numbing than he'd ever experienced with alcohol. He felt her shiver in his arms.

Taking her hand, Nico pulled her away from the lemon groves, through the formal Italian garden, past the roses and burbling marble fountains. The warm sun caressed their skin as he drew her back to the enormous white wedding cake villa that was perched on a cliff overlooking the coast.

He paused for only a moment when he saw Benny Rossini scowling as he was escorted into a waiting SUV by his security chief. Honora watched, her face shadowed with worry and guilt.

Nico ground his teeth. Why would she feel guilty? Rossini himself was clearly to blame for his own bad judgment. But Honora's heart was so tender and kind that she blamed herself for everything.

"Make sure he gets his full salary for the month, and any vacation time owed," he told Frank Bauer, who nodded.

Honora turned to Nico. "I feel bad—"

"Didn't he say he was glad to go to Hollywood?" he said shortly. "He'll be fine."

"But—"

"Honora." As the SUV drove away, he looked directly

into her eyes. "Why do you always blame yourself? It wasn't your fault. Let it go."

She bit her lip, then sighed. "Fine."

He pulled her inside the villa, and the tall oak door closed solidly behind them.

Inside, the two-hundred-year-old classical villa was elegant, stately in its age, and crowded with antiques, the antithesis of his sleek Hamptons beach mansion and stark Manhattan penthouse.

Honora looked with surprise at the foyer's checkered marble floor and frescoed ceilings of cherubs soaring high above. "This is…yours?"

He shrugged. "I bought it with the furniture intact."

Looking around, she gave an amused laugh. "This is the shack you're slumming in until you can buy the villa you *really* want?"

"Until I can build it. I told you. When I get my father's ancestral home, I will raze it to the ground and build something modern and new."

"An ancestral home?" She frowned. "That sounds important. Why not remodel and restore it?"

He looked away. "It's a symbol," he said quietly, "of everything my father did. The place where he seduced my mother, who was a maid in his house. Then he threw her out and refused to take responsibility for her pregnancy. He represents everything that's wrong and corrupt and cruel. I want to burn it all to the ground."

"Oh, Nico," she whispered. "I'm so sorry. No wonder you want to tear it down."

His eyes met hers. "I do. Then I will build a new villa. A new home. With you."

She seemed to visibly melt at his words. Emotion made her green eyes glow. At first it warmed him—but then his heart started to pound. *Danger!* He could not let himself feel emotion.

But desire…

Taking her hand, he pressed it to his lips. "I expect the Villa Caracciola to be mine within the week." He slowly kissed up her bare arm to her shoulder, feeling her shiver. "Until we can build our real home," he whispered, cupping her cheek as he slowly lowered his mouth to hers, "we'll just have to make do…"

Nico kissed her in the foyer until she sagged against him in surrender, both of them lost in pleasure. When he pulled away, he saw her beautiful face was dazed with desire. Taking her hand, he pulled her up the grand staircase.

He'd only visited this villa once, the previous November, when he'd bought it. He was relieved to find he still knew the way to the master suite. It was the only thing he'd refurbished, combining three bedrooms to make a single large modern one.

Huge windows and a balcony overlooked the picturesque sharp cliffs jutting into the turquoise sea. At the center of the room was an enormous bed. The white duvet was dotted with red rose petals. The marble fireplace had been filled with an enormous bouquet of pink and red long-stemmed roses. Nearby, an intimate table for two was covered with chocolate-dipped strawberries, sparkling pink lemonade, small canapés, fruit and tiny sandwiches.

Honora stopped, her sandals almost screeching to a halt on the hardwood floor, her eyes wide as her dark hair swayed over her red sundress. "What's this?"

Nico felt glad in this moment, so glad, that he'd taken the time to ask his Italian housekeeper to set it up. All so simple, and yet his wife looked more touched than when he'd dragged her to Cartier and insisted on buying her a twenty-carat diamond. She looked, in fact, as if she were about to cry.

Maybe he couldn't give her *love*. But romance, romance he could do.

"For you, my darling bride," Nico whispered. Coming forward, he cupped her cheek as he slowly lowered his lips to hers. "Roses and chocolates and kisses. Kisses most of all. Everything I have, everything I am…is yours."

Honora woke up smiling.

Late-afternoon sunshine was flooding through the west-facing windows of their bedroom. She must have fallen asleep naked, she realized, after their lunch and lovemaking. She stretched languorously, loving every sweet ache of her body.

Every part of her felt touched by him, blessed. She didn't remember falling asleep, but then, she'd been tired even before they'd arrived at his villa, with all the passion they'd shared while crossing the Atlantic in his private jet, and before that in his Hamptons house.

Although, she knew Nico would say, if he were here, that it was *their* private jet. *Their* Hamptons beach house. *Their* Amalfi Coast villa.

But the thing she loved most about all of those places was that he was in them.

So where was Nico? Getting out of bed, she looked around her. Unlike the rest of the villa, which had been chock full of antiques, this gorgeous master bedroom was as sparse with furniture as Nico's other homes. Pulling on a silk robe that she'd bought in New York as part of the wedding trousseau he'd insisted on buying her, she peeked into the en suite bathroom.

It was gleaming, modern and new. And empty.

She glanced at the small clock over the bedroom's sleek marble fireplace, above the vase of long-stemmed pink and red roses. It was six o'clock. Almost dinner time, at least by American standards. And she was hungry. Being pregnant really gave her an appetite.

Or maybe she'd worked it up doing something else. Again and again. She blushed.

Taking a shower in the large walk-in shower, Honora relished the warmth against her skin as she scrubbed her hair. So much easier to do here than in that postage-stamp-sized shower on the private jet. Stepping out, she wrapped herself in a thick white cotton towel. As she wiped the steam off the mirror, she looked at herself in amazement as she brushed her teeth.

How had she stepped into this life? She didn't understand how she could be so lucky. What had she ever done to deserve it?

You didn't have to work for it. You're just marrying it.

Her smile fell a little as she remembered Emmie's bitter words, words her friend had apologized for and tried to take back. But it had never been about money for Honora. She would have been mad about Nico, rich or poor! She loved him just for himself!

She loved him. But did he love her?

Everything I have...everything I am...is yours.

Honora shivered, remembering how she'd felt when he'd kissed her earlier and taken her on that bed.

That meant love, didn't it?

Anyway, she didn't need him to say the words. He cared for her; he was committed to her. That was enough. Honora's heart could love enough for both of them. It *could*.

Getting dressed in a pretty, new cotton sundress, she pulled her hair back into a long ponytail and went downstairs.

After some aimless wandering along the villa's hallways, she finally found Nico in a home office with his assistant and several other men in suits, all of them speaking in tense, rapid Italian as they looked over papers spread across a large table. They looked up as she entered. Nico smiled.

"Honora. Did you enjoy your rest?"

Could his men guess why she'd so desperately needed one? She blushed. "Yes."

"I'm just getting some details ironed out for that real estate acquisition. You were asking to taste real Italian pasta, yes?"

"Yes?"

"As soon as I'm done here, I'll take you out to dinner in Trevello, if you'd like."

"Sounds lovely."

Nico's warm gaze traced slowly from her eyes to her lips, down her body to her sandals, leaving a trail of heat wherever they lingered. "I'm sorry I have business with my lawyers. I'll be done soon."

"I'll go wander the garden," she said, not wanting to be a bother.

The formal garden was even more lovely on closer viewing. Standing alone in the middle of the villa's perfect garden, with its spectacular view of the sea, she wished her grandfather could see these flowers. But he was busy with Phyllis, working in the flower shop, redecorating the Queens apartment. They'd decided to turn Honora's old bedroom into a home gym. "I gotta stay healthy to keep up with my wife," her grandfather had told her happily.

Honora looked out at the bright sun, lowering toward the sea. She was glad he was happy. She was, too. She was married and expecting a child.

So why did she suddenly feel so uncertain and alone?

"Stop it," she told herself aloud. "You have everything you could ever have wanted. More than you deserve."

She walked through the garden until it grew dark, then went inside to sit on the sofa outside Nico's home office with an old leather-bound book she'd found on the shelf of the library. By the time Nico shook her awake, it was hours later, nearly midnight.

"Sorry." He gave her a charming smile. "My lawyers took longer than I thought."

"That's all right," she said, rubbing her eyes, trying to wake herself up and be ready to eat dinner when her whole body said she should be sleeping. She felt totally upended by jet lag.

Outside the villa, there were streaks of velvety stars in the dark purple night. Helping her into his sports car, Nico drove her through the gate and out to the cliff road, twisting along the edge of the black Tyrrhenian Sea.

"The restaurant is just up there. The best pasta in Campania, which means the best in Italy, which, of course, means the best in the world."

But as he started to turn into the parking lot, a big RV coming from behind clipped the edge of his back bumper, causing the sports car to spin wildly through the gravel lot, rocking back and forth chaotically.

Their car spun toward the edge of the cliff.

Honora screamed. For an instant, she was eleven again, watching the whole world spin in front of her eyes. It was just like before. In selfishly asking for something she wanted, she'd ruined her life. Killed the people she loved most—

Nico gave a low, tense curse, gripping the wheel hard and forcing it to turn.

The car suddenly stopped. But her screaming didn't.

"Honora. *Cara*—"

She felt Nico's hand on her shoulder, heard his gentle voice. She opened her eyes and saw that the world had stopped spinning. Their car was still. Other than a cloud of dust around them, there was nothing to show that they'd nearly plummeted into the sea.

"I'm—sorry," she choked out. "I didn't mean to scream." Suddenly she was sobbing and his arms wrapped around her.

"It's all right." His voice was tender as he stroked her

hair. "We were never in any danger, but I'm sorry you were scared." He looked fiercely behind them. "Damned tourists should know better than to try to drive this road in that thing."

Honora felt embarrassed, making such a fuss when they were trying to have a romantic evening. Pulling away, she wiped her tears. "I'm fine now."

"Are you sure?"

She nodded, avoiding his gaze. "Absolutely."

Opening her door, he helped her from the low-slung sports car and led her into a charming restaurant, which seemed very local. Perhaps because it was after midnight, the restaurant had no other customers. The owner was thrilled to see him. "Mr. Ferraro! I am so glad you are here!"

"*Grazie*, Luigi."

"My wife, she said you would come and bring your new American bride, your first night in Trevello. I said no, love-birds have better things to do than eat! But my wife, she said, doing those things, one always gets hungry…"

"I can speak for myself," said his wife, who came over, smiling. She had an Australian accent. The two of them were good-looking and gray-haired, and Luigi pulled her into his arms, looking down at her lovingly.

"I will, and I do, and I should always listen to you." He kissed his wife's temple. "To listen as well as I love you, which is infinite and forever."

She looked up at her husband. Luigi abruptly cleared his throat, as if he'd just remembered they had customers. "So Peggy told me you called for a reservation…?"

"Yes. Um…" Nico had the grace to look sheepish as he clawed his hand through his dark hair. "I'm sorry we're so late."

The wife waved her hand, which was filled with menus. "That is no problem. We expected as much, seeing as it is

your honeymoon. We are honored that you chose our restaurant for your first night." Escorting them to an amazing
table by the window, with a view of the moon-swept sea,
the lights of the village of Trevello and a flickering candle
between them, she handed Honora a menu. "This is your
first trip to Italy, *signora*?"

"Yes," she replied shyly. She looked at the menu, then
said, "Nico says this is the best restaurant in all Italy, and
as it is yours, will you please tell me what I should order?"

Luigi beamed at her, then plucked the menu from her
hand. "You chose a good one, Signor Ferraro. *Signora*, I
will be most pleased."

Fifteen minutes later, she was dismayed as they were
served two full plates of portobello mushrooms sautéed
with spinach in garlic and olive oil.

"Enjoy, *signora*!" he said.

"My favorite thing here," Nico said, and dug in.

Picking up her fork, Honora tried to smile. She cut very
slowly with her knife, and she forced herself to take a bite.

"How do you like it?" Nico said, watching her.

"Delicious," she managed to say, trying not to breathe
through her nose or taste the mushroom as she gulped it
down.

He set his jaw. "Honora. If you don't like something,
don't suffer in silence. Be honest. Speak up."

"I hate mushrooms," she blurted out. For a moment, she
was shocked at herself, and even proud.

Then as she sat in the picturesque Italian restaurant with
its amazing view, fear surged through her. What if Luigi's
feelings were hurt by her honesty? What if her husband
was embarrassed, or what if he despised her for not being
sophisticated enough to enjoy this meal? Would he tell her
he no longer wanted such an unpleasant wife who made
such selfish demands?

Setting down her fork, she nervously lifted her gaze.

Her husband smiled at her, his dark eyes glowing. Then he turned, lifting his hand for the restaurant owner's attention.

"Luigi. My wife doesn't care for mushrooms. Please get her something else."

"*Sì, signore.* But of course."

Nico's smile spread to a grin as he reached for her plate of mushrooms. "And I will take care of this."

Two hours later, they finished the most delicious seafood pasta Honora had ever tasted, along with crusty bread and Caprese salad with ripe tomatoes, basil leaves and fresh mozzarella laced with olive oil and balsamic vinegar. She felt happy, relieved. It was strange. Something about Nico made her feel brave, like she had the right to speak up for herself. Like she shouldn't take the blame for things that weren't her fault. Like she wasn't a burden, but a treasure.

Smiling, she drank creamy decaf coffee and finished a cannoli that was as sweet and light as air. Then her smile fell as she saw, on the other side of the empty cliff-side restaurant, Luigi tenderly kiss his wife. She saw his lips form the words *Ti amo.*

And just like that, all her happiness dissolved. Having told Nico that she loved him, she yearned so badly to hear those words back. How wonderful it would be to be loved, now and forever, after her hair had long turned to gray.

But why would she ever think she deserved to be loved like that, when—

She tried to push the thought away. But suddenly she couldn't.

"What's wrong?" Nico asked quietly. She looked at him, so handsome on the other side of the table, shadowed by the flickering light of the candle.

"I don't deserve this," she whispered. "Any of it. I never have."

"How can you say that? Of course you do. You're the

kindest person I know." He gave a grim smile. "If you don't deserve happiness, no one does."

"You don't really know me. What I did."

"So tell me." His voice was gentle.

Honora looked away. Through all the open-air windows, she could see the clusters of lights of Trevello's houses and shops, stretching joyously up from the sea to the sky, twinkling like stars.

"When our car almost went off the cliff, just because I wanted pasta…it all came back." She licked her lips, closing her eyes. "How I begged my parents to take me up to a pumpkin festival in the countryside, two hours outside the city. I thought if we could go, then maybe we'd be a happy family like in the ads."

"What happened?"

"My parents fought the whole time. Just like always. My mother cried and begged as my father drank and criticized her. He drank the whole time we were at the autumn fair, then crashed the rental car into an oncoming truck on the way home. The other driver lived. So did I." She looked up, her eyes filled with tears. "But my parents died because I just *had* to sit on a hay bale and eat pumpkin bread."

"No, *cara*." His voice was gentler than she'd ever heard as he put down his small cup of espresso. "They died because your father chose to drink while he was driving his family in a car. It wasn't your fault. You were a child."

Honora looked up at him, her heart pounding. Then she told him the worst. "They were miserable because of me. They only married because of me. Because I was born. They grew to hate each other. That was why she cried and he drank. They felt trapped but didn't know how to get out. Because of me."

He put his hand over hers on the table.

"It was not your fault," he said quietly. "Your parents made their own choices." He pulled away his hand, straightening his shoulders as he sat back in his chair. "Forget the pain they caused you. Be happy. Live your life only for yourself." He gave her a crooked grin. "That's what I do."

The thought was shocking to her.

"Live for myself?" she said. "But it's the people I love who give my life meaning. My grandfather. Our baby." Her eyes met his wistfully. "You."

A strange, stricken look came over Nico's face, and he abruptly looked away. In the flickering shadows of the restaurant, his jaw seemed hard enough to snap.

"Luigi, the check," he called. Turning back to her, Nico's expression was cold. "Your secrets are safe with me. I give you my word." Tossing his linen napkin down over the empty plate, he rose to his feet. "It's late. Are you ready to go?"

CHAPTER TEN

NICO HADN'T MEANT to hurt her.

Honora told herself that on their drive back to the villa beneath the moonlight, and as her husband made love to her in the darkness, and when she woke alone in bed the next morning. She heard the birds singing in the palm trees overlooking the turquoise sea and repeated it again. He hadn't meant to hurt her.

She'd poured out the most agonizing secrets of her heart, the deepest burdens she carried—that her existence had caused her parents' misery, and her selfish desire to go to a pumpkin festival because of the absurd idea that it would bring them together as a family had caused her parents' deaths.

And all he'd said was that he wouldn't tell anyone. *Your secrets are safe with me. I give you my word.* As if her fears were not only true but shameful, and that if anyone else knew, they would despise her.

Be happy, he'd said. *Live your life only for yourself. That's what I do.*

Nico was living his life only for himself?

What did that even *mean*?

Over the first few days of their honeymoon, Nico worked only in the mornings, and arranged for them to take excursions together in the afternoon. They traveled via helicopter to Rome, and had private tours of the Colosseum and St.

Peter's Square. As they wandered the Roman Forum and tossed a coin in the Trevi Fountain, Honora was filled with wonder and delight, seeing things she'd only dreamed of as a teenager growing up in Queens. And she found herself telling her husband all kinds of stories about growing up in her neighborhood, her friends, her love of books, her interest in flowers and plants. "I had no choice about that," she'd added, laughing, "spending time with Granddad!"

Later, wandering with Nico through the gardens of the Villa Borghese, she talked at length about the best way to care for cypress and pine trees and keep aphids away from roses. She was a little embarrassed later, but it was hard not to talk. Nico was a very good listener.

The next afternoon, he took her to Pompeii. The Roman ruins were remarkable, but seeing where all those people, those *families*, had died suddenly in the eruption of Vesuvius two thousand years before, she became mournful. Nico lifted her spirits afterward by taking her to the most famous pizzeria in nearby Naples, where they shared a margherita pizza with basil and tomato sauce, mozzarella cheese oozing over a crust that was as light as air. As they sat at a small table, surrounded by the hustle and bustle of other customers, she found herself telling him about the disastrous time she'd tried to make pasta from scratch. "Even the neighbor's dog wouldn't eat it," she said with a laugh.

None of her stories were earth-shattering, but it was all of them together that made Honora who she was, so she decided not to be embarrassed. She was glad to share her life with the man she loved. Both afternoons were wonderful and warm, and she loved feeling her husband's presence, whether she was sitting beside him in the helicopter or encircled in his arms in the back of the sedan, chauffeured by Bauer.

It was only much later, after they'd returned to the Amalfi Coast, that it occurred to Honora that she'd done all the talking. Nico was a very good listener, but he'd told her almost nothing about himself, about his own stories and hopes and dreams. The closest he'd gotten was when she'd said in the Pantheon, "You were born here, weren't you? I'd love to see where you grew up."

"Now *that* is ancient history," Nico had said lightly. Then, with a careless smile, he'd distracted her, pointing out the concrete dome, which was apparently special for some reason. And he'd never brought up the subject of his past again.

Looking back, the golden glow of happiness seemed to lose some of its shine.

Honora wanted so desperately for them to be happy. They had everything anyone could want on this Italian honeymoon in this luxurious villa, their baby expected soon. So why did Honora feel like something wasn't right? Something was...missing, and it made her feel empty.

As the first week of their honeymoon passed, then the second, there were no more fun excursions. She watched with mounting dismay as, every day, Nico disappeared into his home office with an increasing number of lawyers and staff. He was apparently having some trouble closing the deal for the Villa Caracciola. Feeling lonely during the second week, she'd once tried to join them. Nico had all but blocked the door.

"I'm sure you have more enjoyable things to do," he'd told her firmly. He handed her two platinum credit cards. "Go shopping down in the village. Or Bauer can drive you if you wish to see Sorrento or Positano."

"Without you?"

He glanced at his lawyers grimly. "I'll be done in an hour or two. Then I'll join you."

But the hour or two was always eight or ten or even, yesterday, twelve. Honora entertained herself by spending time in the villa's delightful formal garden, walking among the flowers. It was perfect in its ornate simplicity, but, she thought, if she were going to design a garden, she would make it more random, wilder. But the gardener clearly didn't need her help, and he didn't speak English beyond smiling at her and bringing fresh flowers into the villa every day—mostly roses.

She got to know the other staff at the villa and learned some basic greetings and questions in Italian. The housekeeper, Luisa, had a little white dog who needed daily walks, and so when the older woman twisted her foot a few days after they arrived, Honora happily offered to take Figaro outside in her stead.

Taking the dog down the steep hillside to the village that clung to the rocky shores that rose sharply from the sea, Honora walked through Trevello alone. For a honeymoon, she thought, it was surprisingly lonesome.

In spite of the amazing sex every night, for which Nico still always found time, Honora was almost relieved when the two weeks finally came to an end. It wasn't so enjoyable to eat delicious meals alone, or sit in the villa alone, or walk along the coastal road alone. She yearned to go home to her grandfather and friends.

Then, the night before they were supposed to leave, Nico suddenly announced that they'd be staying in Italy "indefinitely."

Honora said anxiously, "How long?"

"As long as it takes for me to buy the villa," he bit out. When she flinched at his angry tone, he tried to smile. "On the plus side, it will give us more time in my birth country, so I have decided to host a reception here, to properly introduce you to all my European friends. We'll have music, and dancing..."

Her old insecurity went through her. "You want to introduce me? At a formal ball? To a bunch of wealthy, gorgeous society people?"

"As you said, such social events are necessary, are they not? For the community?"

"I guess so," she said reluctantly.

"The household staff will plan everything. All you need to do is find a ball gown. Excuse me." He glanced back at his home office, which was filled with even more lawyers than before. "I must get back to work."

She didn't ask questions because she feared he'd only snap at her. She wanted to be supportive, to be a good wife. Surely if she was always agreeable and kind, he would love her for it? Surely she should be as small and quiet as she could, no trouble at all, so she wouldn't be a burden?

She'd done that most of her life. She told herself she could do it again.

But suddenly, strangely, she didn't want to. She thought of how she'd felt so powerful in Nico's bed. How he'd encouraged her to stand up for herself, in everything from not feeling guilty over things that weren't her fault, to refusing to eat things she didn't like.

Be happy. Live your life only for yourself.

Okay, she thought, *I'll give it a try.*

So the next day, when Honora walked the dog, she didn't rush right back to the villa in case her husband finished work and wanted to see her. No. She would try to make herself happy.

She took the long coastal path and looked out at the sea.

She could see Le Sirenuse in the distance, the three lonely islands rising from the blue waves. One of the villa's staff members had told her that, according to ancient legend, the rocks had once been inhabited by sirens who'd seduced sailors to their own destruction.

Honora shivered as she looked at the three rocky islands in the distance. How awful to think that someone could be led to their own ruin, simply by following their heart's desire.

It felt good to be out of the villa, and not just falling asleep in a chair with a book in her lap, waiting for her husband to have time for her. Honora felt exhilarated to be in this village, to breathe this air, sweet with lemons and salty from the sea, that seemed so different from New York, or even the Hamptons.

As the days passed, she started talking to people and making friends. Once she tried it, she found it wasn't even hard. Many English-speaking tourists came to the Amalfi Coast, and Trevello's shopkeepers and inhabitants all spoke English to varying degrees, enabling her to chat with everyone, usually about the sweet-natured dog Figaro, who attracted love everywhere.

As the housekeeper rested her twisted ankle, Honora looked forward to walking her dog every day, hiking along the cliff-side path, even window-shopping in Trevello, looking for a ball gown.

Early morning was the best time to walk, she found, before floods of tourists arrived via buses or cruise ships. When the town was quiet, she could walk Figaro and hear his nails click against the cobblestones, as church bells echoed and shopkeepers swept their doorways and restaurant owners sprayed off their patios. She saw elderly women heading to church—stoop-shouldered, with handkerchiefs covering their hair—while other women of a similar age snuck back furtively to their homes, returning from midnight assignations, chic in Dolce & Gabbana and navigating the crooked streets in high heels.

She loved Italy!

Honora met an older lady of the first type coming up the hillside early one morning, pulling a small wheeled basket filled with groceries. She seemed to be struggling to lift it over the crooked curb in front of a tall gate and stone wall.

Honora hurried forward, Figaro trotting on his leash behind her, his tongue lolling happily. "Please, let me help," she said awkwardly in English, hoping the woman wouldn't think she was trying to steal her grocery basket.

The elderly woman smiled at her sheepishly. "*Grazie*. It is not so easy anymore." She looked at Honora's belly. "But you should not be lifting things…"

"I'm fine." She tilted her head, looking up at the large, decrepit villa above them on the cliff. "Do you work up there?"

She gave a low laugh. "It is worse than that. It is mine." She paused as a sad expression crossed her face. "For now…"

"Are you moving? That's a pity. Trevello is so lovely."

"I wouldn't leave by choice." The elderly woman looked down at her wrinkled hands. "Someone is trying to force me from my home."

"That's horrible!" Honora was indignant. "There ought to be a law!"

She helped the woman pull the heavy groceries past the gate and up the long, winding steps toward her faded house. It was not an easy journey. Even Figaro looked tired by the time they made it all the way up the many steep steps.

As Honora bid the elderly woman farewell, it crossed her mind that she'd ask their housekeeper if something could be done for her. Perhaps to have her groceries delivered?

Poor old lady with no family to take care of her, and her awful stepson trying to steal her home. When Honora had asked why her family didn't help, she'd learned that the woman's children had died when they were babies. Pregnant as Honora was, her heart broke even more.

After that, she made sure to check on her every day, just to say hello, but mostly to make sure the sweet old lady didn't break her leg trying to haul groceries up alone.

But one such morning, after nearly four weeks in Italy, changed everything.

It had started out so well. The proprietor of one of the

little shops had found Honora the ball gown of her dreams, handmade in Naples by his cousin, who'd come that morning to do the final touches on the fit. Her belly was huge now, she had to concede. As she left the shop, the owner and his cousin promised to have the dress delivered to the villa. Just in time too, because their formal reception was *tomorrow*.

Walking back up the cobblestoned road, the dog bounding happily behind her, Honora hummed happily to herself. Her husband had promised, absolutely *sworn*, that he'd finalize his business that afternoon. Apparently his acquisition of the Villa Caracciola was on the verge of a breakthrough. His team of lawyers had cracked the current owner's legal objections, apparently by some unorthodox means.

"Unorthodox?" she'd asked.

"Don't worry about it," he'd replied, smiling. "It just means we're going to win."

To celebrate, he was going to sail with her on his yacht to the isle of Capri. She was already dressed for the excursion, in maternity capri pants, a white bateau T-shirt, with a red scarf wrapped around her dark hair.

So after tomorrow night's formal reception, they'd be able to go home to New York. *Finally*. Her baby's due date was growing perilously close, less than a month away. She'd started visiting a doctor in Positano for checkups, just in case, but she wanted to be back in New York when she gave birth. Her grandfather kept sending messages, asking when she was coming home.

Honora blinked herself out of her thoughts when she saw the elderly woman, Egidia, standing outside her gate in Trevello, looking around anxiously. As soon as she saw Honora, with Figaro beside her, the woman blurted out, "Is it true your husband is Nico Ferraro?"

"Yes." She smiled. "Do you know him?"

The white-haired woman's face crumpled. "He is the one who is taking my home…"

Then she'd told Honora a story she'd hardly been able to believe. One she kept thinking about, over and again, for the rest of her dazed walk home.

"There you are," Nico said when she finally came inside. "Where have you been all this time?"

"Out." Squatting down, she let Figaro off his leash, and the little dog raced back to the kitchen.

Nico's forehead furrowed. He seemed confused by her cold tone, as well he should be—he'd never heard it before. "Are you ready to go for a little adventure?"

"Yes," she said quietly, feeling like she'd already had more adventure than she could stand. As she looked at Nico in the checkered hallway of the elegant villa, it was as if she were seeing him for the first time. He was darkly handsome, wearing a blue shirt with the top two buttons undone. His body was so powerful, his shoulders broad. She'd kissed every inch of his skin, as he had hers.

She'd thought she knew him. She'd only known the man she'd wanted him to be.

Frowning at her unusual reserve, he looked her over from her sandals to her capri pants, to the red scarf in her hair, then bent to kiss her on the cheek. "You look beautiful. Were you shopping in Trevello again?"

"I found a gown for the reception." She tilted her head. "I was walking Figaro. And talking to people in the village," she mumbled.

"Figaro?"

Did he really not know? "Luisa twisted her ankle a few weeks ago. Tripped on a stepstool. He's her dog. You haven't noticed her hobbling around the kitchen on crutches?"

Nico looked at her in surprise. "Is she? I didn't notice." He nuzzled her. "I should bring you to work for me," he said lazily. "You're better than a bloodhound. We'd get our deals done faster, and probably cheaper, too, if we knew everyone's secrets."

Honora stiffened. "It's not about ferreting out secrets. It just helps to know what people are going through."

"Helps what?"

"To know how to be kind, and comfort them through it."

Nico barked out a laugh, then sobered when he saw she was serious. Looking away, he said in a low voice, "I'm sorry. I just learned to see people's secrets differently."

"As weapons?"

He gave a brief nod. "In business, if you know your rival's priorities—or better yet, their guilty secrets—it's very useful. If you know someone is running out of cash, you can get them to drop their price because they're desperate. If you know secrets about their banker, their lawyer, you can convince them to do a shoddy job for their employer. If you—"

"I get it." Feeling sick, Honora looked at her husband in the grand foyer of the Italian villa. "So that's what you do? Blackmail people? Hurt them?"

"Blackmail?" Nico looked at her incredulously. "What do you think this is? Real estate isn't about making friends. It's a battle. If I'm disciplined, I win. If I'm not, if I'm weak, I'll be the one who's destroyed."

"You see sharing as weakness," she said slowly. "That's why when I told you about my parents, you said my secrets were safe with you."

He straightened. "I want you to feel safe. To know I'm on your side. I will never let anyone hurt you, Honora."

What about when he was the one who hurt her? she thought.

She was quiet as he drove them to the marina, where they boarded his yacht, the *Lucky Bastard*. She felt Nico's gaze, his full attention. But what she'd learned that morning hung like a dark cloud over the distant horizon.

Maybe Nico was right about knowledge being a weapon, she thought. Because what she'd heard about him from Egidia Caracciola felt like a bullet wound in her heart.

She had to confront him about it, but she feared she already knew what his reaction would be. And if she was right, their marriage might come crashing to the ground. She was afraid it would be the end of everything, because how could she spend the rest of her life with someone so heartless and cold?

The yacht crossed the Tyrrhenian Sea to Capri, the legendary playground for the wealthy just off the Italian coast. Around them, the yacht's staff bustled about, offering sparkling water and fruit, delicious meats and cheeses and freshly baked bread.

But for once, Honora had no appetite.

Nico remained close at her side, touching her hand, being charming, pointing out the sights—particularly the three rocky islands she'd looked at from a distance. "Le Sirenuse," he said. "Also called Li Galli. There's a story about sirens, luring lovestruck sailors to their doom…"

"I know," she said flatly. She felt tears burning the backs of her eyes and blinked fast, looking out at the bright blue horizon. As the yacht skimmed lightly over the water, the beautiful isle of Capri loomed large, and she knew she wouldn't be able to squelch her emotions for much longer. She turned her face to the sun and closed her eyes.

What else hadn't he told her?

Who *was* Nico Ferraro?

"Is everything all right, *cara*?" he asked in a low voice. Blinking, she tried to smile.

"Of course." But the words caught in her throat.

He clearly intended to make this afternoon special and romantic. When they arrived at the marina, he was quick to grab her red scarf when it got tugged away from her dark hair by the wind. Holding her hand, he helped her off the gangplank of the ship and along the dock into the charming seaside village. And he didn't let go of her hand.

As they explored the island together on foot, he was attentive, warm, sweet. But that only made her feel sadder as they wandered in and out of tiny shops, including, at his insistence, the fancy designer boutiques and jewelry stores that filled this exclusive, dreamy island.

Honora preferred the quaint little tourist shops. Trying to avoid his direct gaze, she bought some Limoncello liqueur and gardening gloves for her grandfather, some *cioccolato al limone* for Phyllis and a hoodie and snow globe for Emmie.

"All these gifts for others," her husband murmured, looking down at her, cupping her cheek. "I want to get something for you." He put his large hand gently on her belly. "What do they call it? A push present? I want to get you the best push present in the world, so if you go through pain giving birth to our child, you won't feel it, but you'll only remember the reward."

Honora looked at him, then said in a strangled voice, "*Our baby* is the reward."

His expression changed. "Of course. But I also want to get you a gift. Just for you." He grinned. "Think of it as recompense for all these weeks when I was so distracted."

He thought people's secrets were weapons to be used against them—even against his own family. He thought Honora wanted to get paid for giving birth to their child. He thought he could make up for his absence during their honeymoon by throwing money at her. All of it was adding up in strange ways. She swallowed hard.

"Are you hungry?" he asked. "It's early, but you didn't eat much lunch…"

"If you want," she said, still not meeting his eyes.

They ate dinner at a taverna on the edge of the sea, where she didn't even taste her *linguine con vongole*, and the conversation was stilted. She could feel his bewilderment, that even though he was trying so hard to please her, somehow, it wasn't working.

They finally returned to the yacht at twilight, and sailed back across the sea as the red and orange sun fell into the western horizon.

He pulled her beside the railing, where the staff couldn't hear. "What's going on, Honora?"

"Why do you think something's going on?" she said, evading him.

Nico looked down at her, so darkly handsome that her heart twisted in her chest. "I wanted today to be special. I hoped to buy you a gift you could treasure…"

Feeling the ache in her throat, she looked away at the dark glittering sea. "The gifts I treasure aren't things you can buy."

"Oh, come on," he said, trying to tease her. "A diamond tiara? Your own yacht? A green Ferrari to match your eyes?"

She said in a low voice, "That's not what I care about."

"What is it, then?" Red twilight was turning violet across the Tyrrhenian Sea as he looked down at her grimly. "Tell me what's wrong, Honora."

She took a deep breath.

"I want you to tell me why you're trying to hurt people. And don't tell me it has anything to do with business." She looked him in the eyes. "Why are you trying to destroy your own family?"

After all their days apart, Nico had wanted today to be special. He'd wanted to romance her, if he could not love her.

After weeks of frustration, his lawyers had finally found a way to force the sale of his father's ancestral home. Nico's stepmother had been vicious, keeping the villa tight in her grip, using every trick she could, calling in favors from old friends in law and government, even pulling in environmental and architectural objections. In the last month, Nico had spent millions of euros in legal fees, far more than the property was actually worth.

But now, finally Villa Caracciola would be his. His stepmother was out of money and out of options. The villa was her only asset. She had no choice.

It had been a long, hard fight, but it was nearly over.

Through it all, Nico had missed being able to enjoy his wife's company, since he'd seen her only at night, in the dark heat of their bed. He'd never intended for her to spend the days of their honeymoon alone, or for their time here to stretch to a month. But as he'd told her, real estate was a war, and this was one battle he did not intend to lose.

Now, he was eager to make up for lost time with Honora, with some grand gesture to delight her. And what better place than the famously romantic island of Capri?

Sailing across the sea in their yacht and walking the charming streets hand in hand with his beautiful wife—so lovely in her white T-shirt showing off her curves, and the red scarf pulling back her long, tumbling dark hair—should have been the most perfect day of their honeymoon.

Instead, the day had been useless. Honora, usually so loving and warm, had refused to even *look* at him.

Now, out of the blue, she'd attacked him like this.

Nico pulled away from her on the yacht's railing, feeling strangely hurt. He didn't understand what she was talking about, but he felt her harsh criticism, just when he'd least expected it.

"Trying to destroy my family?" he repeated, blinking in the twilight. "What are you talking about?"

"You never told me you had a stepmother!"

"Are you kidding? *Her?* She's not family."

"Of course she is." She lifted her chin. "No wonder you bought a villa so close to Trevello. You said you were going to knock down your father's ancestral home. You neglected to mention someone was still living in it—a sweet old lady!"

"Sweet old—" He stared at her, speechless. "You've got to be kidding. That woman is horrible. A snooty aristocrat who believes she's better than everyone else."

"If you ask me, you're the one who thinks you're better," she said coldly. "You make your own rules. You want what you want, and don't give a damn who gets hurt while you get it."

Nico stared at her, feeling sick as he stood on the deck of his yacht in the fading purple twilight. Honora's lovely eyes were hostile and angry—the eyes of an enemy. In his home. In his yacht. With his name. Carrying his baby inside her.

Beneath his feet, he could feel the sway of the waves unsettling him, making him feel like at any moment he could get knocked down.

How had it happened that his sweet, kind wife, the woman he'd thought would never challenge him or work against him, was hurling accusations from the same sensual lips he'd kissed so passionately?

"You don't know what you're talking about," he said in a low voice. "Egidia Caracciola is not some gentle, helpless old lady."

"No? She can't even carry her own groceries, and you're trying to drive her from her home without a cent!"

"It's not my fault my father left her a pile of debts."

Honora lifted her chin. Her green eyes glittered in the red sunset. "It *is* your fault, Nico, and you know it. You gathered up all his debts and then demanded that he pay them all in full at once. As his creditors never would have done."

"So what are you saying? That I killed him? That I caused his heart attack? You're doing her dirty work, Honora—using the very words she insulted me with, over his grave."

"She was probably upset, lashing out—"

"I'm the one who should be lashing out. Did you know I called my father after my mother's cancer diagnosis?" His heart was pounding, flooded with emotion he didn't want to feel. "The only time I ever asked him for anything. I begged for money to try to pay for an experimental treatment, and he refused. He said we were nothing to him. And she died."

Her expression changed. She whispered, "Maybe he didn't have the money…"

Nico looked away. "He was rich back then. He just didn't care. So I promised myself that someday I'd show him how it feels, to be desperate and poor and to ask your own blood for help, only to have the door slammed in your face."

"He hurt you," Honora said quietly.

"Yes."

"You've spent your whole life trying to get revenge."

"Yes."

"But your father is dead." She lifted her chin. "Why are you punishing *her*?"

When she put it like that, it did seem strange that Nico would go to such obsessive lengths to get revenge on an elderly woman he'd met only twice in his life. After all, he couldn't blame Egidia for his mother's death—at least not directly.

And yet something in his heart yearned to get the woman's attention, since he could no longer get his father's. He wanted to force his father's wife to admit she'd been wrong, and that she was sorry. So very, very sorry.

He set his jaw. "What do you know about her?"

"I met her a few weeks ago in Trevello while I was walking the dog. I helped her carry some groceries, and this morning she realized who I was."

He set his jaw. "She was probably targeting you all along, as a soft touch to try to get to me."

"No. She wasn't." She glared at him. "She has almost nothing, but you're trying to take her house."

"I did offer to pay her for it. It's not my fault she's forced me to play hardball."

"Is that what you call it? You didn't even *try* to go to court to legally claim your father's estate. He had no other children. That would have been kinder. No, instead you slowly ruined him, *humiliated* him, as you're now doing to her."

"You think I'd want to claim Arnaldo as a father after he rejected me? No. He made me a stranger so I'm taking his estate like a stranger. By force."

"And what about Egidia? His devoted wife of fifty years?"

Devoted. Nico realized he was trembling. "I don't give a damn. She's nothing to me."

His wife stared at him for a long moment in the darkness as their yacht approached the glittering lights of the Trevello marina. "You're lying. You *hate* her. Why? What did she ever do to you?"

Honora was right, Nico suddenly realized. He did hate Egidia Caracciola. With a passion. Gripping the railing, he turned away.

"I saw her with my father once, on the street in Rome. I was just seven years old. My mother pushed me forward, begged Arnaldo to recognize me as his son. Egidia wouldn't let him even *look* at me. She couldn't admit her husband had a bastard son. Because of her pride."

"Or maybe she was distracted with her own grief. She lost three sons of her own. Did you ever think of that?"

Nico blinked, turning to her. "What are you talking about?"

"I asked her why she was living alone in that old mansion with no one to help her. She said long before she lost her husband, she'd lost their three children as babies, one by one." Wrapping her hands protectively over her baby bump, Honora whispered, "Can you even imagine? Three?"

He stared at her, his heart pounding. Then he pushed away what was obviously an attempt at emotional manipulation. "She probably made it up. To try to get sympathy."

"How can you be so cold? Just go talk to her!"

"No." Nico's voice was like ice. The sunset that had been so vibrant and bright had turned dark shades of bruises and blood, and the sea now seemed deathly black. "Put her from your mind. She's not family. You are." He set his jaw, clenching his hands at his sides. "Don't let her drive a wedge between us, Honora. Do you want to be my wife?"

She sucked in her breath. "Now you're threatening to leave me?"

"I'm simply stating a fact." Nico looked at her, and felt nothing. "Either you're with me, or you're against me. You must choose."

"I choose you," she choked out. "Of course I do."

He hadn't realized he was holding his breath until he exhaled. He held out his arms, and after a brief hesitation, she walked into his embrace, leaning her cheek against his heart.

But as he stroked her hair, Nico had the unsettling feeling that something had changed between them.

His sweet wife had betrayed him, attacking him without warning. He would have to be on his guard from now on. Raise walls to protect himself. Make sure he didn't feel too much. Stay distant. Stay numb.

Because Nico would never let anyone hurt him, ever again. Not even her.

CHAPTER ELEVEN

THE NEXT EVENING, Honora looked at herself in the full-length mirror. She took a deep breath.

The formal gown she'd had made for her in Naples was simple but pretty. The length was short, as it was still August, and soft pink, with an overlay of beadwork. Her dark hair was in a chignon high on her head, glossy and sleek.

At over eight months pregnant, she felt like a whale, but her husband's eyes still lit up when he came into the bedroom. "You look beautiful, *cara*."

"Thank you." Her cheeks burned hot. Nico looked almost unbearably handsome to her. His powerful body was barely contained by the civilized, perfectly tailored tuxedo.

Reaching into his pocket, he pulled out a fistful of sparkling jewels. "I brought you a gift."

Stepping behind her, he placed a cold necklace of enormous rectangle-cut emeralds over her collarbone. As he attached the clasp, he lowered his head and kissed the crook of her neck, making her shiver with dangerous desire.

"Perfect," he said huskily.

She wondered if he would think her so perfect if he knew whom she'd invited to the ball tonight.

Honora faced him, her heart pounding. After his ultimatum on the yacht, he thought she'd given up the issue of his stepmother. But she could not let him keep going down the path he was on. It could only lead to the destruction of his soul. And hers.

Last night, after they'd returned to the villa, he'd kissed her with such sweet tenderness, stroking her body so slowly, so gently, taking his time, so when he'd finally brought her to aching fulfillment, she almost couldn't bear the intensity of her own joy.

But even then, beneath it all, she'd known she still had to stand up for what was right. She couldn't remain silently, passively married to a man who was so intent on destroying his own family. After all, if Nico couldn't forgive the stepmother who'd once been too lost in her own pain to do the right thing, how could Honora expect anything but the same for her and the baby—that they'd be punished or exiled for the slightest transgression?

Either you're with me, or you're against me. You must choose.

She was married to him, pregnant with his baby. She was in love with him. She was on Nico's side. Of course she was.

But sometimes, being on someone's side had to mean being able to tell them when they were wrong. Even if it made them angry. Even if it caused trouble.

If you don't like something, don't suffer in silence, he'd told her. *Be honest. Speak up.*

And that had just been about a plate of sautéed mushrooms. This was about the rest of their lives.

But she was afraid. More afraid than she'd ever been in her life. Inviting Egidia was a huge risk. Honora knew that if Nico could just see her, talk to her in person, they would finally reconcile. He would either forgive her and be glad, or—

Or he wouldn't.

"Nico." She swallowed hard. "There's something you should…"

"Yes?" He looked down at her expectantly.

Her courage failed her. She looked down, putting her hand on the cool, hard emeralds at her throat. "They're beautiful. You didn't have to do this."

"Of course I did. They match your eyes, and you deserve every luxury." Leaning forward, he whispered wickedly against her skin, "Especially after last night."

Her blush deepened as she remembered the previous night's passion. Every night of their honeymoon he'd found new ways to give her intoxicating pleasure.

She just prayed Nico would forgive her for the public ambush, and eventually understand why she'd had no choice but to do this, to make him face the past he'd gone to such lengths to avoid…

"Are you ready?" Nico murmured, holding out his arm.

"I hope so." Nervously, she took his arm. Would he still smile at her so warmly when the night was over?

Together, they left the master bedroom and went down the sweeping staircase of the Amalfi Coast villa as guests began to arrive.

They greeted each guest in the foyer, beneath the soaring crystal chandelier high overhead, and above it, the frescoes of cherubs. But there was no sign of Egidia. Honora felt more and more nervous as the minutes ticked by.

Nico seemed proud to introduce her to his glamorous European friends, many of whom were from Rome or farther away still—Milan, Paris, Athens. For once, Honora had no energy to feel insecure when she met the extravagantly thin, gorgeously dressed supermodels and heiresses and female tycoons. She was too anxious about the coming confrontation to care what strangers thought of her.

The villa's ballroom was as exquisite as a jewel box, filled with flowers, and a string quartet was playing music. Holding a crystal flute of sparkling water, Honora stood beside her husband as he spoke to a small group of people, switching from Italian to English for her sake. She tried to smile and nod and appear as if she were interested in their discussion, which was apparently about some land deal in Malaysia. She felt Nico's hand stroking her bare upper back. Her shoulders felt tense. Her gaze kept straying to the door.

Then she gave an intake of breath.

Nico noticed at once. He looked down at her with a bewildered frown. Then he followed her gaze. His body stiffened.

"What the hell—" His voice choked off in a strangled gasp as he saw the new guest in the ballroom's doorway.

"Forgive me," Honora said quietly. "I had no choice."

An elderly white-haired woman, round and slightly stooped, dressed in a formal gown that looked like couture, though it was two decades out of fashion, entered the room. Principessa Egidia Caracciola.

Nico's head was spinning.

For the last twenty-four hours, he'd been congratulating himself that he'd convinced his wife to stop fighting for his enemy, aka his stepmother, and to keep her loyalty where it belonged, with Nico. He'd tried to bind her to him more thoroughly, making love to her last night with agonizing slow gentleness—though it damn near killed him to go slow—and buying her an emerald necklace worth half a million euros, which had once belonged to a tsarina of Russia.

He'd introduced her to the cream of European society, which he'd bulldozed into with his wealth, power and charm. He wouldn't call them all friends, exactly, but they were entertaining, and useful, and anyway, it gave him satisfaction to think he'd earned his way into the aristocratic circle his father had tried to deny him.

For the last hour, he'd watched Honora, in her sparkling pale pink cocktail dress, her green eyes brighter than the emeralds at her throat, hold her own against them all, talking easily to even the most arrogant Milanese heiress. His heart had burst with pride for his beautiful, clever, kind wife.

Nico had started to relax again. Maybe he'd overreacted. Maybe he could still trust her. Maybe he didn't need to permanently be on his guard.

And now...this ambush!

He pulled Honora to the side. His jaw was tight. "Is this about revenge?" he said in a low voice, for her alone. "Is that why you invited her here? To win the argument? To hurt me?"

Honora's forehead furrowed.

"No, Nico," she said, looking bewildered. "I'm trying to help you make peace with your family. With yourself—"

"Peace!" He'd never heard anything more ridiculous. He felt like his heart was about to explode. He couldn't believe she would attack him like this, in such an underhanded fashion, trying to humiliate him in front of European society! What had he ever done to deserve this? Nothing! All he'd ever done was treat her like a queen!

With an intake of breath, he turned back to the grand doorway of the ballroom. Egidia Caracciola. His dead father's widow.

Their eyes met, and his whole body was engulfed in ice.

The ballroom seemed to fall silent, first the guests, then the musicians discordantly cutting off midsong. Nico knew there'd been gossip about the lengths he'd gone to, gathering up Prince Arnaldo's debts, then trying to force the sale of the Villa Caracciola. There had been commentary about the physical resemblance between the two men. Gossiping about secret parentage was always an enjoyable pastime for the jet set, but he'd thought he'd quashed that rumor. Now, he could feel new whispers building around him like wildfire.

"What have you done?" he said hoarsely.

"Please, Nico." Honora's lovely face looked scared. "Just give her a chance. I'm trying to help you. I love you."

Help. Yes, help him into public humiliation. *Love.* Love him into an early grave. He felt his chest tighten and squeeze and suddenly remembered how his father had keeled over of a heart attack last Christmas without warning.

You killed him! his stepmother had screamed at Nico at the funeral. *I hope you're proud of what you've done, you awful, awful boy!*

And now they were facing each other in person for only the third time in their lives. The first time had been on a street in Rome, when he was seven years old. His mother had pushed him forward, both of them hungry, and he'd been wearing clothes that were too small.

Please, Arnaldo, this is your son. Help us.

His stepmother, wearing her sleek designer clothes, had grabbed his father's arm and gasped, *No. I can't bear it. Tell me it's a lie.*

His father had said coldly, *It's a lie.*

Tension pulsed through Nico's body as he faced his stepmother. This was supposed to be a party. A celebration. Around the elegant ballroom, all his so-called friends, men in tuxedos and the women in shimmering gowns, were watching and listening with interest, the better to gossip about later.

He had to pull it together.

With an intake of breath, Nico walked forward, his traitorous wife trailing behind him. His guests parted, creating a path between him and the elderly Italian woman.

He stopped in front of her.

"Buonasera, signora," he said with a coolly courteous nod. "Welcome to my home."

Lifting her chin, his stepmother replied in the same cool tone, "Thank you for inviting me."

But you weren't invited, Nico raged inside. He forced

himself to smile, to take his wife's hand. "We are so glad you could come."

Egidia stood in front of him in her dated gown, her white hair carefully done, and her bright coral lipstick not quite straight on her feathered lips. She drew herself to her full height, which wasn't much, and looked at him, her forehead creased.

Then she sucked in her breath. Her eyes roamed his face, then filled with tears.

"You do look like him," she whispered. "I didn't want to believe it. But you look like Arnaldo when he was young." Her wrinkled face crumpled, as if she were about to cry. "All this time I never realized…" She choked out, "Villa Caracciola should be yours. I will no longer fight it. You are his son. *You are.*"

The old lady moved forward, as if to embrace him. Nico tried to step back, holding up his flute of sparkling water like a shield. But it was not enough.

"Which means…" Lifting up on her tiptoes, she threw her arms around him with a sob. "You are mine…"

Gasps and exclamations rippled through the crowd. Some of the guests had tears in their eyes, obviously enjoying the scene, as if it were some melodrama on television, the reprobate prodigal son being welcomed with open arms by his dead father's widow.

Looking around him, at the way his party had been taken hostage, and his whole life story revealed to people who might somehow use it against him someday, Nico tried to smile and pretend he was calm and pleased. But inside, he was seething with rage greater than he'd ever known. He felt embarrassed, angry, ashamed.

And looking at his beaming wife beside him—so beautiful, *so deceitful*—he knew just who was to blame.

CHAPTER TWELVE

AGAINST ALL ODDS, she'd succeeded.

As Honora watched her husband and his elderly step-mother embrace, tears filled her eyes.

She'd taken a terrifying gamble, inviting the woman here, praying that he could finally forgive her and let go of the resentment and anger poisoning his soul. She'd been so scared that Nico would refuse, that he'd make a scene and toss Egidia from the house, and that he would hate Honora for what she'd done. But she'd been brave enough to risk it anyway.

And this was her reward.

"I'll tell my lawyers the Villa Caracciola should be yours," Egidia Caracciola said tearfully.

"Thank you," Nico said. Looking around at his guests, he added, "I will, of course, pay you the estate's full value."

"That's not necessary—"

"I insist." All the guests smiled approvingly at this ob-vious generosity, of each side making a concession, the picture of family compromise and unity.

Coming forward, Honora embraced her stepmother-in-law. "I'm so happy," she whispered. "For both of you."

"Me too." The white-haired woman smiled at her through her tears. "All this time I was fighting him, I thought I was protecting my husband's memory. But I was wrong. Nicolo is actually his son. He is the one I must protect now."

Honora glanced at Nico to see if he'd heard. He was watching them, his handsome face impassive. He abruptly gave his stepmother a smile.

"May I get you some champagne?"

For the rest of the evening, Honora felt a warm glow of happiness. After the awful last twenty-four hours, she felt like everything would be all right. Their family was healing. The future was bright—for all of them.

The reception had been a greater success than she'd dared to hope, and she was grateful to all his friends who'd come to wish them well. By the time the last guest had finally left at around two in the morning, trailing off into the cool August night beneath a black sky swept with stars, Honora had spoken with every single person who'd attended. From the Milanese automobile heiress—she was actually very sweet—to the pompous duke with dyed black hair—he told such funny jokes—and thought they were all lovely, lovely people. Honora was happy to call them friends.

As the door finally closed on the last guests, collected by their chauffeurs to head back north to Rome, Honora felt like she'd never been so happy. She turned to face her husband, expecting gratitude, or maybe praise, but not needing either. All she wanted was to share their joy, maybe by him taking her in his arms for a kiss.

But once they were alone, Nico's whole demeanor changed.

"How could you."

His voice was a low growl, his powerful body in the tuxedo standing silhouetted in front of the wide windows facing the sea, bathing him in a pool of silvery moonlight.

Honora didn't understand. She came forward in the pale pink beaded dress, the emerald necklace sparkling coldly against her collarbone. "What do you mean? Everything's better now, isn't it?"

He turned on her, his face coldly furious. "Better?" He let out a low, sharp laugh. "I suppose. At least now I know I can't trust you. Ever. Again."

She felt an icy chill down her spine.

"But the two of you made up," she whispered. "You forgave her. You said—"

"What was I supposed to say, surrounded by guests? Did you expect me to knock the woman down? You knew I could not make a scene. I could not show weakness, or even anger that might reveal how much that woman hurt me."

"But you made peace." Honora felt dizzy. "Egidia accepted you're her husband's son. Even though it clearly hurts her, because it proves that her husband was unfaithful, and also it must make her feel heartbroken about her own babies that died. But she still claimed you. In front of everyone."

He snorted. "Because she knew my lawyers were at her throat, and she'd soon lose the villa anyway. She thought she could manipulate me, with this *tender family reunion*." He said the words as a sneer. "And it worked. I had no choice but reciprocity. Now I'll be paying her a tidy little bundle, whereas before she would have been left with nothing."

Honora stared at him in horror. "How can you be so cynical?"

"How can you be so gullible? Can't you see how the world really is?"

"Just your own awful world you've created for yourself, where you believe the worst of everyone!"

"And they so rarely disappoint me." Nico's eyes were as cold as a wintry midnight sea. "I should have known you would be the same."

Honora felt a sharp ache in her throat.

"I was trying to help you," she whispered. "I wanted you to forgive your stepmother, and your father too, so you wouldn't be so angry all the time." She abruptly looked away. "I thought if I could heal your heart, then maybe you could love us. The baby and me."

Love us. The longing in her voice as she quietly spoke those words seemed to echo in the ballroom. Wishing. *Begging.*

Nico glared at her, then lifted his chin.

"Why shouldn't I be angry?" His voice was dangerously low. "My wife stabbed me in the back."

Standing in the ballroom, shadowy and dark but for the silvery moonlight flooding the six tall windows, Honora felt forlorn, suddenly shivering in her fancy beaded dress. She saw confetti at her feet, which had been tossed earlier by their friends, saw some cake that had been smashed by someone's shoe into the marble floor. The remnants and trash of the party, like the bitter aftertaste of earlier joy, were all around.

The ballroom was starting to spin. She put a hand to her forehead, trying to breathe. "I never meant to… But you seemed glad!"

His cruel, sensual lips curled. "I lied." He narrowed his eyes. "And I'll never trust you again. Never."

Honora stared at him in the harsh, cold silvery-green moonlight.

She felt shaken to the core. He saw her as his enemy now, she realized—all because she'd tried to heal him.

Did Nico really have no love inside his soul? No ability to care for anyone but himself?

What kind of husband would that make him? What kind of father?

Nico Ferraro is a selfish bastard. Benny's words came back to haunt her. *He doesn't care for anyone but himself. And sooner or later he's going to hurt you. A man like that can do nothing else.*

Shivering, Honora wrapped her arms around her baby

bump in the sparkly, pretty cocktail dress. "So I'm your enemy now?"

"You ambushed me. Betrayed me."

She lifted her gaze. "And how do you intend to punish me?"

Setting his jaw, Nico turned to a nearby table. He poured himself a drink of Scotch from a nearly empty bottle. He drank a long sip and didn't answer.

She watched him in despair. "I thought you weren't going to drink as long as I was pregnant."

"And I thought you were on my side." He took another sip. "Seems we're both a disappointment."

She had the sudden memory of her parents' arguments when she was a child, as her mother had raged at her father over his drinking, the two of them clashing and blaming each other. Honora had always felt so small, hiding in a corner or outside the doorway.

After one very loud fight when she was nine years old, her mother had taken Honora back to her childhood home. *I never should have married him*, she'd overheard her mother sob late that night in the kitchen. And Granddad, putting his hand on her shoulder, had replied sadly, *You never should have gotten pregnant before you knew what he was.*

He hadn't known Honora was in earshot. But as she'd crept away to her sleeping bag down the hall, she'd known her parents' unhappiness was her fault, because she had been born. Later that night, her mother had found her crying.

She blinked. "I would give anything to see my mother again," she said quietly. "And my father. I understand better now. I wish I could tell them that. And that I'll always love them." She lifted her gaze. "I wonder if that's what you were wanting this whole time, Nico. Not revenge. *Connection*. For your father to acknowledge you. And your stepmother.

It was never about the villa. I think you were just trying to get their attention. I think you wanted...to be a family."

He stared at her, aghast. "Are you out of your mind? I hated them. I vowed to destroy them. And I have."

Honora's shoulders slumped.

Feeling like a burden as a child, she'd done everything she could to be loving and kind and giving, even to the point of eating things she didn't like, and doing things she didn't want to do.

But Nico, feeling unloved, had gone the other way. He wanted to punish anyone and everyone. And he would never stop. Never forgive.

"Now I know I can't trust you, I'm not sure how our marriage can succeed." He drank another gulp of Scotch as he looked out toward the dark moon-swept sea. He looked back at her, his face in shadow. "And it must. For the baby."

Honora's hands froze over her belly. She felt the delicate sparkling beadwork, rough beneath her fingertips.

I'm not sure how our marriage can succeed. And it must. For the baby.

She looked down at her baby bump.

Did she want her daughter to spend her whole life feeling as Honora had—that her parents were trapped in a cycle of misery and blame, all for the apparent benefit of their miserable, blamed child?

She had the sudden memory of her mother's beautiful, sad face when she'd found Honora crying that night in her sleeping bag.

Oh, my darling, don't cry. It's my fault, all my fault. We'll go back home tomorrow. Her young, heartbroken mother had started crying too, and hugged her tight. *Just be happy, Honora. Please.* Her voice had caught. *You have to be happy. For all of us.*

Honora suddenly looked up.

"It was never my fault," she whispered.

Nico's head turned, and she saw his sudden scowl, edged with silver light. "What do you mean? Of course it was. You're the one who invited her here."

Honora shook her head, lost in her own realization. "My parents made mistakes. They did the best they could. But I was never to blame. I was just a baby." She looked down, her hand resting protectively on her own unborn child. "I'll never do that to you," she whispered. "Never."

"What the hell are you talking about?"

She looked at him in wonder. "My whole life, I've felt like I didn't deserve to be happy, or speak out for the things I wanted." She shook her head. "You helped me learn to stand up for myself."

"And you turned against me."

"I was never against you, Nico," she said quietly. "I'm always on your side, even now, though you can't see it. I love you." She looked down. "But you'll never love me back."

Nico's posture changed. His dark eyes looked haunted.

"Love was never part of our arrangement," he said in a low voice. "But I didn't want to hurt you. I thought if I romanced you, with passion and gifts—"

She gave him a sad smile. "I know."

He set his jaw. "But *trust*, watching each other's back— that's what I expected in our marriage. And you couldn't even uphold your end of the bargain. That's what your so-called *love* is good for."

Standing in the ballroom of this elegant Italian villa, pregnant with a much-desired child, married to a handsome billionaire and draped in jewels, Honora had never felt so sad and alone.

She thought of how her mother had loved her, so much that Bridget had given up her own chance for happiness, for her child's sake.

What would have happened if her mother had left her father that night for good, and never gone back? Could

Bridget have learned to be happy? Could her father have cleaned up his act? Would they both still be alive today—blessed to live long enough to learn to do better?

Honora suddenly saw her choice clearly.

Would she stay with a man who considered her an enemy if she said he'd made a mistake? Would she teach her daughter to feel like a burden? Teach her that families should be filled with anger and blame, rather than forgiveness and love? Teach her that wives stayed and put up with misery, no matter what?

No, she thought. No.

"You have no love in your heart," she whispered. "Not for me. Not for anyone. No love. No forgiveness. Nothing."

"It's who I am," he said coldly. "You knew that when you married me."

"But I thought—" She took a deep breath. "It doesn't matter. I can't live like this anymore."

His mouth fell open. He quickly recovered. "You can't leave. Under the terms of the prenup, you'll get almost nothing."

"You think I care about that?" she choked out.

"Everyone cares about money, no matter what they say." His dark eyes glittered. "Money is power, and power is everything."

She gave a laugh that was more like a sob. "Money? Power? It's *love* that matters, Nico. Loving your family, but also loving yourself. It's about being kind and helping each other. Because living can be hard, and everyone has secret bruises and broken hearts they try to hide."

Nico looked at her coldly. "I don't."

Honora stared at him. The pain in her throat felt radioactive. "I realize that now. Nothing I can do will help you or heal you. Because you don't want to be helped. You don't want to be healed."

His dark eyebrows lowered. He walked toward her, and

his handsome face came fully into the moonlight. He looked younger than he was. His expression seemed strangely lost.

"You can't leave." His voice was uncertain.

"I have to," she whispered, "or you'll drag me into your darkness. Drag all of us."

Stiffening, he glared at her. "Just because I protect myself and don't forgive my enemies. Just because I seek justice. Just because I'm angry you went behind my back and—"

She held up her hand, stopping him midtirade. She felt tired and so, so sad. "Maybe I shouldn't have done it. But I can't let you ruin my life—and our daughter's."

"Our daughter!" He drew back, his expression shocked. "I would never do anything to hurt her!"

Honora took a deep breath, fighting to be reasonable and kind when she felt so hurt. "If that's true, you can still be her father."

"Big of you," he said, sneering.

"I'll make sure she knows you never abandoned her. You can visit her anytime you like. I'll wait until after she's born before I start divorce proceedings."

Nico's voice caught. *"Divorce?"*

She looked at him quickly. His darkly handsome face was as inscrutable as ever. She must have imagined emotion in his voice. He would never feel anything, certainly not hurt, let alone despair.

"I won't ask for alimony. I'll take all the blame," she said. "She'll live with me, but legally, we'll share custody. As long as you're good to her. And don't turn her into your enemy, and try to punish her, or push her utterly out of your life any time she disappoints you."

"You really think I would do that?" he whispered.

Honora took a deep breath, blinking back tears.

"It's what you do," she said.

Turning, she left the ballroom. She was proud of herself

that she didn't fall apart, but walked away steadily, without looking back. Pride was all she had to hold on to, and a quiet, desperate hope that someday, somehow, she might climb out of this misery.

I have to stand up for what is right, she repeated to herself desperately, her hands clenched. *To truly love my daughter, I also have to love myself.*

But it was hard for her to even imagine ever being happy, as she left the only man she'd ever loved behind, in the dark, forlorn ballroom where, just hours before, she'd thought they had a future ahead of them of limitless joy.

Nico had never imagined she'd just *leave*.

The villa was dark as he stood in the ballroom. A few minutes later, he heard her final footsteps and the slam of the front door. It crossed his mind to worry about how she would travel, whether she'd be safe. He paced, then called his security chief, who was staying in the carriage house. "My wife is heading for the garage. Take her anywhere she wants to go. Wake the pilot if necessary. Just go with her, Frank. Keep her safe."

But as Nico hung up, his lips twisted bitterly. Why was he worried about her? In the short month that they'd lived here, Honora had made friends everywhere, both inside this house and in the surrounding villages. She would be safe. Everyone loved Honora, because she loved everyone first.

And she'd said she loved *him*. He'd thought he could trust her, that their marriage would last through anger and arguments and pain. He'd never imagined she'd just…disappear.

Or maybe he had. Nico took a deep breath. Some part of him, deep inside, had always been afraid to fully trust her. He'd known he'd always be on the outside, even of his own family.

Nico carefully set down the glass of Scotch. He'd drunk very little—it had been mostly for show, to prove to her that he could defy her, too. Perhaps to prove it to them both, after the way she'd humiliated him in front of their guests.

I was trying to help you. I wanted you to forgive your stepmother, and your father too, so you wouldn't be so angry all the time. I thought if I could heal your heart, then maybe you could love us. The baby and me.

Feeling numb, he pushed the thought away. He slowly walked through the wreckage of the ballroom, with the mess of food, dropped napkins, used plates, colorful confetti and the pile of brightly wrapped wedding gifts. Gifts. How he hated gifts! As if an emerald necklace could ever make a difference, could make her stay!

Grabbing one wedding present wrapped in silvery sparkly paper with a big bow, he turned and smashed it against the wall. Whatever was inside broke into a thousand chiming shards, like crystal.

It didn't make him feel better. Neither did the early phone call he got a few hours later, as he was trying and failing to sleep in the big bed alone.

"I just got a phone call from Egidia Caracciola's lawyer," his head lawyer told him happily. "I don't know what you did, but she apparently left him a message late last night, as she was leaving your party. She'll be coming into his office this afternoon to sign the papers, transferring the Villa Caracciola to you, free and clear. She's not even asking for payment."

"Pay her the full market value," Nico said tightly.

"But it's not necessary—"

"Do it," he said, and hung up.

Dawn was rising over the eastern horizon, soft and pink. Nico felt restless, trapped in the villa, especially as the villa's staff began arriving to tidy up from the night before.

He longed to go for a run, but the Amalfi Coast was rocky and steep, not like the flat shoreline of the Hamptons. Hiking the cliffs and mountains, with their gorgeous view of the sea for miles, would have to do.

Pulling on a T-shirt and shorts and running shoes, he pushed himself as fast as he could, climbing and descending the rocky path, watching the ground so he did not stumble and fall off the edge to his death. His mind was carefully blank of everything but survival.

He went five miles, brutally pushing himself into the mountains as the sun climbed the wide Italian sky. When he reached the top, he looked back at the vast blue sea. The world was fresh and new and he'd never felt so worn-out and old.

Had she ever been his to lose?

I love you, Nico.

He could still remember how her eyes had glowed so dreamily when she'd first spoken the words. And the way her light had faded in his weeks of silence, as he'd never said the words back to her. How could he, when he didn't know what love was? When his heart was stone?

Honora deserved better. Both she and their baby deserved more than a man who had nothing to offer except cold, hard cash.

A noise came from the back of his throat, and he suddenly stumbled over the steep rocky path. Looking down the rocky slope toward Trevello, he saw his father's ancestral villa, the one he'd wanted for so long, and fought so hard to possess.

I wonder if that's what you were wanting this whole time, Nico. Not revenge. Connection. *For your father to acknowledge you. And your stepmother. It was never about the villa. I think you were just trying to get their attention. I think you wanted to be a family.*

No. Ridiculous. He clawed through his hair. What kind of feeble thing would that be, for Nico to still be trying to get the attention of the people who'd hurt and abandoned him as a child? No. He wasn't that weak or spineless. He'd done it purely for vengeance.

And now he had it. His stepmother was giving the villa to him, as a gift. Last night, she'd publicly acknowledged him as her deceased husband's son.

But looking at the Villa Caracciola clinging to the cliff, Nico didn't feel the happiness and pride he'd craved. Setting his jaw, he descended to the villa's gate.

The door was dangling open. Apparently Egidia Caracciola had already left. It was empty.

As empty as he felt.

His shoulders hurt. He felt bone-weary. And something more. Something he'd spent his whole life trying not to feel.

He felt sad.

But as he started to turn away, he heard a noise. Peeking past the gate, he saw the elderly widow collapsed across the steep, crooked stone steps. She was still wearing her ball gown from last night.

Was she dead?

With an intake of breath, Nico rushed forward. He only exhaled again when he discovered she was, in fact, still alive.

Seeing him, Egidia whimpered, "My leg... I think it's broken."

He reached for his phone, only to remember he hadn't brought it on his hike. "I'll go get help."

"No, please, don't leave me." Her voice was a quiet sob. "I've been out here all night. I thought I would die alone..."

"Where's your phone?"

She gestured wildly to a dense thicket of trees farther down the treacherous hill. "Somewhere—over there—I think," she gasped. "After I tripped, I couldn't find it. I... tried."

Her breathing was uneven, her voice weak with her cheek pressed down against the stone. Nico felt a surge of worry. He kept his voice calm. "I'll find it. What does it look like?"

"It's silver, a clutch bag."

He strode to the copse of trees, looking around with a swiftly pointed gaze, and soon found the 1990s-style bag and the barely more modern phone tucked inside it. Turning it on, he immediately phoned for medical assistance. Then he returned to kneel beside her.

"The ambulance is on the way. Everything's going to be fine," he said gently. "Can I help you get more comfortable?"

Egidia's face was filled with pain and panic, but she nodded. He slowly helped her turn over, so her face wasn't pressed into the stone steps. He flinched when he saw her fractured leg bone, stretching her skin. Following his gaze, she tried to laugh.

"Serves me right. I should have sold you this villa last year, after Arnaldo died. The truth is, the stairs are too much for me."

She said the words lightly, but he saw the beads of sweat on her forehead.

"I'm sorry I made you fight so hard," he said quietly. "I wasn't nice."

She looked at him quickly. "Neither was I." Her breathing came quick and shallow. "It was hard for me to admit that my husband had a baby with the maid while I was still mourning all the sons we'd lost."

"Honora—" Nico's throat closed around her name "—told me how you've suffered."

Her rheumy eyes filled with tears. "Three little boys. Two lost before birth. The other died before he was a month old. All had the same genetic disorder. After that, we made sure to have no more children. And then…" She looked down. "Then your mother ambushed us on the street in Rome. She pushed you forward, a sweet, dark-haired boy, and said Arnaldo was your father. He told me it was a lie, that your mother was just trying to get money. I wanted so desperately to believe him." She grasped his hand. "And you are the one who suffered for it. I'm sorry."

Nico felt a strange tightness in his chest. "So it wasn't because I seemed unworthy? Useless?"

"Unworthy?" she gasped. "I looked at you on the street, this proud, black-eyed boy, and I wanted so badly for you to be mine. I would have done anything. All I could think of was how my own body had betrayed me, and would not give me what I wanted so badly." She swallowed. "I couldn't see past my own pain. And Arnaldo…he must have been ashamed."

Nico stared at her.

"It was never about me, was it?" he said slowly. She shook her head.

"You were an innocent child, caught up in the lies of adults. When I saw you last night, I was finally forced to admit you were his. And I hated myself for letting my own insecurities and grief keep me from loving you long ago. As every child should be loved." She tried to smile. "You are the brother of the sons I lost."

In the distance, he could hear the siren of the coming ambulance. In the rhythm of the sound, he heard Honora's voice: *My parents made mistakes. They did the best they could. But I was never to blame. I was just a baby.*

"Please, forgive me," Egidia gasped as the paramedics hurried past the gate toward them. Looking down at her, his injured, elderly stepmother, who'd spent the entire night stretched out on cold stone steps, alone and scared, he put his hand gently on her shoulder.

"Only if you'll forgive me, too."

With a sob, she whispered, "Bless you." The paramedics stabilized her leg and loaded her carefully on the stretcher. "And your sweet wife…"

"I'll call the hospital later to make sure you're all right," was the best he could manage. But as he watched the ambulance depart, his heart felt strange.

It felt…lighter.

After all these years of being numb, of priding himself on his hard heart, he watched the ambulance disappear up the narrow cobblestoned street and felt like a burden had suddenly been lifted. Not completely, but just enough for him to be made aware of how heavy it had been all along.

He'd thought his father and stepmother had made some judgment about him when he was a child, that they had found him lacking. But their reasons for rejecting him had had nothing to do with him. They'd been dealing with struggles of their own.

Was it possible that all the times he'd felt ignored, unwanted, an outsider in his own home, it hadn't been about him at all, but about other people's insecurities and pain? His father's shame? His stepmother's anguish? His mother's poverty and heartbreak?

Had Honora been right? All this time he'd thought he wanted revenge, had he really just been hungering for connection, to know his place in the world, to be recognized and seen?

He'd always believed that emotions were a sign of weakness. Anger was all he'd allowed himself. Was it possible that being courageous enough to feel joy, sadness and everything in between was the biggest strength of all?

It's love *that matters, Nico. Loving your family, but also loving yourself.*

Honora's sweetness, her kindness, her passion…all the times she'd sacrificed so much, and risked even more, in her amazing determination to make Nico happy, to make him *whole*—

His heart was pounding. He felt overwhelmed with emotion. All around him, soft golden sunlight seemed to glow over the village of Trevello with a kind of magic as he thought of her. He could almost imagine her on this street, helping Egidia with her groceries, walking the house-keeper's little white dog, talking to everyone, smiling and kind…

Nico sucked in his breath.

He loved her, he realized. He was totally and completely in love.

This was what love meant. Honora was his *family*. His other half, his better half. He needed her. He would die without her.

With a sharp intake of breath, Nico turned and ran up the hillside. He had to talk to her. Now.

Reaching his villa, he threw himself into a cold shower to wash off the sweat. Pulling on a shirt and trousers, he remembered his private plane was still in New York. Grabbing his phone, he saw he'd gotten a text from Frank Bauer to say that Honora had arrived safely, and he'd dropped her off at her grandfather's apartment at her request.

Dialing a number, Nico told his assistant to charter a jet to New York immediately. After he hung up, he stared at the phone, trying to work up the nerve to call Honora. He yearned to tell her everything. To throw himself on her mercy and beg for another chance.

But what if she said no? What if she said he'd hurt her so badly that she couldn't love him again? His hand shook as he hesitated. Being in love was terrifying. She held his life in her hands.

I hope you fall in love with her, Nico. Wildly and desperately. Lana Lee's vindictive words floated back to him. *And I hope you'll suffer for the rest of your life when she never, ever loves you back.*

His phone suddenly rang in his palm, making him jump. The number on screen belonged to Honora's grandfather, Patrick. He snatched it to his ear.

His former gardener's voice was terse. "Honora's in labor. We're at the hospital. She wanted me to let you know. And to tell you that everything is fine."

Even now, Honora was worried about his feelings? His heart was pounding. "*Is* everything fine?"

Silence fell at the other end, then the old man said, "Look, I don't know what you did to her... She says she doesn't want you here." He paused. "But you should come."

"Why are you telling me that? Going against her wishes?"

"Because, well, damn it, you're family."

And he hung up.

Nico stared at the dead phone in his hand.

You're family.

Those simple words cleared out the cobwebs of his mind, exploding the stone walls around his heart, making everything very clear.

Honora was in labor with his baby. Possibly too early. Possibly dangerously so. Terror looped through him.

Grabbing his passport and wallet, Nico ran to the garage. Jumping into the closest car, he started it with a roar, pressing on the gas, heading to the airport where the charter waited, praying he wasn't too late.

Whatever happened, he had to be there. To take care of them. To show them he lived for them. That he'd die for them.

He loved them.

CHAPTER THIRTEEN

IT WAS TOO early for labor. Three weeks too early.

Honora's heart was pounding erratically as she sat in the hospital bed in Queens, in counterpoint to the rat-a-tat of her grandfather's leather soles as he paced by the window. No matter how many times the doctor and nurses had re-assured her that her baby's heartbeat seemed healthy and strong, and that the labor hadn't been caused by anything she'd done, she was scared.

She'd been on Nico's private plane crossing the Atlantic when she'd first felt contractions. Could the elevation change or pressurized cabin have somehow set off labor? Or had it been caused by the anguish of leaving the only man she'd ever loved?

"Please, baby," she whispered, her hand on her belly. "Please be all right."

"Don't you worry," Granddad said gruffly, stopping his pacing. "Everything is going to be fine."

She felt a catch in her throat. "What if it's not?"

"Your doctor seems like a pretty smart lady, and she said babies come early all the time." He gave a rueful smile. "They say the baby's lungs should be fine, and if there's any problem, they can scoop her up and take her straight to the NICU... Aw, Honora! Don't do that!"

She'd burst into tears. Sitting on the edge of the bed, he patted her hand. "It'll be all right...you'll see."

"But it's my fault…"

He looked astonished. "How?"

Honora looked up at him miserably. "I have been too upset. I've been crying for hours—and I was on a plane. I should have known better. After everything Mom and Dad went through, I shouldn't have married him when I knew he couldn't love me!"

"Stop right there." His hand tightened over hers. "If anyone's to blame for your parents' marriage, it was me. I shamed your mother into marrying him, and hoped he'd grow into his responsibility. But it didn't turn out, though they both tried. And then—" he blinked fast "—I did the same to you. Hauling my hunting rifle over to Nico's beach house like an old fool."

She stared at him in astonishment. Was her grandfather…crying?

"I'm so sorry, Honora," he whispered. "I never should have done that. I should have listened to you. Trusted you to figure out what was right." He gave a tremulous smile. "I'm sorry."

Shocked, she put her hand on his shoulder. "You were trying to help." Thinking of how she'd tried to help Nico, she looked down. "But sometimes you can't help. Sometimes there's nothing you can do, except love someone from a distance."

Looking up, he said, "You're right. How did you get to be wiser than me?" He tried to smile. "You've always had such a big heart. So eager to help everyone. You love people more than they deserve. Me most of all." He looked up, his eyes full of tears. "I'm so proud of you, Honora. You should know that. How much I…love you."

She couldn't have been more shocked if he'd taken off his boot and thrown it at her.

"You…" Her throat closed.

His eyes were watery. "I never was good at saying that, was I? Or showing it. But I've always loved you, kid."

Her grandfather loved her. The thought was like a warm hug. He hadn't just been taking care of her out of his sense of duty. She'd never been a burden. He loved her.

"I love you too," she choked out, and he hugged her.

Patrick drew back, smiling. "Now, I'm about to meet my new great-grandbaby, who I already know is going to be the brightest, feistiest, most loving child. Just like her mother." His green eyes, so much like her own, glowed beneath his bushy gray eyebrows. "And if that husband of yours can't see what he's missing, he doesn't deserve either of you."

A sudden longing for Nico went through her heart. As she sat in the hospital room, she looked out the window. Outside, it was twilight. Fading red light slanted through the half-open blinds over the sterile equipment and easy-wash floor.

"Oh," she choked out, tensing as she felt a new labor pain start to rise.

As Honora started to gasp with pain, her grandfather rose quickly to his feet. "I'll get the doctor, tell her you want an epidural after all—"

"It's too late," she panted. "They said it's too late." She gasped another breath. "I can handle it—"

And suddenly she knew she could. After all the hard things she'd done in her life, she now knew she was tough and brave enough to handle anything. It was love that made her strong. Love for her baby. Love for her grandfather.

Love for herself.

But she couldn't stop wishing if only Nico could have been part of their lives! If only he'd been able to open his heart!

She would go on without him, living in her old bedroom of her grandfather and Phyllis's apartment, until she graduated from college and could afford one of her own. But it wasn't the life she'd wanted.

If Nico had given her the chance, she would have tried to mend his heart. In a strange way, loving him had helped her mend her own. She would have given anything—

She gasped as her body shook with pain. Her hand tightened on her grandfather's, making him flinch. But she couldn't loosen her grip as the agony built, worse than anything she'd ever known, overwhelming her until she cried out.

"Doctor!" her grandfather shouted. "Nurse!" Pulling away, he rushed to the door in a panic. "Please, someone, my granddaughter needs *help*—"

And suddenly, in the corner of her hazy vision, she saw a large, dark figure push into the room. Not a doctor. Not a nurse.

"Cara."

Honora looked up with a gasp.

Was she hallucinating?

Like a miracle, she saw her husband. He rushed to her bedside, and she saw that his clothes were wrinkled, his jaw unshaven, and he had deep hollows beneath his eyes. But as he leaned forward to take her hand, his dark eyes glowed.

"I'm sorry I'm late. Oh, my darling," he whispered, kissing her sweaty temple. "I'm so sorry."

"What are you doing here?" she choked out. "I told you we're through—"

But even as she spoke the words, she gripped his hand desperately.

"I'm here now." Nico glanced back at her grandfather. "I'm here for her."

Clearly relieved, Granddad nodded, then hurried to join Phyllis in the waiting room.

"You don't know what you're—" Honora began, but then couldn't speak anymore against the flood of pain.

Her husband didn't flinch, no matter how hard her grip became. He didn't look away. He looked straight into her eyes, letting her crush his finger bones without giving the slightest evidence it hurt him. He seemed unbreakable, and as she closed her eyes, lost in pain, she could dimly hear his low voice, telling her how powerful she was, that he was in awe of her strength, that she was an amazing woman, an incredible mother. That he loved her.

As the pain slowly ebbed, letting her breathe normally again, Honora looked at him.

"What did you just say?"

He smiled, and his dark eyes looked emotional, even tender. "Hello, *cara*."

Honora felt a different sharp pain, this time in her heart. Had he followed her all the way to New York City just to tempt her, to torment her with what she could not have? It had nearly killed her to leave him in Italy, even knowing it was the right thing to do. She would no longer settle for second best. She could not give her life to a man who was incapable of loving her.

So had she imagined his words?

"What—what are you doing here?"

"I finally figured out what present to give you. The only gift you'd ever care about."

He still thought he could buy her? Her rising hope crashed to the floor. "I don't care about presents."

"I never liked them either. Until now. Because I've found something I really, really want to give you." Holding her hand, he came in close.

"My heart," he whispered. "For you and the baby. I want to give you my heart." His eyes had a suspicious gleam as he tried to smile. "The truth is, I already have."

She looked at him in amazement. "You're saying—?"

"I love you, Honora."

She stared at him, stricken, afraid to believe. Then she

felt the pain rise again, even worse than before. Again, he held her hand, helping her through it, telling her over and over again how proud he was of her, how he couldn't wait to hold their baby, how much he loved her.

When she could finally breathe again, she said, "Why are you saying this? Just because you don't want to lose me? You said you could never love anyone."

"It was myself I didn't love all these years. You were right. But I've learned the truth now. I spoke with Egidia at her villa—"

"You did?" she gasped.

"And she helped me realize that their rejection was never about *me* at all. It's what you said. Everyone has secret bruises and broken hearts that they try to hide." He paused. "You should know Egidia's in the hospital, too. But don't worry, she's going to be all right. She broke her leg on some steps at her house, but I helped her get an ambulance—"

"You helped her?" The world seemed to be spinning. She felt another pain coming. Already. Too soon.

She squeezed his hand, closing her eyes as she endured the agony, surrendering to it. He held her hand quietly, calm and tender and strong. When the pain finally abated, she exhaled.

"All these years I was so wrong, about everything," Nico said. "I thought being hard and cold and numb was the only way to protect myself." Lifting her hand to his lips, he kissed the knuckles as he whispered, "Then I met you."

She felt another rise in pain. Contractions were coming quicker together now, and harder. "Nico—"

"You've changed my life in every way possible. You've changed me, heart and soul." He looked down at her, his handsome face glowing with intensity. "And I swear that whatever it takes, even if takes the rest of my life, I will find a way to win back your love."

She looked up at him, and then her lips parted in shock. "You're crying."

"Yes." He gave a ragged breath, tried to smile as he ran a hand over his eyes. "I feel everything. And what I feel most of all is how much I love you. How much I *need* you," he whispered. "Please, Honora. Tell me I have a chance to win you back. To be the man you need me to be."

He loved her. He actually loved her. The realization was the sweetest feeling Honora had ever known, even as she gasped with agonizing pain. "I feel like I'm dreaming. I can't believe you're even here."

He didn't flinch as she gripped his hand tight enough to break a bone. "Your grandfather told me to come."

"Behind my back!"

"He said I'm family. Is it true, Honora?" He looked down at her. "Am I your family?"

She looked at him.

"Now and forever. I love you, Nico."

Joy filled his dark eyes as he bent and kissed her forehead, her cheeks. *"Cara..."*

Then the pain took over, and her doctor was suddenly there, and nurses, and her doctor was telling her to push, and the pain was so blinding that Honora thought she might die.

Then, suddenly, the pain was over, and forgotten, as a sweet little baby girl was placed in her arms, and her husband wrapped his powerful arms around them both, and all of them were crying.

Many hours later, as Honora held her new daughter, she looked over at Nico. He'd fallen asleep in the hard plastic chair. He had dark circles under his eyes, and scruff over his jawline, and his clothes were wrinkled, and he looked as if he hadn't slept in days. And he'd never been more handsome.

As if he felt her gaze, Nico looked up, then smiled. And the love she saw in his dark eyes filled her heart.

As she held her baby, the dawning sun came in through the window, covering them both with a soft golden glow, and Honora knew that their happiness would always last. They both deserved to be loved. And they'd finally come home to the circle of each other's arms.

The summer sun was bright and hot in the cloudless August sky, as the wild Atlantic waves splashed against the white sand.

Sitting on the grass outside their Hamptons mansion, in the same exact spot where they'd been wed the previous year, Nico looked at the people around him, feeling gratitude and quiet joy.

His wife was snuggled beside him on one of the soft blankets covering the grass, wearing a short, pretty sundress that showed off her slender curves, and a wide-brimmed sun hat. She'd thought of wearing jewelry—nothing fancy, just the golden heart necklace he'd given her for her birthday—but quickly thought better of it the first time baby Kara's hand had wrapped around it and pulled.

No matter. Honora didn't need jewels to make her sparkle brighter than the sun. Nico was dazzled every time he looked at her, as her green eyes glowed and danced while she laughed, her full lips a festive red to match the balloons and streamers.

Their baby sat nearby, wearing a little jumpsuit that revealed the adorable fat rolls at her thighs. She had her mother's green eyes and dark hair. They'd named her Kara, because she was beloved.

Their butler, Sebastian, smiling from ear to ear, had just served sandwiches—tiny ones with the crusts cut off, and fancy cookies with jam, and tea with milk, although their daughter was drinking hers in a sippy cup.

"A tea party?" Nico had asked his wife with amusement. "For a baby's birthday party?"

"Kara likes tea," Honora answered primly, then grinned. "Especially tea with milk."

Now, Nico slowly looked around him at the people who'd somehow become his family.

Honora's grandfather, Patrick, was telling some drawn-out story about the proper raising of lemons, to Egidia, of all people, who'd raised more lemons in Italy than the retired gardener ever had.

His stepmother's leg had completely healed. She no longer had to worry about rickety flights of stairs, as he'd bought her a luxurious single-floor apartment in Rome to live in while her longtime home, the Villa Caracciola, was remodeled and furnished with an elevator. She'd happily accepted Nico's offer to come visit the Hamptons for her granddaughter's birthday. The baby's great-grandmother, Phyllis, was giving Egidia a sympathetic smile, and offering her a cup of Italian espresso and sugar cookies.

His wife's best friend, Emmie Swenson, had arrived in a fluster a few hours before. The two women had laughed and talked together as they'd put up the decorations for the family party, all in red which was Kara's favorite color. Nothing made Honora happier than taking care of people.

Her patience might soon be tested, though, since any minute now, Nico's friend Theo Katrakis was expected for dinner. Which Nico honestly didn't understand.

"Why would *Theo* ever agree to come to a baby's birthday party?"

Smiling at their baby, his wife had crooned, "Because he loves Kara. And she loves her uncle Theo, doesn't she?"

Honora often fretted that his friend didn't have any family to look after him. Nico wasn't worried, but his wife seemed to care about the whole world. It left him in awe. He loved his family, but he couldn't imagine having the capacity to worry about absolutely everyone, not like his wife did.

She'd even been happy to read online that Lana Lee was

dating rising star Benny Rossini. "I hope they'll be happy." She'd smiled. "They deserve it."

That was what Nico had learned from her. *Everyone* deserved love. And he knew he'd spend the rest of his life protecting and caring for her—the heart and soul of their family, and beyond.

And so, an hour before, their family had gathered on the grassy bluff overlooking the sand to celebrate their baby's first birthday. The balloons and streamers were hung high in the trees, where Kara couldn't reach them. Nearby, there was a small pile of presents that they'd just helped their daughter unwrap. None of the gifts were expensive. Beach toys, like a bucket and shovel. A truck. A teddy bear. As Honora had taught him, it was about love, not money.

Good thing too, since Kara seemed mostly interested in playing with the discarded wrapping paper.

They were planning to go down to the beach in a bit and make sandcastles, assuming the star of the party didn't try to eat any of the sand. And later tonight, after dinner, when the sun fell softly into the sea, they'd gather around a bonfire on the beach, roast marshmallows and sing songs before Nico carried their sleepy baby against his shoulder, back to the house, to tuck her into her crib.

And then, Nico knew the rest of his family would finally disappear to their rooms, and he could be alone with his wife. He would hold her in his arms, setting fire to the night, as outside their bedroom's open window the summer stars would sweep across the wide sky and the surf would roar against the shore.

He hoped they'd have more children. Five. Six. As many as she wanted—as many as they could handle. What the hell else was money for? He'd just buy a bigger house. A bigger jet. And be ready for a bigger heart.

"What are you thinking?" Sitting beside him on the blanket, Honora looked up at him suspiciously.

Leaning forward, he whispered in her ear, "I want to unwrap you."

He had the satisfaction of seeing his wife blush, feeling her body shiver. Oh, yes. Six children. Tonight would be just the start of the joy that would last all their lives.

Nico remembered how numb and broken he'd felt in this empty house last summer, and all the gray months before. Then Honora had burst through the door and given him a new dream. A new life.

Now, as Kara toddled nearby and the grandparents laughed at some joke Patrick had just made, Honora suddenly leaned forward and whispered something in his ear.

With an intake of breath, Nico looked back at her, wide-eyed. "Are you sure?"

His wife nodded shyly, glowing with visible happiness. "In February." As he started to gasp and turn towards the others, she whispered, "Don't tell. Let's just keep it between us for now. Our little secret."

His glance dropped briefly to her belly, and he nodded, almost dizzy with happiness.

After years of making big real estate deals, he'd finally found the place that was the hardest to create, and the most precious to hold: a real home. In giving away his heart, he'd gotten back more love than he'd ever thought possible. Love was infinite, he thought, looking out at the wide blue ocean. It never ended.

Nico could hardly remember a time before he loved her. It seemed to him now that he'd loved Honora even before he knew her. They'd been brought together by fate, as she'd once said. And that was the greatest secret of all. The two of them were meant to be.

* * * * *

COMING SOON!

We really hope you enjoyed reading this book.
If you're looking for more romance, be sure to
head to the shops when new books are
available on

Thursday 19th August

To see which titles are coming soon, please visit
millsandboon.co.uk/nextmonth

MILLS & BOON

THE HEART OF ROMANCE

A ROMANCE FOR EVERY READER

MODERN

Prepare to be swept off your feet by sophisticated, sexy and seductive heroes, in some of the world's most glamourous and romantic locations, where power and passion collide.

HISTORICAL

Escape with historical heroes from time gone by. Whether your passion is for wicked Regency Rakes, muscled Vikings or rugged Highlanders, awake the romance of the past.

MEDICAL

Set your pulse racing with dedicated, delectable doctors in the high-pressure world of medicine, where emotions run high and passion, comfort and love are the best medicine.

True Love

Celebrate true love with tender stories of heartfelt romance, from the rush of falling in love to the joy a new baby can bring, and a focus on the emotional heart of a relationship.

Desire

Indulge in secrets and scandal, intense drama and plenty of sizzling hot action with powerful and passionate heroes who have it all: wealth, status, good looks…everything but the right woman.

HEROES

Experience all the excitement of a gripping thriller, with an intense romance at its heart. Resourceful, true-to-life women and strong, fearless men face danger and desire - a killer combination!

To see which titles are coming soon, please visit

millsandboon.co.uk/nextmonth

MILLS & BOON

Coming next month

THE SICILIAN'S FORGOTTEN WIFE
Caitlin Crews

"I wish only to kiss my wife," Cenzo growled. "On this, the first day of the rest of our life together."

"You don't want to kiss me," she threw at him, and he thought the way she trembled now was her temper taking hold. "You want to start what you think will be my downward spiral, until all I can do is fling myself prostrate before you and cringe about at your feet. Guess what? I would rather die."

"Let us test that theory," he suggested, and kissed her.

And this time, it had nothing at all to do with punishment. Though it was no less a claiming.

This time, it was a seduction.

Pleasure and dark promise.

He took her face in his hands, and he tasted her as he wanted at last. He teased her lips until she sighed, melting against him, and opened to let him in.

He kissed her and he kissed her, until all that fury, all that need, hummed there between them. He kissed her, losing himself in the sheer wonder of her taste and the way that sweet sea scent of hers teased at him, as if she was bewitching him despite his best efforts to seize control.

Cenzo kissed her like a man drowning and she met each thrust of his tongue, then moved closer as if she was as greedy as he was.

As if she knew how much he wanted her and wanted him, too, with that very same intensity.

And there were so many things he wanted to do with her. But kissing her felt like a gift, like sheer magic, and for once in his life, Cenzo lost track of his own ulterior motives. His own grand plan.

There was only her taste. Her heat.

Her hair that he gripped in his hands, and the way she pressed against him.

There was only Josselyn. His wife.

He kissed her again and again, and then he shifted, meaning to lift her in his arms—

But she pushed away from him, enough to brace herself against his chest. He found his hands on her upper arms.

"I agreed to marry you," she managed to pant out at him, her lips faintly swollen and her brown eyes wild. "I refuse to be a pawn in your game."

"You can be any piece on the board that you like," he replied, trying to gather himself. "But it will still be my board, Josselyn."

He let her go, lifting up his hands theatrically. "By all means, little wife. Run and hide if that makes you feel more powerful."

He kept his hands in the air, his mock surrender, and laughed at her as he stepped back.

Because he'd forgotten, entirely, that they stood on those narrow stairs.

It was his own mocking laughter that stayed with him as he fell, a seeming slow-motion slide backward when his foot encountered only air. He saw her face as the world fell out from beneath him.

Continue reading
THE SICILIAN'S FORGOTTEN WIFE
Caitlin Crews

Available next month
www.millsandboon.co.uk

LET'S TALK
Romance

For exclusive extracts, competitions
and special offers, find us online:

f facebook.com/millsandboon

🐦 @MillsandBoon

📷 @MillsandBoonUK

Get in touch on 01413 063232

For all the latest titles coming soon, visit
millsandboon.co.uk/nextmonth